SINKING
STEALING

For Faith
"A sister who sings"
with love
Jan Clausen
4/25/87

OTHER BOOKS BY JAN CLAUSEN:

After Touch (poems) – Out & Out Books

Waking at the Bottom of the Dark (poems) – Long Haul Press

Mother, Sister, Daughter, Lover (stories) – Crossing Press

A Movement of Poets: Thoughts on Poetry and Fiction (essay) – Long Haul Press

Duration (poetry and prose) – Hanging Loose Press

SINKING STEALING

a novel by Jan Clausen

The Crossing Press/Trumansburg, New York 14886
The Crossing Press Feminist Series

Portions of this book originally appeared in slightly different form in *Conditions, Fireweed,* and *13th Moon.*

Lines from *On the Road* by Jack Kerouac, copyright © 1955, 1957 by Jack Kerouac are reprinted by permission of Viking Penguin, Inc.

Library of Congress Cataloging in Publication Data

Clausen, Jan, 1950-
  Sinking/stealing.

  I. Title.
PS3553.L348S5 1985   813'.54   85-4158
ISBN 0-89594-160-0
ISBN 0-89594-159-7 (pbk.)

This book is for
Elly Bulkin, Anna Bulkin, Eve Weinblatt,
beloved "non-biological" family,
and for the BASTA Brigade,
sine qua non.

Acknowledgments

My gratitude to the women who helped me in the completion of this project is all the greater on account of the few who did what was in their power to hinder it. For invaluable personal support and for sharing their literary and political perspectives, I especially want to thank Dorothy Allison, Elly Bulkin, Cherríe Moraga, Rima Shore, and Barbara Smith. Barbara Macdonald and Cynthia Rich provided encouragement and editorial advice which were important at an early stage of the writing. Jan Bradshaw, Ros de Lanerolle, and Sarah Lefanu of The Women's Press Ltd. demonstrated their faith in the book at a crucial point; I believe the cuts I made at their insistence improved the finished product. I found Nancy K. Bereano's suggestions useful in completing revisions to the U.S. edition. Kate Dunn has been not only a terrific advocate but that rarest and most gratifying of editors, one who takes fiction seriously.

I also want to thank Kathryn Lazar, Robert Schwartz, David Steinberg, Martin R. Stolar, and Catherine Tinker, attorneys, for their generosity in discussing their respective views of the legal implications of certain actions undertaken by the characters in this book. They are not, of course, in any way responsible for the final, fictional result.

Finally, I am extremely grateful to the National Endowment for the Arts for providing a fiction writing fellowship without which this work might have taken years longer to complete, and to the Millay Colony for the Arts and the MacDowell Colony and the Writer's Room, Inc., where significant portions of the writing were done.

Well if you don't think I love you
look what a fool I've been
If you don't think I'm sinkin'
look what a hole I'm in
I'm sinkin'
stealin'
Mama don't you tell on me
I'm stealin' back
to my good old used-to-be.

                    – Traditional

PART I: SURVIVORS

We are in the mountains.

August, maybe: tenuous warmth of an alpine spring shading into autumn. Sun setting insects ahum in the cramped, marginal vegetation of a meadow, product of ancient glaciation, slung low between hips of hills. Light music of water pouring off distant snowfields. Sierra, this range, or Wallowas of Oregon? Rhea ahead, I know though I can't see the face. And, knowing, feel neither longing nor alarm.

In life we never hiked those trails together.

Higher we move, breathing deep with measured effort, toward peaks with ice on them. A cold, light-burnished clarity is what this path leads to. Up there we will see everything: so it is promised.

We are in the mountains. We belong here. That's the dream.

I have dreamed this often. Details differ, I hike among single peaks or ranges, alone or with other companions – yet altitude remains constant, emblematic. Like the Bomb dreams, variously plotted, but each turning on the axis of that fixed, unsurvivable moment when I gasp full-faced into flame blossoming like predestined Hell in the air.

Somewhere a woman is screaming bloody murder.

I've fallen asleep with the TV on: dreadful habit. That's my first conscious perception, my first rational judgment. Thrashing at the bottom of the pool, accelerating through level upon level of sleep till, my skull piercing the thin layer of surface tension that binds the top of the unconscious, I'm catapulted into the mortal, waking world, my inchoate conviction has been, of course: this is *it*.

I was raped once, years ago, in another city. What seemed remarkable later was the sense of recognition with which I'd greeted the large hand clamped over my mouth and the dull, cruel voice rasping in my ear. Oh yes, this is *it*; of course, this is what I've expected.

And when they called up about Rhea –

Not that I'd expected anything like that to happen. Only that a slight but suspicious haze of familiarity clung about the motions I began to go through then; about everything that started in that moment. No, I wasn't so surprised by that late-night call.

But we're speaking here of public catastrophes.

My preoccupation with apocalypse was acquired early, a natural consequence of a southern California childhood which effortlessly achieved its sun-drenched synthesis of backyard pools and backyard fallout shelters. Like plenty of others who'd rather not discuss it, I grew to be an adult who perpetually anticipates a wide range of full-scale cataclysms: earthquake, liquified natural gas explosion, atomic attack, genetic engineering mishap, tidal wave, volcanic eruption, dam break, nuclear power plant meltdown. I walk intact, unjustified through my days, a tree marked by surveyors left standing in the forest.

Though the TV's on, the screams are not televised. Awake, this much clear, it takes me a few moments to orient myself. I'm standing naked at the window, shivering, peering, panting, dialing 911 from force of habit before I'm able quite to grasp the fact that the danger in the street can't touch me in my tower.

By the time someone picks up on the other end, I've isolated the problem to two small figures grappling beneath my window. By the time I've remembered my address ("I think we got that already," says the operator, dispassionately snapping her gum), a cacophony of approaching sirens has announced – well, if not salvation, the nearest thing we'll get.

The live action, in fact, looks unnervingly like tube fare. Squad cars converge on my quiet, modest block with an authoritative howl of sirens, a businesslike shriek of tires. Cops leap out, hands hovering over holsters. Revolving lights illuminate the field of battle.

The target of this massive retaliation is a short, slight, dark-faced, dark-haired man who appears, in the yellow glare of the street lamp, remarkably quickly subdued. He's certainly more tractable, for instance, than the fellow I once saw wrestled to the concrete floor of the IND platform at Broadway-Lafayette, four big cops on him pounding away at his kidneys while he fought back wildly, a man drowning. From my third-floor sanctuary this guy actually looks rather harmless, hunched, handcuffed, wearing a shabby jacket. *They've got you now. Why didn't you run, brother?* I think this, yes, even knowing what I know. Indelible screams resounding in my brain. *Screaming bloody murder.* I never heard before what the words meant.

Roughly, roughly, they cram him into the car. He doesn't look back at the source of all the trouble, the inevitable female figure.

There, an afterthought almost, a detail appended to the big picture, she lies, inert on her back in ice and dogshit and blood. Hushed, finally, after all that screaming. There's a wide, dark stain on the front of her light coat. Cops confer above her. She might be a child worn out by a temper tantrum, or a corpse rotting on a battlefield. The moon, a day or two short of the full, lofts above the low brownstones opposite, deftly outclassing the streetlamps. They ignore it, her. Will the ambulance ever come? The block is aroused now, its secret collective pulse quickened. Squares of light checker the dark facades; the curious, gregarious, and hardy, hastily bundled into winter jackets, trickle down into the street.

For this sort of thing does not happen on our block—despite what's whispered of depraved New York in the upright cities of the interior. It's an average Brooklyn block in the Park Slope section, neither rich nor poor, a mixture of smallish brownstones and brickfronted eight-family buildings. It used to be solid Italian before the neighborhood "changed." Recently it's bleached out again as white professionals fleeing the rents of Manhattan and the trials of suburban commuting have begun to make inroads. The population currently is, the statisticians of the Block Association will inform you, pleased as though they themselves had legislated the proportions, quite evenly divided between Black and white, with a smattering of Hispanics.

Not that we're strangers to a peace disturbed, to the shrieks of women and the howls of sirens. In the ten or so months I've lived behind these windows (Rhea and I slept in the back of the house, on another block, in what seems another life), I have witnessed a good deal of impromptu street theater. Most compelling of all are these late-night, winter dramas, when cold and the hour have left the stage uncluttered, emphasizing the action: auto collision followed by fistfight; purse-snatching; "racial incident" (six white teenagers taunt a couple of Blacks). I am above all schooled in the ways of impassioned lovers and husbands who yell for the wide world to hear how they'll bash her face in, kick her in the crack, whip her ass, show her, tell her, teach her, kill her, cut her, make her sorry, make her listen, make her pay—if she doesn't shut up, talk, keep still, mind, watch out, pay attention, learn, behave, grow up, start acting like a woman, stop acting like a goddamn cunt. I try to intercede from the gallery, yelling out the window for all the good it does—and generally call the cops. Having been reared where large yards, thick foliage, and well-modulated voices concealed domestic violence from the neighborhood, and where I was inculcated at an impressionable age with the quaint notion that the policeman was my friend (never mind the later lessons of demonstrations), I can't seem to get over thinking that this will accomplish something.

But here's the ambulance, keening Emergency, as though we hadn't known it all along.

The attendants bustle about, efficiently bundling their charge onto the stretcher, covering that light, impractical coat with the thick grey ambulance blanket. Will that make it better, like kissing a child's skinned knee? I take it as a good omen that they leave her head uncovered, though perhaps warm bodies are to be treated with deference until pronounced officially Dead on Arrival. But why in the world is she wearing those platform shoes? Who could expect to run for her life in that getup? Perhaps it's the fault of her own silly vanity that her face, pathetically tiny from this distance, looks paler than any face I've ever seen (I never saw Rhea's, after).

They hustle her into the back. The ambulance goes, screaming as though to obliterate the memory of her screams. Most of the cops have left. Several linger, officiously calming the onlookers. There's quite a crowd gathered by now, women beside their husbands, a couple kids, even. Just like the song says, everybody loves Saturday night.

Watching, I'm struck by the rare camaraderie, the inattention to the everyday caste divisions, typically suspended only in the event of fire, blizzard, or the annual block party. They're mixing so democratically down there in the cold, smoking, stamping their feet, reluctant to go back to bed until they have sifted and fingered every available eyewitness account and every rumor to arrive at their collective and individual versions of this appalling, enthralling occurrence. As though any explanation could protect them.

Nothing helps, I know that, but I too want explanations. I understand their guilt and nervous pleasure at finding themselves untouched. Still there seems no need to go down there at this hour. Any conclusions reached by tonight's ad hoc investigative commission will be sure to be rebroadcast in full tomorrow.

I watch till my neighbors crush out their cigarettes and creep back into their houses. Then I lie down and close my eyes and try to see something besides that creature, pale-faced, being trundled into the ambulance – and the other one, handcuffed, shoved behind the grate, acquiescent, never looking back. As though he knew all there was to know about it.

The alarm wakes me in time to get Ericka. It's eight-thirty; I've slept a couple of hours. I splash water on my face, blunder into clothing. No time for coffee – Daniel grumbles when I'm late.

On the second landing my progress is impeded by Mrs. Catania, the landlord's wife, who's down on her hands and knees scrubbing linoleum. Why she saves this chore for Sundays before mass has always been unclear, along with her reasons for eschewing sponge mops.

She hoists herself laboriously to a standing position, but continues to block my path. "Did you hear the fuss last night?" she demands to know, as I was afraid she would. She approves of me: I am quiet, white, and single. I listen respectfully to her. My rent checks never bounce.

"Who could help hearing?" I reply, attempting to convey by my tone that I'm in a hurry.

"Poor thing. They say she may not make it. It's eleven years since we had anything like this."

"Where is she?" I ask, to be decent.

"They've got her up there at Methodist, in the Critical Care. He stabbed her a total of seven times, that's what the police say."

"But why? Do they know? Did she know him?"

Mrs. Catania shakes her head no. Vein-knotted hands grip the banister. "He wanted money, they claim."

"And she wouldn't give it to him?" I'm thinking I've found my loophole. How dumb do you have to be to turn a mugger down?

"She gave him what she had, a couple dollars. I guess he wanted more. They say he just started stabbing, just like that. He didn't even try to run or nothing when the police pulled up. Must of been some real nut. That, or on dope, I guess."

"And they think she won't live?" I'm resolving to be good, to carry money, never to come home past midnight anymore.

"They don't know." Mrs. Catania sighs. "It could go either way. Such a terrible tragedy. She was just a young girl, too. Lived up here a couple of blocks. Engaged and all, still living with her folks. I didn't hear a sound, if you can believe it. Mr. Catania and I slept right through. Course, we're in the back. Some real sicko, that one. . . . A Portarican fella, from down there." And she jerks her square chin grimly towards Fifth Avenue.

It's starting, it's in the air, and I want to split. I like the woman, and don't want to hear it, whatever's coming next from someone who prides herself on her lack of "prejudice," since she held her ground thirty years ago when Blacks started buying.

"It must be rough for the family," I murmur.

"Poor thing," she laments again, momentarily diverted. "No woman ought to be out alone so late."

7

I make my excuses, flee.

Outside, a rough knot of children—boys, mostly, with two or three hardy girls elbowing in—has drawn tight around that historic spot on the sidewalk. I hear their excited voices, the speculative intensity of their talk, as they grope for clues to the mysteries of grownups.

* * *

"Go into my room, Ericka, and watch TV while I talk to your father for a few minutes."

Once upon a time I would have judged quite harshly the adult who resorted to this ignoble ploy. Rhea and I lived for years without television. But that was long ago, and Daniel's request, phoned in on Friday ("Suppose I could stop in for a few minutes Sunday evening when I pick up Ericka? I've got something I want to talk to you about"), was perfectly explicit. I don't turn him down, these days.

"Would you like coffee, Daniel?" I ought to offer him wine, and there's a gallon of cheap burgundy in the closet. But I don't really want to encourage him to make himself more at home than he has already, lolling on my lumpy, ragged couch.

"Uh, no thanks, that's okay. You don't happen to have any Perrier or club soda around?"

"Afraid not."

"Well, maybe I will have coffee, on second thought."

"Let me warn you, it's instant." The truth is, I have fresh beans in the refrigerator. An electric coffee grinder is one of the numerous small luxuries I've indulged in recently, living up to the limit of my modest but fulltime salary.

"No problem. Don't make it too strong, and I'll take some milk or cream. I have to watch it. I'm not as young as I was."

"Well, neither am I," I announce, arrested by my sudden vision of Daniel, lank, morose, sitting hunched over his perpetual cups of coffee at the scarred, ringed, ancient wooden kitchen table in the ancient days when Rhea and he were married. That table, sanded, refinished, now stands across the room. A twinge of pity—for whom?—surprises me. He's so much more cheerful now than he was then, at what must have been just about my present age.

"Oh you, my god. *You* certainly can't complain. How old are you, anyway?"

"Pushing thirty."

"Thirty. Christ. So we'll have to stop trusting you."

I resent the intimate, jocular tone of this.

"Mind if I smoke?"

"Go ahead." But it's reluctantly that I fork over my one ashtray; I have grown intolerant. Rhea smoked sporadically, and we had so many meetings that the tobacco taint never quite faded from the apartment. In this new place I am pure and solitary, and leave my windows open for half an hour following the departure of even one moderate smoker—which Daniel is, of course. A man of the modern world, he's acutely sensitive to "tar," cholesterol, the nitrosamines in his hot dogs. He's even wearing running shoes today. Not that I imagine he does much running in them, but they do go well with his perfectly faded jeans, the effortless leanness of his long body.

"You wanted to talk?" It's time we got on with it. I'm stirring two cups of instant. Deadly stuff, but I want something in my hand.

"Right. Great, thanks, a little more milk will do it." Daniel, perhaps sensing my dislike of serving him, has come over to join me in the kitchen alcove. "Yes, I was getting to that. It's about Ericka. Do those doors close all the way?" And he points to the heavy sliding doors that divide my small bedroom from the rest of the apartment. "Do you suppose you could—?"

I do as he indicates. Although I soften it, murmuring tactfully to Ericka that we don't want to be disturbed by the TV, I see by the cautious smoothness of her face that she understands we're about to discuss secret matters in which she's implicated.

"It's nothing much, I suppose," Daniel prefaces, settling back on the couch. One ankle rests on the opposite knee; he leans back, thoroughly at home, the way men do in the subway, taking up space. "Brenda went to Ericka's parent-teacher conference last week, and something rather disturbing came up. Apparently Ericka's been . . . pilfering."

Instant relief. At least it's not more nightmares—nor any attempt of Daniel's to pare our weekend visits down. Funny how I always anticipate trouble from him, though actually our relations have been quite smooth of late. "What's she taken, from whom?"

"Nothing of any value, just milk money and pencils, that sort of thing, from a couple of boys in her class."

"The teacher's sure? The kids aren't making it up?"

"She checked it out, even caught Ericka once. Apparently her modus operandi wasn't too subtle," Daniel chuckles tolerantly. "Anyway, the teacher asked if we thought anything unusual was going on with her, and Brenda and I were frankly stymied. We thought it might be a good idea to let you know about this, and find out whether you've noticed. . . ."

"Not a thing," I say, suppressing my resentment. I used to go to those conferences with Rhea. "Did you talk to Ericka?"

"Well, yes. We confronted her with her teacher's report, and she – stonewalled. Simply denied it. Oh, she got upset and cried and said I was mean, but she wouldn't admit anything."

"Hmm, that's interesting." I too can stonewall. "She seemed okay to me. A little manic today, but that was about her birthday."

"So you haven't noticed anything that would indicate – "

I make my voice pleasant. "Not that I can recall." Fool, I'm thinking. You want her. You handle this.

But, as usual, thought of her welfare pulls me up short, forces me to add, "Of course you realize it's been just over a year since Rhea's – "

"Right," he stops me. "No, I've thought of that."

"Ericka hasn't brought it up?"

"Not a word. I guess that's how she's handling it. No, Brenda and I have discussed it, naturally – it's one reason why we wanted to make a special effort for her birthday. She told you about the party?"

"Of course. She hardly talked about anything else."

"Anyway, this petty thievery has been going on for quite some time. I doubt it's related to . . . that anniversary."

Case closed; we won't speak further about Rhea. I'm just as glad. I don't want sympathy, don't want Daniel anywhere near my feelings, and certainly don't want to start hearing about his, about the sorrows his first wife's memory inspires, which he has once or twice already exposed to me with the silly gravity of someone baring the scar from a serious but embarrassing operation.

It makes me furious that he doesn't get it: how Ericka feels, I mean. Oh, he grasps the pathos of motherless childhood, but that's pure convention, the stuff of Hallmark cards. Not being a man of much imagination (a strange deficiency, it always struck me, in a professor of history), he measures Rhea's effect on others solely in terms of his own experience of her. She was, for him, the woman who was *too much,* who upset his plans with her challenges and risks. So he can't see how, for a child almost nine years old, she meant the center of all gravity and safety, all sense of permanence in the universe. Six months of trips to a kiddie therapist and he figures his daughter should be as good as new.

I remark that stealing milk money seems like pretty small potatoes for a kid Ericka's age.

"Yes, don't you think? I suppose it will blow over. And Brenda seems to concur. Still, we wondered if you'd speak to her."

"You flatter me—as if I had influence!" I get this out in just the right tone, lightly sardonic, with a little smile which will be interpreted as self-deprecatory, though it masks irritation.

"Oh, I don't for a minute underestimate your influence." Again, the suggestion of intimacy, that bantering, almost flirtatious approach which makes me so uneasy. Why does Daniel now begin to treat me—well, *like a woman* is how I want to put it. Which is certainly not what I ought to seem to him. He ought rather to see me as neutral, unsexed, a slightly ridiculous, slightly pitiful object. This other approach never fails to catch me off guard, much as I am unnerved on those infrequent occasions when my passage elicits a tremor of interest in a crowd of construction workers. How can it be it's *me* they have in mind? Don't they see who I am, how far from my thoughts they are?

"Well, sure, I'll try to raise it with her. If I can find a time when it seems natural."

"Thanks a million, Josie." Beaming his approval.

"Of course. But listen, I've been meaning to ask: do you suppose Ericka might sleep over with me next Saturday? I thought we could do something special for her birthday."

"What sort of thing did you have in mind? I mean, not that I necessarily see any problem—"

"I thought she might want to have Jasmine spend the night, and then on Sunday I'd take them to a movie."

"Jasmine?"

"You know. Her friend from our old block."

"Oh, right." Though Daniel agreed to my original proposal that Ericka should be encouraged to keep up all those ties, in fact he's never made the slightest effort in that direction. "Well, I'm sure she'd like that. I'd better not say definitely, though, without checking with Brenda. You know she's our household social secretary." He laughs self-consciously, aware of my jaundiced feminist eye on his domestic arrangements.

"When can you let me know?"

"You'll talk to Ericka during the week, I suppose. You could

11

call, say, on Tuesday." But there won't be any problem; like a housewife clever at cadging spending money, I congratulate myself on having learned to pick my moments. "Are you coming to the extravaganza?" he continues.

"Of course. I'll take half a personal day, I guess. Ericka made it clear my presence was expected. The whole thing sounds . . . pretty impressive."

"Well, that's Brenda, you know." He smiles indulgence. "She really gets a kick out of planning these things. And then, as I said, we do want it to be fun for Ericka. Poor kid."

"How *is* Brenda, by the way?"

"She's just fine, thanks. The first trimester was considerably rougher this time around than with Leah—nausea and so on—but she's much better now. Did I tell you we had an amniocentesis?"

"What for? Is something wrong?"

"Oh no, everything's fine. It was just that she'd recently found out about a rare hereditary problem in the family, so we had it checked out. But no problems, apparently."

"So what's it going to be?"

"A boy, so they tell me."

"Variety," I charitably remark, noting his sheepish grin, quickly suppressed. Daniel is the sort of modern father who likes to proclaim the advantages of daughters. They're fascinating in ways sons could never be, he assures you—and easier, given social realities. With boys, you're always sailing against the tide, intervening in fistfights, wondering whether to confiscate cap pistols and, later, *Hustler* and *Penthouse.* Girls, on the other hand, may be encouraged. The future is theirs. Rearing them in this decade, one has a privileged sense of participation in an historic shift.

Yet now this gleam in his eye at the prospect of a son.

No real cause for astonishment, of course. Daniel is simply a man of the upper middle classes, and despite his liberal patina, he is as utterly unremarkable in his ideas of fatherhood as he is in patterns of earning and consumption. And yet I retain my capacity for surprise at fresh revelations of his mediocrity. Somehow he always succeeds in holding out the promise of more than he delivers.

Years ago, about the time of his remarriage to Brenda, Rhea and I developed a metaphor for Daniel: we compared him to a large American car of the sort he himself would not now deign to own, a pre-energy-crisis model with lots of chrome and lots of room, very impressive at first glance in its ability to glide, almost without mediation from the driver, at seventy or eighty miles an hour down the universal American interstate so brilliantly designed to accommodate it. The casual passenger takes a while to notice that such a car gets miserable gas mileage, is incapable of negotiating unpaved roads, is lethal on ice, and requires expensive transmission work at frequent intervals.

Rhea could be bitterly funny in describing her dismay at her belated discovery of Daniel's deficiencies. For she'd married him, when she was confused and twenty, with nothing far short of genius in mind. Brilliance, at any rate, and staunch political commitment—these were the qualities which, fondly, she imagined she detected in the nice Jewish iconoclast with the good grades, the New Left hero who staged such thrilling debates with her stodgy Old Left parents.

And he still possesses traces of these attractions: there's the whiz kid's sharpness in his dark, lean-featured face, the fetching suggestion of radical asceticism in the skinny frame with its nascent pot belly. Given the exercise of a bit of historical imagination, it's quite possible to believe he spent a year in SDS. Having had the opportunity to observe the genus White Male Politico in a variety of West Coast incarnations, I can, for instance, conjure up a picture of him planted firmly in front of a menacing TAC squad contingent: megaphone in hand, he directs the chant, "One side's right, one side's wrong, victory to the Viet Cong." The militant simplicity of this message is appropriate, for one gets the impression that Daniel has never been much plagued by doubt, no matter what he's been doing. This is hardly the same as possessing strong convictions—but who knew that, in the days when Rhea met him?

"A lightweight," she lamented, "such a lightweight." It was more than anything his lack of passion (even a sterile passion for ideas might have commanded her reluctant admiration) which she found hard to forgive. He failed to insist that life mean something large. He settled. Prestige and comfort could buy him off.

For his part, despite his highly affable manner, I suspect Daniel of regarding me with a condescension colored by both irritation and pity: irritation because, as he's made clear all year, it's rather a nuisance to find oneself forced into perpetual dealings with one's difficult first wife's female former lover simply because said lover has chanced to form an attachment to one's daughter; pity because – well, undoubtedly I seem quaint and odd to him, living so marginally by his brownstone standards, working away at my little office job, persisting in thinking of myself as a radical of some sort even now that the Seventies are on the wane, now that the fashion's changed, now that I'm pushing thirty. He can't know many people like me anymore, and he's at a loss to understand it: why I keep on with music when I've never managed to develop it into anything that could reasonably be called a career; how I remain content to renounce the society and sexual love of men on the strength, it appears, of a political whim.

Nonetheless, I must exert some sort of attraction, for we've exhausted amniocentesis as a conversation topic, and he still shows no sign of getting up to leave. In part, I suppose, it's the well-known fascination unavailable women have for certain men: like little boys prodding curled-up caterpillars, they're terribly eager to elicit a response. Then, too, domesticity sometimes palls. Daniel doesn't regret for a moment his life with Brenda; still, he doesn't mind spending an occasional hour or so drinking coffee with a woman of an utterly different type: unencumbered, opinionated, a trifle abrasive – a modern bluestocking. This hour refreshes him. He returns with relief to his wife, his spacious house, as, after a camping trip, one hails with appreciation a civilization which has produced hot showers.

But perhaps most important, I'm his link to Rhea. And she's a persistent itch he never succeeds in scratching to his satisfaction. For no matter how he tells the story of their marriage to his credit, emphasizing what he calls her "craziness," her radical unreason, her sexual adventures – the fact he can't dismiss, and that continues to gall him, is that she was too much for him altogether. Too emotional, too unconventional, too political, too angry – and, in the end, too queer. No fault of his, any of it, so he tells himself, and least of all the last item, which certainly lets him off the hook as far as the breakup goes. Still, it rankles. And she's gone now, out of reach, having skipped town, the country, and the galaxy when he wasn't yet ready to be done with her.

And so, oddly enough, he turns to me, who may technically be said to have cuckolded him. He needs someone who knew her.

I suppose I could get away with a policy of avoidance, having him ring for Ericka and sending her down. But so far I haven't cared to risk snubbing him. And in fact, he could be worse. My one real grudge against him at this point is his handling of things with Ericka, and even that seems more a matter of insensitivity than of malice. And perhaps even partly my fault. In all the chaos of these miserable months, I haven't insisted as I might have done.

While I've been thinking unflattering thoughts about him, Daniel has smoothly switched gears and is now lecturing me on the historical underpinnings of current events in the Horn of Africa, a topic apparently suggested by a headline on a *Guardian* I've left lying on the table. He likes to inveigle me into political debate, then cheerfully inform me that I'm every bit as utopian in my thinking as Rhea always was.

But at last Ericka emerges from my bedroom, perhaps overcome with anxiety at the duration of our "secret" talks, perhaps merely at the end of her TV program.

"Daddy, can we go soon? I'm bored." It's a little like watching a seasoned seductress slip into "something comfortable," watching her slide into this tone she employs with him, the flirtatious tone of prepubescent daughters with their fathers, which contrasts almost humorously with her unsophisticated appearance: childish chunky frame and mop of uncombed hair, wavy and dark like his, falling into her eyes. She lounges against his knee. He puts a proprietary arm around her waist and keeps talking.

Her transformation in his presence is so routine that we have developed a private, joking phrase to describe it, Ericka and I: we say that at this hour on Sunday evenings she "turns into a pumpkin." She knows whom she has to please, I think, watching.

But that's unfair. She loves him, of course. She must.

"We'll go in a minute, sweetheart. I'm explaining something to Josie."

With the leisured air of a pedagogue in control of his audience, Daniel finishes his thought. Then he suggests his daughter go wash her face, she's got spaghetti sauce on it. While she's out of earshot, he ventures how sorry he is: not just about Rhea, that goes without saying, but also about how awful the year's been for me.

I thank him, and then he starts to inquire if I'm quite sure I'm doing all right. But Ericka fortunately comes bouncing out and cuts short the condolences. She kisses me, hugs me, demonstrative all of a sudden, putting off departure.

I can't wait to be rid of the two of them.

"Don't forget about my party," she insists.

"I certainly won't. But I'll talk to you before then. I'll call on Tuesday to check about our plans. You'll know by then, Daniel?"

15

"Right. Come on now, Ericka. See you, Josie. Take care." I ignore his meaningful look.

"Goodbye, Ericka. Have a good week."

"Have a good week, Josie."

This has become our ritual parting phrase, like the bedtime farewell of old, "Good night, sleep tight, don't let the bedbugs bite."

With relief, I close the door. I'm tired, yet I move quickly to expunge the traces of the visitation. I pick up the scattering of books and other objects which Ericka always seems to leave behind, flotsam in her wake. I rinse off spaghetti-draped dishes, open windows to admit an exorcism of freezing air. Nine o'clock already: it seems I've survived the weekend.

I wash my hair and iron something for morning. Then I settle into bed with a cup of tea and the *Times*. Later, I turn out the lights and lie in the half-dark which is all this city's shallow night affords. The view from my window takes in the spectral lift of one of the Slope's many steeples and, looking out on the huddled roofs with that medieval shape looming over them, I can almost imagine myself embedded in some ancient foreign landscape, some slow village life far from dangerous, hectic Brooklyn.

And now it's begun to snow. Small flakes drift past the street lamps.

Soon the flakes are larger, thicker. Maybe they'll even stick, late in the season as it is, mid-March upon us already. I can't imagine what Brenda was thinking of—she's usually so practical—planning a garden party for Ericka.

Have I said how thoroughly New York winters suit me? Despite the fact that Gina, who sits next to me at work, swears I've been humming "California Dreamin' " at my typewriter all winter, the truth is that, wrapped in my blankets, drinking my tea, I'm content. I don't want it to be April, ever.

* * *

It's such an unaccustomed pleasure and relief to leave work at lunchtime on Friday that I mind somewhat less than I ordinarily would the demoralizing trek through the expensive wastes of midtown in search of a gift suitable to be offered up on the common heap at Ericka's birthday party. (In fact, the task is not too strenuous, since this object is to serve a purely ceremonial function; I'm saving the important present, a sweater I've been knitting since December, for presentation on the weekend.) In a Fifth Avenue record store I locate a wholesome-looking Pete Seeger album I hope will do, though who knows what she listens to these days on her father's sound system – punk sex, possibly, or rock 'n roll. Then there's time for coffee, and an interval spent wandering the far, echoing reaches of the Forty-Second Street library, my habitual midtown refuge, before I head for Brooklyn.

My hour in one of the planet's poshest shopping districts has at least had the merit of preparing me for an afternoon chez the professional middle class. So I reflect, arriving on Daniel and Brenda's clean block. Oh yes, this still exists – even, improbably, here in New York City – this universe of comfort and convenience which I tend to connect with California and my childhood, which I solipsistically think of in the past tense, simply because I no longer inhabit it.

Already on its way up in the world when I first made its acquaintance, the block has risen further with Park Slope's ascending fortunes. When Daniel Fein and Rhea Krevsky were new homeowners here, and rented me a room at the top of their crumbling brownstone, many of the buildings were still split up into rooming houses or dark, tacky little apartments. Now they're almost all occupied by single families, some of whom rent out an upstairs floor to help with mortgage payments. The renovators of that early vintage, the ones who took credit for "turning things around," plumbed, wired, carpentered, stripped, and sanded, and endured the foibles of their low-income neighbors (who would shortly be driven off to look for cheaper housing) amid a spirit of pioneering solidarity. Those remaining from that era tend to look down on the more recent arrivals, who have paid a premium for their original detail, scraped floors, and exposed brick. Daniel, no booster and certainly no handyman, evinces little nostalgia for the good old days, but knows he lucked out, buying when he did. He's been heard to remark that the prices would be prohibitive if he and Brenda had to look now – too bad they're not thinking of selling.

Unaware of New York's ubiquitous contradictions, the naive visitor to this "prime block" (in the realtors' phrase, which always makes me think of beefsteak) would scarcely imagine the decrepitude and squalor which flourish a few blocks away. Here the street is innocent of litter and even of dogshit. The identical brownstone fronts, once-deplored soulless tract housing of a century ago, march up the incline with all the chic allure of a Brook-

17

lyn Union Gas ad. Even nature has thoughtfully been made room for. Most of the houses enjoy the luxury of small front garden plots behind wrought-iron fences, and everywhere the Block Association's saplings lift their ugly, ambitious branches, the buds standing out on the tracery of twigs near bursting. The day is warm, almost muggy (for New York knows only two authentic seasons, two poles of climatic discomfort, and March weeks which start by resembling January quite often end up like June), yet no children's games clutter the sidewalk, as they do on my street in good weather. Kids here have rooms of their own, and back yards to play in.

Daniel's house, well-maintained as it's come to be in the years since his remarriage, is as handsome as its neighbors. I study the carved door, compose myself, then ring the buzzer hard. A pause, and Brenda materializes, smiling her hostess smile.

"Oh, hello, Josie. Come right on in."

She's wearing a wide, bright print dress that flares cavalierly over her distended middle; she's lugging Leah, hefty at two and a half, professionally on her hip. Her face and arms look a trifle puffy, her eyes faintly circled with fatigue, but her hair swings out from her high cheekbones straight and shiny and obviously recently cut at some really *good* place in the Heights, or maybe Manhattan.

Aside from marrying Daniel, this knack of hers for visual effect was about the only thing she and Rhea had in common. But Rhea, no matter how striking (some people called her beautiful out loud, even in our circles), almost never appeared particularly respectable, whereas Brenda is the consummate healthy, weary, well-heeled Park Slope matron—in her face the strain and triumph of her calling: chaos of children and marriage crossed, contained, by a scrupulous attention to detail, a loving involvement in perfectible surfaces.

"I'm so glad you're here, Ericka's been looking for you. Come on out back. What a relief the weather's cooperated." Why is it that, no matter how trivial her remarks, she always succeeds in rubbing me the wrong way? As she leads me back through the long parlor floor, I'm busy drawing analogies between her condescending tone and that of the aristocratic mother addressing the cherished retainer, dear old nanny or governess.

I always think of Brenda as being older than I am. In fact, we are almost precisely the same age, but Brenda has put her decades to the obvious use, has successfully completed the transition into that creature I have been known to describe with amused hostility as a "real grownup." Whereas I. . . . Sometimes lately as I walk home from my train I stop for a moment to watch the little girls—sweet, rowdy little girls who block pedestrian traffic with games of "double dutch" jumprope made boisterous enough to rival their brothers' intrinsically livelier stickball—and am seized by sudden confusion as to my true identity, my proper place in this world. Smiling, I murmur hello and prudently withdraw, secretly thinking it seems almost within my power to cross some invisible line and join them, if I chose. After all, nothing official has happened in my life to cut me off from them. I'm nobody's keeper, nobody's wife or mother.

I might add that these minor episodes of vertigo have nothing to do with being what's popularly termed "good with children." As a teenager I disliked babysitting, and even today I avoid getting stuck doing childcare at meetings and conferences. My surprising good luck with Ericka never tempted me to experiment further. It's just that I'm frequently assailed by this inappropriate sense of identification, and don't know what to do with it, beyond smiling and muttering inanities for which I am rewarded by suspicious glances betokening children's natural healthy mistrust of the motives of this lady who lacks credentials, who is not the mom of any of their friends. On the old block, of course, at least they knew who I lived with.

But we've reached the kitchen. An exclamation escapes me.

"That's right, I guess you haven't seen this, have you? They finished the remodelling about a month ago. It took absolutely forever, and what a pain in the neck, but it's so convenient now," Brenda explains.

They've added a counter, stainless steel, and built-ins. Everything gleams, ordered, immaculate; to look at it you'd never guess that a family with young children lives here. Keeping it up must require a semi-heroic effort on Brenda's part, even given the services of one Nilda Campos—the eternal "Nilda" of Ericka's conversation—who makes their two-paycheck family possible.

Strange indeed to contrast this with a former reign: Rhea's loom set up on worn carpet laid over the bare, splintery floorboards by the front windows, the leaking ceilings and the flaking plaster, the problems with the furnace. Rhea, with her far different purposes—she envisioned a free school in these lofty rooms—at least had gotten the basics in order by the time she moved out. Brenda inherited solid wiring and plumbing, and on these foundations built her grand effects.

Actually, I've often wondered how she manages all this on her and Daniel's combined salaries. Another of her innovations has been the addition of a deck which provides access to the back garden from the parlor floor. Here lawn chairs are arranged beside a picnic table heaped with brightly wrapped presents. Six or seven women and one bearded man, the latter looking rather out of his depth, sit watching the children in the garden below. No Daniel, I note.

"Josie, this is Linda, June, Donna . . . Josie is a friend of Ericka's," Brenda explains, disposing with flawless tact of the scandal of my childlessness. No question but what the others are *real* parents. Several of the women even have toddlers hanging on their skirts (there's a very high ratio of skirts to pants in this crowd); sticky faces and fingers menace dry-cleaned laps.

"Have a seat, Josie, and let me get you some wine. I'm trying to make this thing as tolerable as possible for the older generation."

Brenda laughs, intimating she takes in stride the ordeal of arranging an afternoon's entertainment for twenty kids. I accept the glass she offers. To go down into the garden now would be to make myself even more conspicuous than I feel already. Sooner or later Ericka will notice me. I prefer to stay put and sip my wine and watch her from above as she flits in and out among buds and bare branches, a manic debutante; her hair coiffed and beribboned, she's clad in a silly femmy spaghetti-strap dress, but it doesn't appear to slow her down much.

"That cake is absolutely ravishing, Brenda. Where on earth did you get it?" This question, posed by a sallow-faced woman in a chic maternity smock, fairly represents the general level of discourse. The cake reposes on the picnic table beside the tower of gifts. About a foot and a half in diameter, it sports an elaborate two-tone frosting job and the legend HAPPY BIRTHDAY ERICKA – TEN YEARS OLD picked out in a mosaic of nuts and raisins.

"Thanks, I'm glad you like it. I custom-ordered it from Sweet Surrender – you know, that place that just opened on Seventh Avenue. They're very nice, they'll do whatever you want. Ericka was talking about an ice cream cake from Carvel, but I persuaded her ten is old enough to be a bit more adventurous. I just hope the kids eat it."

"Was it terribly expensive, if you don't mind my asking?"

"Oh god, don't make me think! It cost an arm and a leg. Still, they use all natural ingredients . . . really, it's not out of line, when you consider the quality."

A silence while the women mull over this precedent.

"Thanks for telling us. I think I'll look into it," one mother at last announces firmly. "Todd has a birthday coming up next month, and I'm so sick of those cheap, gooey, icky, cardboard-tasting things!"

Nods of agreement at this, and a tinkle of social laughter which, since there's nothing intrinsically funny in the remark, I interpret to mean relief and gratitude. For Todd's mother is Black, yet has managed to introduce the minimum possible level of disharmony resultant from that fact into these pale proceedings. You can see how they love her for being so poised, so attractive in that simple dress and elaborate, sculptural necklace. A cute, plump-cheeked two-year-old in scarlet rompers, hair minutely corn-rowed, clings shyly to her chair. She outshines the general luster. I guess she has to.

And here I sit, in cropped hair and clunky shoes, lumpish, unable to think of a word to say. Isn't that how Brenda sees me, as she watches, vivacious with her half glass of wine, with the triumphant sense of having brought this off to the admiration and envy of her neighbors?

I tell myself I look quite respectable. Haven't I come from work? My pants cost twenty-five dollars on sale. I'm even wearing a bra. Hoop earrings in my ears prove I'm a girl. What more do they want? Should I pluck my eyebrows, tote breath spray in á purse?

Of course it doesn't help that I'm nobody's mother.

Once upon a time, when Ericka wasn't much older than Leah is now, Rhea used to tell her, "You have two mothers." That was an error, of course. I might be many things, might wake with her in the night and guard her play and comfort hurts and read monosyllabic books and praise her and scold her and make her eat vegetables – but children do not have two mothers. Anyone knows that.

So we got it settled: I was not her mother. But neither was I nothing. Which is part of why I now feel the way I do about Brenda. "Brenda is my new mother," I've heard more than once, on some occasion that required an explanation. I don't hold this against Ericka: she has to say it. But I do hold it against Brenda.

For other reasons, too, this competitive resentment I harbor against my child's stepmother is an interesting phenomenon, quite different from my attitude toward Daniel, and perhaps worth analyzing. What, for instance, occasions the irritation I feel when, strolling Seventh Avenue of a Saturday morning, too late to cross the street I glimpse Brenda coming? Engaged in that arduous labor of consumption upon which her family's existence is predicated, she's wheeling Leah in a fancy stroller. And though I know full well how tedious toddlers can be in public, there's something that particularly irks me in the sight of a child who's perfectly capable of walking lolling there like royalty borne on a litter. I smile; I exchange the requisite brief greeting (Brenda's evidently no more eager for conversation than I am); they proceed down the block. I'm left there holding that mixed bag of emotions—prideful scorn, contemptuous envy—which I suppose the drab in the gutter used to feel, splashed by the wheels of the good wife's shiny carriage.

In short: a pox on famous sisterhood.

Not, mind you, that I'd wish to undermine the fundamental proposition that Brenda suffers oppression as a woman. But I run into problems when I try to put my finger on the precise location of the injustice. Suppose one could X-ray her perfect-looking days. Where would the hairline fracture, the suspicious mass, show up? Where's the flaw in this crystalline structure? Where does it hurt? She believes she's chosen this opulent servitude.

And what would Nilda Campos have to say about it, as she stoops to fold yet another load of Brooklyn laundry, and wonders how her own kids up in the Bronx are doing?

But these reflections are destined to be cut short. Forlorn as I look, I tempt intervention. The woman sitting to my right has determined to make a charitable effort. I can see her leaning forward, revving up for it.

"Isn't this just the most fabulous party? I'm enjoying myself so much! I'm just afraid now TeriAnn, my daughter, will expect something really fancy!"

She's a small woman with tiny, almost babyish features framed by a heap of black curls. She rather resembles a miniature poodle, cuteness the effect she's aiming for, I suppose. Her clothes are too frilly for sophistication, and there's an excess of fuchsia-stained cigarette butts in the ashtray she holds in her fuchsia-tipped fingers.

"It looks like an awful lot of work," I hedge.

"Oh, but it's so important to them, their birthday, you know. Especially the girls. At least I know it is to my TeriAnn. Isn't it to yours?"

Rather striking, this assumption that I have "mine," particularly given Brenda's ambiguous introduction of me as Ericka's friend. I decide to ignore the question. "Is TeriAnn in school with Ericka?"

"Oh no." A rueful shake of the poodle curls. "That's a good school they send her to, though, Lincoln Prep. A very good school. Expensive. I'm afraid we couldn't afford it, even if—but we're Catholic. The kids go to St. Saviour."

"So you live here on the block?"

"Oh, no." Once more sorrowful, apologetic. "No, I'm afraid not. It's a lovely block, don't you think? Our block's okay—Second Street, just below Seventh—and we own our place, but it's nothing like this."

"So how did TeriAnn and Ericka meet?" Thinking some insight into my child's other life may be forthcoming; I can't remember her mentioning this kid.

"Dance class, they were in a dance class together last fall. Just for one term, but they've sort of kept up. Not that TeriAnn has much talent in that direction, but I thought it might improve her posture. Actually, I do feel she's becoming somewhat more poised. It's nice now they're old enough to walk to one another's houses, don't you think? Not that I let TeriAnn go *anyplace* by herself after it starts to get dark, though she tells me the other kids do. She's got to that age, you know, where every other word that comes out of their mouth is, 'But Mom, the other kids get to.' Have you noticed that with yours?"

"Which one is TeriAnn?"

The mother points out a thin, braced, bespectacled girl wearing a sashed dress in a synthetic fabric that takes me right back to my own early "party dresses." Sure enough, the child's posture leaves a great deal to be desired.

"And yours?"

"I'm sorry, I should have explained. I don't have any kids. I'm here simply as an adult friend of Ericka's," I manage quite gracefully. It's a gentler awakening than such presumption deserves, but I don't have the heart to be rude. TeriAnn's mother seems touchingly anxious to please, to feel herself at home here in this illustrious circle.

"Oh, I see." She looks uncomfortable as women do when they perceive that the answer to an innocent question tends to reflect discredit upon the person of whom they've asked it. Gallantly changing the subject: "How about you, do you live on the block?"

I divulge my apartment's modest coordinates.

"How do you like it down there?"

"I like it fine."

"I always wondered – I mean, it looks a little – "

I reiterate firmly that it's worked out well for me.

"But didn't I hear – isn't that the block where they had that awful thing happen – a woman got stabbed or something? Of course, it could have been anyplace, the way things are now. And since you don't have kids . . . it's true sometimes you can get a real nice apartment on those blocks that haven't gotten so fixed up yet. The values can be a lot better. Do you have a nice place?"

"Very nice. Just what I need right now." She's right, of course, though I wince at the vulgar wording. Objectively viewed, I am one of those transients whose role in the drama of urban manifest destiny is to form an opening wedge for the relentless drive of brownstoners, contractors, and co-opers eager to "take back" the block, the borough, and by extension, the world.

"What sort of work do you do?"

Here we're reprieved from our laborious chitchat; Ericka, coming up behind, has flung herself on me. "Josie Josie Josie! Guess who!" Her small cold hands cupped tightly over my eyes.

"Not hard. Hello, birthday kid. How are you?"

"Hello Josie, I didn't know you came. I was looking for you. I wondered where you were."

"You were too busy having fun to notice when I came in, I guess."

"I wasn't having fun, I was playing. Like my dress?"

"It looks kind of chilly. Don't you want a sweater or anything?"

"No, I'm *hot*. Honest. It's *roasting*. How do you like my party? Isn't my cake *scrumptious*?"

"It does look good. When do we get to eat it?" I'm none too taken with this keyed-up, showoff mood. Hard to tell, though, how genuine her enthusiasm is. She strikes me as protesting a bit too much.

"Hey Brenda, when are we eating my birthday cake?" she tosses rhetorically over a bare, shrugged shoulder. "How come you didn't come down and say hello, Josie? Is something the matter? Aren't you even going to wish me happy birthday?"

"Happy birthday, kiddo. Want me to give you your spanking?"

"*No way –* " and she darts playfully out of reach. "Daddy did that to me already this morning. What's that you're drinking?"

"Wine."

"Uh-oh, you're gonna be drunk. Can I have some?"

"Ericka, aren't you being a little bit silly?"

"Ericka, come here a minute, please." Brenda's tone is firm but pleasant. Casual: the expert manager. As though I were any childless friend of the family, a novice incapable of self-defense, whom her kid's harassing. I glare, detecting a calculated intervention. Particularly here on her home territory, of course, Brenda wants to avoid a display of my intimacy with her stepdaughter.

Ericka returns more businesslike, subdued. "I'm sorry, Josie, I have to call the kids. I'm opening my presents now, Brenda says. I'll come back later."

She rounds up the scattered herd down in the garden. Brenda is fetching scissors, a wastebasket. I stay put in my chair, content to watch from a distance the rending and tearing, the ritual violation.

Of course I'm familiar with this climactic moment, endemic to birthday parties: the remorseless frenzy of the defloration; the jaded, indifferent gesture with which each gift is laid aside as the young roué gropes about for fresh stimulus. Elsewhere in the world, in kibbutzim and communes, children are not encouraged in these consumeristic orgies, and I've known parents who, with that foreign ideal in mind, strove for a wholesome, socialist atmosphere at their own kids' American birthday celebrations. Rhea and I, however, who belonged more or less to the laissez faire school, used to grit our teeth and supervise the carnage. Gathering up what we could of the wrapping paper for reuse, we told each other Ericka would survive, just as we ourselves had.

But today the inevitable rapacity of the proceedings is emphasized by the costliness and sheer quantity of the gifts. There are complicated-looking board games and fancy jumpers; necklaces and bracelets and rings with real little opals; picture books about horses and the ballet; and from Daniel and Brenda a long procession of objects including a digital clock radio and a tennis racket. The audience quickly grows restless, though several of the girls dutifully finger the loot as Ericka discards it; they frown responsibly at the boys, who are speculating audibly as to the timing of refreshments.

Moving to quell insurrection, Brenda promises cake and ice cream the minute the presents are opened. My Pete Seeger album elicits the usual tepid thanks, along with the observation that Grandma and Grandpa Krevsky have that record, too. By now the deck around Ericka is ankle-deep in wastepaper and cardboard. Soon she's down to the final item, a small box wrapped in heavy, patterned paper.

"I saved this one till last. I think I know—"

"Don't shake it, Ericka," Brenda admonishes.

"Oh look oh look oh I love it. Just what I asked for. Look everybody, what my daddy gave me. You saw it already, didn't you Brenda? Josie, look, a real grownup watch!" And she elbows through the press of kids to show me.

The thing is silver, delicately banded. She particularly wants me to examine the accompanying card, on which sprigs of flowers frame the scrawled message, "For Ericka, with tons and tons of love, Your Father."

"Where is he this afternoon, by the way?"

"He had to work. He'll be a little late. We're supposed to be sure and save him a piece of cake. . . . Hey Brenda, don't forget to save some cake for Daddy." She's expertly casual—glib is the word, I think—almost like a woman with too much practice covering up for a philandering husband.

"Here. Put it on for me."

Obediently I fasten the pretty clasp. TeriAnn's mother looks on.

"There. Oh, doesn't it go *perfect* with my party dress?"

"It's fine, very nice. Better go back with your friends now, so we can all have cake."

We sing "Happy Birthday." Ericka blows out her candles, laughing she won't let us in on her wish. Then Brenda dissects the cake with professional-looking implements, while Todd's mother serves up ice cream. The mollified children subside onto chairs and benches. Soon enough, however, several of the less sophisticated begin complaining that they don't like the cake, it has "things" in it.

"Okay, Jason, just eat your Häagen Dazs, then."

The children settled, Brenda offers refreshments around to the grownups. The predictable wail over calories goes up, predictably resolved by calls for "just a sliver," but in the midst of cutting she's summoned to deal with the arrival of the magician who's been hired to provide the rest of the entertainment.

At first it seems like the moment for a quick getaway, but TeriAnn's mother, who's taken over the serving, won't hear of my not having cake. "Come on, live it up. You're not on a diet, are you? *I* should be, but I'm going to have a piece. Who knows when we'll see another cake like this one, right?" Finally I yield to this cheerful, insistent patter, and the conspiratorial wink which accompanies it.

Brenda returns, nibbles cake. The conversation flows, a broad, complacent stream. Abandoning the lone adult male guest to the morose consumption of several helpings of sugar, we concentrate on the female mysteries, especially reproduction. It develops that not only Brenda but also June and Paula, the other women wearing maternity clothes, have recently undergone amniocentesis.

Having rather enjoyed the element of surprise in her previous pregnancies, June finds she regrets knowing the sex this time, though of course it simplifies the name problem. Brenda, on the other hand, is just glad to know it's a boy, because, though Daniel is so marvelous with his daughters and of course would welcome another, she does think it's nice for a man to have a son as well.

"You don't know what you're in for!" TeriAnn's mother brashly interjects. "I mean, I'm real glad for you and all, but boys are so much harder than girls to raise. They're so much more active, right from the first, and into everything. . . ." She trails off, rather crestfallen; several of the other mothers are regarding her with marked severity.

"Boys and girls raised without sex-role stereotyping exhibit fairly similar development, I believe," the father stiffly corrects her. He's got frosting in his beard.

Brenda, ever tactful, heads the talk in a new direction. Soon her guests are eagerly swapping anecdotes about crimes against property.

"We changed all the locks; we thought it was an inside job—I'd had a mother's helper who had a key—and we waited six months to replace Hank's tuner and turntable, and wouldn't you know it, two weeks after we finally did, *they* were back!"

"*They* must have something worked out with a fence, because every time we've been robbed I've had some valuable jewelry lying right out in plain sight, and *they* haven't touched it—just took electronic stuff."

"*They* know what they're after, all right."

"I just got done paying—oh, let's say a small fortune—to have bars installed on all the windows where we didn't already have them, parlor as well as ground floor. Madge and I have started referring to the old homestead as 'Fort Jorgensen'," the father—Mr. Jorgensen, presumably—puts in, evidently relieved that we've finally hit on a topic he knows something about.

June says she's been considering a dog. "I won't have a Doberman, but Nick says shepherds will do if they're trained properly. I get so nervous sometimes when he's out of town and I'm alone with the kids."

"You've got every reason to be."

"Why not invest in a really good alarm system?"

"You're lucky, Brenda, to have a solid block association. I really believe *they* tend to stay away from blocks where people are organized."

I glance at Todd's mother. She looks politely interested. I can't help wondering what it is she thinks about the shade of the blurred faces conjured up by this unremitting *they, they.*

"I wouldn't bet on it," Brenda laughs sharply. "About six months ago *they* forced the back door – this was before we had the gate put on – one weekend while we were upstate. I think something scared *them* off, so we didn't lose much. But *they* did take some meat from the freezer, and, of all things, Daniel's scuba diving equipment!"

"I wonder what fence handled that!"

"Well, fortunately he hadn't used it for years. Still, you stop feeling safe. . . ."

"Yep, it's sad but true. Nobody's immune." Jorgensen looks determined to face the music. "Not in this town, anyway. You start to wonder whether it's even safe to let your kids out to play. Just last week some punks tried to rip off Pete's ten-speed."

Ericka used to play out all the time, with the other kids on our sleazy old block. She lived to tell it. But I can't say this, of course.

Brenda sighs. "I've lived in the city almost ten years now, and I'm telling you, I've lost patience. I never was crazy about the suburbs, but at least you could send your children to the schools you're supporting with your taxes."

Her comment provokes a plaintive recitation. Apparently a number of the company have experimented with the local public schools, found them lacking, and now feel personally affronted by the failure of their good-faith effort.

I've heard enough. It's high time I went. If only I could disappear and find myself safe on the street, not have to go through the motions of leavetaking, not have to smile at Brenda, not feel their eyes on me.

But, if it can't be helped –

I lean forward in my chair.

"Ericka went to P.S. 321 through the third grade, and she got along fine," I hear myself announce.

They turn to me with that mild, anxious interest the folks on a New York City bus display when a fellow passenger they've judged harmlessly dotty suddenly starts to exhibit threatening behavior. Encouraged, I plunge on.

"She really had some decent teachers. Not that their methods were very advanced or anything, but she liked them, and she learned to read really quickly. She had some friends in her classes. Rhea and I didn't have any problems with the idea of keeping her there."

It's a well-known rule of human interaction that as long as you assume your authority in a given situation, as long as you act like you know what you're doing while avoiding the fatal mistake of explaining yourself, people are hesitant to challenge you. Sometimes, emboldened by bitterness or wine, I can pull off a scene like this.

They smell trouble now, these innocent bystanders. But it doesn't appear to threaten them directly. Only Brenda flounders, panicked, in her lawn chair, and TeriAnn's mother turns to me with her exasperating candor and squeaks, "Rhea?"

Adrenaline is slowing everything, enabling me to admire my own performance. I turn to Brenda and add, quite pleasantly, "Actually, it surprised me that you and Daniel switched her to private school, when she was doing so well."

Goaded, Brenda defends, "Ericka really loves it at Lincoln Prep. And I must say we're very pleased with their approach. . . ."

I permit an awkward silence to ensue.

It's gallant Jorgensen who dashes to the rescue. "Well, I think several of us have had public school experiences that, you know—I mean, you figure, give it a whirl, what the hell, it sure is a heck of a lot cheaper than the other route, but mostly we've arrived at the same conclusion, unfortunate as that may be. Of course it's not so rough in the lower grades, but ultimately you've got to be realistic. I mean, you care about your kid, you want him to get what he needs. . . . Now take Madge and me, we found out pretty fast the administration was not interested in being even remotely cooperative, which is sheer suicide if they're sincere at all in saying they want to keep the middle-class kids. Which, let's face it, in the long run is the only way they'll save the city schools, if they *can* be saved, given how things are going."

The women look relieved, seem to feel released from something. Grateful smalltalk commences, a trickle and then a torrent. A flood tide of trivia swells, drowns the jagged contours of looming controversy.

Sobering, I begin to feel anxious. Yet what can Brenda *do*; what real power has she?

Well, Ericka.

But that nebulous, broad threat is nothing new. All year it's shadowed every move I make.

I must talk to Daniel. I've put it off too long.

"Whose mommy are you?"

The voice, which at first seems to be coming from underneath my chair, startles. Turning, I confront a blond three-year-old: fingersucking, portly, androgynous in overalls.

The question is so much the last straw that I'm tempted to come back with, "Which are you, a girl or a boy?" Little kids, I've noticed, generally can't abide confusion on that score. But, not being a monster of cruelty, I compromise and reply, "I'm nobody's mommy. Whose mommy are you?"

"I'm not a *mommy*" – solemnly indignant – "I'm a *boy*."

High time I went, indeed. I go looking for Ericka. The little prick tags behind me, chanting, "I'm a *boy*."

"Oh, shut up, Greggie," Ericka commands. I've located her in a corner of the deck where she's whispering with a clutch of sticky girls. Dishevelled, wired on sugar, they plot some mischief. "We don't want any spies here!" she orders him off; explains, "Greggie's Melissa's brother. He's kind of a pain."

"I came to say goodbye, and thanks for the party."

"You mean you're not staying for the magic show?"

"I think not. I've got stuff to do at home. But I'll be seeing you tomorrow."

"Gimme a kiss."

"Okay, chocolate face. Here. Have a good time."

I discharge my last duty of the afternoon by thanking Brenda, who interrupts her talk of childcare woes to smile impeccably at me. "Thank *you*, Josie, for taking the time to come." Her tone clearly seeks to underscore the extreme remoteness of my connection to her family.

TeriAnn's mother says she'll walk out with me.

"Wasn't that party terrific!" she enthuses, once we're out on the sidewalk. "But I was beginning to get a little headache, maybe from the wine. I'm not used to drinking in the afternoon! Anyway, I've got to pick up my son at the neighbors', and then my husband will be expecting dinner. TeriAnn can walk back alone, now it gets dark later. Did you enjoy yourself?"

"It was fine," I mumble, to encourage her. Somehow I don't

mind it that she talks too much.

"That cake was fabulous, and TeriAnn's having a ball."

"Oh, the kids seemed to be having a great time."

"But. . . ," she sounds a surprising, hesitant note of doubt. After a pause, she resumes, "I've never felt all that comfortable with Brenda. Not that she's not a nice woman. She's very nice. And Ericka's one of TeriAnn's nicest friends. But . . . I don't know. Maybe I shouldn't be going into all this now. Are you close friends with her?"

"With Brenda? No, not close."

"Oh. From what you were saying about the schools and all, I had the impression you knew each other pretty well. Anyway, it's hard to put my finger on it. I don't know if it's something to do with him being a professor, or . . . but then, it's a classier block. And she always dresses so well. I mean, I don't guess her clothes are really super-expensive, but she always looks so sort of *sophisticated,* you know? I end up feeling ugly and dumb around her. And then I get nervous and put my foot in my mouth. Did you see how they all looked at me when I said that thing about raising a boy?"

"I know what you mean," I try to reassure her. I suddenly want to be worthy of her trust, and am painfully conscious of having indulged myself in secret amusement at her frilly clothes, her assumptions about gender.

"Oh, that's good! I hate to sound weird."

"By the way, tell me your name. I keep thinking of you as 'Teri-Ann's mother'."

She laughs. "Donna. Donna McInerney."

"And I'm Josie Muller—so you'll know, just in case we run into each other somewhere around the Slope."

"I'm sure we will, I sure hope so. It's been *good* meeting you, Josie. Look, I guess I'd better run in here and pick up some meat for dinner."

Her odd, voluble friendliness has kindled a small glow that warms me a minute or two after I've watched her glossy curls bob off to disappear inside the butcher's. Then I'm alone with my worries.

I let things slide after the accident. Belle and Sam, Rhea's parents, flew up from Florida, and after the funeral they took Ericka back down there with them for a brief stay. Then Daniel said he wanted her over at his place. Nothing was ever made very definite. He talked about a period of adjustment and used the word "flexibility" a lot, and I, having no rights, clung to that. He said we could work things out better after we'd all had a chance to recuperate. Meanwhile, Ericka would be spending regular time with me. I was stunned and heartsick; I didn't press anything.

I miss Rhea so sharply in these moments, when I see how I counted on her in any trouble. And I'm afraid to fight, to feel too much. But none of that matters; I've got to say to Daniel: look, I'm here. I'm Ericka's parent, too.

I don't want to go home just yet. The traffic-pulse pounds toward evening, the dinner hour. Soon, night, but I'm expected nowhere. I want to walk the streets for a long time; to let motion tumble and sort my thoughts as water sorts and tumbles pebbles in a stream; to stare into the shop windows and lighted, familial houses; to peer into the faces of the others, the hurriers rich and poor, the shoppers, workers, mothers and fathers, the *real* grownups, the people with obligations.

* * *

As arranged, I reach the house at five p.m. Daniel opens the door. He's the Weekend Father in his stocking feet, a drink in one hand, Leah's small pink paw in the other.

"Step in, Josie, she's still getting ready."

He bellows upward that I've arrived and disappears behind doors of stained oak. I detect the thin mutter of the television.

Though I know from experience what nasty tricks it plays, I can't resist taking a look at myself in the built-in mirror bordered by glossy carving. Even in the soft, tactful light shed by the two wall lamps with their old-fashioned glass shades, I strike myself as looking washed out, my shoulders hunched in the infamous tall-girl stoop Mother always preached against, my mouth drawn down in mug shot resignation.

Ugly dyke: the vicious caption flings out of nowhere, more obscene than a curse.

No, mirror, you're quite right: I don't belong here. Wasn't formed, it seems, for gracious brownstone living.

I wonder which Ericka I'm about to see, what sort of mood she'll be in. Always this suspense before our meetings. It would seem more natural to go upstairs and find her, not languish here in the entry like a boyfriend kept waiting by his date. But that isn't done. I await her appearance.

She has described her new room to me, however, and I'm very familiar with it. On the third floor, it's the one I once rented. There Rhea and I used to make love on my lumpy mattress, while we listened with half an ear in case she woke up early from her afternoon nap downstairs.

Finally she materializes on the landing. She's lugging an overnight case. "I'm sorry to hold you up. I had to pack." She's so reserved and formal, so sophisticated in her belted jumpsuit – a practical style I approve, despite my suspicion that it's the height of spring fashion – that I feel rather lucky to receive her cool kiss.

"Hello, kiddo. You look very nice."

"Josie, would you maybe carry this for me?"

"Part of the way. Then you can carry it the rest. What did you pack in here? Jesus, this weighs a ton."

"What's Jesus got to do with it? *I'm* Jewish –" and she ducks into the other room to say goodbye to Daniel.

Now this is a joke, but mildly obnoxious, because meant to signify distance. It's a subtler version of the old *you're not my mommy.* One of the major drawbacks of our current schedule is that the testing period she often seems to require before she can be sure of who I am, who she is in relation to me, sometimes extends over the better part of the visit. We just get settled when she has to go.

Once out on the street, I try light conversation. "So how did your party go?"

"Okay. It was cool." She accompanies this with a blasé little shrug.

"And the magic show?" I attempt.

Another shrug. "Okay. I mean, pretty good, I guess."

"The other kids had a good time?"

"Uh-huh."

It seems to be a law of our interaction that I wax cheerful, cajoling, as she grows sullen. I suppose I overdo it, like a mother plying a delicate child with food. But I can't seem to help it – she does seem delicate to me. Over the year I've gotten into a habit of anxious watching. I couldn't say exactly what it is I fear to detect – the crack across the heart, the shadowed X-ray, an almost nineteenth-century foreboding as of pleurisy or consumption.

"I see you're wearing your new watch."

"Uh-huh."

"Did your father get his cake?"

"Yeah. But he came home after the party got over."

"Oh, how come?"

Another shrug, resentful. "Had to work, I guess."

Here is perhaps the clue to her moodiness. I feel the old bile rise: so he spoils my time with her. Like the early days, before Brenda, when Rhea and I were always having to repair his damages. Ericka would come home from a visit with him overtired or with a stomach ache and we'd be the ones to pay.

I stop trying to talk, allow the silence. After a while she asks about my week.

"Pretty average. Same old boring stuff at work. We're putting together a new coffee table book. Collectibles, this time."

"What's that?"

"Yesterday's chochkes at today's prices."

"You don't like your job that much, do you? How come you don't go work someplace else?"

Not for the first time, I try to explain real life. "I just don't like doing most of the things I know how to do to make money. A new job most likely wouldn't be any better."

"My father and Brenda like the jobs they have."

"They're very fortunate."

"Couldn't you play your flute? You used to do that."

"Not for a living."

"But you could. You play good. . . . How come you never want to play anymore, anyway?"

"That's not entirely true. I play with Katya."

"But you hardly ever."

"Well, I don't know. It's too noisy here." This sounds like a feeble excuse, but there's a good deal of truth in it. When I first moved to New York, I was never especially bothered by the cosmic racket the city generates. Like everyone else, I took it for granted. Only lately have I begun to notice, realize it's been eating away at me all this time like some unsuspected chemical pollutant, corroding my ear, dulling my appetite for sound. When my fingers twitch with the habit of intricate patterns waiting to be worked out on cool keys and my lip expects the pressure of smooth metal, when I crave the exercise of difficult etudes, when some spore-like, airborne phrase fraught with melodic possibilities invades my ear, more often than not I put away the impulse. What's the use of my frail, idealistic music in the face of this implacable universe of radios, traffic, shouts, sirens, and subways, of toilets relentlessly flushed and garbage grindingly collected?

But Ericka wants me to promise I'll play for her.

"Sometime, yes."

"Tomorrow?"

"We'll see."

"*Please.* For my birthday."

"Don't beg, Ericka. I said we'll *see.*"

We're picking Jasmine up on our way back to my place. I've been thinking of this as routine. It's only now, as we turn the familiar corner, that I realize how I've tensed for the encounter with the block. The two of us haven't been down here in four or five months, not since the last time Ericka played with Jasmine. It was easier then, in a way. Now the memories are stiff, scabbed-over.

Barren of trees or any sort of shrubbery, eerie in failing light, the street is bleaker than I remembered, a narrow canyon defined on either side by the scalloped cliffs of brick eight-family houses pressed tight against the sidewalk. Abandoned buildings, their windows tinned over, are scattered among the still-occupied ones like mold spots spreading on fruit. In the middle of the block one stark facade gapes open, unsealed, raw, sinister as a chancre.

A few more stoops and then our old place. "It's for sale!" Ericka cries.

And sure enough, there squats the realtor's sign in the window of the Negron's ground-floor apartment.

Poor Mr. and Mrs. Negron! What unimaginable catastrophe can have overtaken them, forced them to put up that sign?

They had bought the place shortly before we moved in. They were older people, near retirement, and looked on the property, which they'd saved for decades to own, as their chief security. I heard them talk about leaving it to their children, and how they had faith in the block despite its problems—they were sure it would soon be "coming up" like the rest of the area. They kept in readiness for this expected future; valiantly they battled dirt, roaches, petty vandalism, and the endless spontaneous decrepitudes of old flimsy buildings. Patched, cobbled—basic repairs were beyond them—their house still managed to hold its head high.

Our relations with them were not particularly affectionate. Mrs. Negron, especially, cast a suspicious eye on our manless ménage à trois; if we had a night meeting, she was sure to complain about "parties." At the time I keenly resented the harassment, yet now I feel for her. If only they could have hung on a few more years. . . .

Three doors down from the Negrons' a group of teenagers clusters on the stoop. A distinctive contrast of masculine grumbling and feminine giggling is audible as we turn in at the gate. I stiffen, anticipating an awkward moment. Jasmine's bell is chronically broken; we'll have to holler up.

Then Ericka says, "Hi, Jasmine," and I spot her.

She's tall, suddenly, blends right in with the teenagers. Except that I decide, on closer inspection, that a number of these kids are in fact prepubescents who are practicing very hard at teenager-hood as they ply their Afro combs and pop their gum; move, in the warm air edged with evening chill, gently to the staticky disco beat that pounds from a small radio on the top step.

"Hi," Jasmine greets, without enthusiasm.

"Hello," I say brightly. "Are you about ready?"

Silence. Blank look. Then a thought: "Oh wow, you mean it's *to-day* I'm sleeping over?"

"What did you think we're here for?" Ericka demands ungraciously.

"Oh shit! I went and forgot all about it."

The kids on the stoop are convulsed by appreciative titters.

Just as I'm thinking Jasmine really wants out of the deal, she mounts a saving display of energy. "Hey, lemme out of here, I gotta pack. Catch you all later. Josie, do I bring my party dress?" Not waiting for an answer, she whisks into the entry. Her friends ignore us, fan out across the stoop.

After a short, uncomfortable interval, a window above flies open with a loud, protesting creak. A woman's head pokes out. "Come on upstairs, no need to stand out there in the street. That Jasmine got no manners."

Relieved, I lead the way in. Ericka and I climb the dusty, sagging staircase through layers of cooking smells to the door on the third floor right, where we're ritually examined through the peephole. Jasmine's mother opens. "Hello, how you feeling?" She's wearing slippers, has her hair tied up. Her lined brown face is thinner than I remember.

I am glad to see her, and want to say something, but, "Fine, thanks," is all I come up with.

While I lived on the block, she and I always maintained a polite, nodding acquaintance, perhaps slightly exaggerated in its correctness. ("Why do you call her 'Mrs. Webster'?" Ericka once queried, sharp enough to note that there weren't many women I dignified with the old-fashioned title.) She knew Rhea, knew we were not sisters; of course I assumed she'd formed some sort of opinion about us, but whatever it was, she kept it to herself. I was grateful for small favors.

"Why don't you go sit down in the front room," she directs now. "I guess Jasmine ought to be ready pretty quick. I want you to know I do appreciate you taking her out like this, and I know she appreciates it too, even if she don't act it. Now if you'll excuse me, I was just getting dinner."

I know her apartment's layout intimately. A railroad setup, it's the mirror image of our old place. The string of open rooms is an arrangement singularly deficient in privacy, as Rhea and I discovered. Here, with five kids, the crowding must be intense. Ericka and I negotiate a dark passage huddled close with bunkbeds. The front room, thronged with furniture, is very neat. A meager oasis of snakeplants and philodendron subsists on a shelf beneath the dingy windows. We perch on armchairs swathed in slippery plastic. They confront a massive, old-model television which focuses the surrounding furniture.

This gives Ericka ideas. "Can I watch TV?"

"No, please, let's not start that now."

"How come?"

"It's not ours, kiddo. Just be a little patient."

She frowns. I see she wanted to lose herself, blot something out.

At last Jasmine shows up. "Okay, I'm ready!"

Like Ericka, she seems prepared for a grand tour. Her accoutrements bulge from a giant shopping bag.

"Great. You and Ericka wait here a minute. I want to make sure your mother has my phone number, and let her know when you'll be back."

The kitchen is shabby, clean as scrubbing can make it, yet dirty with the soot and grease of decades ground into its every crevice. Mrs. Webster stands at the window, her back to me. She faces out toward black, budding branches. Behind them, buildings; behind, a grimy sunset. A padlocked gate protects against intrusions from the fire escape: good security against burglars, but potentially disastrous in the event of fire. Her arms half-raised, she grasps the barrier in an odd, suppliant gesture.

"We're on our way," I announce, over the hiss of whatever she's got cooking.

She jerks around, startled. "What's that you say?"

"I said, we're on our way out. I just wanted to make sure you have my phone number, and let you know I'll bring Jasmine back tomorrow around four-thirty or five."

"Oh, that's fine. . . ," she gropes, recovering. "I got your number written down, I guess."

"You want me to give it to you again?"

"No, that's fine. You don't have to bother."

Somehow I don't quite want to leave it at that. "Look, I was wondering—how have you been? I mean, I haven't seen you in quite a while. All the kids okay and everything?"

"Yeah, we're all right," she asserts heavily. "I been having some more of this gall bladder trouble, is all. So I'm not quite right today."

"I'm sorry."

"Thanks. I'll be okay."

"You've been to a doctor about it?"

She shakes her head no. "But that's all right. I've had it before this. They never tell you nothing different, anyhow."

I feel she's tired, in pain; I ought to go. "I saw that For Sale sign up on our old building. How come the Negrons are selling?"

"He had a stroke, here, a couple months back."

"Oh no."

She nods. "It's a shame all right."

"He's going to be okay?"

"They say they don't know. That's these doctors—all they charge, you think they'd know more. Anyway, he's pretty sick now. He ain't working. They can't keep up the payments. How's she gonna maintain that big old place, all by herself? And she's got to be tending him."

"He wasn't that old."

"No, he wasn't. . . . Seems like they tried so hard," she summarizes.

I say I'd better be going.

"Say"—to my surprise, she moves to detain me—"How about you, you doing all right?"

I wonder how she means it.

"I mean," she fumbles, embarrassed, but why I'm unsure, "you and Ericka and all . . . her losing her mother . . . I felt so sorry for the both of you, after that accident."

I'm touched. "It's been a tough year, but we're doing okay."

"Well. . .," she seems at a loss.

"Look, I won't keep you." I leave her there, propped painfully over the stove.

"You take care now," she calls, after a moment.

"And you feel better," I answer, uselessly.

Still, I feel somehow strengthened by her unexpected acknowledgement, better prepared to cope with ten-year-olds.

Back in the front of the house, I find said ten-year-olds absorbed in conversation, but of course they clam right up when I appear. The walk home is rather strained, with Ericka addressing most of her remarks to me while Jasmine lags behind, a diffident stranger.

Anticipating their problems in getting reacquainted, I've made plans to involve them in dinner preparations. The strategy seems to work; by the time the kitchen is in ruins and the hamburgers are on the table, they appear much more relaxed with one another. At dessert, however, we hit another snag. Ericka, possessed by what evil impulse I can't imagine, begins a detailed description of the refreshments and entertainment which were featured at her party.

Jasmine veers from judicious disbelief ("Come on, girl, you know you didn't have all that!"), to frank envy, particularly of the famous magic show, to thinly-simulated indifference. I finally intervene at that dangerous stage at which Ericka is pressuring her to substantiate her dubious, frantic claim that, "I had stuff just as good as that at *my* birthday, anyway."

I feel, of course, like hauling Ericka off by the ear and standing her in a corner. Instead, I produce my present, the sweater I've been saving.

"Oh, Josie, it's pretty," she approves, rushing to try it on.

"I'm glad you like it. It took me a while to knit."

"You didn't knit this."

"I certainly did."

"But me and Brenda saw one almost like this in Bloomingdale's."

"Brenda and I," I correct intolerantly.

"Brenda and I. They were having them on sale. I almost got one, in case me and Daddy go skiing in Vermont next winter. He said he might take me. And I could wear this."

I repress any outward sign of irritation at the prospect of my honest gift being employed for this obnoxious purpose. My diversionary maneuver appears to have succeeded, for Ericka drops the subject of her party, and Jasmine brightens up. The two of them resurrect a favorite entertainment involving Beebo and Red Emma, who, having grown complacent in their virtually child-free middle age, look none too thrilled at being made to "walk," "talk," and clap their paws together in games of "pattycake."

Finally I take pity on the cats and dispatch their human tormentors to my room to watch television. Reading my book, drinking my wine on the couch, I can hear periodic bursts of live mirth resounding over the grating sit-com laugh track. Already I anticipate the necessity of reading them the riot act, issuing the strictest of injunctions against bouncing on my mattress.

In short, the weekend promises to be a hit; I envision return engagements. Only it's difficult to arrange such occasions when my time with Ericka is so severely limited.

That one has an obvious solution. I've got to speak to Daniel, wring some concessions from him.

*   *   *

Following a classically inane matinee at Radio City, I take my charges out for classically gooey sundaes. Then we hurtle back on the IRT to Brooklyn.

Ericka wants Jasmine to stay to supper, and Jasmine guesses her mother wouldn't mind, but I veto the proposal. I noticed Ericka yawning on the train. She and Jasmine were up pretty late, and I'm well acquainted with the negative effects which, predictable as a chemical reaction, fatigue produces in her. Besides, I want us to spend some time alone.

"We'll do this again soon," I cheerfully promise, pretending not to notice their dramatic scowls and groans. We stop by my place to pick up Jasmine's things, then walk her home. The pre-teen crowd is camped on the stoop once more, and she dashes off to greet her true, indigenous cronies.

Ericka is taciturn, thunder-faced.

I begin to feel rather injured: some thanks I get. "What's wrong, kiddo? I thought you had a good time."

"Nothing."

As we pass a store, I ask what she wants for supper.

"Nothing."

"Ericka," I begin in arctic tones, "I think you can make up your mind either to discuss your problem with me, or to be a bit more pleasant."

"You should know my problem!"

"Well, I don't. I'm sorry, I'm not a mind-reader."

She marches a block or two without reply. I remind myself to stay calm. After all, I don't have very long to put up with this. Her father will come for her in a couple of hours.

In a sense, though, that's part of the difficulty. Whatever's going on, we don't have much time to fight it out.

"How come Jasmine couldn't stay to dinner?"

Now I know this can't possibly be at the root of it. Nevertheless, it puts me on the defensive.

"I think you're mean! It's supposed to be my birthday. . . . And Jasmine doesn't like me anymore," she adds presently, with belligerent satisfaction.

"Now wait a minute, I think that's pretty silly. The two of you may have had a little trouble at first, but I thought you ended up getting along very well."

"Yeah, she's such a terrific friend, she hardly even says good-bye to me!"

"Oh, Ericka, come on. You know it was just because those kids were there. I think maybe she felt a little embarrassed in front of them, showing up with us. You'll see her again soon."

But intimations of hope only strike her as fresh insults, ingenious attempts to thwart her further, when she's bent on pure despair. She flings herself against the high iron fence of a grey stone church we happen to be passing and collapses, sobbing emphatically.

A hot shock of resentment surges through me. Why must I always be the grownup with her: so much blotting paper to soak up her rancor, all her real or imagined slights and wrongs and disappointments? Why must I rein in my seething irritations while she rides hers full throttle?

Sometimes, in fact, I used to give in to my baser impulses, and rail and threaten, when Rhea was around. But not now. Things seem too delicate.

I approach her gingerly. "All right, all right, sshhh, Ericka, calm down." Grudgingly I stroke her wild hair. At least tears represent a sort of progress, like the breaking of a fever.

She shakes her head, won't have any comfort. Her sobs are harsh animal bellows. Mucus pours, a sticky hemorrhage. Passers-by are turning around to look at us. I search my pockets. Not a single Kleenex.

"Nobody likes me, I don't have any friends – "

This simple narcissism makes me want to smile, but at the same time I'm starting to get worried. She seems so energetically bent on misery.

"Ericka, listen, try to calm down. We can't talk about it till you – "

"I don't want to talk about *anything*."

She breathes raggedly, gulping in air, diptheriac in self-lacerating frenzy.

"Ssh, ssh. . . ." Against her will I hold her.

She chokes and sputters. Gradually she calms; dribbles; drips; sniffs; wipes her muddy, sad, flash-flooded little face unselfconsciously on the back of one plump arm, the wrist of which the "grownup watch" still graces.

I feel more tender, somehow softened by her tears. "Well, kiddo, that's better. Let's get on home now. We can talk about all this while we're having supper. Goodness! Look at your face, good thing you didn't melt." I muddle on, afraid to stop talking; ease her along like a skittish horse that might bolt.

She's still not prepared to concede there's any hope, but at least she takes the hand I hold out to her. Our progress punctuated by loud sniffles, we hobble home at the invalid's pace she sets.

Upstairs, I dispatch her to the bathroom to clean up while I start supper. After several minutes of vigorous nose-blowing she emerges with a relatively composed if still desolate countenance, and huddles in silence near the stove where I'm fixing creamed tuna and toast, a bland, somehow comforting dish which, because I associate it with childhood illness, now seems appropriate. Inspired, I even locate a can of peas far back on a shelf.

"Hey, Ericka, you want to have a picnic on my bed?" That was something she and Rhea and I used to do occasionally for a rainy day diversion.

"I don't care."

So I carry the plates into my room. Ericka settles back against the pillows. Deliberately, with excruciating slowness, she sets about spearing a mushy grey-green pea on each fork tine.

I am still rather shaken by the recent upheaval, and would rather not disrupt this joyless peace. However, it's got to be done; just as Rhea and I used to be obliged despite her howls to extract the splinters she acquired running barefoot over the wood floors, so now I must dig for the source of her misery.

Clumsily, I begin to break her down. She won't feel better till she talks, I threaten. There must be more to it than Jasmine.

The tears flow again, as they must, but more slowly now: singly they splash into congealed white sauce. Rather bored, I bide my time, watching her spear those peas and thinking what an odd notion of vegetables informed my childhood.

Then something surprising. She heard Daddy, she says.

"Heard him what?"

"Tell you about the money."

"The money?" I know what she means, but I need more to go on.

"Last week. You know. The milk money and stuff."

"Oh, that." I'm now in a delicate position: she may take offense if I indicate I believe him, may once again deny all the charges. "I'd almost forgotten about it," I say truthfully.

She seems encouraged by this. "It's not fair. . . ."

"What's not fair? That he talked to me about it?"

"I don't know. Everything's not fair. Everything's just horrible and yucky."

"Suppose you tell me about it. Why you took the money."

"You'll just get mad," she artfully suggests.

"I don't think so. It's not the stealing itself so much as the reasons why you did it and how unhappy you seem that I'm worried about. Are you so upset because of what you did, or because you didn't feel like you could talk to your father about it?"

"I don't know. Both, I guess."

"Were you mad at the boys you took the stuff from?"

"No, not really. How could I be? I didn't even know them." Odd, but she's suddenly dry-eyed, competent.

I decide the time is ripe for some amateur therapy. "I want to try an experiment," I tell her. "Shut your eyes."

"What for?"

"So that the eminent Dr. Josephine Muller may, by dint of her formidable diagnostic acumen, learn what dismal and arcane affliction has the dubious distinction of having rendered a sanguine young person such as yourself a quasi-basket case!"

"No, Josie, really!" she protests—but coyly, preparing herself to be seduced. We have played this game before, and my mock pedantry always seems to entertain her.

"Never mind, you'll see what happens. Now go ahead, close your eyes. Good. Now I want you to relax a minute, then try to think back to how you felt when you took the milk money."

"Wait a minute. Are you hypnotizing me?"

"No, I solemnly promise I am not hypnotizing you. I left my hypnotist's license at the office. Now go ahead, remember how you felt. What were you thinking about? Did it remind you of anything?"

More quickly than I expected, she nods vigorously.

"You thought of something?"

"Uh-huh. Can I open my eyes?"

"Okay. What?"

"Do you remember when Mommy used to steal?"

Dismayed, I hesitate. After Daniel's session with me, I naturally puzzled over his report and arrived at some tentative conclusions about what might be going on. Ericka's upset over the recent drastic changes in her living situation, I thought; perhaps inadmissible anger at the Feins. But I never made the connection to Rhea's shoplifting—nor, despite my comments at the time, did I seriously consider raising the subject of her mother with Ericka.

The insight is unwelcome: I am rather like Daniel. I too have been guilty of preferring not to look too closely at her messy, incurable grief. And have taught her by example to mourn in secret.

It was different at first. This has happened gradually.

"Don't you remember?" she's prompting.

"Of course I do, kiddo. I'm sorry. I was just thinking."

Rhea shoplifted for years. She'd started sometime before I knew her; it was standard for the period, of course. I tried too, in fact, but it scared me in a way I didn't enjoy—I don't like horror movies or roller coasters, either—and I stopped after a few experiments. Rhea, however, discovered a true vocation. Expropriation, she claimed, afforded a unique outlet, particularly when she felt depressed. Dressed as decorously as she could manage—in her "Park Slope housewife outfit," as she said—she'd hop a train to Manhattan and return a few hours later, the Macy's shopping bag she'd taken with her for the purpose stuffed practically to overflowing with small luxury items that showed up piquantly against the background of our general austerity. In obedience to an odd superstition, she refused to steal the basics. Only things we never would have dreamed of paying for showed up in that bag of hers: scented soaps, artichoke hearts, packets of saffron, books of art reproductions. I still drink coffee from a stunning grey cup with blue anemones hand-painted on it.

But the risk she was taking increasingly bothered me. Almost from the beginning I refused to accompany her on her expeditions, and soon I asked her not to tell me what she had planned until it was safely over. Which didn't help much—I always guessed. We used to have terrific fights about it. She quit finally, but it took an arrest to convince her.

"Mommy almost had to spend the night in jail, remember?" Ericka is reminiscing. Of course Rhea and I had to explain the whole thing to her; she must have been six or seven at the time. How we struggled, impaled on her childish absolutism! Stealing was wrong, she insisted.

"But what did all that about Rhea have to do with your taking stuff from those kids?"

"I don't know what it had to do with it. It's just what taking the stuff made me think of, like you said."

"Did you feel like you were doing what she did?"

"I don't know, not exactly. . . . Josie, how come, if it's okay to steal, like, from some big store, it isn't okay to steal from other people?"

"Suppose you tell me what *you* think."

"But those kids wouldn't hardly even miss that stuff I took! Their parents are rich, honest. They live on the Promenade in Brooklyn Heights, at least one boy does. And I heard this other kid say he gets ten dollars a week allowance!"

"Oh, Ericka—" But I scarcely know how to put it.

"What? See, I told you you'd get mad."

"No, kiddo, that's not it. I'm not mad at all."

"What, then?"

"Look, let's forget about the stuff you took. You're right, the kids probably didn't really miss it, only don't do it again. It's not fair to them, and it makes you too miserable. What's more important, though, is what you were saying about how everything's horrible. . . ."

"Huh?"

"I mean, it's been such a terrible year for both of us. We haven't stopped missing Rhea. And it's such a long time since we even talked about it."

In reply, she picks up her fork, starts toying with cold food.

"You know what I'm saying, don't you? I'm sorry. It's my fault, a lot."

"What good does talking do." She makes it a flat statement.

"Well, not much, in a way."

"So don't talk."

Glancing at my watch, I see it's a while yet till Daniel's due. I want him here already, I want her gone. The distance between us now seems unbearable, and I feel drained, weary, utterly lacking the energy required to keep battering away at her admirable defenses.

No: it's worse than that, if I'm honest. I'm apathetic, with the dangerous apathy that signals loss of hope. So inevitably we seem destined to be strangers.

In any case, something has to fill the time until Daniel shows up. Ericka wanted to hear me play the flute, I remind her.

It's okay, she says, it doesn't matter now.

But I'm determined. It seems better than talking. "Really, I said I'd play for you and this seems like a good time. I'll be ready in a minute. Lie down, if you feel like it."

Taking my flute down from its hiding spot behind a row of books where I hope it would go unnoticed in the event of a robbery, I see Ericka was right in her accusations. It's been so long since my last duets with Katya that an incriminating layer of dust has had time to accumulate on the case. Well, nothing to be done about that now: time, emotion, talent down the drain. No use crying over spilt ambition. And here's a nasty scratch I never noticed before on the real gold mouthpiece which, warmer than silver, produces the finest tone. That mouthpiece seemed so utterly thrilling a badge of accomplishment and earnest of triumphs to come, back in the days when I was planning on growing up to be a famous flutist and my teacher informed my parents that I was ready for a professional instrument.

A few warmup arpeggios, then I launch into a Bach sonata. It's one I once learned by heart for a competition, and I never quite stopped cherishing a secret affection for it, not even during the subsequent period when I was influenced by a climate of opinion which held classical music in disrepute for a variety of political reasons: as Western, elitist, or reprehensibly male.

I wander around the apartment as I play, glad to escape Ericka's morose surveillance. I'm getting the notes out all right, but only just. They ring on my critical ear thin, breathy, mechanically reproduced. I feel my fingers stiff, my embouchure flaccid. Which is after all precisely what I deserve: I haven't been practicing.

Finishing the Bach, I stand looking out the window. Beneath me under the street lamp the wild boys still pursue their raucous pleasures. I can hear their howls of *chickenshit* and *faggot*.

I start noodling around, stringing notes together. Gradually I can feel the music warm, loosen, take on a breath of spontaneity. I seem to glimpse certain possibilities.

But they can wait until after Ericka goes. First I will make one more effort. I place the instrument carefully in the center of the table, where the cats won't knock it off, and go in to her.

She lies on her stomach, face buried in my pillow, exhaustion scrawled in inert and crumpled limbs.

Poor tired kid. But she's got to stay awake.

Down I sit beside her, stroke her hair. "Hey, kiddo, don't fall asleep now. Your father will be coming pretty soon."

When, not asleep at all, she flings herself into my lap, besieged by weeping, rocked with the single question, over and over, the last thing I want to hear:

"Josie, why did she have to go and die?"

* * *

We have wept together, holding one another, in the oceanic darkness of the bed, as we did in those first strange hours after Rhea when the two of us seemed fused in radical grief, our sorrows open and touching one another. We have wept our fill, our emptiness of tears. We have huddled silent under the fraying quilt, in shadow patched with a distant square of lamplight.

We have started to speak in whispers. She has wanted the old stories. I have told about Ericka Huggins, the brave Black Panther woman whose name she shares—that is, what I recall of

46

Rhea's schematic version, the one designed for a five- or six-year-old, the one she used to ask for over and over. For tonight, I know, she's after the ritual of it.

"And I was named for her, sort of, wasn't I?"

"Well, partly. And for your mother's grandma Eva."

"Tell me about the mountains."

So I've spun my fairytale of Yosemite: how in June the flowers poke up through melting snow and the alpine firs straighten, shrug off their ice-burden. How clear the air is, how violent the storms. How ravenous the mosquitoes, how steep the high peaks. How early the winters close in, and how frail and tough is the thin veneer of growth stretched over rock above treeline. How deep in the night-pit burns the galaxy, the thrilling indifference of those untouchable worlds.

(But always, promoting this legend, I think of smog: how it creeps, inexorable, inland, a few miles further each year. Think, and exclude from mention.)

Now how can this urban child possibly believe me, possibly credit that such places do exist? But she has remembered to ask, as she used to ask, when I will take her there.

When she's big enough, I've said, as I always say.

This time she hasn't been satisfied with that. "Really, Josie, when will that be?"

"When you're thirteen or fourteen, maybe—if it's okay with Daniel and Brenda."

And I've made her put her shoes on, and wash her face. And Daniel has shown up, tardy and jovial, and noticed nothing amiss. But watching them, I've satisfied myself that this week, at least, he does not claim her fully.

I have locked them out. Cleaned my flute and put it away. Laid out my clothes for morning. Brushed my teeth. Finished the paper. Watched the ten o'clock news.

And fallen asleep, into a dream of Rhea.

She's been in prison. She calls me to say she's out. I'm to meet her somewhere in midtown Manhattan. I have to take all sorts of transportation to get there: a bus, a subway, at last a helicopter. Finally I give up and start walking. The traffic is absurd; even on foot, I can hardly get through the crowds.

It occurs to me that there must be some sort of crisis going on.

I locate the coffee shop where we're supposed to meet. Inside, I find Rhea at a table with a lot of other people—women from prison, I gather. There must have been a general amnesty.

Or perhaps there's some connection with all that traffic? In a crisis, mightn't they turn the prisoners loose, give them that chance at least?

I'm disappointed not to find Rhea alone, but I suppress the reaction, judging it individualistic and selfish. She greets me warmly, and I cheer up. "Don't worry," she assures me, "we've got plenty of time." All around us women are eating enormous plates of blintzes with sour cream. Look at all that food, I tell myself. Things must be all right.

She excuses herself, saying she has to pee. I wait and wait but she doesn't come back. After a while I go looking. The restroom is vast, tiled, silent. Inside the last stall I find a revolving door, like an office building entrance.

I exit to the street. It's winter now. Snow is heaped up, trackless, immaculate: not city snow.

But the city is empty, I notice.

Whatever the crisis was, it's apparently been resolved. Still, I did see Rhea. She's got to be around. . . .

Clutching my souvenir glimpse of her bright, sweet face, I wake in Brooklyn darkness.

* * *

Okay. Rhea, then.

I was twenty-one and fresh off the plane when I met her. In the bravest act of my ignorant young existence, I had recently dropped out of college and abandoned the evergreen hills of Oregon for the grey synthetic bluffs of the Big Apple. I spent the first few months of my Eastern exile sleeping in a studio apartment in Astoria and taking an interminable elevated train ride into mid-Manhattan each morning. My biggest mistake, aside from renting in Queens, had been to mortgage my future to an employment agency which had secured me a clerical job "in publishing."

Concealing from my parents my grim determination never to return to school, I had simply given them to understand that my desire to spend some time on the East Coast had a lot to do with my musical aspirations. I told myself this, too. In fact, I was a fugitive of sorts, but one who could scarcely have explained to her own satisfaction what, exactly, she had to get away from.

I had come resolved to immerse myself in music. But thanks to the extortionist employment agency, I found myself virtually without discretionary income, and for months my concerts were pretty much confined to WQXR, the jazz stations, and the hopeful streetcorner bawling of Greenwich Village "folksingers."

Meanwhile, problems developed with a neighbor, a retired civil servant who was always home in the evenings. He had decided that my music interfered with his digestion, and would bang on my door and threaten to call the super whenever I tried to practice—or "compose," as I dared to hope I was doing upon occasion. The threat was absurd, of course, but it wrecked my concentration, and for a while there I didn't play much.

I had cherished the usual youthful fantasies about the bohemian, politically-charged atmosphere New York could be expected to offer. Needless to say, both Astoria and midtown failed me in this regard. I knew exactly one person in all the five boroughs, my friend Luce, also recently arrived from the West Coast, who was then crashing somewhere on Avenue C in circumstances so squalid that one visit scared me off. Once in a while she'd phone me up about some Women's Liberation "action," and I would meet her and march around, fist clenched, yelling militantly (I'd learned how to do that much in Portland at least). Afterwards we'd go somewhere for coffee. But she seemed to know her way around so well that I was intimidated. And I couldn't quite feel myself a real feminist: not because I had any quarrel with the movement's aims so far as I understood them, but because I hadn't yet surmounted the nagging feeling that perhaps there were some tacitly understood membership requirements which I failed to meet.

Inevitably, I gravitated to the Village, where, though nothing much happened, I always felt it might. I got into the habit of going there after work. I would walk downtown from my office, partly for exercise, partly to save the thirty-five cent train fare, and partly because it still thrilled me to struggle with rush-hour traffic. I can't remember now how I managed to locate my first women's bar. Perhaps it was mentioned in one of Jill Johnston's *Village Voice* columns, which I read religiously. At any rate, I at first got a great charge out of these excursions into a milieu I was pleased to regard as exquisitely decadent. Any knowing Villager who happened to observe my passage through that unlabelled, conventional-looking, yet notorious portal might, I thrilled to reflect, suppose me a Lesbian. I even liberally allowed that I would not be at all averse to trying sex with a woman, should a chance present itself. Examining my own responses, I had long detected intermittent twinges of seeming bisexuality, and I was curious to find out what they might mean—whether I'd simply been overstimulated by drugs, Janis Joplin stories, and the laissez-faire ideology of the moment, or whether, as I hoped, I was really a bit — *that way.*

But depravity rarely pounces with the convenient simplicity of an Ann Bannon plot, and since I did nothing more aggressive than to sit discreetly ogling the dancers from my observation post at one of the small tables, weeks went by in which nothing much happened. I simply sat there sipping my very expensive drink, and smoking a very occasional Marlboro (in the context of the bar, these mild intoxicants once more took on something of that aura of irresistible wickedness they'd possessed in my young adolescence, before grass and hash and acid and psilocybin). Gradually I grew inured to the spectacle of female couples locked in emotional tete à tetes over their beer glasses, women dryfucking on the dance floor to the pantingly heterosexual lyrics of the slow numbers. Occasionally I would enter into desultory conversation, all very businesslike. Once when I made some sarcastic remarks about Queens, the young woman I was talking with advised me to try Brooklyn. "The rents are much cheaper there than in the city, especially in Park Slope. That's where all the young, hip people are moving."

Though I smiled at the word "hip," which reminded me of high school, and though I rather dreaded abandoning my secure if boring beachhead out in Astoria, I soon began checking the classified ads. And thus it came about that, six months or so after my solitary, apprehensive debarkation at the space-age Ellis Island of Kennedy Airport, I rented a room with kitchen privileges on the top floor of Daniel Fein and Rhea Krevsky's decrepit Park Slope brownstone.

Brownstone: how I relished reporting I lived in one. The architecture itself seemed to make me a real New Yorker. The place had until recently been a rooming house, and there were about six toilets, one in every bedroom. The walls were noxious shades of green and pink. The lighting fixtures were fluorescent, the floors covered in layer upon layer of cracked linoleum. The owners were doing their own renovations. The building had been delivered to them empty, they took care to emphasize — they weren't displacing anyone. Nor, though they rented to me, did they wish to be in any kind of power position.

I noticed too that Daniel, who had been until recently an adjunct lecturer, doctoral candidate, and part-time politico, still appeared a bit sheepish and apologetic about his new fulltime position at NYU. His wife, I thought, seemed more to be trusted. Her politics were surprisingly good, I judged, for her advanced age — twenty-seven then — and the bourgeois family setting in which I found her. (Though my own political involvement during college had been minimal, I had absorbed certain purist notions from the atmosphere around me.) I did rather look down on her for having married, but at least she'd kept her name, a decision fairly unusual at the time. She ran an informal Free Nursery School for Ericka and other neighborhood two-year-olds, wove densely textured fabric on her loom, puzzled out how to improve the ancient wiring and plumbing, attended demonstrations, and fabricated cheap, surprisingly tasty meals out of beans, grains, tofu, vegetables. We shared the standard oppositional stance which held that everything currently in existence was irrevocably fucked, corrupt, "fascist," and unfair, and in need of being replaced wholesale rather than piecemeal, by some spontaneous and magical process of combustion. We regarded with uncritical admiration an outlandishly ill-assorted revolutionary pantheon including Che, Emma Goldman, Karl Marx, Germaine Greer, Jimi Hendrix, Chairman Mao, Kate Millett, Fidel, Madame Binh, Eldridge Cleaver, Carlos Castaneda, and Angela Davis.

Rhea seemed to like having people around. She confided she'd have preferred to live communally, but Daniel had vetoed that. Though I was the only roomer, and at first ate separately, there was often a crowd for dinner, seated around a table made of plywood and sawhorses. The company seemed to disagree with Daniel, who would scowl at his plate and finish rapidly, afterwards withdrawing upstairs to prepare his next day's lecture in the conjugal bedroom, at that time the house's most rehabilitated zone. He'd leave Rhea to clear off the table and shoo away the raggle-taggle multitude, which might be comprised of kids from the block, women from her C-R group, childhood friends, nursery school parents, food co-op members, or politicos in transit. She would wash the dishes as she performed all domestic chores, with an insouciance which seemed to belie their oppressive implications. Once she said rather defensively to me that, after all, the big dinners were *her* idea, not Daniel's. And anyway, he was the one supporting the household, except for the little her weaving sometimes brought in.

I wasn't entirely convinced; although I didn't contradict her, I secretly suspected that these arguments would not hold water with, for instance, Luce's militant coterie. I felt free, as I've said, to judge Rhea. But even as I did so I was rather in awe of this compact, small-featured woman in the bright shawls and skirts, dangling earrings, flamboyant hats. She was older, grownup, a mother. She had a knack with people. And she *was* New York to me: that is, the alien, ethnic, fiercely political East which I, the raw and rootless West Coast kid, so much admired. She negotiated the subways with a fearless ease I despaired of ever attaining; made matzoh ball soup, baked mandel bread and challah; was unafraid of the water at Brighton Beach; knew where to get underpants by the dozen on the Lower East Side, where to go for Chinese tea lunches, what to order in Indian restaurants. Though she evinced scant reverence for any sort of tradition, Jewish or otherwise, at intervals fascinating Yiddish expressions I couldn't remember having heard before from Jewish friends in Portland or LA would issue from her lips: *tsuris, naches, schmate, treyf, potchke.* Loathe to inquire and display my ignorance, I would look them up later in the pocket Yiddish-English dictionary I'd purchased as part of my effort to educate myself in the customs of the country. (My parents, I might mention, are lukewarm Congregationalists; I remember my surprise and naive dismay at learning this fact qualified me as "Christian," as New York reckons such things.)

Though Rhea had the normal Sixties anarchical contempt for rigid structures and party orthodoxies, she nevertheless seemed to be well up on the histories of local political groups, their programs and lines, their myriad feuds and splits. She had actually gone on the famous Pentagon march, the one immortalized by Norman Mailer. And when she happened to mention off-handedly one day the circumstances in which her parents had left the Party ("You mean Communist?" I'd blurted gracelessly), I was so impressed I could hardly contain myself.

All the same, at first I resisted Rhea. Being shy, proud, lonely, and very young, my initial impulse was to keep my distance from all this splendor and dazzle, Rhea's circle—sometimes it struck me as more of a maelstrom—of friends, lovers, neighbors, whatever they were. (It was difficult to tell, for she greeted almost everyone who came in the door with the same enthusiastic kiss and hug.) I was renting a room, not joining a commune, I thought. But she was no less friendly to me than to anyone else ("What a time I had breaking down that damned indifferent goyishe facade of yours," she'd rib me later), and I slipped into the habit of sharing cooking, watching Ericka occasionally when she and Daniel went out.

Ericka was the first toddler I'd been around since my own brothers were little. Even in high school I'd never been much of a babysitter, and recently I'd been traveling in circles where kids, the consensus had it, were symptoms of convention, irremediably "bourgeois." Now, with this flesh-and-blood child, I felt nervous, excessively eager to make a good impression. I envied Rhea's off-hand manner with her.

The Fein-Krevsky marriage, I shortly learned from Rhea, was the resolutely unconventional union typical of the period. She and Daniel had married in the mid-Sixties with the usual assumptions, but in recent years had agreed to be nonmonogamous. Rhea was frank, even humorous, about the problems this presented. Each was jealous, she admitted, when it came to the other's adventures. At least Daniel usually pursued his in the city, discreetly, at a distance. "But I'm in Brooklyn. . . ," she smiled, with the self-deprecating gesture of the immobilized housewife.

We were lovers within months of my move to Park Slope.

In the end, I was the one to bring it up. I tried to make it all seem as casual as possible, matter-of-fact in our liberated age, a point of information—"you know, I really feel sort of attracted to you"—in the kitchen, always her kitchen, after weeks of tracking the movements of her body beneath the flowing clothes, her small soft breasts under the tie-dyed T-shirts; weeks of tingling attention each time she kissed me hello.

"Oh lord," she sighed, smiling, "life's already so complicated," and I laughed in a show of terrific sophistication, hiding my chagrin.

But several weeks later, on a day when I'd called in sick and holed up in my room to play music (I'd gone back to the flute again since leaving Queens, and Rhea was encouraging me in it), she climbed up to the third floor on some inconsequential errand. And we ended up making love on my narrow Goodwill mattress on the dusty rough floorboards beneath the curtainless window.

I was far too scared that day for easy pleasure, afraid of doing it wrong, flunking some test—but enormously relieved to have touched a woman at last, and electrified by the thrill of experimentation, breathless as any sixteen-year-old with excitement of new tastes and textures. I recall her breasts against a backdrop of furniture, cinder blocks and orange crates, hovering just above eye level. I remember, mostly, how her mouth astounded me, after the hard mouths of men. And after, my sense of exultant outlawry.

So we began an "affair," with the usual resolutions to live only in the moment, not worry where we were headed. Daniel made no public scenes, but grew increasingly sullen. At night in their room, Rhea told me, he would accuse her of a subconscious desire to humiliate him by taking up like that with a woman right there in the house. Would he rather she'd taken up with a man in the house? she quite sensibly retorted. Well, if she had, he maintained, not really addressing the point, at least he would not feel so subtly mocked – he was beginning to wonder if she really liked men, anyway. If the opposite sex weren't so sexist, Rhea declared, she might indeed be more enthusiastic about the prospect of including its representatives among her lovers. Oh god, said Daniel, now I'm a sexist pig too, I suppose. Is that what you talk about in your women's group?

Rhea wavered, guilt-torn. She would give me up: a necessary concession. No, she wouldn't give me up. It wasn't fair. . . . I was not her first woman lover, but I'd come at a crucial point. She was getting fed up with Daniel, with married life; she'd begun to look for something. There were months of agony and indecision, but the upshot was that we rented an apartment and took Ericka with us.

I still wonder what she saw in me. Not only was I young, I had spent most of my life in milky, homogenized middle-class environments which thwarted my ever-intensifying craving for strong impressions, contact with "real life." So far most of my attempts to satisfy this itch had been by way of vicarious participation in the exploits of angry boys who lent me paperback copies of Kerouac and Mailer, played their B.B. King and Velvet Underground albums for me, taught me to suck cock and roll joints. As for the famous political eruptions which were transforming the social landscape, despite my attendance at various demonstrations, my work on an underground newspaper, I seemed to have witnessed these through some transparent barrier, so that I could watch the lips moving, the fierce gesticulations, but could not quite hear the shouting, not quite smell the fear.

Maybe what Rhea saw was simply that I would love her. It scared her sometimes, what she felt with me, the depth of it, she said. It took her back. She found herself letting her guard down, admitting her longing for a basic grounding and security she'd had some brief sense of in early childhood. Her first solid memories from three and four and five were of being the well-loved baby of the family, with warm sensible Belle always there like a caricature of the all-American mom – except plumper, maybe, and darker, but pretty, smiling – in the cramped, warm, tidy kitchen cooking something, letting a little girl lick the bowl. "You'll laugh," Rhea said, "I know it's what you had, and you saw the other side, all that Fifties bullshit, but I ate it up. That was really my notion of safety and being loved, that picture of her and her kitchen. Pretty trite, I guess, isn't it? God, it scares me sometimes to think about Ericka – wondering how she'll grow up to remember all this. I suppose it's inevitable she'll be angry on some level about my leaving Daniel – that's got to be her fantasy paradise, hasn't it, the time she can't really remember when the two of us were married?"

Rhea's own childhood idyll was very soon over, with Belle gone back to teaching elementary school someplace in Staten Island, coming home distant and tight-lipped in the late afternoons. The older kids, put in charge after school, were resentful of looking after a bratty baby sister, and there was no way for a first grader to grasp that the chilly, ungenerous atmosphere at home wasn't really a matter of being deprived of the birthright suggested by the images of blonde, beaming mothers featured in the pre-primers from which she would soon learn to read, mothers of pink, priggish children with ridiculously simple problems and strangely truncated names, not the Irwins and Esthers, Evelyns and Leonards, of Rhea's experience. But in fact the sudden tension was due to large events: the busybody Cold War poking into everything, even their quiet corner, its bony obscene fingers; the mean and prosperous Fifties coming on like gangbusters with blustering Joe McCarthy revving up, so that all the grownups, her parents and their friends, soured and tightened, grew stern and sharp with fear.

And yet there were plenty of kids on the block, other Jewish kids who lived in small apartments like the Krevskys', whose parents seemed not to dread or even notice the deepening gloom and chill, so that it felt to Rhea as though she and her family were under that cloud in the Al Capp cartoon, a very special private cloud meant just for them and all the other "progressives." It was because they were different, she came to understand – and hated, temporarily but passionately, this "progressiveness" that shrivelled common pleasures.

She had plenty of other memories from the early Fifties: friends of her parents over, after her father lost his printing job especially, everyone sitting around in little worried bunches, conspiratorial over sour cream and herring, quick to change the subject when their offspring came barging into the room on some pretext or other – but the children caught the dire, mysterious phrases, "subpoena" and "blacklist," "witchhunt" and "pogrom." And then there was the day she went skipping into the front room with a handful of red and yellow leaves which she intended to press in one of the heavy books with gold-lettered spines that clustered together in their place of honor on the shelf, the works of Marx, Engels, and V.I. Lenin. But those books had disappeared; there was only a wide, empty spot where they'd been, with a little ugly vase squatting in the middle. She'd gone to Belle about it, and Belle had answered her, in a sarcastic tone that meant something more than the words said, that those books had been taking up more than their share of space, and how about using the Sandburg life of Lincoln?

Or Larry Meislin, whom she'd never liked anyway, but was always expected to play with since he was her same age, brought over by his folks one Sunday afternoon when they showed up for one of the grownup worry sessions: how he tortured her with tales of the Rosenbergs, described how it felt when they strapped you into the Chair, pointed out Julius and Ethel were somebody's parents, too, and taunted maybe *her* mom and dad would be next. And she'd stood up to him — *I bet they get yours first* — and had wept in terror, later on in bed.

But the child who wished for a family like other families grew into a dissenter; the child who longed to escape from politics had politics under the skin. For a time this too would distance her from her parents, her father in particular remaining staunchly Old Left in outlook long after he'd resigned from the Party. When she began living with me, it created fresh trouble. "Okay, so do what you want," Sam angrily blurted, "do what you want in the privacy of your own home, but don't tell me about it!" He calmed down considerably after a talking-to by Belle, and things were smoothed over. Both elder Krevskys were very civil to me, but I was always nervous around them; partly because they were living in Florida, I didn't get to know them very well.

Still, I liked them both, especially Belle. I liked her formidable competence at life, which I saw reflected in Rhea. I liked her blunt tongue and her tart, oblique kindness. I enjoyed her frank gossip about the Old Left ("The Dennises — now, not that we really *knew* them, I don't pretend we were on *that* level — but people talk, and I never felt Gene was fair to Peggy"). Rhea's older brother Art and sister Etty were apolitical, and I think Belle revelled in her youngest child's feminism even as her letters sped north, their recipes and news of gardening interspersed with cautions against "going too far" and reminders that "men are not the enemy."

For Rhea and I had plunged into the women's movement. As far as I was concerned, coming out had been like clearing the decks for action. I had committed myself, made a statement, and was no longer embarrassed or defensive, even in front of Luce. I was full of energy. I joined a socialist-feminist study group, a reproductive rights action group, a group of lesbian musicians who attempted to conduct a comparative investigation of the historical relationships of women to music in various Eastern and Western societies. I took self-defense, walked the neighborhood rape patrol. Meanwhile, Rhea got involved in a new C-R group, all lesbian this time, trained to do rape counseling, and soon became involved in planning and organizing a shelter for battered women which she eventually directed for several years. So Ericka, too, entered a heady political milieu, and words like "demo," "boycott," and "benefit" early on assumed their place in her vocabulary.

I was callow enough at the time to have been over-impressed with the rigor of separatists and sectarians; fortunately for my development, then, Rhea was resolutely non-doctrinaire. She approved of Emma Goldman's famous dictum that political change should not preclude dancing. Erratic in the view of her detractors, she was perhaps no more self-contradictory than anyone else. It was just that she was singularly unafraid of her own inconsistencies. When she'd finished quoting Emma, she liked to cite Marxist theory in support of her opinion that contradiction is what makes change possible.

She knew how to bring things off with her dramatic sense of timing, her surface self-confidence. Sometimes I judged her reckless, as when she shoplifted, or when she would rush out of the apartment in the middle of an argument, no matter the hour of night, to stalk the streets with short, vehement strides that would take her for miles before her rage abated. She was relatively indifferent to material security, and never complained about leaving Daniel the house, for instance, despite all the work she'd put into it. Sometimes we clashed over this attitude. I liked living frugally, but it was important to me to have reliable health coverage, to be sure where our next month's rent was coming from. Rhea tended to assume that things would work out somehow.

Another cause of sporadic conflict between us, at least initially, was Ericka. Certainly it made things easier that she was so young when the three of us started living together. Even so, the divorce upset her, and she was jealous at times of my claim on Rhea's attention. As I struggled to insinuate myself into the mother-daughter nexus, there were many moments when I felt like a hapless organ transplant besieged by an indignant swarm of antibodies. In the end, all three of us were very lucky, for by the time the dust of an almost ritual confrontation had settled, Ericka and I had discovered that we rather liked one another.

Daniel fortunately showed no interest in custody. He saw his daughter from time to time, but ignored Rhea's suggestion that he establish a regular schedule of visits. Anything reminiscent of their lost life together was, he intimated, too traumatic to be borne. He was feeling terribly injured, and I suspected him of malingering, but was too guilty over my magnificent good fortune at his expense to press the point with Rhea, who, steeped in her own guilt, tended to humor him. He took to dropping by without advance notice, and would loll around our kitchen, holding Ericka on his lap but not really looking at her, barely attending to her frantic prattle. His reproachful glances at Rhea were most eloquent. He smoked a lot and seemed to have lost a few pounds, which, given his already lanky build, made for an impressive concavity of feature. We privately nicknamed him "Heathcliff," and would explode in relieved, satirical mirth the minute he was safely out the door.

Ericka seemed upset by these lugubrious visits, and finally I urged Rhea to ban him from the premises.

"If I do, he'll never see her," she objected.

"Would that be so terrible? Look how anxious she gets. At least you could go out or something when he comes, not subject yourself to all this manipulation. Besides, maybe you're wrong, maybe he'd shape up if you'd quit catering to him."

Matters improved with time and a change in Daniel's fortunes. Brenda entered the picture shortly after we heard that he'd been promoted to Associate Professor. He became a lot easier to deal with and started taking Ericka one day each weekend.

"He wants to show the girlfriend what a terrific father he'll make," scoffed the by now thoroughly disillusioned Rhea.

"Never mind," I told her, "now you can relax. He's finally starting to realize how much happier he'll be without you in the long run. Of course you've never been what he wants, not really. Aside from those unfortunate *tendencies* of yours, you're just too damned unconventional."

The truth was that at times her "unconventionality"—sexual, above all—would trouble me too. She saw other women during the time we were together, a situation I found no easier to deal with than do most enlightened but insecure partners. Still I always believed she loved me, and we somehow got through the rough spots.

And so I get to keep on wondering what would have happened in the long run. Maybe, I tell myself—unsure whether to take heart or grieve afresh at the thought—we'd have parted anyway, embittered and disillusioned. Or perhaps we'd have lasted, she'd still be here with me, we'd slog on into the future, exemplary in our quirky fidelity, to become a legend, a mythic pair sitting rocking on the porch of the Lesbian Old Age Home which, as we used to joke, poetic justice required she end by administering, another sort of battered women's shelter, a Veterans of Domestic Wars retreat—and she a charming, wrinkled relic whose food I'd chew in some ultimate geriatric intimacy, I younger and sound of tooth, who had not grown up with Brooklyn candy stores.

But no matter what, no matter if we'd quarreled, denounced, wounded, hated, parted on the most destructive terms—were she alive, were she breathing, here, in this city, or in any other corner of the planet, I would have some way of moving toward or away from Rhea. She would be a mortal woman among women, to make peace with or forget. And it didn't happen like that. This disappearance of hers, this unconscionable evasion, this subtraction of Rhea from the universe, is a lump in my throat I can't swallow or choke up, a shard of reality I can't assimilate. Made out of granite, encased in shatterproof glass, it's a strange exhibit, out of place in my tranquil apartment, though I've learned to walk around it, sleep nearby, set magazines and beer cans on top of it, and tactfully indicate its significance to nervous visitors, like a woman I once knew who entertained a python in a terrarium she kept in her living room.

As Rhea's image recedes, unchanging, into the distance, I sometimes feel as though I recede, too. Or—

But no. That doesn't really describe it, either.

She had gone upstate for a conference on family violence. She was supposed to get back around ten on a Sunday evening. I waited up for her in the living room, where I was listening to a Mahler symphony on a scratched library record; I had decided for some reason that it was time I knew about Mahler. I remember sitting there patching a pair of jeans, trying to ignore the scratches and focus on the music.

She didn't come by ten, but it wasn't until I'd switched off the record and put on the eleven o'clock news that I really began to worry. Even then, at first it was only a minor wrinkle of anxiety, a grudge I could pleasurably nurse, planning how I'd berate her, once assured of her safe arrival: "You might have called! Didn't it occur to you I'd wonder where the hell you've been all this time?" And then I forgot all that and lay down on the couch, thinking I might take a little nap—it was very late, now—but instead found myself concentrating on the varied, arcane creakings of traffic on the stairs, each sound grown familiar through years of repetition. In counterpoint, the wind-driven rain rattled the front windows in their half-rotted frame. Cars idled promisingly down in the wet street, and the front door groaned open, banged shut. But no one mounted to the fourth floor.

When the phone finally rang, I sprang on it in relief and irritation.

But a strange woman's voice: operator, maybe.

Did a Miss or Mrs. Krevsky live here? Yes? Was I her roommate? Well, then. This was something-or-other office, State Highway Patrol.

She'd been traveling south on the thruway. There was sleet interspersed with rain. South of Albany, between exit such-and-such and the so-and-so service plaza, a truck and trailer rig in the oncoming lane had swerved out of control. Mrs. Krevsky, in the driver's seat. . . .

Here I had the first of what would be many encounters with the consolations of the word "instantly."

The voice went on. Angle of impact . . . two passengers, one stable one guarded . . . need to contact Mrs. Krevsky's next of kin.

We started arguing over this last point. Dimly, I felt I should call Belle and Sam myself, and declined to give out their number. The voice on the line begged me to understand the need for relatives to be officially notified. It seemed to me that I was a relative, but of course I couldn't say so, and we went round and round for a surreal interval while all the time some detached piece of my brain was remonstrating with me: the lady's just doing her job, don't give her a hard time. And still it seemed I couldn't get out of it, till at last she hung up with an ill-humored exclamation. And I put the phone back and sat there staring at the slip of paper on which I'd dutifully jotted the number to call about funeral arrangements—*funeral arrangements,* how absurdly stuffy it sounded—wondering, out of skeptical radical habit, now how do I know this is true, suppose there's some mistake, do I really call up these old folks in Florida at two o'clock in the morning on the strength of such a bizarre phone conversation?

And all the time just wanting Rhea home, wanting her assistance and advice, her reliable sympathetic outrage when she heard how I didn't count as a relative. And no pain, exactly—I was already checking symptoms—but only that dazed outrage that is with me yet: *how is this possible, it makes no sense, how can they ever get away with this?*

But knowing I would have to call Florida. And then it would start, the machinery of mourning.

In the end it was fairly simple. Belle and Sam, as though familiar with tragedy, seemed to know what to do. They said they'd catch the earliest plane they could. Sam volunteered to double-check with the authorities, and Belle firmly instructed me to get a friend to come and stay until they arrived. I tried Luce, who came immediately. She was ruthlessly practical as a seasoned nurse, and made coffee, and awkwardly held me, all the time exhorting: you've got to think, kid, they'll be swarming all over tomorrow—the relatives, Daniel—you've got to think *now*.

Which was excellent advice, but I couldn't then—not about anything except how to tell Ericka, who became, in that instant before I was to lose her, more my child than ever. Because always before there'd been a higher authority, a final arbiter and miracle-worker; if nothing else would comfort when she woke with a bad dream, I had always known I could calm her down with, "Go to sleep, we'll tell Mommy in the morning." That night I inherited the curse on mothers: whatever I couldn't fix would go unmended.

I woke her with the news before dawn. Better, I finally reasoned, the brutality of this method; better for her, later, not to feel anything had been kept back, not even for a night, than to wake to the betrayal of innocent-seeming morning.

But it was bad for a few minutes, like some hideous surgery. Childlike, she resisted my efforts to rouse her, and even when I finally had her up was too groggy at first to get it. She finally did, and that seemed even worse, and we cried together and dozed and woke and cried. And slept and woke, and the room filled up with light, and Luce cooked some sort of breakfast, and Belle and Sam called from the airport; they were taking a cab over. And I jumped up and started sweeping floors, afraid that Belle would disapprove my housekeeping.

The Krevskys handled the details. Belle informed the family, including Daniel, whom she tactfully dissuaded from rushing over. Sam arranged things with the funeral home. For people like the Krevskys, for whom rationalism had been the religion of their youth, cremation seemed the logical procedure, and I didn't contradict them, though I've wondered since if it mightn't have been better to have had some spot to visit, some marker in one of those tenement-crowded New York cemeteries. This way, Rhea's disappearance is complete, no slate or marble to weight her drifting bones.

The Krevskys stayed with us for about a week, and in that time I got to feel especially close to Belle, who had the tact to indicate immediately that of course since there was no will it would be up to me to figure out what to do with Rhea's few possessions. Still, I knew she didn't see our relationship as quite on a par with marriage. She seemed rather dubious about my ability to cope with her granddaughter, whom she "took off my hands" at every opportunity. That naturally bothered me, but at least I thought her offer to take Ericka back with her to Florida for a week or two made some kind of sense. I needed time alone to begin to sort things out.

Before they left town Daniel called up, pointing out that the two of us should talk. I'd known this was coming, of course, and had broached the topic with Belle; the two of us had had some long discussions about Ericka's future, had caucused in the kitchen after putting her to sleep while Sam sat in the front room methodically reading the *Times*, habit his only bulwark against sorrow. To my astonishment, Belle mentioned that the two of them had considered suggesting Ericka come to live with them in Florida. They apparently feared her father might not want her (though Belle put it tactfully, simply referring to his "new situation" with Brenda and Leah); it simply hadn't crossed their minds that I would be prepared to bring up "someone else's child." When I'd succeeded in convincing her that I wanted Ericka with me—part time, of course, if Daniel preferred it that way—but was anxious about my lack of legal standing, she expressed the optimistic opinion that her former son-in-law would "be reasonable."

And reasonable he seemed, or at least encouragingly vague. We had our talk while Ericka was away, and he came out with something like this: "I'm no ogre, Josie, and I'm certainly not about to snatch her away from . . . everything she's used to. On the other hand, she *is* my daughter, of course. But don't worry, I'm sure we can work something out."

I knew I should have talked the situation over with Ericka, but I hadn't wanted to face it, had preferred to imagine her mercifully unaware of all possible complications. I learned better when she timidly inquired, long distance from Florida, "Josie, who will get custody of me?"

Knowing she dreaded more than anything the prospect of fresh loss, I rejected the dire language, echoed Daniel's assurances. But in fact he ran the show when she came back. The coup was bloodless. I had no leverage, and certainly no emotional surplus to expend in losing battles. I tried to appeal to Belle at one point, but she seemed distant, reluctant to interfere, and I understood that she was still rather impressed by the natural rights of fathers, even those for whom she had no personal fondness.

I took what terms were offered. A lack of choice was even a sort of relief. I went out and got a fulltime office job. I packed my things and moved to a smaller apartment, one where the rent would be easier to manage, not to mention the memories.

*　*　*

I'm slipping, I decide. I'm out of shape. Too passive and re-moved from things, too much given to rueful self-satisfied con-templation of the disasters outlined in the *New York Times*, sketched on the TV news. Rather like someone embarking on a moderate exercise program, I decide to start going to demos.

A call comes through soon enough from Lesbians for Reproduc-tive Freedom, a group on whose phone tree I remain an honorary twig though I haven't attended a meeting in two years. A five p.m. picket and rally are scheduled three days hence in front of the Waldorf Astoria to protest the arrival of a certain right-wing Latin American leader who's stopping in New York on his way to Washington. LRF feels it's particularly important to support this action given the U.S. role in victimizing women throughout Cen-tral and South America . . . and so on and so forth, a breathless two-minute rap designed to persuade me that American im-perialism is really a sort of international rape or battering, hence worth my opposition. If I'd care to join them, they'll be there with the banner.

I decide to go on my own, avoid LRF. The group did some de-cent coalition work a few years back, but recently has suffered an influx of rosy-cheeked, energetic baby dykes whose talk is all "gynergy," "vision," and "patriarchy." "Process" is another of their watchwords, and at the last meeting I attended I felt so tyran-nized by raging structurelessness that I fled in dismay.

The Waldorf's a brief walk over from my office. Arriving, I pause on the curb across the street from the blue police barriers to survey the situation. A good turnout, evidently; already the picketers seem cramped into the one short block we're allotted. Their chant rings loud and clear: *Jimmy, Zbignew, you can't hide—we charge you with genocide.* Plenty of cops, a dozen or so on horseback, but the atmosphere's calm, everyone's clear on the rules. This isn't '68 or '69 and nobody's head's about to be split open, nobody expects to be trampled by killer horses in front of the Waldorf on a nippy April evening.

Luce and her gang, I note, are nowhere to be seen, but I soon make out the LRF banner: patchwork letters dancing on a lavender ground, a relief to the eye, I admit, after the leftists' rectilinear layouts and clenched-fist graphics. Signs lettered on oaktag sound the familiar note: "NO TO PORN, RAPE, AND PHALLIC IMPERIALISM," "PATRIARCHAL $$ ARE KILLING OUR LATIN SISTERS." I smile and let them pass, then take the plunge, fall into place sandwiched between alien slogans, glad to mingle, anonymous, nonaligned, in the crowd of white leftists, Black leftists, supporters of Puerto Rican independence and advocates of Zimbabwean liberation, feminists, pacifists, Trotskyites, anti-militarists, marshals, button sellers, newspaper hawkers, and undercover agents, all of us matching our steps to the time-honored rhythm: *El pueblo. unido. jamas será vencido. El pueblo. unido. jamas será. . . .*

My pleasant obscurity turns out to be short-lived. Hailed by name from the sidelines, I turn to confront a tanned, broad farm-girl face, a couple of short pale pigtails, and a Fifties bohemian-style beret and poncho. It's my friend Wendy, back in town after an extended absence. She introduces me to her companion, a young Asian woman in a down vest bright with political buttons who's got a kid in a stroller.

Wendy and I met in a study group a few years back. She's a painter, and after the study group dissolved the two of us used to get together once in a while to discuss music and visual art and politics, utility and truth, and our common origins in middle America. Having grown up on a family farm in Indiana, she shared with me a lingering, dazed sense of relief at the luck of having *gotten out.* By the laws which governed the world of our childhoods, even art should have been beyond us, let alone activism—yet here we were in New York, doing both. Not that we spoke directly of our good fortune; it would have struck us as unseemly, I suppose, to have celebrated openly our escape from those fabled worlds of all-American privilege.

I've always liked Wendy's deliberate way of moving, as though she simply declined to take note of New York's imperious demand for speed; the contrasting intensity of her conversation; her vintage "beat" getup superimposed on the solid grace of a Hoosier just in from the cornfields. Still, our friendship has been casual, oblique; I haven't heard from her since she left town. Now she suggests we get something to eat later, and I agree despite my distaste at the prospect of filling her in on my recent miseries. It never fails, I notice: just when I'm convinced everyone's finally heard about Rhea. . . .

I fall back into line – what I'm here for, after all – and we trudge around in the faithful revolutions of oxen grinding grain, our major entertainment the brief crescendos of chanting for the benefit of the TV camera crews. At last there's a break for the rally, and Wendy resurfaces. The sound system is bad, nobody can hear the speeches, and finally we take off for a coffee shop.

On the way, she fills me in on her recent travels. She spent about six months in Mexico, worked hard on her Spanish there, then traveled to Guatemala. Saw what she could of what was happening, tried to make connections with women, did her best to blend in, be unobtrusive – a difficult trick, given her coloring: "At least I'm fat, thank god. That was the only plus! Damn, talk about stereotypes – I even met a few people who refused to believe I was American, thought I must be German or Scandinavian or something, partly because I spoke halfway decent Spanish, but mostly because of my weight. Female American tourists belong in Acapulco in itsy-bitsy bikinis!"

In a plastic-covered booth over sandwiches, I tell her about Rhea. Over the months I've come to think of this announcement as a kind of standardized test which I've administered to enough subjects to have come to expect a certain range of responses. Wendy scores quite high on my scale, since she doesn't seem horrified, tongue-tied, or embarrassed, look eager to escape, or assume lugubrious airs. She just says simply how sorry she is; Rhea always seemed like a good person, though she didn't really know her. She'd like to hear more, if I want to talk about it. She's surprised, she adds, at not having been told sooner. "I've been back for almost a month, you'd think somebody'd have mentioned it to me."

I explain the facts of life. "Mostly, people don't want to think about it. Rhea knew a lot of New York feminists, and there's this way I feel like the whole community freaked at having to confront anything that final happening to someone. They dealt with it by holding this big memorial event and then contracting total amnesia."

"Hey, that's a drag – especially for you."

"Yeah. Well, I guess it's probably not all that unusual – I mean, in terms of how people react to death. But frankly, I'm pretty weary of that subject. Suppose you tell me more about your trip."

Wendy says she found Guatemala by far the heaviest politically. You had an incessant sense of impending disaster there, she says, sort of like New York feels too sometimes only incredibly magnified, the mass anxiety of a packed subway car when it stops too long in an underwater tunnel—but all the time, everywhere, in the countryside, the streets. Mexico was better, despite the poverty. There's been some liberalization since the Sixties. A small gay movement's starting to take hold.

"How was it, being an American down there? I mean, aside from people thinking you belonged in Acapulco?"

She flashes a grimace, a neutralizing grin. "Not terrific, on a lot of levels. I felt ashamed a lot, and angry—at myself, at all of us. But most of the people I met were incredibly kind, I mean they didn't seem to hold me particularly responsible, on a personal level, you know? Que yo soy norteamericana, gringa—it was like that was just my karma, so to speak. The disaster is there, it's enormous, it's almost like there isn't much sense in individual blame."

"You look like you're in pretty good shape."

"How do you mean?"

"I don't know. More self-assured, maybe."

Wendy nods. "I feel more like myself, I guess. I mean, I'm just this white protestant American farmer's daughter, blonde and blue-eyed as they come. There's no use whatsoever pretending otherwise, so it's like, okay, where do I go from here?

"I might as well have been to the moon and back. Not that any of those places seemed so different, in a way, even though everything about them was different from here. It was like they were so solid, their own reality . . . oh, it's hard to explain. I always knew the rest of the world existed, but I didn't really *know*. We get such a warped perspective. I mean, I don't care how bloody radical you think you are, when you live in this country, especially New York, you can't help absorbing a little of the notion that everything, for evil if not for good, revolves around you. It dawned on me finally that being over-impressed with our wickedness isn't that far different from being over-impressed with our virtue. I mean, it's true, the empire *is* this ghastly machine, and it has all these dreadful effects. But there are other things happening, other centers of reality. Radicals here, and that includes feminists . . . it's like we're always on the lookout for some kind of ultimate *answer,* some unifying equation that's going to explain it all. We're still trying to save the world with one bold theoretical stroke—though if Marx couldn't square the circle in the nineteenth century, I don't see why we should expect to pull it off in this one.

"As if anyone could logically expect to put it all together in New York or Boston or Berkeley or Chicago. As if change of that magnitude could be orchestrated. God, the arrogance—it's as ridiculous as those science fiction movies that are always showing extraterrestrial life descending on some upper-class suburb. It always seems self-evident to me that intelligent aliens would be at least as likely to want to know what's going on in Sri Lanka or Tanzania . . . but look, I'm rattling on."

"It's perfectly okay. I'm fascinated." I also discern an amusing irony. Wendy's talking fast now, almost as fast as Rhea used to talk when involved in some hot topic. Having had her revelations, here she is back home in the Big Apple, trying to chart it all, take it all apart and put it back together over cups of restaurant coffee. That old radical fervor, sense of ourselves as shock troops. She reminds me of what I've been missing these months of hibernation.

"So what will you do now?"

" 'What Is To Be Done?' " she lightly mocks, her beret at a rakish angle. "Well, I'm afraid it's not very edifying, but I'm flat broke and I've got to make some money. I'm also looking for a place to stay, maybe sublet, if you hear of anything. Then I'm dying to paint, of course. I haven't done anything except sketches in over a year, and I have oodles of ideas based on things I saw: faces, fields, markets, women doing physical work. A lot of the rural stuff had Indiana echoes for me, different as it is. I want to explore all that."

"And politically?"

"I haven't got a clue. Something around Latin American women, I think."

"Here I was counting on you to tell me you'd finally achieved our famous synthesis of art and activism!"

"Please, are you kidding? If anything, I've just gotten a little more resigned to the contradictions, that's all. It's fairly easy to be philosophical now, but I'm sure I'll get sucked back in, bogged down. The options haven't changed much, have they?"

"You mean, between the rock of the left and the hard place of feminism? To tell you the truth, I'm not sure I'd even know. I've been really out of it. This must be my first demo in six months at least."

"But you've been playing music?"

"Off and on. Duets with Katya. . . ."

"Performances?"

"Uh-uh."

"Too bad. How come?"

"Oh, you know. Partly the usual. Everybody's into 'women's music.' I'm too esoteric, classically oriented. 'Elitist' is the technical term, I think."

Wendy makes a face. "Fuck that shit."

"Easier said than done."

"No, seriously . . . all those bullshit categories of correct art, you've just got to ignore them. They'll never go away; why let them run your life?"

We talk of other things, but on the way to the subway station Wendy remembers that a woman she knows who runs a small art gallery has approached her about the possibility of showing some drawings there. If that happens, possibly in the fall, might I want to do some performances in the space?

Maybe, I tell her, warily pleased. And find myself inviting her to dinner next week.

But high on a D train strung like a line full of clothes against the soaring roofs of lower Manhattan skyscrapers, I suddenly feel anything but encouraged. Wendy seemed so lively back there in the coffee shop. She's been expanding, putting out new growth — and I can't help seeing by contrast how I've shrivelled on the vine, how long it's been since I knew myself a part of some daring commando assault on the problems of the planet.

* * *

When things go well with Ericka, I feel terrific, easily inclined to congratulate myself on my powers of nurturance. When they don't, I feel rotten, a washout as a parent and perhaps as a human being. In the days when we lived together, I used to oscillate frequently between these poles of enthusiasm and alarm, and could never decide whether Rhea's comparative equanimity should be ascribed to a different temperament, or rather to her security as the official Mother. Since Ericka's birthday weekend, I'm back on the old seesaw. Something, somehow, shifted for me then. I made up my mind I wouldn't let her go, not without a fight, anyway.

Though I haven't yet spoken to her father, I imagine I already notice a change in the weather between us. Sometimes we seem much closer, at others only more intimately at odds, wrangling and sparring like a pair of crochety siblings. The latter mode initially prevails when she comes for another weekend, Daniel and Brenda having elected to park her with me while they travel overnight to Cleveland on some unspecified business.

To begin with, of course, my pleasure in the visit is marred by irritation at having had the offer of it sprung on me midweek, requiring me to cancel dinner plans with Luce and reminding me I'm viewed in certain quarters as a glorified babysitter. The offense is compounded when the buzzer jerks me awake at 7:30 Saturday morning.

Ericka comes thumping up the stairs, dragging her overnight case as though it were a serious burden. Impeccably dressed this morning, her hair well-brushed, barretted, she leads with her pointed chin, a misanthropic sprite.

"Ssshh," I greet her crossly, "you'll wake up the whole building."

"I can't help it if this thing is so heavy."

"I thought your father was going to drop you off after 8:00."

"Their plane got switched or something. What's for breakfast?"

"I haven't got that far. The buzzer woke me up."

"Can we go out? *Please?*"

"I don't think so, not this morning. We'll cook something here. How about French toast?"

"Yuk. You always make it with whole wheat."

"What's wrong with that?"

"I like how Nilda makes it."

At least I know enough to ignore that one. "What's going on in Cleveland, anyway?"

"I dunno. Daddy had work."

"How come Brenda went?"

"I dunno. Well, see, it's hard to explain. She said she was freaking out or something, so Daddy said he'd take her and give her a little rest. I think that's it, anyway. Leah's been being sort of difficult, she's in the Terrible Two's, Brenda says, and she has these obnoxious tantrums."

"So where is Leah staying?" I can't resist pumping, though I feel a bit guilty—not because I expect to elicit any state secrets, but because I intend her innocent replies to fuel my resentment of Daniel and his doings.

"At Brenda's mom's on Long Island. *Please* can we go out?"

"Ericka, you heard me the first time."

"How *come?*"

"There's plenty of stuff to fix right here in the house. We'll be going out later to do some errands. Now I'm going to get dressed, so why don't you figure out what you want in the meantime. We could have eggs, pancakes. I could make matzoh brei."

"It's soggy, how you make it."

"Then you come up with something."

When I emerge from the bathroom she's "watching cartoons," her rigid, mirthless features two feet from the grey screen.

"Aren't you a little old for that stuff? Decide what you want yet?"

As though intent on some riveting sports match, she declines to turn her head. "Lox and a bagel. That's what *we* have."

"Sorry, kid. Not on the local menu. I'm fixing myself some pancakes. Let me know if you want any."

As I work, scattered bursts of animated mayhem assault my cringing eardrums, but to make her turn the thing down would invite further trouble, and on days like this one picks one's skirmishes. In the end, of course, she elects to eat with me, and though I eye disapprovingly the provocative volume of butter and Log Cabin syrup with which she anoints her two modest pancakes, I keep my mouth shut. Best give her credit for minimum compliance and the fact that she doesn't mention the real Vermont maple syrup Brenda probably serves.

"You don't seem to be in a very good mood," I venture at last.

She shrugs, masticates pancake. "Neither do you."

"Maybe we should both try starting over."

"Fine with me." Another belligerent shrug.

"Did something happen to upset you before you got here this morning?"

"How could it? There wasn't time. Brenda just woke me up and kept saying hurry this hurry that help Leah hurry hurry hurry and then we got in the car."

"Something last night, then?"

"Everything's dumb, that's all. I dunno."

Eventually we adjourn our struggle session to my usual laundromat, which, early as it is, is already jam-packed, a mini-inferno appropriate to our mood: close, steamy, rife with peevish kids and sour, impatient mothers, with blows and imprecations aimed at malfunctioning machines, and bitter competition over access to those that work. Will the family wardrobe get washed and dried without major incident, without some cheap dye running and wrecking a whole load, without mechanical failure before the "spin" cycle? Will the day in which so much is to be accomplished proceed relatively smoothly, or merely as a series of escalating frustrations? Such are the stakes in an urban laundromat.

Ericka manages to lay claim to a broken plastic chair in a far corner and sits there reading her Judy Blume book. Her expression suggests she's above this vulgar turmoil, and for forty-five minutes I let well enough alone. Then, at the point where I've decided to give up on the feeble dryer and fold my damp clothes, I risk calling her over.

She helps me fold with sharp, resentful gestures—"These clothes are still soaking"—then suddenly takes up our breakfast conversation as though she'd never let it drop. She *is* mad, she says. Nobody wants her. And she bets *I* would feel horrible if no one wanted me.

I agree it's a dismal fate to be unwanted, but dispute her melodramatic second premise. After some probing I'm able to discover that when Brenda decided to go to Cleveland with Daniel, she at first asked Nilda to sit. Nilda had family responsibilities and declined. Ericka subsequently overheard part of a discussion between Brenda and Daniel as to whether they could ask Brenda's mother to take both her and Leah. Brenda felt this would be an imposition, so Daniel gave me a call.

"So I come here and you don't want me either!" The tone of grievance whines into her voice like the note of gears downshifting for a hill. "Everybody should just say the truth: they wish I'd disappear. I'd camp overnight in Prospect Park, that's what!"

"Oh, Ericka, don't be silly."

"Well, all you could do was act like I got there too early and everything."

"I'm sorry, kiddo. I was half asleep. It's not your fault, but it makes problems for me when your father doesn't let me know his plans. He told me one time and dropped you off at another. It's just like when he called me about this weekend—I really wanted you to come, but because he didn't let me know till the last minute, I had to switch some plans I'd made with Luce. It doesn't mean I don't want to see you."

This gives her pause, but only briefly. "Anyway, why couldn't he have called you first thing! I can't *stand* Brenda's mom."

"Did you let him know you didn't want to stay there?"

"Uh-uh. See, I wasn't really supposed to hear them talking about it. But I don't think she likes *me* that much, either, so how come she always has to come over and hug me and make me call her Grandma? Some of her perfume even rubs off." She wrinkles her nose, graphic in distaste. "You could choke, how that stuff stinks."

"It doesn't sound too pleasant," I allow. She's watching me to see whether I'm inclining to rebuke or to encourage this unprecedented critique.

"I think your father and I need to have a talk. I really do want us to spend more time together, and I'm hoping we can set up a different schedule."

"You mean, like have me sleep over more and stuff?"

"I'd like that, if you want."

"How come I stopped sleeping over every week, in the first place?"

"Your father wanted you over there more."

"Why?"

"He never did explain very well. Basically he said since it was a hard time for you he felt it would be better for you to be more in one place."

"That's a dumb reason."

We proceed home with the laundry through warm, spring-festive streets. By the time we arrive, Ericka has dropped her pose of aggrieved hauteur, and when she asks if we could do something "fun" today, I surprise myself by immediately agreeing.

"Could we see — ," and she names a current box office hit which, I gather from subway ads and TV commercials, nostalgically pretends to re-create the teenage working-class culture of twenty-five years ago. She already knows two of the songs, she says. Lots of kids in her class went.

"I don't know, Ericka. How about something we could do outside? The weather's so nice."

"But how come not the movie?"

"Because I've seen the ads for it, and for one thing I'm not crazy about films that exploit women."

"What's *exploit* mean?"

"Treat like a piece of shit."

She giggles at my daring, then reflects, "Oh, you mean, because they, you know, *do it*?"

"They what?"

"You know, *do it*, the boys *do it* with the girls. TeriAnn's mother said she couldn't go because she heard the boys and girls . . . you know. . . ." Unnerved, she trails off. "She said it was too *sexy*."

"Well, not exactly." How do I put this? "I mean, just like in a lot of other movies, they try to make you think girls like to spend all their time dressing up and acting silly to make boys notice them."

"Yuk, that's stupid. I wouldn't think that."

"Let's figure out something else you'd enjoy doing."

We end up on the F train to Coney Island. The very name invokes the desired note of magic, the aura of pure, wholly irresponsible pleasure required for a celebration of spring. And Ericka seems satisfied with the idea. I've never taken her on the rides out there, though she's been with various friends. Rhea and I used to make an occasional pilgrimage to wander beneath the neon-lit ferris wheel, to witness the crawl and plunge of the world-famous roller coaster with its shrieking passengers, to inhale the reek of the matchless fast-food stands, with their catholic arrays of clams and pizza, knishes and sausages, calzone and corn on the cob, and to draw a definitive sense of participation in summer from proximity to acres of beached flesh, boardwalk multitudes, and the Spanish-speaking families thick on the pier: their encampments of blankets and pillows and kids and coolers, their crab-traps baited with hunks of raw chicken.

Ericka assures me that the rides will be functioning; apparently it's knowledge common to every Brooklyn child that Easter weekend, just past, is opening time out there. On the way she teases me by reciting a litany of harrowing rides. The train gropes up from its familiar underworld into the strong light of extreme south Brooklyn, and I bask in our jerky progress toward the earth's blue end. It's been months since I've voyaged to anywhere but Manhattan, and on a day like this when the seasons are in flux, even a ride to the beach can feel like significant travel.

But a sudden question commands my full attention: "Josie, what does *sexy* mean, really?"

"Well, different things," I attempt, totally unprepared. "Something to do with sex, or that makes people think about it." I'm aware of providing a circular definition; though of course she knows, for instance, where babies come from, that doesn't seem quite the point.

"Am I sexy?"

Amused and alarmed both, I scrutinize her. She's looking a rather young ten years at the moment, hair now an unkempt mop, a residue of lunch lingering around her small red mouth. Not for the first time it occurs to me how little I know about her, her world of fantasy and social intrigue. One day in the Slope not too long ago I found myself walking behind a clutch of schoolgirls, aged perhaps thirteen at the very most. They were wearing the plaid skirts and kneesocks of parochial school pupils, and were engaged in a voluptuous consumption of ice cream cones, a giggling speculation as to what their mothers would do if they ever "found out." It took several blocks before I could discover that their tremendous secret consisted not in the fact of having spoiled their dinners with sweets, or having cut some class, but rather in having "made out" with boys at a birthday party. I thought, then, of Ericka, with a fatalistic sense of how the gap between us seemed foreordained to widen, Daniel or no Daniel. And it seemed to me that the work of the women's movement over the past ten years should have made more of a difference in the world than I suddenly felt it had, looking at those sweet, sticky-faced, ignorant little girls.

"Josie, am I sexy?" she pursues. "See, I'm almost starting to have . . . tits." She pokes out her bony rib-cage, half-serious, half-clowning. "Saundra in my class has real big ones already."

" 'Sexy' isn't exactly one of my favorite expressions," I begin, trapped now by my failure to define the term and alert to the danger of seeming a hopeless prude. We're only a stop or two from the end of the line and the car has emptied out. Our companions now consist of one family group, a teenage boy standing vigil at the doors, and a man across the aisle who's reading a Russian paper.

"Why not?" she naturally has to know.

"It's a word I feel like men use a lot to put women down, even though we're supposed to think it's a compliment." I know I'm missing her real question, whatever that is. "You're very nice-looking, and you're strong and smart," I try to reassure her.

"Brenda said I might get my period soon."

"Yes, I guess you might. It's hard to tell."

"She gave me a box of sanitary napkins to soak up, you know, the blood. She said when she was my age they had this stupid kind with a belt that was really uncomfortable, but now they make them different, they stick to your panties, sort of. Josie, how did you get to be a lesbian?"

"Let's talk about that later, when we get home, okay?" I feel guilty putting her off, but the car is far too quiet. Beyond the screen of his Cyrillic columns, the newspaper reader may well understand our English, and as for that tall youth in his spiffy creased jeans, who knows what he's capable of?

At last the train grinds to its final halt, the conductor proclaims our arrival, and we take the concrete ramp that leads down to the vast, empty station, forlorn in the absence of its hot-weather multitudes. Outside, stores are closed, some gutted: everything in abeyance, waiting to begin. A block or two; the rides, maybe half of them open; then the empty beach, the token strip of water.

Coney Island in this season reminds me of LA's Pacific Ocean Park in December or January. Like that pivotal staging-ground of my adolescence, it is clearly a haven for drifters, the unemployed, and lovers so furtive or impoverished that they welcome the chilly charms the location offers. Only a few young parents loiter by with strollers in the alleyways between the kiddie rides; only a few hopeful dark-skinned boys weigh opportunities to "test their skill" and win green plush bears, pink rabbits. Seduced by thin sunshine, everyone seems to be shivering in light, inadequate garments. Only the peripatetic radios blaring disco hits of last summer or of next enter fully into the pretext that we've gotten over winter. But Ericka moves happily to the beat, and I buy her a big blue cloud of cotton candy to mark our descent into ultimate decadence.

For a while I get away with standing by and applauding her bravery on the tamer adult rides, but eventually she prevails on me to "try" a lethal-looking arrangement called the Hammer. Business is slow, evidently, for a serious-looking young man in spectacles and dreadlocks has to put aside a copy of *Pedagogy of the Oppressed* in order to strap us into the cab of a mobile torture chamber that slams us back and forth for an endless several minutes, while Ericka claws at me and bleats ecstatically for it to *stop.* After, she pops out not visibly worse for wear, and begs to know wasn't I *scared* to *death,* and couldn't we maybe go on the roller coaster, just one little time?

In fact, I *was* quite sufficiently terrified, though I'm not about to say so. The mere fact that I couldn't recall having read of any fatal accidents in Coney Island didn't seem to reassure me that this rusty-looking contraption with its preoccupied attendant wasn't even more likely to self-destruct than the average American car, airplane, or nuclear-powered metropolis, unsafe at any speed. Luckily my companion's zest for death-defying amusement seems easily deflected. She agrees when I suggest I'll choose one final ride before we call it a day. I pick the Wonder Wheel which is, despite its creaks and crotchets, wonderfully soothing by contrast with the Hammer. Hung in a bucket, we rise like a shaky sun into the blank air above the densely inscribed boroughs. This time we hold hands calmly, given to sane, detached, visionary pleasures: below us the crawling, self-obsessed human landscape, pocked with industry, pitted with fretful commerce.

"Josie."

"Yes."

"Don't you feel . . . powerful?"

"How do you mean, powerful?"

"I feel like I feel in an airplane when it's taking off, or when me and Daddy went up to the top of the World Trade Center. Like I could stay up here forever. Like being a king or something."

"A king?" I shy away from the imagery, but in fact I understand her. Why else do drug users talk about "getting high?" Or, as I generally end up reflecting when I'm hiking in the mountains: no wonder Satan chose a high-altitude site when he took it into his head to tempt Jesus.

"Well," I allow, "I feel sort of like that too. But unfortunately we're just regular old people, and we've got to live down there."

"I know that," she answers soberly, as though I weren't joking, but stating a basic truth, one she wants to show she's old enough to grasp.

The wheel turns, brings us in for a quick landing. Sated with enjoyments, we take a direct route back to the train station, and before we know it we're rattling down once more into the old familiar hole. When we emerge into light at Seventh Avenue, it's to find the streets silver-streaked with sudden rain. We sprint back to my apartment and arrive soaked, giggling, pleased, but thoroughly chilled.

"I can't stop shivering," Ericka objects.

"Dr. Muller prescribes a hot shower, followed as soon as practicable thereafter by a piping hot bowl of soup."

"Yuk, I don't want soup."

"How about the shower?"

"Could we take it together?"

"Well, I guess so."

We used to do this often in the old days, when she would kick up a fuss about taking showers on her own because she was little enough to have trouble getting the water properly adjusted. But it's been a long time, and we've both grown self-conscious. I can sense in the careful way she keeps her eyes off me her secret interest in my unexceptional breasts, the impressive achievement of hair in places she doesn't yet have it.

"Brenda's really fat now," she volunteers.

"Is she?"

"Yeah, you should see her stomach. Her breasts got big, too."

This, I suppose, is intended to put me on notice that she hasn't forgotten our afternoon conversation, or my promise to discuss certain matters later on. I soap myself and brace for rich adventures.

Early as it is, we both put on pajamas. I pour apple juice, brew tea, scramble eggs. We take our plates into my room to eat with the TV set turned on low at the foot of the bed.

Slowly Ericka relaxes against my shoulder, flannel on flannel. "That was a fun day," she says. It is her highest tribute.

"I'm glad you enjoyed it, kiddo. I enjoyed it too."

"Did you ever used to like rides when you were little?"

"Yes, though when I was 'little' I never went on anything like that thing we were on today. When I was a teenager I used to go to an amusement park near the ocean in LA that had some really scary rides like that."

"You went with your parents, then?"

"No. With friends."

"Like who?"

"A boy I liked, and some other kids."

"What was his name?"

"Michael."

"And what did you do there, just go on rides?"

"No, other things. Wandered around, hung out."

"What else?" she challenges, emboldened now.

"We smoked dope sometimes," I concede; I'm not about to admit the speed, the acid. "We'd sit out there on the beach in January, wearing thin sweaters—that was California, of course, but it still could get pretty chilly. And we'd rap about how we were going to be great when we grew up, like Albert Camus or Woodie Guthrie or Allen Ginsberg or Kazantzakis."

"Who're all those?"

"Men we—well, men Michael and his friends used to admire. We smoked Pall Mall non-filters, or hand-rolled Bull Durham, either of which is awful for you, of course. It's a wonder I have any wind left to play the flute with."

"How come you did it if you knew it was bad for you?"

"We were unhappy. Miserable, mad at the world."

"I don't get it. How come?"

"We didn't exactly know ourselves how come. Everything just seemed pointless. We had to grow up, obviously, but we didn't know what we wanted to do or be. The Vietnam War was in full swing. We blamed adults for the mess things were in."

"But you could have had demonstrations or something to try and make it better."

"Well, thanks, kiddo, that's a good suggestion, but we didn't understand that at the time. Some people did, but we hadn't caught on. I wasn't raised like you were, going to meetings and demos and rallies in Washington." It feels like another century I'm describing.

"Was Michael your *boyfriend*?" she dares.

"Yes he was."

"And did you and him—?"

"Did he and I—?"

"You know. Like those kids in that movie we didn't go to. Did you. . . ." Her voice trails off against the backdrop of TV noise, and I have to ask her to repeat the question.

"Did you *do it*," she manages, delicately.

I admit we did; I am totally at a loss, though when she screams *fuck you* in moments of anger I take it in stride.

"But did you like it, though?"

"Yes. Well, that depends . . . sometimes I liked it." How would I tell the truth, anyway? Would I emphasize authentic, raw desire? Or mechanical ignorance and frightful risk of days when illegal abortions and homes for unwed mothers provided the only backup if the quality control was under par at the Trojan receptacle tip condom factory? Or the blundering ideology of it all, derived from those books we read?

Or my wild, repressed horror at being the *girl* in all this?

"But . . . how did you get to be a lesbian, then?"

"It's not that simple, kiddo. People aren't always just one thing or the other. And I didn't know I had a choice back then. I'd never met anybody I knew was a lesbian. Girls were just expected to have boyfriends. Besides, I used to think boys had all the interesting ideas and got to do all the fun things. It took me a long time to figure out how much I like women."

"And that's how Mommy got to be a lesbian too?" She bites her grubby knuckles, overcome by a case of fidgets. I see we're finally getting to the point.

"Basically, yes. We sort of decided together."

"What did my Daddy say?"

"Well, he wasn't too happy at first. But I think everything worked out better for all of us, after a while."

She bows her head, peers up through tangled hair. On her face, a grimace intended for a smile proclaims she isn't really serious.

"Josie, what do you think *I'm* gonna be?"

I feel the full honor and weight of my responsibilities. I'm the only one in the world she thinks she can ask that question.

* * *

April: the leaves coming on the trees. Sneaky, in the night, when I can't see them, or maybe afternoons when, shut up in the office, I'm staring at the partition that separates my desk from Vi's, over which I've plastered an Alaska travel poster, an unattainable terrain of crags thick with Dall sheep.

Or perhaps I'm just unobservant, from LA and unable to get the hang of these rigorously delineated Eastern seasons. I don't know what to look for, the alchemy eludes me.

Anyway, it's the month of the unexpected. I'm only mildly surprised when Daniel breaks precedent by calling me at work one afternoon. He's in Manhattan, he says, has meetings in midtown. There's something to do with Ericka he's been wanting to discuss. Suppose we have a drink after work?

I'm annoyed, but suggest we meet in a coffee shop. Part of my new strategy involves maintaining a more businesslike, reserved stance in my dealings with him, and a drink sounds much too cozy.

It's only after hanging up the phone that it dawns on me why I should have postponed this, or at least tried to find out what the man has on his mind. Now I'll walk into it cold, will have to make an on-the-spot decision as to whether it's a propitious moment to raise the issue of Ericka's schedule.

"Got a date?" asks Gina, ever hopeful. It was she who took the call. She knows how seldom I get calls from men.

"Not exactly. More like a business meeting."

Though I'm five minutes late to the coffee shop assignation, I end up having to wait, standing out on the sidewalk pressed up against dirty brick. Daniel's tardiness, I realize, might have been foreseen, along with the fact that I'm starting to feel very dowdy and outclassed and secretarial indeed as I watch the midtown hordes pour past on their way to Grand Central in their crisp, perfect clothes. Finally he comes strolling up the block.

"Hi, Josie. Terribly sorry to be so late. I got hung up with a couple of grad students. Earnest little buggers, some of them. But why didn't you go in and sit down? It never occurred to me you'd be standing out here all this time."

"That's okay, I've been sitting all day. Anyway, it always makes me nervous to have the waitress hovering," I explain for some reason.

"What's the problem? Just tell her to get lost and call her back when you're ready," he instructs. "Here, go ahead."

He holds the door; what can I do but enter? We settle down in an empty booth near the back.

"Coffee," I tell the waitress. Daniel asks to see a menu.

"Just coffee? How spartan of you. If we weren't having company for dinner, I could use a cheeseburger . . . terrible admission, isn't it? How's the cheesecake, anyway? Do they make it themselves?"

"No idea, I've never had it."

"I should have known *you'd* never stoop to anything quite so decadent. What the hell, I'll try a piece with coffee."

"So what's up, Daniel?" I prompt, the minute he's placed his order.

"Ah, yes. What's up is—" He pauses to fumble for a cigarette. "Well, this is a bit—wait a minute, here comes our coffee."

Only now it hits me that he's actually nervous. But I don't have more than a minute or two to enjoy the unusual spectacle of Daniel discomfited. He doses his coffee with milk and two sugars, then gets to the point.

"I've accepted a job in Cleveland for the fall. So we'll be moving out there. I guess it'll be—oh, early or mid-July. Depends how soon we can get rid of the house."

I look at him. Does he know what he's saying? I can't take it in yet. His tone sounds so ordinary.

"The whole thing really came up very suddenly. Brenda and I are still in a bit of a daze. Of course she has mixed feelings about moving away from her mother, and it won't be the easiest thing with the baby due. But basically, we think it's the right move, and I don't know when I'd have gotten a better offer. . . . Anyway, I just assumed you'd want to know first thing."

He stops. I'm supposed to say something, evidently.

The waitress brings his cheesecake. It looks good, with crimson viscous cherries bleeding all over. I want some. I want him out of my sight.

"You've talked to Ericka?"

"No. We're going to within the next couple of days. As I say, I wanted you to know immediately."

"How long have you been planning this?" I accuse.

"It came up very suddenly, Josie, I assure you. Oh, granted Brenda and I had been kicking around the idea of moving for a while, but nothing definite. I mean, things have been getting out of hand in the city—we all recognize that, right? We knew we weren't going to be able to hang on forever. And now, with the baby coming—well, Brenda really wants to be someplace where she can send the little kids out front to play without having to worry. I can't blame her for that. The situation affects Ericka too, for that matter. She's been wanting a ten-speed, for instance. Now how the hell is she going to ride a new ten-speed around the Slope without getting it ripped off? And then the school tuitions—with Leah coming along, that's not going to be a joke in the next few years unless we relocate someplace with decent public schools. Of course Cleveland has its own big-city problems, but where we'd be the schools actually have a terrific reputation.

"As I say, we're not eager to go, even though it was obvious we'd have done it sooner or later. But we really hadn't begun to think about it concretely. This offer I got was totally unexpected, a chance to go into administration with a pretty decent increase, so I didn't feel I could very well pass it up."

"I see."

"In fact, it's less than two weeks ago that I first heard of it as a possibility."

"So that's why you made the trip to Cleveland last weekend."

"Well, yes, in fact. Of course I didn't feel it made sense to say anything to you while things were up in the air."

"Of course not."

I have nothing to say to the man, no speech potent enough, no way to plunge him into the cold pit of my fury. If only I knew how to open the deep freeze behind my ribs, I could blast him dead on the spot like a mastodon, fork still in his hand. Failing that, I want to get out of here fast, but I grip my coffee cup and sit tight, bound by some archaic habit of prudence, some irrational hope that if only I hear him out. . . .

"Josie," he's appealing.

"What now?"

"Josie—oh, I was afraid of this. Look, I do know it's rough in terms of how you feel about Ericka. Believe me, I know."

"Do you? Do you really?"

"I don't want you to think I don't understand. But it had to come sometime, after all, didn't it?"

"What? Your moving?"

"A break, a—well, a parting of the ways, to some extent."

"I fail to see why."

"I mean, I fully appreciate that the two of you have been close. That's been important for Ericka, and I don't mean to discount it, not in the least. But you couldn't realistically expect the attachment to continue on the same level indefinitely, given Rhea's death and the new living arrangement. A child that age can't live with split loyalties forever."

"*Split loyalties?* I don't believe this, Daniel. What do you suppose her whole life has been about? Ever since the divorce, ever since she can remember. How would you have felt if Rhea had said she didn't want you to see your daughter anymore because the *split loyalties* were too painful?"

I'm shaking, my voice is shaking. But Daniel seems perfectly calm, all trace of his earlier nervousness gone as he patiently informs me, "Brenda and I have tried to be as accommodating as possible, even at times when it's inconvenienced us. But there's no avoiding this now, I think you can see that. So even though I recognize it's bound to be a bit traumatic for you and Ericka both, I do hope you at least, as the adult, will be able to appreciate what's happening as a natural sort of break. To the extent that you're able to help Ericka see it in that light as well, I think you'll do her a tremendous favor. It will make a tough adjustment that much less difficult."

I muster my words with effort. "Daniel, don't you get it?"

"Get what?"

"Don't you understand that I think of Ericka as my child, too?"

"I understand that you care for her a great deal. But that's precisely why I —"

"Did you *hear* what I just said?"

"Josie, commitment and connection are all well and good. As I've emphasized, I fully recognize your importance to Ericka. Especially given Rhea's flightiness at times, I think having you around has been a lucky thing for her. But I *am* her father, after all."

I glare. "You're her father all right."

He's finally beginning to look annoyed. "Look, Josie, you and I both know there are certain social facts, hard realities, if you will . . . I mean, come on, be a little reasonable."

"I'm being more than a little reasonable. The point is, I've *raised* Ericka. I've lived with her for well over half her life — much longer than you, in fact. You don't just suddenly veto that, cancel it, make it disappear."

"No, of course not. And that's why Brenda and I have facilitated things so you could keep seeing her, as you wanted to. Not everyone would have done that, I hope you realize. I mean, given the . . . unconventional nature of your relationship with Rhea. All things considered, I think we've been pretty fair.

"Besides, nobody's suggesting putting up some kind of wall between you and Ericka. You'll be in touch through letters and phone calls, and of course we'll come back for visits. If you want to fly out to Cleveland for a few days, I'm sure we can work that out."

"Daniel —"

But it's no use, I can see by the looks of him, by how composed his handsome face is, perfectly sure of itself above the brown tones of his handsome sweater. He really doesn't get it. This is one of the fatal consequences of that lack of imagination Rhea and I always remarked on.

He doesn't *have* to get it—that's part of it, of course. He's never going to be this powerless, this naked.

I hear my voice go on, repeating arguments. "Just because I haven't any legal rights to Ericka, just because I can't *say* what our relationship is, label it with any socially-approved title—well, Daniel, I'm sorry, but I refuse to act as though—"

"You're really not listening, Josie. I'm not dismissing it. I'm crediting the importance of that past connection, but asking *you*, from your adult vantage point, to recognize that things are different now."

"No they're not, not in the way you mean! I'm entitled to a say in what happens next. And what about *her* feelings, anyway? Are you going to ask her what she thinks about moving away from me a year after losing her mother?"

My voice is rising now; people are starting to notice. His own tone low, tight to rein me in, Daniel snaps back, "Come on, Josie, you can't seriously mean that you expect an entire family to base its choice of residence on proximity to the husband's ex-wife's former lesbian lover! The Sixties are over, remember?"

"Thanks, Daniel." I stare hard across formica, trying to compress the force of all my feeling into the one long look. Anything I might say, any curse I chose to hurl, would only be used against me.

A gun, I'm thinking. That's what he'd listen to.

Somewhere in his neck a muscle twitches. He's worried now, suspects he's said too much.

He can do what he damn pleases. Okay, so I'll go away . . . the West Coast, maybe try San Francisco this time. Or Oregon, east of the mountains, that empty desert. A job in a truckstop, or one of those cannery towns.

"Hey Josie, wait a minute, I—"

How easy it is to slide out from under the table, snatching my coat from the hook beside the booth, not stopping to put it on, no farewells taken nor explanations tendered. How natural and appropriate the continuity of motion up and out the door, dignified in defiance of turning heads, not having screamed, nor broken anything.

Let the motherfucker pick up the check for my coffee.

* * *

I have, it turns out, a single dime in my pocket. I dial from a wall phone in the guts of the subway as an uptown train roars in across the platform.

To my great relief, Luce answers – sounding, however, at least an ocean away, and hassled into the bargain.

"Listen, Luce, it's Josie. Something's happened. Do you suppose I could come over?"

"Jesus, Josie, where are you calling from? The connection's awful, I can't hear a fuckin' thing. Look, is this really urgent? I've got an emergency meeting going on here."

"Yeah – well, yeah, it's important. You don't have to interrupt the meeting, I can hang out till you finish. I'm just really freaked, and I'd rather not go home."

"Okay, come on over. The door ought to be open downstairs. I've got to get off now. See you later."

So I take the F to Brooklyn. Luce lives a couple blocks south of Fifteenth Street in a not-yet-fashionable section of second- and third-floor apartments over storefronts, of bars and pizza joints and corner groceries and Italian bakeshops. A full block almost directly across from her place is taken up by Our-Lady-of-Something-or-Other and its outbuildings, a coincidence she humorously pretends to regard as a personal affront since she herself was raised Catholic. This block is the focal point of the neighborhood: its weddings periodically strew the streets with rice, its funerals block traffic, its parochial school pupils clog the sidewalks at three o'clock each weekday. There are white boys hanging out on the corners, white men talking in front of the bar and the post office. American flags are prominently displayed for Veteran's Day, Memorial Day, and the Fourth on the modestly prosperous sidestreets, racist slogans splashed on the asphalt near the park where the white kids go to cut school, drink beer, hassle joggers.

"Good solid white working people" was how Luce used to characterize the neighborhood, five years or so ago when she first moved here. She spoke proudly then of her own class background, identified herself as a Marxist-Leninist. But her "pre-party formation" has since changed its line, switched its dialectical bet to a different horse. It now considers the white working class, if not beyond redemption, fundamentally irrelevant to the *real* revolutionary struggle, the one being waged world-wide by peoples of color. Therefore she no longer talks much about where she came from, but regretfully alludes to her white skin privilege. Now this neighborhood is merely where the rent is still low enough, where she holds emergency meetings, maintains her shelter for itinerants both feline and human, and crashes for the night.

Her apartment is above a hardware store. I enter the building, grope my way up. The hall is dark, the bulb burned out on the second-floor landing where cartons and boots and a folded baby stroller booby-trap my path. This place, I recall, belongs to a battered woman who occasionally takes refuge upstairs with Luce when she and her husband "argue." I've watched Luce bandage wounds, commiserate, advise—all without a trace of rhetorical moralizing. It's as though in moments of crisis she reverts to an order of behavior learned in some other world than the intensely ideological one she nowadays inhabits.

Approaching the third floor, I detect the contentious murmur of a meeting well into its agenda. I knock, bracing myself for scrutiny. There's a brief pause while I'm scanned through the peephole; then the door cracks open on a long dark room full of white faces, some of them familiar. The air is heavy with cigarette smoke and a sour inkling of catshit. Luce barely nods as I enter, while from a sofa leaking stuffing a dark-bearded young man I've never seen before continues to hammer home some telling point.

I expected all this, but still I'm uncomfortable, aware of a warning hand laid on the speaker's arm, of unflattering glances sizing me up as I pick my way among coffee mugs, full ashtrays, empty shoes, notebooks, and outstretched feet in hole-filled socks, and with relief duck into the kitchen. I'm known to most of this crowd, by sight if not by name, from a hundred past political events—known, I wouldn't doubt, as Luce's backward friend, the one who has consistently declined all opportunities to join their study groups.

Safe in the kitchen, I clear a little space by pushing dirty dishes to one end of the table, transferring stacks of leaflets off a chair. Cats, scrawny and ubiquitous, regard me misanthropically from various surfaces. Luce likes to take in strays, and the visitor never knows how many will be found in residence. Sitting down for a moment to consider my next move, I'm immediately accosted by the one friendly feline, Apparatchik (Chickie for short), a permanent resident who's been with Luce since his kittenhood in the nonaligned days when she still had a political sense of humor.

Eventually he tires of being petted and scampers off. I rouse myself, scrounge around for a clean saucepan, and put on water for tea. Fragments of jargon waft from the other room. There's a bit of entertainment to be had in trying to deduce the nature of the crisis that occasioned this meeting.

A sudden lull, then Luce, emphatically: "I'm telling you, it's cool."

But this would appear to meet with some objection. After a minute her head appears in the doorway. "Mind if I close this?"

"Go right ahead."

"Just a routine precaution," she half apologizes.

I'm amused, irked, only mildly surprised. These people are famous for their paranoia.

With difficulty I locate a rumpled Lipton's tea bag, pour hot water, and head for the bedroom. What chairs there were in there have been borrowed for the meeting, and there's no bed either in the strict sense, just a double mattress on the floor in one corner. Arranging jumbled sheets and blankets preparatory to sitting down, I consider just why the fact that Luce, at thirty-two, chooses to sleep on the floor should strike me as a reproachful commentary on the fact that I possess a decent bed.

I'm always intrigued as much as I'm repelled by the total effect she achieves: clothing strewn across a moldy carpet, venetian blinds out of alignment affording a segmented glimpse of the dark hulk of the church across the street flanked by commercial neon, cups half full of coffee or burgundy in which drowned cigarette butts float. Her radical squalor hints at the stern view that even minimal expenditure of energy on one's private life, one's physical well-being, is frivolous, a distraction from serious revolutionary purpose. Not that Luce would put it in so many words. Her story is simply that she can't be bothered.

It occurs to me to escape, go out for a little walk, but I'm not up to wading through that meeting again. Unfortunately this means most of her books are inaccessible as well. She consumes printed matter rather less sparingly than she does the general effluvia of the capitalist marketplace, and I can often amuse myself for an hour or two by going through her shelves, which are in the front room. Now I'm stuck back here with the rejects, dogeared paperbacks tumbled into cartons. A survey reveals a discouraging lot indeed, a high-toned college smattering of Castaneda, Hesse, and Marcuse alongside the real dregs, stuff like *Steal This Book* and *The Greening of America*. After an unsuccessful effort to interest myself in a tattered *Story of O* in which paragraphs and phrases have been painstakingly underlined as though for some literature course, I give up, go back to the kitchen, and start washing dishes.

It's no use: I can't avoid Daniel's news.

But at least I can keep moving. When Luce comes in sometime well after eleven, I've about completed the herculean task of cleaning out her refrigerator.

"Hey, what's all this for? What's the big idea, you wanna upset my roaches?" She eyes with mock suspicion the minor mountain of clean dishes on her drainboard. "Shit, I'm pooped," and she collapses at the table. She's looking properly revolutionary tonight in olive drab and checked flannel and those ridiculously affected-seeming dark glasses which are supposed to have some medical purpose or other, dark hair straight and stringy to her waist, cigarette dangling toughly from her lower lip, my home-grown Tupamaro, Red Brigade sister. Despite her claim, she radiates energy. Except when actually ill, Luce overflows with vigor, wired for the political treadmill, sustaining her eternal round of meetings, demos, and fulltime typesetting jobs on a regimen of coffee, beer, brown rice, Burger King, tobacco, speed, and five hours' sleep a night.

"You know me: compulsive as they come. And then there wasn't much entertainment around here, and obviously I couldn't set foot in the parlor, not unless I wanted your company to think that the Feds were in the building."

"Sorry about that." She looks a bit embarrassed. "It's nothing personal, of course you realize. We do have to have a few security rules."

"Never mind. How'd the meeting go?"

"All right. What's with you? You sounded bad on the phone."

"Daniel's moving to Cleveland."

"No shit."

"They made him a job offer he just couldn't refuse. Besides, you know how rough the city's getting. He wants me to understand that times have changed and I can't expect to be close to Ericka forever. I'm supposed to kiss her goodbye and write cheery notes."

"Heavy duty." Luce whistles emphatically.

"Yes, isn't it? Especially when I was just screwing up my courage to talk to him about how little I've been getting to see her as it is. God, I feel like I've been so bloody gullible."

"Look, Josie, I'm starving, I'm going to fix a sandwich. Suppose you start from the top and tell me the whole thing. You didn't throw out the ham that was in a paper bag on the second shelf of the refrigerator, did you? Oh, here it is. It's still good, I guess. No, Chickie, beat it, you can't have any."

While Luce prepares her dinner, I tell my sorry tale. I'm still talking as she wolfs it down, punctuating mouthfuls with indignant grunts in response to Daniel's egregious behavior. When I'm finished, she wants to know, like a good materialist, what it is I plan to *do*.

"*Do?* You tell me. What choices do I have?" Right now I only want to be consoled.

"Come on. There's always choices," she insists.

"Sure. Like I suppose I could have *chosen* to waste the bastard with an astutely placed karate chop, and gotten busted for assault, instead of just walking out on him like I did."

"Yeah, that's one option."

"Oh, I have all sorts of options. I could just forget about Ericka altogether, cut my losses, so to speak—after a while I guess she'd forget me too. I could go along and do it Daniel's way, write letters and run up a phone bill and see her once a year for a day or a weekend, when they come to town to visit relatives. I imagine I could even move to Cleveland and keep on seeing her the way I do now, if I wanted to press the point. Daniel wouldn't like it very much, but I might get away with it. He prefers to look liberal."

"How about having her spend part of the year with you, did you ask him about that?"

"I wasn't in any position to do much asking. The man was *telling* me."

"What makes you so positive he wouldn't buy it? Is Brenda all that hot to be a stepmother?"

"I can try, Luce, but I don't think it'll work. Daniel's just not in a mood for compromise. I mean, the basic tone of his presentation was: I'm her father, and I've got every social, legal, and moral right and privilege in the book, so you can just fuck off, sweetheart, because you have served your purpose and you are henceforth obsolete. The patronizing creep did just about everything but hand me a gold watch for my faithful years of service.

"Hell, they don't want me socializing any child of theirs for even a couple months out of the year. It could screw up everything. She'd have this whole other point of reference they're counting on her never having access to once they get her off in that white-washed surburban heaven they're headed for.

"Look, Daniel wants to put as much distance between him and all the challenges Rhea posed as he can possibly manage. He doesn't need a daughter boring from within, asking a lot of embarrassing questions as she gets older. He doesn't want her hanging around a fire-breathing manhater. He doesn't want her playing with Jasmine Webster, and neither does Brenda. The two of them went along with her seeing me as long as they lived here because it wasn't practical to separate us totally. It would have meant an enormous hassle. But now Daniel thinks he sees a painless way out. He's not going to let that go."

I hear my voice overloud with the need to convince Luce. I'm always a bit unsure of her sympathies when it comes to Ericka. Of course she agrees with me in principle, but it's more than principle I want right now. She has always led the absorbed, irresponsible life of the rebel bachelor girl, and falls back too readily on abstract analysis.

For now, she's neutral as a therapist. "Suppose you're right about him. What do you want to do?"

"Oh, fuck. Split to the West Coast. Go can crabmeat in Alaska. I don't know."

"Hmmmm." Lips pursed, chin on fist in her strategizing posture, Luce considers for a moment. I know from years of watching her at this how her grey eyes have narrowed to contemplative slits behind the opaque glasses. "And take Ericka, you mean?"

"No, Luce, I meant by myself." I can't resist a short ungracious laugh at the gap between our characteristic assumptions. It's true that in the first weeks after Rhea died I sometimes thought of just going off somewhere, taking Ericka with me. But those were wild daydreams. I knew I was half-deranged. I never literally thought of stealing her. "Still, it's an intriguing fantasy, isn't it? Expropriate a child from patriarchy."

"I wasn't joking. I thought that's what you meant."

"I know you did. That's what seemed so funny. You've never *lived* with kids, let alone been underground with one."

"Oh, but I've known fugitives with children." Luce matter-of-factly hints at classified anecdotes. "But never mind, I'm certainly not trying to talk you into it. The opposite, in fact. It would be fucking dangerous."

"Since when have you been against breaking a law or two in a worthy cause?" I bristle, suspicions aroused by her unaccustomed prudence.

"Well, it's one thing in a revolutionary situation, but this –"

"This what?"

"Splitting with someone else's kid – pardon the expression, I mean biologically someone else's – is technically known as kidnapping, I believe. That's a fairly serious federal charge you could get slapped with."

"What were these fugitives you knew facing?"

"That was a little different."

"Different, how?" My tone is accusatory.

"Christ, Josie, what is it? Did I say something wrong?"

"I'm just beginning to wonder how seriously you take any of this."

"Don't I sound sufficiently sympathetic? Didn't I say I think it's outrageous, what Daniel's up to? What was I supposed to do, tell you I thought you *should* take the kid and run?"

"Oh, fuck. No. It's a lunatic idea."

"So then what's bugging you?"

"Never mind. It's too complicated."

An edgy silence descends. Luce gropes for a cigarette. With an impatient nudge, she expels poor Chickie from his happy perch on her lap, then falls methodically to picking off cat hair. Her face looks sickly, grey in harsh fluorescence.

"You'd better say what you're thinking," she warns at last.

"All right then." I feel she's asking for it. Somewhere in the wall a pipe knocks imploringly. "I don't believe you really understand what all this means to me. I mean, yes you do *sympathize,* and you think Daniel's a shit, and all that. But you don't really get it. You do fine as long as you can sit up there with your analysis of the bourgeois family as a property relation, or whatever the line is on it this month, but when you're faced with an actual example . . . then it isn't a goddamn 'revolutionary situation'!"

"Josie, I don't get it. What do you want from me? You're jumping down my throat for no reason."

"I'll tell you what I want from you: support! It isn't real to you, what I feel about Ericka. You think being involved with kids is a nice thing to do as long as it doesn't cause problems – otherwise, a self-indulgence, a waste of time. I know damn well you think it's about time I snapped out of my depression, forgot about Ericka if necessary, and went out and did something politically useful."

She doesn't try to deny it, only says, "Well, or . . . I mean, if you *want* to be around kids, Ericka's not the only option, after all."

"They're not interchangeable parts! She happens to be the 'option' I care about."

"I'm sorry I said anything." Luce is now officially pissed. Resentfully, she grinds out her cigarette. "If we're going to list grievances, you haven't exactly displayed the ultimate in reverence for some of *my* choices either. What was that crack about 'this month's line'?"

"Oh, fuck."

"What?"

"This is not what I need right now."

"Me neither. It wasn't my idea."

I decline to answer. Silence thickens between us. A burglar alarm down the block whoops monotonously. I can hear car engines revving along the park, the poltergeist plumbing knocking inside the wall. Luce has piled a tiny haystack of cat fur on the grooved, grimy tabletop.

"It's late. I'd better get going."

"Are you sure? You can sleep here," she suggests without warmth.

"Thanks but no thanks. I'll get my coat."

Much to my surprise, she moves to block my exit. "Josie, wait. Come on, it's after one. I think you should sleep over. I'll open up the couch. It only takes a second."

"Don't patronize me. I can make it home."

"Calm down, just relax a second. Of course you can, but why the hell should you go running off when you're all upset like this? You've just been hit with some pretty serious news."

I glare at her, half-hoping to be convinced.

"I'm sorry," she adds, "if I've been insensitive."

Coming from Luce, this is quite an apology. "I thought you were pissed," I remind her.

"Well, so I was pissed. It's been known to happen between friends. It ain't exactly . . . an antagonistic contradiction." She grins wryly at the in-joke.

I smile warily back. "Okay, Chairman Luce. Hope you know what the hell you're talking about. I'd hate to see class war break out in the wee hours."

A minute later I'm sobbing in her arms, drenching her rough hair and flannel shoulder with tears of temporary relief and ultimate desolation, beginning at last to reckon with a hurt I could put off feeling as long as I quarrelled with her. I'm tolerant of her awkwardness with grief. She's about my height, substantial. Her solidity comforts me.

"Do you want to talk about it?" she offers – gallantly, considering the hour and the fact she too has work to face, come morning.

"Not now. It's nothing new, you know. I'll be okay in a minute."

I calm down and finish getting ready for bed. Soon I'm ensconced in a tattered sleeping bag on the sagging, faintly piss-scented studio couch that has harbored so many waifs and fugitives. It's hot in the apartment, the radiator blasting though the night outside is temperate enough. The open airshaft window gives inadequate ventilation, and the atmosphere still reeks of cigarettes. The cats have sprung to life in the yeasty dark, and are making a great to-do, racing one another up and down, pouncing, hissing, and spitting. Somewhere in the building a radio emits a twangy, commercialized country-'n-western lament. Finally I renounce the hope of sleep, turn on the light and pick a book at random: *Fanshen,* which takes me half a world away, to a land of material wounds, objective struggles.

Shortly before dawn I drop off, to wake at a quarter to eight with my hostess standing over me, naked in her large, loose body, holding a coffee mug.

"Howdy, ma'am. You plan on going to work?"

"Shit, I guess. I'm gonna be a zombie."

"Well, better try to look alive and drink this. Sorry I can't send you off with a steak-and-eggs breakfast, but at least the instant coffee's on the house."

"Do you have a blouse or something I could borrow? I hate to show up wearing yesterday's clothes. Gina always gives me such a look."

"A *blouse?*" Luce hoots at my hopeless gentility, comes up with a shirt only two sizes too large. With it, she offers a small gelatin capsule. "Dex. It helps. I just dropped one myself."

"Thanks, pal. I guess I better not."

"You sure? It does help get the old workday off to a more energetic and intriguing start."

"Well . . . maybe once won't hurt. I certainly could use a little mood elevation. I feel like I got kicked in the head last night."

"Here you go. Have a good flight. Just remember to watch out for a bumpy landing, along about lunchtime."

I gulp the capsule with my tepid coffee. Side-by-side, hurriedly, we dress, in something like the comfortable morning silence of old familiar lovers.

I'm ready first. She follows me to the door.

"Luce, thanks a million for last night. I know I was obnoxious."

"De nada, de nada," she dismisses it. "Take care, Josie. Let me know what happens."

We hug. I start downstairs, but then she calls me back.

"Look—what we talked about. That trip you mentioned."

"Trip? What trip?"

"You know, the one I said I thought was too expensive . . . to plan on taking a kid. The one we had the argument about."

"Oh, right. *That* trip. What about it?"

"I gave it some thought last night before I fell asleep, and I just wanted to say . . . we could discuss it again, if you're interested after considering the alternatives. I might be able to help you figure out a way to plan it so it would be a lot cheaper. My resources, as they say, are at your disposal."

"Oh, thanks. I can't imagine—but thanks anyway, Luce. Look, I'll call. I really appreciate it."

And I do; I'm gratified that she took my reproof to heart. I'm also amused at her conspiratorial airs, though I suppose in fact there's some sense in the notion that, especially if you're a diehard ultra-leftist, it's unwise to discuss too openly even the most hypothetical of kidnappings in the hall of your apartment.

The station, when I reach it, is packed solid. Evidently there's some delay in the inbound service; people are grumbling, checking their watches, and leaning out precariously over the platform's edge to peer into the tunnel.

But I don't care. The speed is starting to hit.

The F train picks us up, flings us at Manhattan.

*   *   *

Gina, who misses nothing, elevates her remorselessly plucked brows when she sees me coming, and generally hints by her quizzical attitude that she detects something in my rumpled appearance, or perhaps merely my atypical lateness, which warrants an explanation. But I brazen it out with a cheerful, opaque hello, and busy myself in remote file cabinets till she goes back to her carbon sets and white-out.

For an hour or two I'm ambitious with dexedrine, but the minute I start to droop she wants to know if I'm okay.

"I'm fine. I just didn't get enough sleep."

"Oh, is that it. You look a little funny, like you maybe had a hangover. But I didn't think it could be that—I bet you don't even drink, all that health food you eat and stuff."

"Something was bothering me, it was hard to sleep."

"Want to talk about it? You know, it's bad to keep it bottled up inside. I've been reading about this, they're discovering all sorts

93

of stuff about what stress does to people. The worst effects are when you don't talk. You've got to get it out, work it through."

"Thanks, Gina. I'll be okay, though."

But here a distant bell heralds the coffee wagon. Determined to press her advantage, she insists we take a break. She'll buy me something, she says; maybe that'll cheer me up. She herself is starving, having skipped breakfast. It's hell on her diet to keep snacking like this, but on the other hand if she doesn't eat now she's all the more liable to overdo at lunch.

So I trail her out to the hall by the elevators, where the secretaries throng like kids around an ice cream truck. She buys each of us a plastic-swathed danish and, back inside, perches on my desk, the sturdy thighs which prompt self-deprivation crossed in a holiday posture. "Let Irma get it," she scowls at the nagging phone. She picks her pastry into yellow fragments with long bright fingernails and deposits the crumbs daintily in her mouth.

"Romantic troubles?" she hints.

I explain I'm upset about the little girl she may recall my having occasionally mentioned, the one I used to live with, whose mother died. Her father's moving out of state with her.

Gina is sympathetic. "You know, I could always tell you were pretty attached to that kid, the way you'd talk about her, even though you didn't say much. You're a hard one to figure out sometimes, Josie. How old is she? Can't she visit you?"

"She's ten. It's just rough. She's been almost like my daughter."

But of course no one can really believe this. "Do you ever think about having your own kids?" my colleague innocently muses. She tells me how she once had an abortion. "I used to go out with this guy — I guess I probably never told you this, I don't talk about him much. Vinny. We went together most of the way through high school. He was a real old-fashioned type guy, wanted us to get married and make babies the minute I graduated. Well, I didn't go for that. I wanted some college. . . ."

Her tale is long, suspenseful, and full of heroism, though I'm not in a fit state to appreciate it. Vinny got her pregnant, naturally. "Actually, I always kind of suspected him of trying to knock me up on purpose, hoping I'd quit school and marry him. When I told him my decision, he threw a fit, I mean a *fit*. He wasn't a violent type or anything, but for a while I swear I was worried. He tells me, so help him, if I kill his baby he's never going to say word one to me after that. So I say, okay, so don't. But it's my body and my life and I'm going ahead and do what I have to do.

"By that time, see, I was getting a little stubborn, throwing in some women's lib here and there. And I paid for that procedure myself and everything. But sure enough, a month or two later he comes along and wants to have a 'talk.' Well, I wouldn't look at him. I said, so what do you want with the woman who killed your baby?

"I did feel kind of guilty, you know, for a while there. I'd walk down the street and see girls pushing carriages and think about that kid, how old it would have been. A lot of my girlfriends from high school were starting to have families. . . . But I got over that."

"Good for you," I tell her, glad she doesn't seem to notice how poorly I repay her confidences.

But she shakes her head, as though plagued by second thoughts. "Vinny wasn't such a bad guy. Emotionally, he was like about ten or twelve, but he had a good heart, know what I mean? He would have made a pretty good father.

"And here I am going to be twenty-six, I've had my two years of college, I've spent the last five sitting in front of an IBM Selectric . . . I mean, I've been to California and Aruba, I've met some fun guys and all that. I've got my own apartment, it's cute how I've fixed it up. But it's not like I can point to these past few years and say I did, you know, one big thing to make it all worthwhile. Once in a while it just kind of grabs me – for *this* I had that abortion?"

An inspection of her fingernails reveals some flaw to Gina. She whips out a bottle of polish from her desk and gets busy making repairs. As usual, I marvel at her industry; the "look" she favors requires so much intervention. While she strokes on color, she continues thinking out loud, "If you have a kid – well, it's *yours* at any rate. Nobody can take that away from you."

But here a vigorous, richly wrinkled visage, framed by grey hair, lately Bahama-tanned, looms suddenly above the low partition: Julia Lampe, division head, our boss. "No messages for me while I was upstairs, girls?"

"*I* didn't take any, but you should ask Irma. We've been taking our break." Gina breathes on her nails, determinedly indolent. The moment the apparition vanishes, she swings down from her perch with a guilty grin. "Guess that's the signal, we'd better get back to work, huh? I'm glad we talked, though, Josie. I wish you'd let me know anytime I can be of help. And just remember, it isn't healthy to sit on your feelings."

Noon marks an inauspicious watershed. Upon my return to my desk with a cup of soup from Smilers, I feel rotten enough to say I'm sick and split, but decide that freedom would be worse than bondage under the circumstances. I resolve to *look* busy. Physical work I find almost soothing, just so it's repetitive and therefore easy on my stiff, depleted brain, which only wants to drift and brood at random.

While typing a series of low-priority letters, I'm replaying my scene with Daniel, regretting my failure to use certain arguments. While presiding over the copy machine's officious clicks and whirrings, I'm thinking about the West: how free I could feel out there among evergreens and mountains, self-contained, stripped of belonging and belongings. Yes: why not burrow back into the provincial woodwork? How restful to picture myself in the primeval, anonymous grip of some British Columbia hamlet, Alaskan bush village. Not California: I want the real thing, the deep North, subsistence, isolation. I want to sling hash in the arctic winter night, process shrimp twelve and fourteen hours a day. Desertion was always my vision of perfect freedom. What will Gina make of me, I wonder, when I fail to report for duty one fine morning? Will she claim she had me pegged all along despite my reticence?

At five, out of habit I join the great stampede, though beyond the elevators I've no destination in mind. I wander south, the logical direction. Soon it becomes apparent I'm headed for the Village, and a bar begins to seem like a good idea. I settle on one just off Sheridan Square. It exactly suits my mood to linger now, famished, disdaining dinner, over a gin and tonic; to watch the youngsters disporting themselves on the postage stamp of dance floor, returning to the side tables to quarrel in harsh whispers.

But the youngsters seem younger than usual tonight, and I take my drink up front to the thinly settled bar, where I can monitor the doings of the sweetly butch bartender, she of the serious muscles and molten eyes, of the wide belt buckle and greying pomaded hair, of the cupid tattoo on one pale, hairless forearm. Business being slow, she strolls back and forth at leisure, setting liquor bottles in precise order, dumping ashtrays, swiping at water circles with a sour grey rag, and dispensing advice on how to keep a lover.

"Whatever you do, never live with her. That way you'll always maintain that level of interest." This is addressed to a languid, tall person clad in direst black whose limp blonde tresses trail practically in her drink.

"It's so expensive," she sighs, "keeping two apartments."

"So get a roommate. Figure out other ways. You want to make it, don't you?"

"Well, of course I do. But . . . Esther's pressuring me. To her it's a sign of commitment, living together."

"Yeah, that's how she sees it *now*."

"But what about you and Callie? Look what happened to you."

The bartender smiles ironically, fingers the bristling keyring she wears suspended over one solid hip. "Honey, I don't furnish a warranty. I'm just trying to give you the benefit of the stories I hear, working in this joint. Call it a distillation of experience.

"Look, Callie had her own ideas—if you could call them that. Hot pants and a short attention span, and looks that let her get away with murder. When a woman's like that, not much you can do about it. But you and Esther—you've got possibilities."

And so they proceed, strategizing for happiness. But I've heard enough. I drink up my watery gin; no use putting off going home any longer.

In the train, I remember the cats, and am horrified. The poor things haven't eaten since yesterday morning. Guiltily, I rush home from the station. As the dingy drapery on Mrs. Catania's glass front door flutters in my wake, I can hear a telephone ringing upstairs. Out of purely irrational, compulsive habit—what can it matter who's calling?—I sprint up the staircase, fumble the door unlocked, and, flanked by a shrilly plaintive furry escort, pounce on the receiver.

Ericka. She too sounds rather plaintive. She almost hung up, she says, I took so long to answer.

"Hi, kiddo. I just walked in the door."

"I tried you before. How come you got home so late?"

"Oh, I just walked down to the Village on my way home from work."

"How come?"

"I stopped off in a bar there for a few minutes."

"Eew, what for?"

"I just felt like it, that's all."

"Your voice sounds funny."

"I'm tired."

"Oh . . . Josie, I'm coming over to see you on Saturday, right?"

"That's what our schedule says, doesn't it? Didn't you mark it down on your calendar?"

"Yeah. Josie . . ."

"What?"

"Are you mad at me?"

"Of course not. Why would I be mad at you?"

"I dunno. You sounded weird, that's all. What's all that noise?"

"Just the cats, kvetching."

"You mean they didn't even eat yet? Wow, they're making a racket!"

"Well, you know how they are. I've got to get off in a minute and go feed them. I haven't had my own dinner yet, either. Anything more you wanted to talk about?"

"I dunno."

"How's school going?"

"Okay, I guess."

"Well, look, I guess we'd better say goodbye for tonight, then. I'll see you Saturday."

"Bye, Josie." She kisses me through the phone.

"Bye, Ericka. Love you. Good night."

Evidently she doesn't know yet. But just as clearly, she senses something wrong. And so she tracks me like an anxious lover; calls me up, aimless, just to hear I'm there; dreads most my anger or indifference.

And anticipates nothing of my real treachery. In the end I will bind her over, yield her up – and tell us both I had no choice in the matter.

* * *

Saturday morning dawns clear, heartbreakingly blue and serene, the pink, puffy clouds rolled back from a shell-translucent atmosphere absolved of smog by last night's fitful rains. Arriving on time in front of Daniel's house, I immediately spot the small intent figure immured within the double wall of glass formed by the two sets of heavy doors. She's been watching for me in the entryway. Stripping off her necklace of keys, she quickly lets herself out, locks the door behind her, and rushes down the steps, almost as though to prevent me from coming closer.

"Good morning, kiddo," I manage in normal tones. All the way over I've been getting more anxious, almost as though the whole thing were my fault. If she turns out to be distraught, it will be my job to console her.

But another possibility seems worse: suppose she's not so upset after all, suppose she's managed to take the whole thing in stride? Maybe the promise of a brand new ten-speed and a huge yard and a swell school and an all-American lifestyle will have proved enticement enough.

Disdaining salutations, she flashes out at me, "Daddy told you on Wednesday, didn't he!"

It's a frank accusation. "About planning to move to Cleveland?"

"Yes, about moving. How come you didn't say anything to me, how come you just behaved like—"

"On the phone when you called the other night, you mean?"

"Yes, on the phone. You act so dumb sometimes!" She darts in front of me, jerks open the low gate. Helplessly I trail her down the sidewalk.

Around us is being hatched a perfect day. The prosperous, high-stooped street is festive with bright tulips and pastel shrubbery. Early joggers shuffle virtuously past in their color-coordinated track suits and costly, cushioned sneakers. Some, their aerobic stints already completed, are trickling back from Seventh Avenue bearing little bags of croissants, fresh-minted copies of the *Times*.

Ericka declines to look at me; I'm compelled to address myself to her haughty profile: "Ericka, it wasn't up to me to tell you about the move. Daniel only said he wanted to let me know, and that he and Brenda would be speaking to you soon. When did you hear about it?"

"Last night. We had a *talk* at dinner. Daddy said he spoke to you. But I knew there was something weird going on. They kept having all these private conversations, ever since last week. *Everyone's* been keeping secrets from me."

"How do you feel about moving?" I try to probe, much though her charge rankles.

"I don't know. Just leave me alone, why don't you!"

I sense I'm going about this all wrong. Surely I ought to tell her how *I* feel, abandon this role of sensible, calm adult. Perhaps I'm infected by Daniel's poisonous logic: why make things any harder than they have to be?

"I've been very upset," I assure her. "I really hate the idea of you moving so far away."

"That's a lie," she brutally murmurs.

"It's not a lie. It's not a lie at all."

"Then why don't you make my father stop!"

I'm flooded with relief, with love for her. We want the same things, of course we do.

"Ericka, I argued with your father for quite a while the other night. I appreciate the reasons why he wants to make this move, it's attractive for him and Brenda, but I don't believe it's fair to you and me. I explained how much I'd miss you—"

"What did he say?"

"Truthfully, I don't think he paid the slightest attention to anything I told him."

"Oh."

She falls silent. We have reached a delicate juncture. I'm sure she understands; in fact it's precisely because she does understand that she draws back now from the verge of the tabooed discussion, the one we've never had, in which her father would be directly criticized.

I idly ask if they've bought a house already.

"No. They picked out a neighborhood they thought would be good for us. They have to go back again and look at houses. Or else we might rent and have a place built." She speaks quite coolly now, as though it were all settled.

Around us, the walls have faded to shabby brick, the glad gardens vanished. But the pinched, ill-nourished block is enfolded in generous air, above us still the sky's universal exuberance. Nonetheless, the street is empty: kids in watching the tube.

"Will you really miss me?" she ventures wistfully.

"Yes, of course. Won't you miss me?"

"Yes. Will you miss me . . . as much as you miss Mommy?"

The question alarms me at first, as I used to be alarmed in the days when she would sometimes try to establish grades of affection, and I would feel, obscurely, caught out in some treachery. Then I see it's all right: I can give her what she needs.

"Oh, Ericka, I can't measure it. More than I ever ought to have to miss—you or anyone, that's all I know." And then, grown reckless—damn the paternal image—"I think it's terribly wrong, your having to move."

"You could come live in Cleveland," she offers, low, not looking at me.

"Thanks, kiddo, I'm—"

"Would you, Josie? Would you move to Cleveland?" She grips my hand so hard it almost hurts, so hard I'm sure she knows it's a doomed effort. "You could live right near us. I could see you, just like now."

I answer as I must: my life is here.

"But you could make new friends. That's what Daddy says we're all going to have to do. I could stay overnight with you more, like we talked about. You don't like your job that much, anyway."

"It isn't that simple though, kiddo. Part of it is that I don't think your father really wants us to keep on seeing each other that often."

"How come?"

"He told me he thinks it's confusing for you. He feels it's simpler if you just live in one place."

"But that's stupid, it's no fair at all!"

"No, I agree, it's certainly not fair."

"You mean, if you moved to Cleveland he said I couldn't even *see* you?"

"I'm not saying that. We didn't discuss it, exactly. The main thing is, I don't feel—I'm in his power, does that make sense to you? I'm in his power, and it's like the way things have been this past year, he calls all the shots when it comes to my seeing you. He has the legal right to keep you away from me if he decided to, even though we've been important to each other for such a long time. I don't have any say-so. Moving to Cleveland wouldn't fix that. I could pick myself up and schlep all the way out there and he'd still have the power."

"Well, I'm in his power too."

"I know you are."

"I'm even more in his power, because at least you can decide where to live and everything."

"That's one of the few advantages of being a grownup, I guess."

"I could live with you part of the time."

"How do you mean?"

"Like, part of the year. I could come here in the summer, maybe. That's what this girl in my class does, she spends the summer with her father in Wisconsin. She doesn't get confused."

"Sounds like a good plan. It's what I'd like to do. But again, I'm afraid your father isn't very likely to agree."

Ericka is studying the sidewalk, playing the game in which cracks are ritually avoided. As though her mother had a back to break. "You could ask him," she proposes.

"Yes, I'll be glad to. But I think you should, too."

"Well. . . ." She's clearly uneasy at the prospect. "How come he thinks I'd get confused, anyway? Because you're a lesbian?"

"I'm sure that's part of it. That, and just the fact that he figures since he's your father that gives him the right to make decisions without somebody who's not a blood relative butting in."

"But that's stupid. *You're* like a relative."

"Well, it's not an attitude I happen to think much of. Pretty typical, though. Of fathers in general, I mean."

"Was your father like that?"

"He certainly shared a lot of the same ideas. It was a long time ago, though, and things were much different."

"Like, how different?"

"The same problems just didn't come up in the same way. My parents stayed married. We just took being in a regular family for granted a lot more than people do now. I'd never heard of lesbians, when I was your age."

"Then what did you call it, when women loved each other?"

"It never consciously occurred to me such a thing was possible."

"Wow," she marvels at the ancients' unfathomable mores.

"But we're getting off the subject. You *will* ask your father?"

"Yeah, okay. If you'll ask him too."

"Of course, I'll be glad to. But you've got to ask first. That way there's a better chance he'll pay attention to me."

She looks reluctant enough to stifle the little hope that sprang up in me when she pressed her eager plans. Why should she be so unwilling to approach him? I know he's not going to get mad at her. No: he will be pleasant, amused, aloof, and probably, in the final analysis, impervious to suggestion or entreaty. And it's her own impotence before his remote power she can't bear to face. She desperately wants to believe I can do it all somehow, use my adult magic to make him understand.

Later, over an afternoon game of chess (she's pretty good at it — Daniel taught her), she complains once again that she doesn't know what to say.

"Say the things you said to me this morning. Let him know how you feel about moving, leaving me, leaving all your friends—"

"But I know he'll just tell me I'll get over it. He already told me this story about how they moved when he was little, and at first he was scared and everything, and then when he got over it he liked it there better. But that was in the Bronx."

I'm merciless. "You've got to try, kiddo. I can't promise you talking to him will work, but if you want to have a chance of making him understand—"

She still whimpers, "It's hard to remember stuff."

"I know it is. But I also know you can do it. And I want you to promise you'll talk to him tonight. That way I can call him within a day or so and set up a time for us to get together."

Certain she'll lose her nerve if she delays, I remind her once more of our agreement as she prepares to leave. (Needless to say, Daniel waits downstairs; he's lost his appetite for chitchat on my couch.) Now we've made up our minds to contest this, I'm determined to follow through, which requires of both of us that we ignore the probable futility of our efforts.

Spend the summers in Brooklyn? But that's not why people move, why they pay for suburbs, for space and fresh air.

She's as good as gone, this erstwhile child of mine. But as Luce and Gina imply, I can always get another. What is it we women are for, after all, with our absurd bodies?

* * *

"I'll wait to order, thanks. I'm expecting somebody."

It's now Thursday evening. Gotten up in a freshly ironed shirt and my best silver earrings, early on purpose, I'm waiting in a deep oaken booth in the restaurant Daniel picked for our encounter. Beneath a forest of suspended foliage, white hets ogle white hets over beef and alcohol or quiche and Perrier; a row of wool- and leather-hung backs, robust and masculine, lines the polished bar. It's a momentary diversion to guess at occupations: therapists and artists in well-trimmed beards, clean-shaven computer software specialists and ad copywriters. . . . If Rhea were here, I would say, in our private shorthand, "God, the O.T.O. comes to Park Slope," and she'd know exactly what I meant by that.

For though Rhea and I always griped about places like this, we ate in them sometimes, in our early, penniless days. On those infrequent Sundays when Daniel had Ericka for the afternoon, we would take advantage of the half fare to travel in to the Village and, after browsing in shops or bookstores for an hour or two, would locate some restaurant of this general type in which to have a meal. We would order liberally, tip well, and stroll out afterwards without paying – a stunt which of course precluded our return, and accounted for the generic "O.T.O." or "one-time-only" by which we designated fashionable, overpriced American eateries. To tell the truth, the suspense of our undertaking never did much to enhance the food for me, and I was just as glad when our finances improved enough for us to become regular, paying customers in several modest ethnic restaurants. But Rhea got a kick from such adventures. And, just as she promised, by looking respectable – we always got dressed up for these occasions – we were never caught, never even challenged.

It was in an O.T.O. that Rhea once deposited a message, carefully written out on a paper napkin, at the table of a nondescript male and female pair who'd had the misfortune to locate themselves near us. Her note reported that a meticulous field study intended to provide insight into the courting behavior of a certain sort of biped showed that in the course of a twenty minute period in which the male of the species had expounded on the history

103

and present organization of the Audubon Society, enumerated bird-watching sites accessible from the metropolitan area, and recommended retail outlets for optical equipment, the female had ventured no more than five remarks, three of them brief questions. Though naturally amused by this prank, I reproved Rhea later for having placed an oppressed member of our sex-class in a difficult position. In those days I could be awfully earnest sometimes. Now, looking around me, I can make out quite a few members of my sex-class, arrayed in soft, tasteful feminine drag, whom I wouldn't mind seeing taken down a peg or two.

At least I'm prepared for Daniel this time around. Not intending to feel myself at any needless disadvantage, I dressed for this encounter as though for a heavy date. I anticipate ordering food and eating it, too, and above all being a model of rational argument. My theory is that, regardless of Daniel's behavior, I'll have the satisfaction, later on, of knowing I did everything I could. I've alerted Luce to what's happening, and she's promised to stand by, in case I need to talk.

And here's the man himself, nearly punctual this time. He's different tonight, much more formal, all trace of last week's affability vanished. He's feeling put upon, I gather I'm supposed to gather—though whether because I walked out on him, because I incited his daughter to insubordination, or because, on top of everything else, I have inconvenienced him by requesting this conference, it's hard to say as yet. He curtly nods, plunks his briefcase on the table, slides into the booth without bothering to remove a new-looking suede coat, folds large-knuckled, hairy hands, and leans forward slightly in an uncompromising posture.

I'm starving, I announce. I'd like to order.

"Okay. We need to make it pretty snappy, though, or I do anyway. I'm due home for dinner." He beckons to the waitress, who complies.

I order a hamburger deluxe, which comes with french fries. They make good fries here, the thick, sophisticated sort; from the street, through gauzy curtains, I've noticed how nice they look on the heavy oval plates, and thought perhaps I'd try them out one day. My adversary, with an ascetic air, requests a glass of seltzer. I barely remember to specify separate checks as the waitress crams her pad into the ass pocket of skinny designer jeans.

"Now then," Daniel prompts.

"Did Ericka tell you about the conversation she and I had on Saturday?"

"Yes, she mentioned it."

"Did she say what we talked about?"

"About the move, I believe."

"Did she explain the idea she came up with—that she'd like to spend summers here in Brooklyn with me?"

"Let's see now." He actually appears to consider. I have to hand it to him: he knows how to make me sweat this. "What she said was, if I recall correctly, something about your suggesting that she spend time with you during the summer vacation. She didn't characterize this as her own idea."

"Well, it was, in fact." Trying to keep up an optimistic tone in the face of Daniel's attitude feels a little like trying to maintain a relaxed smile while arm-wrestling Arnold Schwarzenegger. "What happened was that she seemed quite upset when I picked her up on Saturday. She'd just found out about your moving plans. I think she felt bad that I'd heard about the whole thing from you the previous Wednesday, yet of course hadn't mentioned it when we'd spoken on the phone. Obviously she was very worried and upset at the thought of a drastic separation from me, though I certainly think there's more to it than that—Brooklyn is home, Daniel. All her friends are here.

"At first she wanted me to move to Cleveland. Naturally I had to explain I didn't think that would be very practical. Then she came up with what really seems like a perfectly workable plan: she'd spend the summer months here. She compared it to the way some of her friends spend time with parents who live in other cities."

I pause. Daniel declines to take a hint.

"Well, what do you think?"

"Out of the question." His calm is provocative.

"Did you discuss this with Ericka in any detail? Did she tell you how important it is to her?"

He shifts impatiently under my questioning, like a horse aggrieved by the sting of a small fly. Evidently he's gotten over last week's embarrassment. "Look, Josie, I can understand Ericka. Of course she's feeling anxious. A move like this isn't trivial. But I must say, given your expressed concern for her welfare I'm a bit surprised at the role you seem to be taking in this. I thought I made my position clear last week. The very last thing that poor kid needs is to be shuttling back and forth between here and Ohio like some pint-sized Henry Kissinger."

"Even though the alternative is losing a part of her family?"

Daniel frowns. "You're overdramatizing. In fact, the two of you will be in fairly close touch, I should think—that's up to you, of course."

"Letters and phone calls? The kid is ten years old. A short visit in a year or two, when you and Brenda come back to see relatives? Have you forgotten what a year means at that age?"

"I don't believe this is getting us anywhere." Clocking my folly and his own indulgence, he glances at his wrist. "And, frankly, encouraging her in unworkable fantasies—"

"Could you just explain what you see as unworkable? Alternatively, I'd be perfectly delighted to have her spend the school year here and the summers in Ohio, but I more or less assumed you'd want her in school where you are. Either way, I'd get a bigger apartment. If she came in the summer, I'd arrange to take time off. She's been telling me she wants to go camping."

My nemesis frowns, gulps seltzer. There's a faint haze of fresh beard misting his jaw, extending down to the knot of the Adam's apple. I've a quick flush of distaste at all that peculiar equipment. Sitting here inches from his clenched, abrasive features, I recall the rasp of other stubbled faces, how they felt against my skin.

"What you're basically asking is that I should okay Ericka's spending the summer in a cramped city apartment, running around the streets without supervision while you're away at work."

"There are day camp programs," I hear myself plead. "Thousands of single mothers and their kids make it through summers in the city every year."

"Undoubtedly so, but most of them have no choice."

Here we're interrupted by the arrival of my order, and there's a further brief reprieve while I negotiate for ketchup. As I dribble the bottled gore over my heaped plate—the food looks fine, though I've lost my appetite—it strikes me I've come to the end of my strategies. I'm filibustering now. That's all. And any minute Daniel can cut me off by announcing he has to get home to dinner.

Nothing for it but to up the ante, as Luce puts it when talking political struggle. "I'm sure you've seen some families with joint custody arrangements. You know this could work out; you've no really valid objections. All you're doing is invoking property rights."

His face, a fist already, somehow tightens. I've scored. I brace myself for the comeback punch.

"Let's get one thing straight right this minute. Joint custody arrangements are concluded between a child's divorced parents. You are not Ericka's parent."

"Daniel, I am. In fact if not in name."

"Look, this is absurd. I don't even know why I'm bothering to go over this again. Let me put it this way: I, as Ericka's father, and Brenda, as her stepmother, are satisfied that we've devised the healthiest, most consistent living arrangement for our daughter. Now that's about all I have to say on the subject."

"Healthy? Consistent? What are you getting at?"

He looks almost alarmed. "I'm not getting at anything."

"You mean a dyke like me might contaminate her?"

Stiff, offended: "I don't think that's the point."

"I wonder, I really do."

"Don't twist my words, Josie. I mean just what I said. Now it's true that it doesn't seem to me that spending a good portion of the year in . . . your particular milieu . . . would exactly facilitate her adjustment to suburban Cleveland. I think even you would have to admit that the transition could be rather difficult. However, leaving aside questions of *lifestyle*, there are other factors which—"

"Damn right, there are other factors. Like my politics, my low-status job, the fact that I happen to have been your ex-wife's lover—and then of course there's plain old garden variety opportunism. You know you can get away with what you please, since I don't have any legal claim to Ericka. I'd say homophobia per se is probably only about 50% of it."

"*Homophobia.*" His sneer puts it in quotes, as though he suspects me of having coined the term. "Don't give me that crap, Josie. I'm certainly no bigot, and I won't be guilt-tripped."

"It's got nothing to do with guilt trips. I'm just asking you to think about Ericka for a minute, I mean really *think*. Put aside your preconceptions about all those terrific advantages you're offering her and tell me how you fucking justify ignoring what she wants, what she needs."

Daniel looks pained, perhaps at my bad language. "You know as well as I do Ericka's too young to know *what* the hell she needs. And vulnerable enough and confused enough, after all she's been through, to be manipulated."

"You know goddamn well I'm not manipulating her."

"Hey, hey, calm down. No need to shout."

People he knows eat here, I realize. "I don't feel like calming down." But I've lowered my voice anyway, I notice.

"This is getting pretty pointless." A warning glance at his watch.

"Pointless, I'll say. You've invoked father right. Which is about as convenient and enlightening as executive privilege. You haven't given me reasons."

"*I don't have to give you any fucking reasons.*" It's the rubberhose treatment with the invisible bruises, his face a mask, voice dropped to a near-whisper, nothing that would carry as far as the next booth, as he drains his seltzer and reaches for his check.

"*Don't leave now,*" I tell him, plea or warning.

"Then better make it quick."

"Oh, you're incredible, Daniel."

He glares at me. I want to taste blood.

"How come with all your damn rhetoric you never make me believe you actually *care* about her? What is all this shit? We both know perfectly well it's not like you couldn't bear to dispense with her for a couple months out of the year. You were never such a fucking attentive father when Rhea was alive.

"It's all about control, ownership. And you've got that down, oh, have you got it down. You probably don't even begin to guess how fantastically you've succeeded in shutting us both up, making us behave and do things your way, all this past year. You can't imagine how frightened I've been."

"Well, at the moment you're not being terribly coherent," he observes almost mildly, obviously amazed.

I'm furious, reckless, inspired now, and doomed, past calculating effects. "Just listen a minute. I'll be plenty coherent. I want to talk about what it really means, all this 'health' and 'consistency' and so on you plan to offer. Let's talk about how absolutely terrific it's going to be for Ericka Krevsky in Cleveland, stuck way out in the white-on-white suburbs with all the gorgeous green grass and the idiot fresh air. How healthy it'll be for her to spend her teen years babysitting your and Brenda's brats and hanging out playing shopping mall video games with a bunch of nerds from that middle American dreamworld, who don't know the first thing about the experience she comes from. With one dead lesbian mother, one faraway dyke pen pal, and a couple fantastic, heterosexual parents right there on the spot to provide healthy, consistent role models, who want a package marked 'daughter' but completely ignore what goes on inside it.

"She's Rhea's child, Daniel. Even if you won't admit she's mine, you've got to admit that. You're not just going to be able to fucking amputate her first ten years. You'd do it if you could, but you can't. It's in her blood — Rhea and this city.

"And while we're at it, incidentally, I'd like an explanation for the outrageous way you've lied to me all this time, acting like everything could get worked out with a little give and take, acting like I have some rights, when really you've just been waiting for your chance to pull this stunt. Forget Ericka's welfare. Let's talk about how gloriously it suits you to *finally* have an opportunity to get back at the woman your wife left you for."

If you aim for the groin, just make sure you don't miss. That's the excellent advice generally offered in self-defense classes, but right now, sitting here shaking, I don't care about the risk. It's enough for me that the blow delays his exit.

"Look, Josie," he snarls, soft-voiced still, "I really hadn't intended to get into this. But you're . . . you've really pushed me. So I'm going to be pretty direct.

"I'm not about to answer your absurd charges. I only want to say that it's absolutely crucial you find some focus for your life other than Ericka. I'm not about to allow this neurotic fixation of yours to mess *her* up, but if you don't get it under control I'm afraid it's going to have serious repercussions for *you*."

"Daniel."

He can't hear, I guess, the warning tone in this. Doesn't, at any rate, heed it, but keeps on running his mouth as he slides out of the booth, briefcase and check in hand: "If you must have a child in your life, you might consider having your own, you know — though it wouldn't hurt to get your head straightened out a bit first.

"I realize conception could be a bit tricky for a person of your . . . militant convictions. But if it's a real priority I'm sure you'll figure it out."

"Don't you dare give me advice you presumptuous motherfucker."

Somewhere an ill-bred female is screaming this as I rise, inexorable, coldly murderous, to my feet; the plate, crockery, oval, on my palm arcing up in one clean economical gesture slammed high to the pillar of his insolent chest; the impact solid, authentic, gratifying as the famous slam of the door on a well-made car. And then I turn, balletic, springing nimbly clear of soaring pickles and flying grease, hearing crash and shatter reverberate behind me as I seize my coat and flee, threading the tables, in slow-motion dreamtime toward the distant door.

Have I killed, maimed seriously? One backward glance provides reassurance: he stands there, freeze-frame, stupefied in the aisle, clutching his fouled briefcase, ketchup dripping off his coat, french fry caught on a button, hamburger perched on a shoe. While waitresses gasp in poses of simpering horror.

And then I'm out in the blessed cool night, adrenaline-blasted, rocked by helpless rage like a million hot, excruciating volts. Wishing I'd had the nerve to go for his face, knowing I chickened out in the last second only out of some instilled womanish dread of wasting something, making too big a mess, splitting his precious skull, spilling his fucking brains.

I'm walking, fast, south. I don't dare run, not even when I detect a clatter of light footsteps. The steps accelerate to a near-trot; then a slight, white, perfectly-groomed hand alights on my trembling arm. I turn to meet whatever this menace is.

The pretty head is level with my shoulder.

"Excuse, me," it gasps, "I don't mean to disturb you, but I couldn't help overhearing a little of what happened back there. I was paying when you . . . left, and I felt I had to come after you and say—" She hesitates, daunted. "—I mean, he's trying to take your little girl away, isn't he? I gathered that. Forgive my eavesdropping. I'm sure you're terribly upset, I oughtn't to have stopped you. The thing is, I had to tell you . . . I know what this is like."

I look at her in frank disbelief.

"My husband tried to take my little boy. I just felt, you know, you might need some support."

"Thanks, I'm fine," I say discouragingly.

"That's what I thought too, but I was a real wreck. I just wanted to say, you know, there's ways to fight this. Even though the courts do tend to listen to fathers a lot more than they used to."

"Look, please—"

But she seems to have gathered courage. "I won't keep you a minute. I just—oh, I don't know. Men really can be awful, can't they? Sometimes I wonder why we marry them. But I really believe, and I think in the end the courts will have to accept this, in nine cases out of ten, the kids belong with the mother. Even though the fathers generally have more money, and. . . ."

I laugh and laugh. It's cruel, but I can't stop. The misunderstanding is simply too exquisite.

Her face crumples. Still she bravely tries. "I only thought, if you wanted to take my number . . . I mean, you might need a fellow mother to talk with sometime."

"You've made a mistake, lady. I'm nobody's mother. Nobody's mother, just a neurotic dyke." And I leave her there in the middle

110

of the sidewalk, as appalled and hurt, I suppose, as if I'd slapped her.

* * *

May is upon us in all her ironic profusion. "Merry," as in that ballad Joan Baez warbles in her limpid, inflectionless young virgin's voice on the ancient warped folk record I still have in my collection.

"So you've chosen a life of crime," Luce insinuates. Her face winces with subtle humor beneath the disguising glasses. She leans back against a tree trunk and draws on a cigarette.

"I didn't say I'd *chosen* anything. I want to talk it out."

We're sitting on real grass. Through new leaves, stippled sunlight rains upon us its warm, shifting patterns. We face, down a gentle slope, a vista of white and pink trees; women our age and younger who, picturesquely imprisoned on blankets, guard babies and picnic provisions; men, older children, and dogs freely cavorting; soccer players caucused; joggers grinding along; schools of cyclists wheeling, sharp-nosed, predatory, around the green perimeter. A breeze caresses us, redolent, alternately, of cut grass, fresh dogshit, and marijuana.

"Hold it right there, I don't want to hear another word over the phone," Luce cried when I called her up with my request for an audience. She wouldn't even have me in her apartment, but rushed me out to the park as though I were a package suspected of containing some powerful and delicate explosive.

"Do you mean to tell me," I ventured, once we were in the street—by now she almost had me whispering—"that you actually believe your place is bugged?"

"Of course not," she crisply replied. "It's purely a precaution. Expect the worst and you won't be unprepared if it turns out the bastards are really on the ball."

"So what made you change your mind?" she now inquires.

"I haven't, not exactly. I mean, I still feel it's a lousy plan on a lot of levels. It's just that I can't seem to stop thinking about it. Ever since I tossed that plate at Daniel . . . I guess I really hadn't let myself feel how furious I am. It's like all this time I've been clinging for dear life to this pretext that I live in some halfway normal situation, in some halfway decent, rational world.

"But the other day—I don't know. Something snapped."

Luce cracks a smile. "Preconditions for revolt."

"If you want to put it that way. I've really had it."

"So what have you come up with?"

"Well, I should say, first of all, that *if* I decide this is what I want to do—and that's one major *if*—then everything still depends on Ericka. She'd have to make the ultimate decision."

"How do you rate the odds?"

"Of her going along with it? I can't begin to guess. I mean, I certainly think it's possible. It would be pretty hard for her to go against her father."

"And if she does, then what?"

I grin at my advisor. "Suppose the trees are bugged?" The whole thing seems suddenly silly, melodramatic, though last night when I lay in bed going over everything for the umpteenth time it seemed a simple question of material problems to be solved, of sublets and money, maps and timetables.

"The trees are fine," Luce says. "I had them checked this morning. Come on, babe. Shoot."

"Well, my first step would be to patch things up with The Man. I'd have to call him up, apologize, sort of hint that it was only a very precarious mental state that sent me into hysterics and made me ruin his new suede coat. I might even bring myself to thank him for his insights, though perhaps that's overdoing it. Basically grovel, with some finesse, of course."

"You think he'd go for it?"

"Sure. Why not? I mean, there it is, just as he suspected—he's got it all together, I'm this slightly unstable broad. I'd stop being a threat. It would flatter him, when you think of it, in a way. And as long as he thinks he's getting rid of me. . . ."

"You've been in contact since the—what shall we call it, the Ketchup Rebellion?"

"No, it's been ten days and we've totally avoided one another. I expected he'd try to get back through Ericka, but he's evidently either too smart or too chickenshit for that. He still has to try and look a little liberal, to her if not to me. So he hasn't interfered. I saw her last weekend; I'll see her again tomorrow."

"What does she say?"

"Not a hell of a lot. She's pretty miserable, but blocking the whole thing. I told her he'd vetoed a compromise living arrangement. She didn't seem to want to know the details, which was just as well, considering."

"So you go to Daniel now and say you're mighty sorry."

"Right, in a week or two. And after I've softened him up—I'd allow a decent interval, of course—I ask if I can take Ericka camping once school's out. Four or five days away — no big deal. He knows she's been wanting to do that with me, and once he thinks he's won he should be able to feel he can afford a last magnanimous gesture."

"So the two of you take off."

"We split. Abscond. Elope."

"Like rolling a drunk, as they say."

"Taking candy from a baby."

"And then?" Luce looks severe behind her shades.

"It would give us a few days. Then I send Dad a message. Tell him I'll be in touch, and not to bother calling out the posse."

"But he *will* try to find you. And he'll be mad as hell. And life on the run — it's no pleasure cruise, friend."

"Oh, I'm definitely not planning on making a career of it. I'd never even be considering this in the first place if I thought it would last more than a couple months. After he's had a chance to think the situation over and sort of generally contemplate his sins, I'll try to negotiate."

"What makes you think he will, though? He's got the law behind him."

"Yes, but the man *does* know me. As much of a prick as he's capable of being, I don't assume he's automatically going to treat me like an armed, dangerous stranger."

"I don't know. . . ." Luce shakes her head. "You're putting yourself in an awfully vulnerable spot. I'd say you can't discount the possibility he'll talk himself into thinking you *are* dangerous. Didn't you tell me he already said something about neurotic fixations? That could lead him directly to a stance of, you know, no negotiations with terrorists, that mentality. Or he could promise you various things, then renege when you bring her back.

"Just suppose he does go the legal route, you can be charged, number one" — she ticks off on nail-bitten fingers — "with kidnapping, which carries a maximum life sentence. Number two, he could accuse you of child molestation."

"Really, Luce. Now *that's* paranoid." Swathed in her drab clothes, masked in her green glasses, a reproach to the vivid festival of the day proceeding all around, my old friend puts me in mind of an ultra-leftist raven croaking with bleak satisfaction her radical *nevermore*.

"Not paranoid at all."

"He knows I wouldn't hurt her."

"Face it, sweetheart, what counts here is, you're queer. You're a filthy lez, and you're not the kid's mother. The sky's the limit in

terms of what he *could* do. Now I'm not saying he *will*, I'm talking
worst-case scenarios. But committing to something like this is
like starting a game of chess. You're setting in motion a complex
chain of forces, and you'd better fucking look ahead a little, address yourself to the possibilities."

The urban guerrilla is counseling restraint. "I thought you offered to help," I remind her. "That morning on the stairs, after I'd
slept over – did you mean that, or what? Are you going to sit here
all morning threatening me?"

Luce shakes her head cloaked in its rough brown hair. She's in-
terring the remains of a smoked-out cigarette in a little heap of
dirt she has scratched up with a twig from a bald patch amid the
scant grass. Nearby, on a blanket spread with picnic provisions, a
man and woman are trading rapid Spanish. Their small son,
wearing a billed Yankees cap and a T-shirt which bears the
legend, "Yo Tengo A Puerto Rico En Mi Corazón," is trying to inveigle us into a game of peekaboo. But we're mean, we won't
play, and his mother keeps calling him at intervals: "Ven acá!
Tengo un ham sandwich para tí."

"I *will* help," Luce concedes. "I'm not threatening. I just want
you to be very realistic about all this."

"I'm realistic, all right. It's like anything else, having surgery or
driving a car. No guarantee you won't end up a statistic."

"I think you're underestimating the enemy, Josie. From
everything you've ever said about him this dude sounds like a
class A prick."

I find myself in the odd position of defending Daniel. "He really
isn't all that special, Luce. I mean, right now I sure hate his guts,
but I know basically he's just a white middle-class American
father who doesn't exactly, shall we say, lead the examined life,
and who has too much power in this situation."

"Like I said," she repeats drily, "a class A prick."

"But a prick with a liberal image to maintain. He'll call me
neurotic, he'll take Ericka from me, but that's not to say he'd slap
me in jail. Besides, I suspect he'd be anxious to avoid anything too
public, anything that would make the papers. You know, 'lesbian
kidnapping case,' that kind of thing. I mean, Rhea's still a sore
point in certain ways, and I don't think he, or Brenda for that matter, wants to dredge that up."

"Which brings me back to a point I made before. You *are* a
dyke. If it ever *did* come to trial—"

"I didn't mean I count on his good will. I'm not planning on getting caught."

"Fugitives don't, in general."

"After all, I'm not exactly Angela Davis. It shouldn't be *that* hard to pull it off. I'm certainly not planning on hanging around the East Coast."

"Hold it right there." Luce flashes a warning gesture. "I don't want to know where you're headed."

"Fine. I wouldn't dream of telling you. My point simply was, this should work for a little while. It's definitely a gamble, I know that. I just hope once he sees I'm not going quietly—and neither is his daughter, for that matter—it may dawn on him that having me around on a regular, limited basis could actually be an improvement over this sort of melodrama."

"And how about Ericka? How far can you trust her?"

"What do you mean, trust her?"

"You're over Tulsa, or Omaha, or Denver. You have a disagreement. She says she wants her father. She starts crying and threatens to call the flight attendant. She'd have you over a barrel."

Now this is classic Luce, for whom children might be Martians. "She wouldn't, Luce. These things don't work that way. Maybe at three or four, but not at ten. Anyway, she'd always be free to go back. That would be one of the ground rules. . . . And I'm not flying, either."

Fingers clasped, head bowed, Luce ponders. In her cross-legged posture, draped in her dark tresses, she looks like an ascetic Maoist nun. Why, I always wonder, does she tolerate that hair? Even in its utterly straight Anglo-Saxon severity, not a wave or curl in sight, it seems a kind of luxury or excess, something for cops to grab when a demo gets out of hand.

Around us the bright day buzzes, charged with language. The soccer players are flinging back and forth their lively island English, while on a bench across the way two matrons converse in Italian. Our friend the Puerto Rico and Yankees fan has gone back to eat his lunch. And we're scarcely aware of this, or of the flowering trees; we might as well be back in Luce's lair, intent as we are on grey patterns in our heads. Such is the life of New York, abstract, political, all simple sweetness perishing around us while we plot our dense strategies.

"You've got guts at least," Luce announces.

I feel the comment sentences me to something. "But I haven't made up my mind."

"You sure talk as though you have."

"The whole thing scares me stiff."

115

"But I thought you said—"

"Oh, it's not the legal stuff. Or not mainly."

"What else is there?"

"Difficult to say. Convention, I suppose. It's one thing to decide you don't believe in God, another to blaspheme against the Holy Ghost. You know? I've never stolen anyone's kid before." It's hard to admit to this staunch rationalist the vertigo I experience, the sense of earth lurching sickeningly beneath me, when I think how easy it sounds: just hop on a bus. So plain and familiar and commonsense an act.

I'd become responsible for everything.

To my surprise, Luce replies sympathetically, "It's always hard with—well, anything illegal. There's a kind of panic reflex that doesn't necessarily even have much to do with the actual danger involved. It's more just the fact of defying authority—stuff you've internalized from way back. And then, you know, deciding on your own. 'To live outside the law you must be honest.' "

"That's catchy. Who said that?"

"Dylan. Blonde on Blonde. 'Sweet Marie.' "

"Oh yeah? It sounded familiar, but I'd have guessed Gandhi. Wow, kid, you haven't lost it, have you?" It is a longstanding joke between us that Luce's famed ability to cite chapter and verse from a range of radical texts pales beside her skill at coming up with appropriate epigrams from the folk and rock sages.

She smiles, acknowledging the compliment. "The boy's a born-again Christian, beats his wife, but he did manage to get off a good line here and there."

By her shift in tone, I perceive I've cleared some hurdle. "You *will*—take my 'case'?"

"Your 'case,' my ass," she grumbles, still crusty on principle. "Yeah, if you decide you really want to go through with this foolishness, I guess I'll take your 'case.' I suppose you'll want me on your defense committee too."

"Of course. I thought you could run it in your spare time."

"That's a good one. But look, seriously. There's a lot we have to consider."

"Like?"

"Money, for instance."

"I've got some savings, not a whole lot. Enough for a couple months."

"We'll discuss that more later. You can't have too much cash, underground."

"*Underground*! I'm not a Weatherwoman."

116

"Nevertheless, you should start thinking like a fugitive. There's ID. You'll need a couple pieces. Social Security, driver's license, of course. I'll see what I can do. You should start thinking about what name you want to use, something you'll remember and feel comfortable with."

Her diligence makes me smile. "Luce," I say.

"Yeah."

"You seem awfully enthusiastic all of a sudden, for someone who thought this was a bad idea."

She shrugs, sheepish. "Well, I can get into it."

"I guess so. A good thing for me."

"The fact is, I know it's unprofessional and romantic and individualistic and all that – I mean, folks having to go into hiding is certainly nothing to cheer about under any circumstances – but I always kind of dug the whole fugitive bit. Probably it goes back to being a kid. When I was in junior high we lived in this place for a while, big old beat-up place, about a quarter mile away from some railroad tracks. And even though my mom kept warning me to stay away from there – or maybe *because* she did – I was always sneaking off to play around there with the boys. It had a fascination. We'd count boxcars, you know, walk on the ties. There was a little bridge – an overpass, really. We'd dare each other to cross that when a train was coming.

"But the main thing was, I always had these heavy fantasies about running away, hopping the freights with my girlfriend – well, she wasn't really my girlfriend. But she was my friend, and I was crazy about her. And her father hit her too hard, I thought she should get away. I figured she could have a better life with me, riding in those boxcars, cooking our dinner over campfires at night beside the tracks . . . I had it all figured out."

Half-reclining against a tree, Luce speaks softly. Her glasses are off, eyes closed. Thus stripped, she looks amazingly vulnerable.

"How about you," she continues, "didn't you ever want to run away? But then, you were leading the high life out there in suburbia."

"I wanted to run away all right, but not till high school, I guess. By then I was horribly literary. You know, post-Kerouac, *that* scene. Secondhand Zen, watered down Existentialism. Even so, there was something powerful about it. That image of taking off. Of being totally free."

"Well, it ain't that way," she says, flat, suddenly bitter.

"I know. I know."

"Just bullshit dreams." And then her hard look dissolves in the old wide wolf-grin, and for a moment I can see the ancient Luce: the young dreamer, I mean, the one not yet ground down by the hundred thousand losing battles, the million and one criticism-self-criticism sessions that have, as much as fast food and late hours, weighted and slowed the flesh. Incalculable, the depleting effects of that grimly held resolve not to give in, not to be like, think like all the rest. More than that, to construct belief that permits action. "The Sixties are over," says Daniel. But Luce grins, baring her long good teeth, and just for a second they're not.

"Luce, you're fantastic."

I'm really going to hug her; but she, seeing the danger, and embarrassed as an adolescent boy in an overly intimate moment, punches me lightly on the arm. "I've got to run, have to be on the Upper West Side in an hour for a meeting. Let me know the minute you make your mind up, so I can get started on that ID."

"It's not just up to me. There's Ericka."

I watch her go, and stay in the park a while, regarding the composition of bright figures and tender leaves with the detached avidity of the professional traveler, she who knows she's merely passing through this life.

*   *   *

It's in the park, too, that I speak to Ericka.

All morning she's sustained a ferocious output of kinetic energy, as though on purpose to fend off our discussion, the looming prospect of which is supposed to be my secret. Though perhaps I emit some warning sign or scent? Fail, despite my efforts, to mask my mounting panic?

But at last the frantic sequence of bicycling, Frisbee, and cartwheels on the grass comes to an end. At last I have her cornered, parked on a wooden bench tonguing a frozen object whose red, white, and blue striations justify its lurid title: AMERIPOP.

The dreaded moment. I force myself to begin, feeling as though I'm proposing: marriage, or something indecent. Whatever it is, it's something final, fatal.

"Ericka, remember—"

"Do we have to sit here, Josie? It stinks like dog doo." Wrinkled nose, regressed theatrical giggle.

I flash her my sternest nonsense-abating glare. "Yes, we do have to sit here. We have to talk."

118

"Really? Hey, did I tell you about my social studies project? I got the only A."

"No, you didn't. Tell me about it later. There's something we have to discuss." My voice is working badly.

"If it's about my father and moving, I already know all that."

"Know all what?"

"I hafta do what he says."

"That wasn't what I was going to say at all. I had a new idea."

"What, then." She stolidly picks a scab.

"Even though he didn't like our plan . . . do you still want to live with me, part-time?"

Blank look. "I don't get it. You said he'd have to —"

"I thought so. But there might be another choice." Here it comes: a life of crime, kid. "We'd have to run away."

"Run away?" She's at least not horrified.

Hastily I pile on the intriguing details: how we would head out West, how we would make up new names, how we would masquerade as mother and daughter, how we would live on hard-boiled eggs and sandwiches, sunflower seeds and apples. How we would sleep in our rocking Greyhound seats, waking to snow-mantled mountains and painted deserts. How I'd try to get her father to see reason. Then, fearing I've seduced more than informed, I counter with warnings, disclaimers: that she'd probably find the trip very tiring and boring, that she wouldn't be able to see or talk to or write to her father or Brenda or anyone else she knows, not for a very long time. That in the end it might all be for nothing, she might have to go back to Cleveland.

I ply her with problems, occasions for doubt and refusal. She doesn't have to want this, I insist. Really she doesn't.

Is LA near Disneyland, she wants to know. Do I think her father would miss her.

"Yes it is, and yes I think he'd miss you. But if we can get things worked out, nobody will have to miss anybody so much."

"How come we can't fly? I like taking planes."

"Planes are more expensive, for one thing. On the bus we can get a one-month travel pass. Besides, we don't want to attract any more attention than we have to, in case someone's looking. I have a hunch we'll be less conspicuous this way."

"Who would look for us? My daddy, you mean?"

"Whoever hunts missing kids. Cops, possibly."

Clearly this is a new and rather alarming thought. "You mean we could get in trouble from the *police*?"

"Not you, kiddo. You're not the guilty party. I could, theoretically, if—well, if they did find us."

"What would happen?"

"They'd send you home, I guess."

"To Cleveland," she corrects. "What about you, though?"

"I don't know." But she has to hear the worst. "I don't think anything much would happen, I think if it got that far your father would just be concerned about getting you back. But if they really wanted to, they could try to put me in jail."

"What for?"

"Kidnapping. Stealing you."

"But that's not kidnapping!" She's indignant at the illogic. "Kidnapping's like when somebody with a gun makes you get in their car, or a man says come with me and I'll buy you a bunch of candy. Then they make you stay when you don't want to."

"Well, you and I might think so, but the people who made the law have different ideas. They say it's kidnapping if I'm not your legal parent."

"But couldn't I tell them you didn't make me go?"

"You certainly could try. I don't know whether they'd listen. But let's not worry too much about all that. It's a very distant possibility, even if they did find us, which I don't expect will happen." I'm not lying, downplaying it like this: didn't Luce's lawyer-friend, the one versed in federal law, assure me the Feds wouldn't touch this sort of thing, a mere family dispute, unless some other issue were involved? No FBI to contend with, in other words; either some local cop would have to stumble on me ("you'd practically have to turn yourself in"), or Daniel might resort to a private detective. Of course, she added, in the disparaging tones of a cancer specialist diagnosing a paltry case of measles, if I *were* caught the whole thing could conceivably be prosecuted under the state kidnapping law. But even then, only if Daniel pushed it.

Ericka seems satisfied for the moment. "It's funny to think of a *grownup* running away."

"What's funny about it?"

"Well, like, usually, you know, you talk about a kid running away from home."

"Grownups can get just as exasperated."

"Daddy'd be mad though, I bet."

"I expect so. At me more than you, probably."

"Poor Daddy." Pity's conventions cloud her face. "But," she brightens, "there'll be the new baby. That should cheer him up.

Jeremy, that's what they're calling him. I think it's sort of a dumb name."

"That's another thing. The baby. You know you wouldn't see him for a while. Do you think you'd miss being around when he was born?"

She shrugs maturely. "I could care less. Leah'll have a hard time, I'll bet. She's used to being spoiled, getting everything her way. She'll probably have lots of tantrums and stuff. I'd just as soon skip it."

Such total indifference leaves me skeptical. "I expect you'd find you missed them, even if it doesn't feel that way right now. Of course, even if we did go, you could always change your mind and come back. But that's tricky, because if we did that and your father got really mad at me he might not let us see each other at all."

She sits silent.

"I know it sounds scary."

But after all, maybe that's not it. "Tell me again how we'd go," she begs suddenly, with the air of one awakening to delicious possibilities.

Thus authorized, I improve my original story, conjuring up for myself as much as her a vision of the continent opening westward from New Jersey, yielding up its secrets. Days and nights pass; heroic, we plough on, grubby, cranky, exhausted, yet charged with the energy of cities consumed, suburbs squandered, rivers and forests and valleys strewn behind us like gnawed bones tossed over the shoulder. Till at length, winded, gasping, worn to the nerves' limit, we throw ourselves on the flat, hard-bitten mercy of up-against-the-Pacific Los Angeles.

But where would we get money, she wants to know, sober with ten-year-old practicality.

"I've got some saved. Enough for a few months. But it wouldn't be like living with your father. We'd have to be thrifty."

"I can be thrifty. I know how to shop for bargains."

"I know you do. I'm sure you'd be a big help. But the important thing now is for you to figure out what you really want to do about all this. If you decide you're not interested, fine, no problem. But if it seems like you might be, then I want you to give all this some very serious consideration over the next week or two. Before you make up your mind you've got to be sure how you feel.

"Of course it's also terribly important not to say a single word about this to anyone but me. Understand? Not just Daniel and Brenda, *anyone*."

"Don't worry, Josie. I know how to keep a secret."

It's past time for lunch. We head back to my apartment. We've gone a block or two in sober silence—no trace in Ericka now of her former restlessness—when she shyly bursts out, "I *think* I want to."

Appalled, I remind her she's to think it over. At which rebuke she's quiet for a moment, then catches me off guard by inquiring whether her daddy and I had a fight.

"When we talked, you mean? What makes you think that?"

"Well, he came home with his coat all greasy, and Brenda had to have it drycleaned, and—I heard them talking, sort of."

"What did they have to say?"

She's diplomatic. "I couldn't hear, really."

"Then how did you decide we'd had a fight?"

"Well, I heard them say your name, and Daddy swearing. Then he waited downstairs the next time he picked me up from your house, and he looked mad whenever I'd mention you."

So I supply a brief, expurgated version of the Ketchup Rebellion, which she appears prepared to view in the light of an uproarious situation comedy. "No wonder he was *pissed*!" she daringly comments; she can't stop laughing at the thought of her father standing there, the contents of my plate cascading down his chest. "And you didn't even get to eat the hamburger! Who paid for it, though?"

"I guess he did." I laugh along with her, guiltily savoring her disloyalty.

But as the afternoon wears on, I do attempt to challenge her evident assumption that our future together is settled. "Leah will miss me, I know," she proclaims, breaching security by alluding to our secret as we wait in line at the supermarket checkout. Admonished, she waits till we're back in the apartment to make some practical inquiries: "Who'll tell Grandma and Grandpa?" and, "Poor cats, poor Beebo and Red Emma, they'll be so lonesome without you, who will feed them?" and, "Do they have bathrooms on those buses, or do we wait?" More than once she kiddingly calls me Mom.

"Hold your horses," I caution her, as my own mother chided me, in LA freeway-land where there were no horses. "You haven't made a decision yet, remember? I want you to think about all the things that would be hard about this trip, like not being able to settle down in one place for a while, and not having kids to play with, and missing your father."

"But it's not like I'd *never* get to see him *again*."

Of course I'm glad she wants me. And all that's genuine enough. What bothers me is my sneaking suspicion that our "running away" is as unreal to her as the exile to Cleveland must have seemed all along. From the very first, she must have hoped for magic. And now when I mention hardship, she doesn't hear a word.

"Would we have to wear wigs and stuff like that?"

"Ericka, you watch too much TV."

"We'd be sort of outlaws, wouldn't we? Wouldn't we, Mom?"

I can't resist her grin, that's obvious. But what happens when she finds out I'm not her fairy godmother?

PART II: OUTLAWS

"Take the bus, and leave everything to us."
　　　　　—Greyhound motto, c. late Seventies

It feels strange to wake up in Josie's bed.

Everything's so peaceful, like the country, or like Grandma's in Florida, where there's a lot less cars. For a minute I can't remember where I am.

Then I get it. We're still in Park Slope. Daddy dropped me off last night with all my stuff. Today's the day we leave for California.

The light looks funny too. I guess it must be early. I reach over on the little table and get my birthday watch. Only twenty-five to six it says, and it hasn't stopped, I can still hear it ticking. I could of had a digital watch instead if I wanted, but Brenda says this kind's more elegant. Only you have to be very careful not to wind it too tight. But I'm always careful. It's made out of real sterling silver.

Even though it's so early I could tell right away I can't go back to sleep. I'm too excited, that's why. About the trip and everything. Go right to sleep and don't get up till I call you, Josie said, and took the alarm clock in the other room with her. You'll need your rest, she said. She sounded just like Brenda. You might have trouble sleeping on that bus.

I forget what dream I had. An okay one, though. Not like times when I dream something bad, then wake up feeling like I couldn't breathe. Sometimes I'm even scared I might of screamed, but I don't, anymore, which is good because Leah sleeps practically right next to my room and I hate to wake her up. You should hear how loud she yells, it hurts your ears. At first I used to have a lot of nightmares and I had to go to Dr. Turbo who's this psychologist.

It's not my fault I'm too excited to fall back asleep. I've never been on a Greyhound bus before, and I've never been to California. I'm not that used to running away from home!

Besides, they're supposed to have bathrooms on those buses so you could go anytime you want. I have to pee now, but I don't want to bother Josie. I don't want to make her mad, especially not this morning. We're going to pretend like she's my real mother, and I'm supposed to help her out. We're in this one together, kid, she says.

That's what she calls me sometimes, kid or kiddo, like Grandma Krevsky calls me rutabaga, which is just this joke we have because when I was little I used to always make her keep on reading me this story I liked, about a rutabaga and a turnip that rent an apartment together. She said after a while it made her think of me every time she was in a store and saw some rutabagas! I'm her only grand-daughter except Leah, Aunt Etty has boys. Daddy calls me honey sometimes, especially when he's in a good mood. Brenda only calls me by my name.

If I had my book in here I'd read it now, but I left it in the other room where Josie's sleeping. It's called My Name Is Jennifer and I Have This Problem. *See, it's about this girl named Jennifer whose parents get divorced and at first she stays with her father but then she goes to live with her mother who's got this new boyfriend and stuff. I guess she does have a problem, but it doesn't really seem like such a big deal. Anyway, I don't know hardly anybody except TeriAnn, and her family's Roman Catholic so they're not supposed to get divorced anyway, who lives with both their real father and their real mother. Lots of families have problems.*

The birds outside are getting all excited. I never noticed them so loud before. They're what woke me, I bet, flying from the lamp pole to the roof to the tree branches and back and singing and making noise like they're talking to each other. I bet we'll see a lot more birds in California. It might be sort of like Florida there, I think. Josie told me some stuff about it, it's where she lived when she was my age. All the houses are just on one floor. But they have mountains there, lots taller than Vermont. That's where I want to go. At night you lie there in your sleeping bag and look up at zillions of stars. It's near Disneyland, also, which is sort of like Disney World.

I still call Josie Josie to myself, but really I'm supposed to call her Mom or Mother and she's supposed to call me Cindy. We practiced last night. I like Mom best, it sounds the most grownup. Mommy's only for my real mom. There's a picture of her on Josie's bedside table. I'm bringing along my necklace of a Jewish star combined with a woman's symbol that she gave me, I'm going to wear it all the time. From Daddy of course I have my birthday watch.

One thing I like about the idea of pretending like Josie's my real mother is then I won't have to keep explaining to people or kids I meet all the time about Mommy being killed in a car crash. Passed on, some people say, which I think is a dumb expression, since you don't really go anyplace. Dead as a doornail, that's another one.

In a way it feels weird though, every time I say Mom to Josie. Cindy and Laura Cole, that's who we're supposed to be. I'm not sure why I picked Cindy instead of Rachel. I guess I just thought it went good with Cole. When I play the Cindy game, I'm Cindy Anderson, but when I'm Rachel I'm just Rachel, I never thought up a last name to go along with her. I play when I'm lying in bed trying to fall asleep, and I try to play Rachel on Friday nights especially, because that's Shabbos, when Mother and me light the candles. We've cleaned the house and baked loaves of challah bread and cooked a special dinner, even though it can't be too fancy because my father is a rabbi, wise but penniless. But it doesn't matter we're poor, because we love each other.

My mother is beautiful, even in one of those wigs, and when we light the candles and say the prayer, it gives me a special feeling to be her daughter.

When I play I'm Cindy we're not poor at all. My mother and father and my older brother Bob and me live in this huge white house right in the middle of this sort of park, with grass and trees and flowers like the Brooklyn Botanic Garden. Only it belongs just to us so it's never crowded or littered or polluted. Since we don't have muggers or anything like that, you can go for walks by yourself or ride your horses (which I have two of: Flicka and Black Beauty). My father is usually in the city at his job, and my mother has hobbies or something, so I'm by myself a lot. Sometimes I spend the day up in my treehouse, reading, but once my brother Bob came up there and made me do something nasty—not what you do to have babies, but something with your mouth, like these kids were talking about one day in school. Sometimes I go for walks in the woods and meet this friend of mine, this girl who's a little older. There's a pond deep in the forest where you could skinny dip.

I guess Daddy will miss me. I don't want to make him mad. I was going to write him a letter and try to explain I'm not doing it against him, I just don't want to move to Cleveland. But I didn't know what to say, so Josie's going to write to him instead, and her friend Wendy will mail the letter after we've been gone a couple days. I asked her to write to Grandma and Grandpa in Florida, too. She says Daddy will call my Grandma Fein in Boston.

Once I even asked him if he'd miss me if I went away someplace. He laughed and asked had I made some reservations, but I said really, so he told me yes he would. I also asked him did he think he'd like to live in California, and he said he supposed it would be okay, though the lifestyle didn't appeal to him that much, hippies and hot tubs. I wanted to say, but Josie and me aren't hippies. But of course I wouldn't give away our secret! He's going to be surprised, that's for sure.

I'm looking at Mommy's picture. I wish we could take it along. It's kind of big though, and the glass might break. She looks so pretty, I think, even though she's wearing this silly floppy hat. She's laughing and holding up a big sign, only you couldn't read the words. It was taken at a demo for Gay Pride. We used to go to lots of those before.

They cremated her—the corpse of her, I mean. I wondered things like did they do cremation because she was so smashed up and stuff like that. And do they leave your clothes on when they do it. But I didn't know if I was supposed to ask. It didn't hurt, I mean the accident. That's what everyone kept saying. She died instantly.

*When you're dead you're dead. Period. The End. I know that's true,
but it doesn't make much sense. Like, how you could be doing
something like eating ice cream or walking down the street one second
and the next just turn into nothing. TeriAnn thinks the part that's
really you inside goes someplace when you die, that's what Catholics
believe. It's a consoling superstition, Daddy says, whatever that
means. Anyway, we're Jewish.*

*It's getting more light out now, and I can hear Josie turning over on
the couch and coughing, so maybe she's awake too, trying not to
disturb me just like I'm doing with her. Every so often I hear this
loud meow, which is Beebo or Red Emma asking for their breakfast. I
feel sad to leave them here, but Josie says Wendy will take good care
of them. Wendy's who's going to stay in the apartment.*

*I keep hearing Josie turn over on the couch, saying ssshhhh to
Beebo and Red Emma. I can't help if I have to get up, I've got to pee
real bad.*

*I tiptoe into the bathroom and go as quiet as I can, then I tiptoe over
to the couch and look down at Josie lying there. "Christ, Ericka, it's
early," she says, keeping her eyes closed.*

*She's supposed to call me Cindy not Ericka, but I don't want to
make her mad.*

"I woke up and I can't fall back asleep."

"How hard did you try?"

"I couldn't. I was hungry." It's the truth, my stomach was *growling.
I'd like to crawl in Josie's sleeping bag with her, just for a minute or
two.*

*"Well, Beebo and Red Emma claim they're hungry too. Looks like
sleep's a lost cause around here. You go get dressed. I'll make
breakfast in a minute."*

"Can I wear my yellow shorts?"

*"I guess. Just be sure you have a sweater handy, in case you get chil-
ly later. The bus will be air conditioned."*

*I like getting dressed without listening to Leah's fussing. At home
it's usually my job to help her in the mornings. When I'm dressed I
wind my new watch up real careful. I fix my hair in a high ponytail.
My shorts look good, I think, especially with my platforms. Brenda
usually won't let me wear them except to go to the beach. They're too
skimpy, she says. I already have a pretty good tan. I think I look like I
could belong in California.*

*Josie makes fried eggs, not exactly my favorite breakfast. When I
sit down in front of my plate, they look like two big ugly pinky-yellow
eyes staring up at me, and I lose my appetite.*

"You just complained you were too starved to sleep. Anyway, we won't be having lunch for a good long time, so you'd better eat some breakfast." Josie sounds strict, so I stick my fork right in the middle of both eggs like I'm stabbing them or something, and the yolk comes gushing out like yellow blood.

Afterwards Josie says she has to wash the dishes and straighten things up. I don't see why, if we're not coming back. "Check your things and make sure you're all packed," she says, but I did that already.

The phone rings. Josie just stands there at the sink.

"Aren't you going to answer?"

"Just leave it alone," she snaps.

"I am."

Nothing happens. It keeps ringing. Finally it stops. Josie looks so cross, which isn't fair. I didn't make it ring.

It starts again.

Josie picks it up right away, still with dish suds on her hand.

"Hello. Oh, no, it didn't—maybe you dialed wrong? Hold on, I'll get her." It's Brenda calling, she says in this cheerful voice, but giving me a look.

I take the receiver, wet from her wet hand.

Good morning, Brenda says, did I sleep okay, she just wanted to call me up to tell me to be sure and have a good camping trip, and be sure and wear my warm jacket if it gets chilly at night, and be sure and be careful if we go swimming, and remember I can give a collect call any time I feel like it.

Where's Daddy, I ask. He had to leave very early this morning for a meeting in Albany, she says. I kiss her through the phone.

"What did she want?" Josie looks upset.

"Nothing."

"She must have had some reason for calling."

"Just to say goodbye, and tell me to wear warm stuff. How come you didn't answer the first time?"

She doesn't say, just turns on the faucet hard.

"Didn't I do okay?"

"You did fine. I wasn't expecting a call from her, that's all."

"You can trust me, Mom."

"I know I can trust you, kiddo."

I'm sort of glad it wasn't Daddy, though. It's harder not to tell him things than Brenda.

But you have to be able to pretend and stuff, if you're going to be outlaws. Outlaws take risks, that's what Josie said. My mother took *risks, and Grandma and Grandpa Krevsky.*

They don't put kids in jail, I know that of course. Anyway, Josie says not to worry, there's no reason we should get caught.

Besides, when we're in California how could anybody guess Josie's not my real mother?

* * *

Panic at Grand Army Plaza, where, in the course of ten or fifteen minutes, two packed Seventh Avenue IRT expresses depart the platform without us. Suppressing as I am the terrified apprehension that some acquaintance will spot us any minute, I'm hard put to be patient with Ericka, who keeps asking whether we're going to miss our bus. Of course I've prepared a plausible cover story: we are on our way to New Haven to meet my friends, the ones with the car and the tent for our Vermont camping trip. Nevertheless, I want to be out of Brooklyn.

The third train pulls in, doors creaking open only to disclose the discouragement inscribed on the faces facing us: no room, we've won our place, now let us be. But here basic survival instincts come into play and, affirmed in our resolve by shoves from the rear, Ericka and I mount a successful assault upon a yielding density of flesh. When at length the doors shudder closed, stranding angry multitudes, we recognize ourselves among a fortunate minority.

Minutes later, we're trapped beneath the East River. Captive, sweating, wedged upright far from handhold, physically abased as though we crawled this gauntlet ourselves, on our own bellies, we endure alongside other humiliated flesh. I school myself to ignore my companion's predictable, tedious appeals—it's hot, I can't move—and the scowls which the office-bound, the lightly-burdened, direct at our bulky, toe-imperilling luggage. Never again, I'm exulting, almost savoring this last insult. Westward, ho: to hell with toiling masses, mass transit, wretched refuse, the whole bit. . . .

Till at last we blink in Times Square's humid light, morning coffee goading the clerical crowd, Ericka tilting precariously along beside me on those ridiculous platform sandals permitted by Brenda, in her arms her bulging, badly-rolled sleeping bag, while I labor beneath the weight of my North Face pack as though off to the Himalayas. Good day to get out of town: too hot already, and yesterday's blue air, steam-cleaned by thunderstorms, has

132

already begun to contract within a sphincter of brown horizon, starched Manhattan's familiar ring-around-the-collar. Despite the absence, this early, of leering New Jerseyites, three card monte artists, and porn barkers, Forty-Second Street exudes its characteristic raunch. SEXTACULAR ACTS, LIVE GIRLS, the marquees blare (are DEAD GIRLS hawked somewhere in the neighborhood?). We shoulder our way through the oncoming foot traffic, eyes modestly averted from the lolling caricatures of our sex, ourselves, emblazoned on the posters.

Ericka's presence sensitizes me, of course. Always when I haven't spent much time with her recently I tend to forget the double consciousness she provokes, this uneasy habit of monitoring the world as one would the violent corruptions of TV, this sense of my responsibility to provide some helpful gloss on society's outrageous, inexplicable shortcomings.

Somewhere near Eighth Avenue I'm accosted by one of those derelict figures, familiar to the point of archetype, whom more fortunate New Yorkers tend to regard as too fantastically wretched even to register on our scale of credible and appropriate misery. Beard matted, rags bound around ulcerated calves, overcoated, yes, in this weather, the supplicant, who happens to be white, might easily be mistaken for a ghastly refugee from the pages of some drastic nineteenth century Russian fiction. (Indeed, he's just the sort of lurid phantom who used to impress on me New York's fundamentally Old World character, back in the days when I was fresh from that mild, ahistoric coast where poverty and madness are so much more discreet.) "Nickel, dime," he mutters, extending a filthy palm. I brush past, feeling denial freeze my features. Another half block and we're safe in the terminal.

It's a good thing I've allowed plenty of time. The line at the ticket counter barely inches forward. Finally, resolved to forget my cares in the day's catastrophes, I send Ericka off on an errand to the newsstand. But despite the stern authority of close print, the classy understatement of its headlines, I find that the *Times'* front page falls flat this morning. I'm strangely indifferent to certain momentous conflicts which generally can be counted on to provide the fillip of foreboding, the chilly shudder of reality that assures me I'm awake. Given where I'm going, my usual meticulous ingestion of current events seems an ironic formality rather on the order of the condemned prisoner's last meal. Soon I will be one with multitudes content to understand the impingements of the great world upon their malls and shopping centers in light of whatever pap may chance to be dished up in, say, the pages of the St. Paul *Pioneer* or the Seattle *Post-Intelligencer.*

This line of reflection demonstrates, of course, that I've fallen prey to the local news cult, a brand of metropolitan chauvinism against which even the intense cynicism of radicals appears to offer little immunity. (To her credit, Rhea was an exception to this rule. She regarded even our reigning Organ with exemplary detachment, contended she had a pretty good idea what general sort of shit was going down without getting mired in specifics, and added the unanswerable observation that if they're going to blow us up they'll blow us up, never mind what is written. "If a tree falls in the forest and the *Times* fails to report it. . . ," was her usual quip when political meetings degenerated into lamentations over media betrayal; she laughed at the rites of textual scrutiny to which some politicos bring the bitter zeal of State Department hacks decoding *Izvestia.*)

At least the paper affords me a temporary bulwark against Ericka's fidgets. But once our ticket-buying business is transacted, I discard it in the nearest trash can. We still have time to kill. I stop for coffee to go at a shop on the lower level, a hole-in-the-wall advertising freshly made doughnuts. Within, the bored counterman lounges at his post amid an overpowering atmosphere of yeast, grease, and hot sugar, while the white-aproned baker, comb stuck high in his flour-dusted Afro, bops to WBLS at the cutting board in back.

Ericka confounds me with the ingenious argument that if I'm having coffee, which is bad for me, she's entitled to something which is bad for *her*—to wit, a jelly doughnut. We dispute this briefly till I give in, rather pressured by the counterman's frank amusement.

"Right, miss. Jelly it is, you bet. *Jelly, jelly. . . ,*" he hums suggestively, snapping open a waxed paper bag in a parody of efficient, gracious service. "A jelly doughnut for the lady. Something else?"

"Nothing, thanks, but the coffee."

"No doughnut for yourself?"

"Nope. Thanks."

"Now that ain't right. Jelly for the young lady and you're not getting anything except an old cup of coffee, black, no sugar? I mean, look at it like this: this here's no common, ordinary greasy spoon you're in, uh *uh.* You happen to be standing right smack dab in the jelly capital of the Big Apple, if you grasp my meaning.

Open twenty-four hours. Get it hot. Satisfaction or your money back. And here you're settling for a plain old—"

"My change, please," I say drily, half amused, half dreading a humiliating scene, and in front of Ericka. My head's a computer matching the precise tones I'd use automatically if he were white. But he's not, and we're both aware of complications.

"Of course, of course. Whatever you say, miss. But I'm warning you, you're making a mistake."

Or maybe I'm wrong, maybe it's simple for him, has nothing to do with color. Maybe he just happens to be in the mood to put any woman who walks in that door through this.

"It's not too late to change your mind," he's almost baiting.

"Oh shut up, Red," the baker growls from the back.

"Hey, what's everybody getting all uptight about? I'm coming, I'm coming." He makes a great show of ringing up the purchase, extracting my small change from the register.

"No offense, now? No hard feelings? I'd hate to think I'd made any enemies so early in the morning." His hand with the money hovers out of reach.

Coward, I smile for my change.

Ericka and I retreat hastily. "Did that man make a pass at you?" she has to know, almost anthropologically eager to fathom adult customs.

"Well, not exactly. He thought he was being clever. After all that aren't you going to eat your doughnut?"

Already a line has formed behind the door marked "St. Louis," but we seem to be near enough to the front of it to count on sitting together. I'll let Ericka have first turn in the window seat. Highway travel always fascinated her, poor underprivileged waif inured to a maze of city streets and subway limbo, her childhood so different from mine, which was spent in the back seat of the current station wagon, nose pressed to the glass, watching the world whiz by—unless, indeed, as happened too frequently, my mother assigned me to the unenviable center position straddling the "bump," where I formed a buffer between two warring brothers.

The line, lengthening rapidly behind us, proves to our gratification that we arrived in the nick of time. Serious, seedy, economy-minded tourists with cameras strung around their necks talk German, British English, Japanese. American mothers steel themselves for the journey; some, evidently worn out before the ordeal is fairly begun, already threaten their offspring with dire, hackneyed punishments. Close by, a radio reiterates that ubiquitous disco hit which has formed the background to all public life since sometime in April or May, the number which is destined forever to signify this particular summer in the aging nostalgic memories of now-teenage millions.

Ericka, nearly on the threshold of adolescent interest, sways to the rhythm, snaps her stubby fingers—the nails of which, I notice, sport flaking pink polish. Now that we're standing still and I have a chance to get a good look at her, I'm a bit taken aback at the shortness of her shorts, the width of pale stomach beneath her halter top. With those exaggerated sandals and her curls swept up in a pert ponytail, she wears something of the aspect of an underage hooker, an impression our location does much to reinforce. I can't quite think how I let her out in that getup.

But the shock has less to do with her attire than with my sudden perception of just how soon she's destined to outgrow the slight convexity of midriff, the childish plumpness of thigh—and the saving lack of sophistication intimated now by a streak of rosy jelly above her rosy upper lip. Already Daniel's lean genes coil to strike in her. Already she's rehearsing for the two-bit Mysteries. She's going to be a teenager.

"Jesus, Ericka, you're going to freeze to death in the air conditioning," I can't seem to help remarking, though there's nothing to be done.

"Mom, I'm *Cindy*," she reprovingly hisses. "Anyway, you *said* I could wear these shorts."

Yes, I did say she could wear the shorts; and indeed, she is Cindy Cole, and I am her mother Laura on the new ID which, thanks to Comrade Luce, reposes in a black plastic wallet in the front pocket of my overalls: Laura for a great-grandmother on my mother's side, Cole for no special reason beyond the need for something flat and unobtrusive and Anglo-Saxon, something that would signify—on either coast, in the heartland's barren reaches—precisely nothing, or as near to it as possible. Cole seemed safely colorless, odorless, and tasteless as a meal at Howard Johnson's, and so became the common ground of our official kinship.

"Hey, Mom."

"Yes, what?"

"How long will it take us to get there?"

"To St. Louis? We'll be there early tomorrow morning."

"Not St. Louis. Los Angeles, I mean," she fairly broadcasts. For all her zest for using our aliases, she keeps forgetting my admonitions not to divulge where we're headed.

"I don't know, kiddo. We'll see how fast we travel, whether we stop very much or not."

"I wish we'd start."

"Relax, we'll get going soon."

I recheck our luggage. Everything's there: my pack with the sleeping bag strapped underneath; my airline bag full of books, sweaters, lunch, dried fruit, nuts, toothbrushes, changes of underwear; Ericka's day pack and sleeping bag, her Adidas carryall. In my overall pocket beside the forged ID rest the contents of my late savings account in travelers' checks in the name of "Laura Cole." My real ID, and everything else I own, I've left behind with Wendy, who's housesitting.

Except for Luce and a friend who lives in Manhattan who's agreed to let me use her for a mail drop, Wendy is the only person to whom I've explained my plan, and even she doesn't know where I'm headed. She's been extremely sympathetic all along, and offered to forward letters, dismissing the risk involved.

Ericka nudges me, snatches up her burdens. "Hey, come on, it's time."

And indeed, they've opened the door, at last we're moving. There's a brief halt outside while we wait to check our luggage. The bus is clean, shabby, stale-smelling. We claim our seats and watch through tinted glass while below in the smoky dusk of the terminal the driver officiates at final preparations. A tall, austere-featured Black man in a fresh grey uniform, he's obviously an old hand at this. Deliberately he draws on his cigarette, unhurriedly drains his coffee. Then, crisp after all with the high ambitions of morning, he fairly bounds to his seat—"We're off!" my child cries—levers shut the door, and with practiced assurance whips his ungainly steed through the corkscrew intricacies of the terminal. We emerge into the dense summer light of the extreme West Side.

Now details transfix me—or rather, as one does in final moments, I grasp at them like straws: old man stretched out on a chipped stoop, dead drunk or asleep, his worn, baggy pants hiked up almost to his knees revelatory of bony legs projecting at a weird angle out from firmly-planted feet, as though he'd sprawled backward from a sudden blow—who, even in this condition, clutches his brown-bagged bottle as a sleeping baby might its formula; two cute, sweetly tough young Latinas, arms linked, giggling on the steps of a decrepit, half-boarded-up brick building. Everything bathed in acute romance of heat—dirty sunlight, a rumor of sex and music—always more appreciatively perceived, of course, in small doses; from behind the glass; in the cool of the air conditioning; at June's end rather than August's; departing, not returning.

Right now I'm viewing this intricate habitat as I haven't since my earliest months here, before I'd converted it into something more or less like home, which therefore need not be noticed: the forest that gave me shelter, the ocean that let my gills breathe. And realizing this, I'm hit by the oddest sensation we're getting out just in time, just before whatever that last catastrophe is that's forever been threatening. Before houses topple, towers subside into sullied rivers.

But Ericka's already complaining of the cold. And by the time I've finished rummaging through my bag to locate her sweater, it's all over, my famous New York life. We're watching the bloody gleam of brake lights reflected off the white tile walls of the Lincoln Tunnel.

Ericka wants to know how you build tunnels under water. I have to admit my ignorance on that score.

"I bet my Daddy would know."

I wince at this, though it's quite uncalculated. "We could try to find out," I suggest.

"How?" Oh, she is ruthlessly practical. "There aren't encyclopedias on this bus."

And then, after stops and starts and flashing lights and tow trucks, after she's thought to inquire what would happen if this tunnel ever caved in, after a baby in the seat opposite us has set up a harsh, monotonous wail clearly destined to accompany us across several states, we ascend into drab New Jersey. The bus labors up the circular ramp, for a moment giving us Manhattan spread out, an unpeopled monolith, sharp and uncomplicated there in the hot light beside the sparkling water. Fixed on the future, Ericka doesn't notice, but I have to look back. The legendary buildings are at their posts, all right: Pan Am, Chrysler, Empire State — and there, counterweight at the island's tip, the blunt-edged twin phalli of the World Trade Center, that doubled monument which has ruled my days, looming over Flatbush Avenue.

Our resolute skipper heads us into traffic. We have before us a continent's worth of turnpike, thruway, freeway sprawl and tangle — how many thousand miles of asphalt, billboards, fast food, and disgruntled babies between us and the Pacific?

Ericka wants to whisper in my ear.

"Okay then, what is it?"

"Josie, I mean Mom, are we outlaws now?" She's grinning with mischievous pride, full of that same touchingly naive anticipation with which, when she was five, she'd want to know, "Josie, are we in the country yet?" as we'd approach Huntington on the Long Island Railway.

*　*　*

It doesn't feel like we're really on our way to California, not yet. I mean, it's just hard to believe I'm not going home, like tomorrow or the next day or the next day.

The bus is comfortable, I guess, except for this baby across from us that keeps making all this noise. Her mother—I guess it's a her, it has little gold earrings in its little brown ears—keeps looking embarrassed, like she wishes she could pretend it belongs to someone else. I bet I'd know how to distract her. I do when Leah fusses.

It seems like everywhere I go there's got to be some crying baby. After a while it gets pretty boring.

The Greyhound actually isn't that different from the buses they rent when you go to Washington for demonstrations, which me and Mommy and Josie did a couple times. We went to the one about Bakke I remember, everyone yelling, we won't go back, send Bakke back. *Then on the way home we stopped at Howard Johnson's.*

I'm glad I'm by the window, I like looking down on top of cars and trucks. I saw two Winnebagos, also. You see them down in Florida all the time, but mostly parked in front of people's houses. I don't usually see them going. Just now I saw this man and lady in one, the man was driving and the lady was drinking something from a mug, she had her hair up in rollers just like she was at home. I think it would be sort of farout to be able to get out of bed and just drive down the highway in your bathrobe.

There's this girl on the bus called Sukey. She's got this real pale skin with about a zillion freckles, I don't think I ever saw so many freckles on anybody. She has red stringy hair in these barrettes that look like kissing mouths with lipstick, the color of her hair and the red of the barrettes don't go together that good. She seems like about my age. I know her name because her mother and her have seats a little ways in front of us, up behind the bus driver, and I could hear them talking. It's funny because her mother's kind of fat with brown hair turning grey, you wouldn't expect her to have this skinny redhaired kid. Sukey and I kind of look at each other when she goes past my seat on her way to the bathroom.

Then when I have to go too, she's waiting by the door when I come out.

"Hi," I say.

"You sure took your time."

That's not a very polite remark, I don't think. I couldn't help it if it took me a minute to figure out the lock and how everything worked. I was startled when I pressed the "flush" button and it made this roaring noise and this blue stuff came whooshing out!

But I don't say anything except excuse me. She's standing in the way of me going back to my seat.

"We're going to Indianapolis," she announces. "Where are you guys going?"

None of your beeswax, I think. But I keep quiet.

"Whatsa matter, cat got your tongue?"

This lady in the next to last seat is frowning at us, I guess meaning Sukey's talking too loud. I say excuse me again and squeeze past her. When I get back to our seat Josie's sitting over by the window, leaning against the glass with her eyes closed, so I can't find out what I'm supposed to say if Sukey asks me anything again.

Sukey's pretty rude, that's all. When she comes back I'm not looking at her.

I wait and wait and still she doesn't come. Even if she had to shit, I figure she should be out of the bathroom by now.

I turn around and look, but I don't see her.

Then Josie gets up to go to the bathroom, and I move over by the window. Pretty soon I feel someone come up and just stand there by the empty seat. I mean, I'm pretty sure it's Sukey, I can sort of see her out of the side of my eye. But I just pretend I'm looking at the road.

She taps me on the shoulder. "You play cards?"

It seems like maybe she really is trying to be friends, she just doesn't know how very well. Maybe she's insecure.

"Yeah," I say after a minute.

"Like, what games do you know?"

"Oh, Hearts, War, stuff like that."

"You ever play Pee Knuckle?"

"Play what?"

"Pee Knuckle."

"Never heard of that." I feel weird about even asking what it is. It sounds more like a nasty joke than a card game.

"You never heard of Pee Knuckle?" She says it like you'd have to be a real nincompoop not to. I'm beginning to be mad at her again, but then Josie's back, so she goes back to her own seat. I can't really see either her or her mother from where I'm sitting, but after a while I *see her mother's hand reach down for her handbag and get out a package of something, M & M's it looks like.*

"Did you make a friend?" Josie says.

"No. Well, sort of." It's too complicated to explain how I don't even like Sukey, and I'm embarrassed to ask if she ever heard of Pee Knuckle.

"Well, Cindy," she says, in this reminding kind of voice, "I think it's nice if you find someone to talk to. Just don't forget the rules of the road, that's all."

Like maybe I'm dumb or something.

"Don't worry, Mom," I say. I don't bother asking her where I'm supposed to say we're going, because I don't plan on speaking to Sukey anymore.

But she's waiting again, next time I come out of the bathroom. It seems like both of us have to go a lot.

"Want some M & M's?"

They're the different colored kind. It looks like her mom gave her the whole big bag.

"Whatsa matter, you don't like chocolate?"

I'm looking up front, but I can't really see Josie, the seats are too high. I don't know what to tell her.

"I'm kind of allergic," is all I can think of. TeriAnn's allergic to chocolate. I know Josie's going to be mad if she sees me eating candy, especially before I've even had lunch.

"Here, just a couple?"

"Well, okay. Let's sit down back here for a minute, though." There's nobody in the very last seat, and if you scrunch down over by the window they couldn't see you from up where Josie's at.

"What's your name, anyway?" Sukey asks, when we're sitting down. I keep looking at her freckles, she's got so many. She's got some chocolate showing on her mouth. I'm careful where I put my M & M's, so I won't get a chocolate face too.

"Ericka," I tell her.

"That's kind of a funny name. Like Eric, only with an A on it."

My hand flies over my mouth, but it's too late. I already went and said it.

"Hey, what's wrong? You bite your tongue or something?"

I shake my head. I try to look cool.

"Really, what is it?"

"Nothing. I just remembered something, is all."

"Oh." She picks out the orange and yellow M & M's. "Here, you can have more."

"Thanks." I have to come up with something fast. "I was going to say—my real name isn't Ericka, see."

"What?" Sukey doesn't look that interested.

"Ericka isn't my real name. That's just sort of a nickname, because, see, my—father's name was Eric. So my mother calls me that, once in a while. But my real name is Cindy. That's what I go by."

Brenda always says I'm a lousy liar, so I'm surprised when all Sukey says is, "Hey, Cindy sounds a lot like my name. My name's Sukey."

"I know."

"How?"

"I heard your mom call you it."

"What happened to your dad?"

"He—died. A while ago in a car wreck." I'm just crossing my fingers it's okay to say that.

"Were you in the car too?"

"Of course not. Look, I'd rather not discuss it."

Thank goodness it works. She decides to change the subject. "You said you play Hearts, didn't you?"

"Yeah."

"Wanna play? I'd rather play Pee Knuckle, but—"

"Well, okay." I wipe my mouth good. We go up front. Sukey's mom gets the cards out of her bag. Her face is red and puffy, her hair's sort of greasy.

"You eat up all that candy already?" she asks all of a sudden, giving Sukey and me both a strict look.

Sukey doesn't say anything, so neither do I.

"Remember what I told you, I'm not buying you nothing later."

Sukey still keeps quiet, but when we're walking back to the back she whispers to me, "She will so buy me something, just wait."

I start to shuffle the cards. She laughs at my shuffling. So you do it then, Miss Expert, I offer her, trying to hold my patience. Finally we get started.

It's nice here in the way back of the bus, kind of more private. You can look out the window and see where you've just been, even if so far it's only dumb New Jersey.

I don't know if I'd want to have Sukey's mom. She seems sort of weird. What kind of mother gives you a whole big package of M & M's right before lunch?

*　　*　　*

It's midafternoon: several hours, yet, to Pittsburgh, and already interstate travel starts to pall. Ericka is busy being wooed by a tense, skinny, freckle-faced child; I'm just making time disappear now, staring through tinted glass at dusty trees and streamlined futuristic service stations, at June-green hills fast fading beneath the discolored sky, at distant shopping centers and intermittent patches of tract housing, cyclone fence and a swatch of DMZ grass separating the lush or balding yards with their swing sets and plastic wading pools from the six dense lanes of motion. Beneath us swarms the cloud of lesser traffic: compact cars minuscule from this height; complex vacation rigs with automobiles towing trailers which in turn are towing boats; massive, lumbering RV's.

At the time I moved away from the West Coast, recreational vehicles hadn't hit big yet. Now they dominate their ecological niche; the scenic coastlines are clotted with parking lots designed to accommodate them, paved enclosures replacing the modest rustic "campsites" which were our stylized Fifties notion of wilderness. Mom even wrote recently that she and Dad have been considering getting a Winnebago—a small one, of course, a "Mini Winnie"—"Your father needs to relax." She added that "after Hank and Carol have the baby" they might want to make use of it for brief excursions, and wound up, rather defensively, I thought, with a nervous little joke about the convenience of having a rolling roof over one's head when the San Andreas fault blows and the sea forecloses on California.

Strange to be out west and not see family. Except to visit Mom and Dad, I haven't been back to southern California since I went away to college, and I don't know much of anyone there anymore, though Michael, my high school boyfriend, is rumored to be driving a bus in North Hollywood. Hank and Carol are temporarily in La Jolla, where Hank's finishing up a sociology doctorate; my other brother's in Hawaii being a marine biologist. Even my parents have moved out near Pomona, far enough from anywhere we might stay to make me feel safe from chance encounters. I've sent them a letter saying I'll be away, and not to be concerned—futile advice, of course, but I couldn't think what else to do.

I'm still not quite sure why I picked LA over other destinations, unless by some homing instinct, some attraction to the safety of childhood landscapes. That and the mythos of easeful California living, which so many Californians themselves are seduced by. It's going to be tough without a car there, though.

I'm too tired to worry; I want distractions. Groping for an apple in my bag, I happen to turn up a book I impulsively stuffed in at the last minute: a paperback, its brittle, yellowed pages, half of them unglued, confined by a rubber band. (It was already well-thumbed back in the mid-Sixties when Michael pressed it on me, how-to manual and sacred text.) Eighty-five cents is the price printed on the cover above the sketch of a tall, dark-haired, square-jawed, Levi'd boy who slouches against a curvaceous Chevrolet. Smoke curls vigorously skyward from the butt (or is it a reefer?) that depends from his curling lip. At his side slumps a wasp-waisted maiden in "pedal pushers," her black sweater stretched taut over sharp breasts, her bright yellow hair yanked back into a ponytail so merciless that it perhaps accounts for her dyspeptic expression. ON THE ROAD, BY JACK KEROUAC, stark lettering proclaims. THE BOLD, BEST-SELLING NOVEL OF CONTEMPORARY YOUTH. A TOWERING ACHIEVEMENT.

Carefully I remove the rubber band, open at random, and come upon the words:

> I went to sit in the bus station and think this over. I ate another apple pie and ice cream: that's practically all I ate all the way across the country. I knew it was nutritious and it was delicious, of course.

That's it right there, the root of the contradiction. That's why I'm trapped on this stuffy Greyhound bus when I might be busted flat in Baton Rouge or romantically crouched in some freezing midnight boxcar among the enlightened hoboes, why I'm stuck with an eagle-eyed ten-year-old chaperone when I might be coming on to waitresses in truckstops across the land. I have always been concerned with prosaic details, vitamin content, protein versus sugar. Pie and ice cream across the country? Come off it, Jack.

"What's that book?" my long-lost child demands, bouncing suddenly back into her seat. "Ooh, sex-ee," she whistles breathily at sight of the cover drawing.

* * *

I'm sitting with Sukey in the way back. We're playing Hearts but she keeps on saying it's boring and she'd rather be playing that other card game. I wish she'd shut up about it.

Finally I ask her did she ever play chess.

"Chest?"

"Chess. *You didn't?*"

144

"Uh-uh, I never."

"See, you play it on a board like for checkers, but you have different pieces, kings and queens and stuff."

"So?"

Sukey always goes so like that when she doesn't know what to say. She never did a lot of things, I found out already. She already told me she's never flown in a plane, or had Szechuan food, or even Häagen Dazs. She didn't even know what a co-op apartment was. I'm beginning to think Indianapolis must be in some kind of a time warp.

"I know how to play pretty good," I start to explain. "Me and my father—"

I remember, and stop. She's giving me this look.

"I thought you said your father—"

"Yeah, I know. He died. But before the accident."

"Oh."

"Before, we used to play chess all the time."

"So?"

"So, nothing. We used to, that's all."

"I thought of an idea for a game."

"What kind of a game?"

"Wait. You'll see."

She goes back to where her mom's sitting and comes back with a Barbie and a Ken doll! I'm floored, frankly. Leah's got a Barbie.

Sukey seems to be reading my mind though, because right away she says, "Don't worry, we're not playing baby games." She has Barbie get dressed up with high heels and makeup and all this fancy stuff, and then Ken comes along and toots his horn. He's driving a Coopdaville, Sukey says. They're going to a drive-in.

Just because I don't know what a drive-in is, she has to act snotty about it, but finally she explains. At first she makes them sit in the front seat, eating popcorn and Milk Duds and watching the show. But then she says Ken's really hot cause Barbie's so stacked, and he wants to get in the back seat and Barbie says no way cause she thinks it'll look cheap, but finally they do, and then she pulls Barbie's skirt up and Ken's pants down and lays him on top of her. Then Barbie starts saying, ooh, ooh Kenny, and making all these noises like they do on disco records.

Finally she makes them both get dressed again, and then she spanks them and says shame on them, they're not even married. Then she whispers Barbie found out she's in trouble, and Ken can be the doctor when the baby gets born.

"Can't the doctor give her an abortion?"

Sukey sucks her breath in. "Are you kidding? That's murder!"

"But it's not a baby yet, it's just a foetus."

"Doesn't matter. It's still a Human Life, and it counts anyway."

"Who says?"

"Sister Mary Emanuel."

"Who's she?"

"Teacher in my school."

"But that's dumb. How can a little piece of crud smaller than your toe that doesn't know anything or anybody, be the same as a real person?" Brenda would of gotten an abortion if there was anything wrong when she went and had that test, the one that showed Jeremy's going to be a boy. People in my family are not murderers. But I can't say that to Sukey without giving away our secret.

* * *

Dean and I are embarked on a tremendous season together. We're trying to communicate with absolute honesty and absolute completeness everything on our minds. We've had to take benzedrine. We sit on the bed, crosslegged, facing each other. I have finally taught Dean that he can do anything he wants, become mayor of Denver, marry a millionairess, or become the greatest poet since Rimbaud. But he keeps rushing out to see the midget auto races.

That's Kerouac's "Carlo Marx" speaking there. At sixteen, I was enchanted, discerning in this vigorous if puerile program evidence that somewhere there existed the moral and intellectual intensity I'd been looking for—"reality," I suppose I would have called it, my highest accolade. Emerging from a childhood of many advantages, I was bitter, suddenly, against my parents, on account of certain experiences withheld from me: Smith Act trials overhanging my formative years; alcoholic binges; steamy dramas of marital infidelity; the benny-popping, reefer-puffing role models they might have been, tearing back and forth across the continent with infant me asleep in the back seat. Never mind polio vaccine and private lessons; my background had been deficient.

My father, born in the same year as Kerouac, had come to work, in the palmy City of Angels, in the palmy postwar boom of the aerospace industry, as an engineerforLockheed; it was all one word, one familiar if vague job title, as pronounced by the kids who lived in our "subdivision." It described what almost all the fathers did, what made possible that sunny, well-yarded existence. Later, when trouble came to the industry, when government contracts were cancelled and heads-of-household laid off,

146

property values would plummet, yards and paint jobs be neglected, and the realtors' signs bristling on the lawns would give the area a forlorn, tentative air. But that was years in the future, after my own defection, after I'd escaped to Oregon and college. All through my childhood the facade remained in place, pre-fab shiny, without a scratch or chink. The starched, clean-shaven fathers drove off to work each morning. The bare-limbed children splashed in the cool sprinklers, clustered in the available backyard pools, played on trikes and bikes in the quiet cul-de-sacs, breathed trustingly the air our mothers called "hazy."

Our mothers, of course, were home, homemaking. They reproduced and maintained the labor force, hosted Brownies and Cub Scout meetings, took the cars in to be serviced, kept track of dental appointments. And they performed certain social rituals which seemed almost archaic in the context, where each family was armed for self-sufficiency with its ranks of appliances, armies of doctors and sitters. They had their cups of coffee from kitchen to kitchen, their friendships and feuds, their festive or somber markings of those domestic watersheds: pregnancy, promotion, transfer. The men might talk politics in the carpool, might toss around sports scores when they chanced to meet over the borrowing or return of some piece of yard equipment, but it was the women who, out of slight synthetic fibers, doggedly rewove the social fabric; recreated here, in the ranch-style wilderness, some semblance of lost communal life.

My own mother, I see looking back, never fit in very well. It wasn't just her B.A. from the University of Idaho that seemed to set her apart—other mothers had been to college—but the fact that she had (in the rec room) a bookcase filled with nineteenth century English and Russian novels; that she played classical music on the hi-fi, not to impress anyone, but just because she liked it. My brothers and I understood that other women were secretly to be pitied if they saw fit to watch game shows while ironing, or subscribed only to women's magazines. We got *McCall's* and *Ladies Home Journal*, but Mom supplemented them with *The Reporter* and *Saturday Review*, much as she supplemented our breakfasts of Kellogg's cornflakes and pale Langendorf toast with multi-vitamin tablets.

Her social convictions, too, distinguished her. Of course the area was overwhelmingly white, though I think it was considered integrated on account of one Spanish-surnamed family living a few doors down, and some Japanese a couple blocks away. When at long last the first "Negro family" bought, it was Mom, usually reticent in civic matters, who organized the welcoming committee. I overheard her instructing Mrs. Macneice and Mrs. Carlson to act just as though they were meeting any new neighbor; then, clutching a "scratch" coffee cake, she led the charge herself. When she returned triumphant an hour or so later, beaming with relief and Mrs. Hinson's niceness, I can recall thinking proudly that she seemed vaguely in league with the Mississippi civil rights workers we'd been hearing so much about lately.

We never, of course, doubted we belonged, questioned our right to be magnanimous. We didn't even notice our recentness, our lives shallow and flimsy and new as the basementless, barely insulated, one-story wooden structures so presumptuously flung down on land yet scarcely broken to roads. Besides, I was a child, quintessential arriviste; so the instantness of everything around me ("brand spanking new," Dad said of our tract house) seemed perfectly natural. I was not yet used to the work of history, the effort of ferreting out what lies beneath surfaces. I definitely preferred Grandma and Grandpa Washburn's neat, white, two-story residence in Boise, with its wraparound porch, its flower and vegetable gardens, to Grandma Muller's dark, high-ceilinged, fiercely scoured apartment in a working-class Minneapolis neighborhood.

I was not exactly ashamed of Grandma Muller. She was too distant for that. Only, like a child used to the bland comforts of Campbell's soup and Kraft American cheese, I wrinkled up my nose at the sharp taste of her life, her heavy cooking, her tales of sadistic bosses, her embarrassingly literal Christianity—by turns harsh and saccharine—and the hint of a German accent with which she still spoke.

I knew there was some sort of problem with being German. When asked my background on my father's side, I always answered very quickly, "Swiss-and-German," as I'd heard my parents do. Not, as I say, that it really bothered me. *We* were Americans. We always lived in new houses.

*　*　*

It's the morning when we finally get off at the bus station. St. Louis is a pretty small city, compared to New York. There's this wide river, that's the Mississippi, and this huge gigantic arch thing that reminds me of McDonald's.

I didn't sleep that good on the bus. I kept having these weird dreams about nuns and stuff. That's what Sukey was talking about, before she and her mom got off. We were playing Hearts, then we started discussing what we're going to be.

I said I might like to be a jockey. Or maybe a scientist, I'm good in science.

Sukey goes, "I'm gonna be a nun," her voice getting all holy suddenly.

"What for," I go, "and wear those weird clothes?"

"It's called a habit, not 'weird clothes'."

"Well, I guess you could dress just normal if you want. Some of the nuns do at my friend TeriAnn's school."

"That's okay, I want to wear a habit."

"What for?"

"I think it looks better."

"Why?"

"I mean, you are the Bride of Christ."

"The what of who?"

"Bride of Christ," she goes.

That's dumb, he's dead, I thought. How could he get married? But I didn't want to start an argument. "What would you do all day, sit in the subway, like those ones in Manhattan, asking for spare change?"

"No way!"

"Then what? Teach Catholic school?"

"I'm not staying in Indianapolis. I think I'll join a missionary order and travel overseas."

"Like where would you go?"

"Maybe Africa or something."

Lucky Africans, I thought. Still, I miss her, in a way.

Anyway, we're in the bus station. Josie's not in such a pleasant mood. She gives me a look when all I say is, I hope Luce's friend who's supposed to pick us up didn't get mixed up about what day. Then I sit on the floor because there aren't any seats, and she insists it's dirty.

Finally this short Black lady in a pantsuit and dangly earrings comes over and asks are we Laura and Cindy Cole. It feels weird, some stranger asking that. "Our Brooklyn friend sent me. I'm Martha."

Josie switches from frowning to smiling. They shake hands.

"You must be tired," says Martha. "I wish you could see a better side of St. Louis. I'm afraid you're arriving in the middle of an outrageous heat wave." She picks up some of my stuff, and we follow her out to the car.

She seems nice. I didn't know she would be Black. "How does Luce know her?" I whisper to Josie.

"Never mind," she uses her warning voice, "we'll discuss it later."

Martha's right, it's awfully hot outside. We get into her VW. She asks would we like to go have some breakfast, and before I can say yes

Josie says something about doesn't she have to be getting to work soon, but Martha says there's time.

The place we stop at is Sweetie's. Our waitress has a name tag on that says, "Hello there! I'm Your Sweetie Lois Gromp." I order Cheerios. They taste weird.

Josie says eat them, Cheerios are Cheerios. But these ones taste different. Stale, maybe.

Martha drives us over to her place. It's this big old house with a porch and vines on it, not joined to the rest like houses are in Brooklyn. The block is all Black people, or all I could see anyway. A boy looks at me funny when we get out of the car.

Martha's apartment is on the top floor. The ceiling is low, it's hotter than downstairs. Martha shows us where the fan is, and says we shouldn't bother to answer the phone if it rings. We can eat anything we want out of the refrigerator. She'll be back right after work.

Josie gives me my choice where to sleep. I choose the couch, which has the fan by it, and she goes in the bedroom and shuts the door after kissing me goodnight, even though it's morning. I take off my clothes and lie down in just my panties on top of a sheet Martha spread out.

The fan makes a little wind and a lot of noise. I don't feel very sleepy, and after a while I get up real quiet and go look out the window. I can see roofs and people's backyards, with vegetable gardens and flowers, and even some chickens in one. There's kids out playing, I can hear their voices. The sky is kind of grey like in New York, smoggy I guess, but it doesn't look much like New York in other ways. It looks like someplace I've never been before. Even the trees are different.

I wonder what they're doing at home right now. Daddy's there, he's not teaching summer school. Brenda still has to work, but Nilda comes in a little later. I bet just him and Leah are having a late breakfast—French toast, or maybe pancakes. He makes those things on the weekends usually, but only him and me and Leah eat them. Brenda has a poached egg, less calories. She cuts Leah's breakfast up for her. Leah eats with her fingers and smears syrup all over. Daddy reads the Times and drinks coffee while Brenda gets Leah cleaned up and dressed and clears the table and puts stuff in the dishwasher. I think that's fair, since Daddy made breakfast.

It's funny they think I'm just camping. Josie's letter explaining everything isn't going to get there till just before I'm supposed to come back. I wonder how upset they're going to be.

Right now I'm looking at the telephone, which is sitting on the floor beside the fan. Brenda said I could call collect anytime.

Daddy wouldn't have to know, he'd think I'm calling from Vermont. He'd probably ask a couple of questions about camping, and I'd just say we're having fun and stuff. I could say hi to Leah. I bet she's going to miss me.

I take the phone way over in the corner, as quiet as I can. But then I wonder whether Josie really had time to fall asleep yet, so I go over by the bedroom door and say her name. She wouldn't understand, she'd only get all nervous.

I go ahead, but I get a busy signal. The operator says to try back later.

* * *

I'd thought I might be too keyed up for proper rest, but when I roll over on damp sheets and open my eyes halfway, the digital clock on the bedside stand reads three-eighteen. I want to slip back, immerse my brain once more in the amniotic fluid of REM sleep. But it's stifling hot and, in the other room, above the buzz of the fan, a small noise alarms me.

With an effort of will, I locate myself in space, focus on the meaning of sounds familiar anywhere on the continent: click of a receiver replaced in its cradle, then the pause as it is lifted once again, the lingering rasp of the dial. Still hoping she's calling the time or the weather report, I stop breathing and count past seven digits. I hear her give her name to the operator.

I don't move.

They're not answering.

I force myself, fling on underpants and T-shirt, snatch open the bedroom door.

"Ericka."

Surprised, she whirls, phone clutched to her pale flat chest, as though its plastic curves could cover her nakedness.

"Nobody home, huh?"

She shakes her head.

"Who're you trying to call?"

She shrugs, panicked, obviously guilty. I go over and pry the receiver from her sweaty little hand.

"*Who,* Ericka? This is important." I hate her for imposing the task on me: the necessary torture.

She still doesn't answer. I run over my calculations. Who could it have been but the obvious? Belle and Sam, but why? Not TeriAnn.

"Look Ericka, you don't just go around making collect calls. You know perfectly well we could get in a lot of trouble.

"Now if you want to go home, okay. There's still time for that, nobody even knows we're gone. But do me a simple favor and let me know first."

The words said, it seems so obvious. What a monumental mistake this trip has been. We'll start back tonight. They won't have to know, maybe.

She turns away. Her mouth starts to tremble. "He wouldn't guess. He'd think we're just camping."

"You mean to tell me you thought you'd simply call your father up for a little *chat*?"

The tears spill over, choke her. "But I just – "

"You *just*. Right, you *just*." I'm terrible with fright, an avenging angel. "Didn't you hear what I said before we left, that if they find out where we are, you'll have to go back? I trusted you. I thought you were old enough."

"I *am* old enough! I don't want to go back! I was only going to call and say hello. I would of said we're having fun, camping. He wouldn't guess. You don't have to get all mad!"

Slightly mollified – at least she's not deserting – I tell her the obvious: she should have known better. "Maybe he wouldn't have, but it was much too risky. Anyway, they would have been able to find out later on where a collect call had been made from. I was counting on you to show you had some sense."

She hangs back a moment, sullen beneath my scorn, then bitterly bursts out, "You just think I'm dumb or something! You just think I don't have any idea what I'm doing! You think – you think – oh, you're so mean!

"I thought about all that stuff before I called. I thought about what to say. I know how to be an outlaw too, you know, just as good as you do!"

Her vehemence unnerves me. "I *don't* think you're dumb – "

A pause; then, sobbing afresh, she hurls herself on me. "Oh Josie, don't send me back. I want to be with you."

It's the work of ten minutes to get her calmed down. Finally I manage, taking advantage of the opportunity to extract from her a solemn promise not to make any more long distance calls, to come to me first if she ever starts thinking about wanting to go back. Then, wreathed in the tolerant afterglow that generally follows such emotional outbursts, we shower together, dress, and go through Martha's refrigerator.

I wander around the apartment eating a sandwich as I idly scan walls and bookshelves for clues to the politics of our hostess. I don't know what I'd expected from Luce's St. Louis "contact" — something more flamboyant, I suppose. Hard to imagine BLA members or Puerto Rican Independentistas using as a way-station on their underground journeys this tidy, spare place with its lovingly framed photographs of family in the bedroom, its few, unrhetorical posters on the walls: Nelson Mandela, Assata, Blood on Your Hands Pinochet. I'm inclined to think like Ericka, who sniffs around and points out, "But Luce has so many roaches in *her* kitchen."

Martha arrives around six lugging beer and a bag of groceries.

"You folks hungry for supper?"

"We ate something already, thanks."

"Great. Help yourself to a beer if you feel like it. I'm going to fix a quick salad for myself. Then we can figure out what you want to do until it's time for your bus. You know what occurred to me, Cindy, as I was sitting behind my typewriter in that air-conditioned office and thinking how hot you people must be back here?"

"No, what?" She looks startled by the "Cindy."

"Well, it seemed to me maybe you'd be more comfortable with short hair, especially in this weather. I mean, you know, summer's just getting started. What do you think?

The shaggy urchin looks unenthusiastic. "But it's gonna be cool on the bus, and in LA —"

"Ericka, what did I tell you about saying where we're going?" I reprimand, perceiving my own error through her triumphant glance.

"*Mom*, you're supposed to call me —"

"Come on now, people, I think I'll just pretend I didn't hear any of that," Martha cheerfully intervenes. "To return to the subject: haircuts. Not only would you be lots cooler, but we'd get a better view of your earrings. Here, push back your hair. Like that. Oh, that does look nice." The flattery is just subtle enough; immediately I'm prepared to entertain the farfetched supposition that Martha harbors ten-year-old fugitives every week.

Ericka, still skeptical, starts to waver.

"I have a friend who used to work in a beauty parlor. We could stop over there on the way to the bus station. I know she'd do a fantastic job on you."

"Well. . . ."

"You could grow it again, you know. That's the great thing about hair. There's always more where that came from. What do you say?"

She squirms, relishing her power. "Well . . . okay."

"How about you, Laura? Care for a free haircut? But your hair's pretty short in the first place."

"Actually, I'm thinking of letting it grow."

"Hurry up and grow it, it'll make a better disguise," Ericka pipes up, then looks slightly horrified.

"You're perfectly right," Martha reassures her. "And *your* haircut will help things out too. Now you get ready while I finish my dinner."

Luggage-laden, we struggle down to the car in the hot evening of stolid home-bound workers, of housewives or jobless or earlier-arrived arrayed stoically on vine-shaded porches fanning themselves and downing cold drinks and watching, waiting for something—the day, the heatwave, the season—to be gotten over with. "And it's only June yet," I can almost hear the murmur. Just June, and fearfully humid. Even the teenagers skulk off into the shade. Only the youngest kids retain some vital drive that props them upright in the steaming streets, spins them on through jumprope, tag, stickball.

The way to Martha's friend's house lies through similar shabby neighborhoods, the populace lightening, darkening, then bleaching out again. American apartheid: the usual divisions. On the surface, it all seems obvious enough. It's the architecture and the shapes of leaves, not the life of the street, that's different from New York. Yet I keep thinking there's something underneath. Tonight this ugly city where South and Midwest fuse seems richly dense and inarticulate, permeated with a sweet, fatal genius of stasis, an indigenous drowsing sickness which holds it under the sway of all that is dreamlike, unconscious, involuntary. Here in what begins to be the middle, far from notorious, goal-obsessed New York, I more easily recognize for what they are the expressions and gestures of sleepwalkers. It's here, I imagine, one might search for proof: some telltale outcropping of that vast, bedrock spirit of futility and inadvertence which must secretly undershelve the industrious continent.

* * *

We're back on the bus. It's cool, anyway. My birthday watch says ten after eleven, but I don't feel sleepy.

Josie's acting different. Not cross, exactly, but far away, like she's thinking about something. I keep getting the idea maybe she's mad at me, because what happened about me calling home. But when I ask her what she's thinking about, she just says "nothing special" and pats my arm and goes on looking out the window, where it's pitch black so you can't see anything, now we're past the houses.

I keep reaching up to touch my hair, which feels funny. I'm used to twisting a piece around my finger, and now it's not there. Martha's friend cut it in her kitchen. She was white and lived in this crazy big old house. She made me sit on a stool and she snipped real fast, and all the time she and Martha were drinking iced tea and talking a mile a minute. I was petrified she'd snip my ear or something. She had a bunch of kids that were playing out back in the sprinkler in their bathing suits, "brats" she kept calling them. They were making Kool Aid popsicles in the ice cube trays, which didn't get frozen before we had to go.

I am definitely not that crazy about this haircut. It's shorter than I ever had it before. It looks like lesbians get theirs cut sometimes. I bet Sukey would make some dumb remark if she could see me now.

"My haircut looks funny, Mom," I complain to Josie.

"But I think it looks very nice." I knew she'd say that. After Martha's friend finished cutting it, she showed me in a mirror, and all of them said how good they thought it looked. "That's what we used to call a pixie when I was your age. I had my hair cut like that every summer."

"This short?"

"Well, just about."

"Mom?"

"What?"

"Who's that lady anyway?"

"What lady?"

"You know. Martha."

"What do you mean, who is she? A friend of Luce's. I told you."

"But how do they know each other?"

"I have no idea. I didn't inquire, and Luce didn't say. But that reminds me, I was going to tell you"—Josie's talking so soft I can hardly hear her, even though everyone near us is asleep—"you mustn't ever tell anybody we stayed there. Under any circumstances."

"How come?"

"She could possibly get in trouble."

"I don't get it. What for?"

"Sssh. For . . . I don't know. For harboring fugitives."

"What's fugitives?"

"Sort of like runaways."

"You could get in trouble for that? But we never said we were. How is she supposed to know, then?"

"No, I meant . . . look, it's hard to explain. I just have an idea she helps out other people who are running away sometimes, and that

*means if anyone found out about us staying here, it would make it
more likely she could get in trouble about the others."*

*"You mean, like, other lesbians with kids? I didn't know she was a
lesbian."*

"Sssh. I don't know whether she's one or not."

"I still don't get it then."

"I'll try to explain it later, when we're not on the bus."

"We're always on the bus."

"Don't whine at me."

*Josie's in a bad mood all right. You can't even talk to her. It's really
late, but I still don't feel sleepy. I make believe I'm Cindy Anderson,
only this time our house is right in Los Angeles, so I can lay out by
the pool and get a real good tan and we have our own tangelo trees
and stuff. I go to Disneyland anytime I want. I ride one of the horses
over there.*

*I wish I had somebody to play with, though. Even though Sukey
could be obnoxious sometimes, I think it was mostly just to get attention. If she came over I'd let her saddle Flicka.*

* * *

"Josie, I mean Mom?"

"What, kiddo."

"Tell me a story about when you were little?"

"Not right now. I'm trying to rest, okay?"

"But your eyes are open."

"Never mind, I can rest just sitting here. Why don't you put
your head down and try to go to sleep?"

"I can't, I already tried."

"Then just rest."

"Will you later?"

"Will I what."

"Will you tell me a story about when you were a little girl,
later?"

"Okay, I promise. Now let's just be quiet."

Two minutes pass.

"Can I ask this *one* thing?"

"All right, one thing then."

"What do you think my Daddy's going to do?"

Night goes along like this, with a little sleep in it. Finally it's
morning, Tulsa, time for breakfast. Not much liking the looks of
the station snackbar with its Saran-swathed sandwiches, I suggest to Ericka that we take a walk. Within a few blocks we're

rewarded by the discovery of a classic greasy spoon, the EAT CAFE according to the legend emblazoned on a large Coca-Cola sign above the door.

My companion naturally wants us to sit at the counter on the old-fashioned chrome and leather stools which, as she begins enthusiastically demonstrating, "spin all the way around." I'm delighted with the place for other reasons. The walls are painted hospital green, the floors and counters grubby with the respectable grubbiness of age. Refrigerator cases display glinting trays of Jello and runny puddings. No air conditioning, but a large propeller-like ceiling fan, inadequate even this early in the morning, lightly agitates the fly-studded No Pest Strips. Survivors merrily strafe the sticky pastries. There's a calendar, "Fred's Auto Parts" above a bucolic scene, hanging opposite me; up front, behind the massive cash register, a small American flag and a framed photograph of someone I optimistically conclude might be Franklin D. Roosevelt—though he might in fact be just about any broad-shouldered white man in a business suit, for all I can tell at this distance. Clad in a clean white T-shirt and dirty apron, the beefy grillman sweats expertly over his orders in full view of the clientele, men in work clothes bent upon platters of meat, potatoes, eggs. A few of them hotly debate the respective merits of two baseball players I've vaguely heard of, while the rest listen appreciatively. In short, Jack Kerouac would be right at home.

Ericka and I alone represent our sex, except for the one waitress who, in yet another miraculous coincidence with the conventions of picaresque fairytales, is very young, fresh-looking, and even pretty. Or she's cute at any rate, in her blue uniform with her dark blue eyes and shining ponytail, and the firm curvaceous ass any literate, footloose boy would be sure to note in his memoirs, "Julie" spelled out in gold cursive lettering on a chain around her neck.

Don't cruise the waitress, baby, I can hear Rhea say.

"Know what you want yet?" Julie pulls me up short, hands planted on luscious hips, her blue-shadowed eyes with the careful Maybelline lashes impeccable in their professional detachment.

I feel at a disadvantage. "Did you decide, Cindy?"

"Uh-huh. That. Country Griddle Cakes." Pointing to the faded purple ditto beneath the plastic cover, she glances at me to see how strictly I plan to enforce nutritional standards.

"Okay, pancakes. Two ought to do it. And a glass of milk."

"Short stack, Henry," Julie flings over her shoulder. "What'll you have, ma'am?"

We've really left the East if I'm ma'am instead of miss. "Well, coffee, two eggs scrambled and—" But here I pause, covered with confusion. I've very nearly committed the absurd error of requesting a toasted bagel in Oklahoma. "—I mean, what kind of Danish do you have?"

"What kind of what?"

"Danish. Over there."

"Oh, those sweet rolls," she corrects me crisply. "Let's see, I got a butterhorn. I can heat it if you want."

"Never mind." I'm looking at the flies. "On second thought, let me have rye toast."

"No rye toast."

"Whole wheat, then."

"We just got white, ma'am." She taps her pad impatiently with her pencil. A tiny diamond winks on her ring finger.

"White toast, then."

"Two scrambled, Henry. And I got a side of bacon working for Mr. D., don't forget that."

"Bacon *working*," Ericka mouths in wonder. "Pancakes have protein," she adds defensively.

I eat rather quickly, goaded; my companion is convinced for some reason that we're in danger of missing our bus. When I pay at the register I have the opportunity to note that the visage grinning down from the green wall is not FDR at all, but blue-eyed Billy Graham. Signs flanking him proclaim, "Jesus Is Salvation, You Bet Your Life," "We Issue Credit Only to Those Over Eighty Years of Age, and Then Only When Accompanied by Their Parents," and "Support Our P.O.W.'s - M.I.A.'s."

Back in the bus station with plenty of time to spare, we hit the restrooms, distinguished by stopped-up sinks, towels crumpled on the floor. As I hand tissues under the partition to the neighboring stall, I find myself wondering whether I'm remiss in having failed to pass on all those ancient maternal injunctions against fraternizing with public toilet seats. Mom always made me use the "sanitary shield"; come to think of it, I haven't seen one of those wall dispensers in years.

This reverie is shattered by an unseen voice. "Josie, I mean mom, what's fell-at-eye-oh?"

"What's *what?*" Then I get it: she's reading the graffiti.

"F-E-L-L-A-T-I-O."

"Fell-ay-show," I pronounce, playing for time.

"It says here a number to call if you want any."

* * *

158

Something bad happens after breakfast, something scary. And all because I ask a simple question. Did Josie like it when her family lived in Los Angeles.

"I guess so. At the time, anyway."

"You moved there from someplace else, didn't you?"

"That's right, Seattle. My father switched jobs."

"Hey, just like my father."

"Well, sort of. Fortunately at least your father doesn't work on missile systems."

"What's missile systems?"

"Machines for carrying bombs."

"Your father worked for the Army?"

"Not exactly."

"Then how come he made missiles?"

"Because he worked for a private company that made lots of money doing jobs for the Army. Actually, it took me a long time to understand that. They always said he was an 'engineer,' and even though I knew it didn't have anything to do with trains I always thought of Casey Jones, something simple and heroic. I don't think it was till I was in high school that I consciously realized he helped make those things we had the air raid drills for."

"What's air raid drills?"

"Ah, youth." She explains how when she was in kindergarten and stuff, they used to have to hide under their desks to practice for nucular war.

"What's nucular war?" I say for some reason. Even though I think I sort of know.

"Nuclear," she says. "Nuclear war."

"Some boys in my grade play this game called World War III. They play, like, that one of them's President Carter and one of them's this important Russian guy and they've got these big huge bombs and they try to blow up New York. But I wasn't sure if it was real or not."

"I'm afraid it is real."

"But we don't have those drills."

Josie doesn't answer. She's looking out the window.

"I'd go down in our basement," I say. "It isn't locked." Then I remember we're not in Brooklyn anymore. They might not even have basements in California.

Josie starts explaining about something called radiation, how atoms break up in these little tiny pieces. But I know all that, we studied it in science.

"Grownups are stupid," I tell her. "Why don't they get rid of those things?"

Josie doesn't look that comfortable. "The truth is, I'm afraid there's a few people that would rather see the planet burned to a crisp than give up any power."

All of a sudden I remember something. My father and Brenda had this party once, for people from NYU. I was helping Brenda pass the crackers and dip and stuff and listening to them talk. And this one professor was saying "it" was bound to happen by the year 2000, only I wasn't sure what "it" was. But now I think he meant a nucular war. And they were all arguing about whether "it" would be "the end of history." When I asked my father about it later, he didn't explain at all, he just went, "Oh, that's merely Paul Goldberg, the cockeyed pessimist, pay him no attention."

I feel scared all over. The planet, Josie said.

I don't want to ask, but I have to anyway. "Do you think anybody could ever kill everyone in the whole entire world?"

"Theoretically," Josie says, in this weird voice.

"What's that?"

"Possibly—under certain special conditions. But I don't expect that'll happen."

"Why not?"

"Everyone is billions. I expect some folks would make it."

I think she might be lying, but I don't say anything.

* * *

Reboarding the bus after Oklahoma City, we find ourselves across the aisle from a family of five kids and a distracted, nagging mother. "Just straighten up and fly right," she keeps haranguing. "Just straighten up right now, hear, or we're turning right around and going home, and you won't see Grandma and Aunt Dodie and the horsie." She repeats this over and over, like a frantic missionary invoking hellfire in an effort to keep the skeptical natives in line; her offspring clearly have good reason to suspect that Greyhound buses do not change course merely on account of a little juvenile wickedness.

"Can't we *move?*" moans Ericka disdainfully, as the threats finally give way to slaps and wails.

"See any empty seats?"

"Uh-uh."

"Well, then."

Behind us in the smoking section, worse trouble soon develops. Ericka twists to gawk, reports back, "That man in the soldier suit is fighting with that lady."

160

"Don't stare," I instruct her automatically.

"Aw, come on, baby, don't *be* like that." The soldier, if in fact he is one, keeps repeating this theme with subtle variations. I can't quite get the drift of the woman's replies, equally monotonous in tone. Closing my eyes, I reduce this to abstract sound: a pair of birds, each bound to its two notes.

Ericka suddenly discovers she's got to go to the bathroom. Reports back, with suspicious alacrity, "I *saw* them."

"So? What do they look like?"

She shrugs. "The lady has a lot of makeup."

"How about saying 'woman' instead of 'lady'?"

Ten minutes later, I take my trip to the bathroom. They're terribly young; maybe she's out of high school. He's tall, hemming her in, black boots propped in the aisle. His uniform, his tan, his air of aggrieved self-absorption, accentuate the glamor of a handsome, brutal child. She's pale, not very pretty, with a tower of teased hair, pancake makeup slathered on bad skin.

Just as I pass he grabs her fragile chin, hauls her stubborn face toward his. "Baby," he bawls absurdly.

I decide it's about sex.

On my return trip they're silent, he fiercely smoking. She studies her scarred face in a compact mirror.

"Did you see them?" my seatmate demands. "Did you see *the lovers?*" She rolls her eyes, satirical, embarrassed.

"Never mind them. We've got our own problems."

But they start up again, and it sounds serious. I notice the driver keeps glancing in his mirror. All-American fantasies besiege me. The boy will have a gun. He'll take hostages.

"Do you think he's going to *hit* her?"

"Sssh, be quiet. Sit still."

We'll sit by the highway for hours, I'm thinking, with the air conditioning off, sweltering, thirsting, peeing in our pants, while the driver curses his luck and the corporation: why the fuck didn't they put *this* in the manual? . . . We'll be front page in the Oklahoma papers.

The monotonous injured rant goes on and on. "Don't get me uptight now, babe. You know I'm trained to kill."

Would he listen to reason? Let children go, for instance?

A sudden calm. We shift uneasily.

"Sonofabitch!" the female shriek resounds, a heart-stopping exhale of the collective panic.

Ericka digs her nails into my arm.

Dead silence, except for the engine. The impression of time momentarily suspended, though the vista of fields continues to unreel beyond the glass. Slow grind of large tires on the gravel shoulder.

Leaving his motor running, the driver rises from his seat and makes his deliberate way down the aisle. We all turn to look; we can't help ourselves. He stands his ground in front of the offenders: a short, pudgy, pink-faced man in a string tie and sunglasses, thumbs hooked in belt.

"Now hear this," he starts, quietly enough. "This kinda thing don't go on my bus. You understand? No ifs, ands, buts, and I don't care what kinda problems you got, or what brand you been drinking, or who your mother is, or nothing else! We all got problems, we all got differences of opinion from time to time. Fine. But settle it somewhere besides my bus. Either that, or talk it over real nice. Because the other passengers, see, they got their rights too.

"Now I'm telling you something, so listen good, because I'm only gonna say it this once. If I stop this bus again for you two jokers, for any reason whatsoever, you're gonna walk. Walk, you got it? I got to make my schedule. And it's warm out there today, and I hear the hitching ain't much along this stretch. So let's relax, and we'll all enjoy the ride."

Our hero, a teacher who knows how to handle the class, he makes his deliberate way back to his seat. The moment seems ripe for a bullet in the back, but he hasn't misjudged matters. Peace ensues; our terror shades back into normal Greyhound boredom. What happens later is the girlfriend's business.

*   *   *

Amarillo, armadillo.

That's the words to this song I made up, since Amarillo was our next stop. The song has a tune, but just those same words, you sing them to different notes. I sang it a bunch of times, till Josie got impatient. I didn't mean to bother her, but I needed something to do.

I wouldn't like to live in this area, I don't think. Just looking out the window makes me feel all hot and thirsty. It reminds me of those tortures on TV, where they tie people up outdoors in the blazing hot sun, and ants eat them, and buzzards.

In Amarillo, the heat takes your breath away. I think the bus station ought to have one of those halls that moves, like they usually do in airports, that attaches to the plane so you don't have to go outside. Even though the driver said this was our dinner stop, I don't feel much like eating. Josie said our stomachs must be on a different schedule, and even though it's hot we should walk and stretch our legs.

We walk a couple blocks. My legs feel sort of funny. There's not that much to look at, not many people out. They must be home eating dinner now, I guess. I bet they all have air conditioning. Most of the stores are closed for the night already. It's actually sort of a creepy neighborhood.

"Can we go back now?"

"Just another block or two."

We always have to do what Josie wants.

The next block I spot this little dog. It's lying on the sidewalk, tied to a parking meter. It looks like part husky, with pointy ears. When we get up close I see it's still a puppy. It seems like it's got something wrong with it. Its eyes are closed, its tongue is hanging out. Then it looks up at us, and one eye is normal, but the other one has this white stuff all over it. It sort of tries to get up, but then it seems too weak. It drags its tail back and forth on the concrete, and makes a whimpering noise.

It doesn't even have a collar, just the rope.

"What's wrong?"

"I don't know. Maybe it's thirsty. Stand back, now. Don't touch it."

It does seem thirsty. It's panting really hard. It looks at us, like it's trying to say something.

"But that's cruel to tie it up there like that. There's not even any shade. Can't we get some water for it anyway?"

Josie looks around. "I don't know where we'd find it. We don't have so much time before our bus. I'm sure the owner will be back."

I knew she wouldn't want to get involved.

"Please. Look, it's sick."

"It does look pretty feeble."

Just then this boy comes around the corner. He's maybe about fourteen, super-skinny, sunburned. He's got this purple birthmark on his neck.

"Oh hello," Josie says. "Does this dog belong to you?"

He barely nods and starts untying the rope.

"Okay, then, I guess that solves the problem. We were worried, it looked sick."

But I can't just desert that poor dog. I don't like how the boy's face looks anyway. I can't think what else to say, so I ask what kind it is.

"Mutt," he growls, like saying go fuck yourself. "Come on, you, move it." He tugs on the rope. The dog is having trouble standing up.

"I think your dog is thirsty," I point out, real polite.

"She's okay."

Josie goes, "We'd better head back."

The boy pulls harder. "Git over here," he orders. He really says "git," like cowboys on TV. "Git over here, you lazy old dog." The poor dog finally gets up, but she has trouble walking.

"Come on," says Josie, grabbing at my hand.

"But the dog is sick. Can't you see that?"

"I think she'll be okay."

"How do you know?"

The boy is pulling. The dog is lying down. "Git over here," he says. "Git over here, you mutt."

"We've got to do something. She'll die without water."

Josie gives a look, like it's me she's mad at. But she says excuse me, walking towards the boy.

He just ignores her. "Excuse me," she says again. I don't see why she has to be so nice. "It does look to me as though your dog needs some water right away."

"She's fine," he insists.

"But see how hard she's panting."

"Look, lady, you notice any water in the vicinity? She'll be okay. She's lazy."

"Well," Josie says, "I hope you know what you're talking about." That's all. She starts walking. I follow her.

Traitor, I'm thinking. "How come you let him go?" I turn around to look. He's dragging along that dog.

"I tried, kiddo," she says. "You saw what happened."

"But why didn't you—why did you just let him get away with it?"

"What was I going to do? How could I have stopped him?"

I feel like crying, everything's so unfair. It wasn't my idea to take a walk, anyway. "Don't ask me," I tell her, "I'm not the grownup."

"I think you're being a little unreasonable."

"You don't even care about the dog!" All of a sudden I'm ready to explode. I just stand still. If I move, I'll fly to pieces.

"Oh, just stop it." Josie speaks sharply. "I'm not any happier about the dog than you are, okay? I'm in no mood to hassle about this."

I stand there like a statue.

"Come on, I want to get back to the station so we'll have time to pick up some sandwiches or something."

Sandwiches.

"Let's go. Come on."

"HOW CAN YOU BE WORRYING ABOUT GETTING SOMETHING TO EAT WHEN THAT POOR SICK DOG DOESN'T HAVE A DRINK OF WATER?"

"Hey, look." She pulls my arm, rough.

No. You can't make me.

That's exactly what I feel like saying to her. That's all you can do, is say no, if you're the kid. Make up your mind you won't obey, no matter what grownups threaten to do to you.

"I don't care if we miss the bus. I don't care if a car runs us over. I don't care if we get arrested. I don't care what you do, Josie, even if you go and leave me all alone right here in the middle of the street in Texas. I'M NOT GOING ANYWHERE."

Josie acts all reasonable, of course. Claims she doesn't get it, doesn't see what my problem is. I scream at her she does so know my problem. Fucker. Bitch. Pig. Stupid asshole.

Part of me's yelling at her, but what's weird is it's like a little, quiet part is up above someplace, flying around, looking down at us, Josie standing in the middle of the street looking scared and mad and me shouting.

I won't, I say. Won't. It feels good. I can't stop, like when you pick a scab.

She grabs me by both shoulders. "Cindy Cole, this is very dangerous."

"Dangerous, to you! But you didn't care about—"

"Stop it right this minute."

She slaps me hard, once, on the butt. I take a great big breath and scream as loud as I can. Eeeeeeeeeeeee is how it sounds.

I feel like I could scream forever. At least until I started to pass out.

I stop after a while. She's still holding me. I say, "That's child abuse, what you just did."

"Look, listen to me." Her voice is a punishment. "You can stop this carrying on right now, control yourself and start acting your age, or you can go right back to Brooklyn. It's just too dangerous in this situation. I won't put up with it."

"Okay, go right ahead. Send me back."

"Is that what you really want?"

"Who cares? You're the one that makes all the choices."

"You know perfectly well that's not true."

"Well, didn't you just say you'd send me back?"

"You know I didn't mean—I don't want to send you back. But I won't put up with tantrums. We've got enough things to worry about, without you carrying on. Now let's get going. The bus is leaving soon."

So I go, but I look at the ground, I won't talk. I'm crying hard. I don't care who sees, either.

What I'd like to do is follow that mean boy, find out where he lives and steal that dog. Then take her to a vet and see she gets well, and the two of us could go someplace and live.

By ourselves. Period. Fuck selfish grownups.

* * *

165

I am reading the Texas papers, or trying to; Ericka's listless presence makes it tough to concentrate. I'm furious at her, but also I'm worried, especially about that threat to send her back, which in retrospect seems a dangerous escalation.

I wish I weren't so alone with all this. Meaning, of course, if Rhea —

Finally I try, "I'm sorry I yelled at you."

"It's okay," she answers bleakly. But things ease up a bit. Gradually, side by side, we enter a mood of drained acceptance. Silently we share the machine-dispensed sandwiches. The sun toward which we flee collapses into a spectacular puddle of light upon the black horizon. Night cracks down.

The bus is quite empty, emptier than it's been at any other point so far, and when my antagonist and victim starts to droop against the window, limp as the nodding junkies on the IRT express, I move forward to claim the empty seat in front of us; I want to be alone. I recognize we've hit that low point of cross-continental travel where monotony of terrain and flagging endurance conspire to call the whole effort into question. As though all energy pulsed from the populous coasts, while inertia ruled the center, and now threatened to capture us.

Dead tired, I curl up, fold limbs like cramped wings. Fall into the pit where none of this matters.

And, somewhere in New Mexico, dream the dream.

This time it's from bluffs overlooking some virginal blue beach that I watch the pillar of cloud lift up, boil over. All in slow motion, sound track switched off. And I'm not even afraid. I'm just the eyes, watching.

Then I get the punchline, how history's turned out — and in that instant it happens, the universe flies to pieces: sound, light, heat, expand through all of space, as hugely and immediately as though they originated, not out there somewhere but in perception's exact center, as though the brain itself were what detonates.

The blast hurls me flat at the rockface of consciousness. And I'm here, tachycardic, choking back the cry. The old, fantastic impulse to fling myself over her.

You *must* protect the child. Though you cannot.

Ericka. She's gone from the seat beside me. Terrified, I grope through viscous seconds; then, remembering, glance back to find her slumped on the cold floor, flushed cheek against fake plush, softly breathing in dim, benign light.

Drenched with remorse, I get up and haul her as gently as I can back up onto the seat. She hardly stirs. I cover her with sweaters.

166

Of course I've only seen it in film clips myself, but in high school I knew several kids who'd lived in Nevada in the Fifties and had watched the tests there. They told how the families would congregate in yards, on patios, settling down in lawn chairs, swigging Coke and Coors, to watch the free show. The mothers, to be sure, never got over a certain nervousness they themselves admitted was irrational, and the children, after the first such experience, were bored and uneasy both. But the fathers seemed to be in their element. As they loaded up their cameras, they patiently explained (for not even their wives ever seemed quite to remember) how it was the atom worked, and what fission meant, and fusion.

That was togetherness. Who expected leukemia? I remember well enough how my brothers and I were once pried out of midnight beds in order to contemplate a much-advertised piece of hardware as it traced its stellar path against the dowdy galaxy. These sights were considered wholesome and instructive. See there, kids? Science at our service. Don't worry, we'll beat the pants off those sneaky Russians.

When I wake around 6:30, we're already in mountain country: not peaks by any means, but substantial pine-clad slopes. We've disposed of all New Mexico in the night. I have some vague recollection of Albuquerque: harsh lights and passengers getting off.

Ericka's wide awake. "Is this the West?" she greets me.

"Well, sort of. The Southwest. Arizona."

"I thought the mountains would be taller."

"They will. Just wait."

Shortly after seven the driver announces our breakfast stop. The town of several hundred is called Biddle, an abbreviated sprawl of ugly modern dwellings, mobile homes and such, at its center a street of dignified old two-story wooden houses set on irrigated lawns. The Greyhound ticket office is in Biddle Mercantile, across the street from the one coffee shop.

We shake ourselves and obediently stagger forth, gritty-eyed but eternally optimistic, toward caffeine and food. I'm half-expecting the heat of Amarillo, but it's cool here yet, of course, won't warm up till the sun hits. It's about to be a perfect western day: blue, blue sky with a few high scrawls of cloud. Which are called what, cirrus? I used to know these things.

The coffee shop is plastic-clean, appealing, with Glen Campbell bleating from the jukebox, chrome-studded individual selectors for which are stationed in each booth. I sip coffee and feel almost cheerful. Amazing what a few hours' sleep will do. Besides, the place serves hashbrowns, the hallmark of western breakfasts. Ericka says she likes them, though "they're different than home fries." Once she's finished eating she goes outside to wait.

I accept a coffee refill and consult the Flagstaff paper, which is short on news, long on syndicated females; Dr. Joyce Masters, for instance, writes sympathetically about the problems of a self-styled "average he-man" who has fallen in love with a "very feminine" transsexual.

Gradually the other passengers are starting to head back toward the bus. In no hurry to re-embark, I've been keeping an eye on our driver. His solid rear end planted firmly on a stool, he's enjoying himself, smoking, luxuriously tapping ashes into a mess of egg yolk on his plate, cracking jokes the two matronly, grey-haired waitresses seem to feel obliged to smile at. His loud complacent sallies irritate me, and finally I pay the check and go, humming "Here Comes the Sun," out to wait with Ericka.

She isn't with the others on the sidewalk. Thinking maybe she's taken a stroll across the street, I walk around to the other side of the bus. But she isn't over there, nor does she leap out at me in one of those childish ambushes she consideres entertaining.

It occurs to me she must have gone back inside to use the bathroom, in fact probably passed right by while I was buried in the paper. After a minute, I go in to check. Behind a door marked "Cowgirls" are two toilet stalls. Under the first door, large, flat grownup feet. Under the second, nothing.

I hurry back outside, sure I'll find her there. She'll probably want to know where *I've* been.

She's still not there, though the passengers have gathered outside the closed bus and are starting to get restless. Through the coffee shop's front window I can see the driver at last rising slowly from his stool. He fumbles in his pocket for the tip while one waitress still hangs poised, counter-rag in hand, awaiting release from his coercive humor.

The street is empty. It's early. Everything's normal.

She's up to some trick, evidently. But right now —

Suppose she took a little walk up the street? Suppose she turned a corner? Then she'll be back directly. There's obviously no place in this little town to get lost.

But impossible to shake this cold panic, which is going to look so foolish in five minutes. Of course she'll be back any second. Reason says so.

When I get my hands on her.

Suppose – what? A Buick with tailfins. Car pulls up to the curb, engine idles. Two men inside. Curb window rolls down. "Little girl – "

Horror tales from my childhood. Things they scared us with. She's Brooklyn-hip. This is Biddle, Arizona.

No, it could still be perfectly innocent, she just got bored, wandered off, misjudged the time.

What I thought that night with Rhea.

Driver's coming. He's going to load now.

I pick someone, anyone, woman standing next to me, mid-fifties, bermuda shorts, tennis shoes. "Excuse me," I hear myself, voice oiled to absurd politeness, "could I ask a favor of you?"

"Yes?" she peers.

"I have to – I mean, I seem to have lost my daughter."

"Oh no, dear! Where?"

"Well, I don't suppose she's lost, actually, but she does seem to have wandered off. I think I'd better go around the block and take a quick look. Do you suppose you could see the driver waits a minute? I'll be right back."

"Well, of course."

"Meantime, if she does show up – she's ten years old, kind of small – "

"Has real short hair, dark and curly?"

"Right. Her name's Cindy."

"Don't worry. You run along."

I walk two blocks. Turn right. Turn right again.

Sure the town's small, but I can't see everywhere.

The thing is, I haven't the faintest notion what comes next. Society has more or less prepared me for all sorts of emergencies: drownings, fires, cardiac arrests. I know how to proceed if somebody chokes on dinner. But nobody's ever explained what it is you do when you're on the lam and you suddenly lose your kid.

I circle back to the bus. Nearly everyone's boarded. Only the woman in bermuda shorts is still standing outside with a man – has to be her husband – also in bermuda shorts.

"You didn't find her?" they chorus. Full of genuine concern. (They won't forget this later on, either.)

The driver saunters up. "All aboard." I ask how soon he's leaving.

"Right about now. You in any hurry?" he quips.

The woman steps forward. "We can't," she says firmly. "Her little girl is lost."

He sizes me up. My hair, my overalls. Hippie type, not your run-of-the-mill mom.

"I could wait five minutes," he offers.

"But supposing her daughter isn't found by then?"

"Then I can take her luggage off. She can always get another bus out later in the day."

"But she's—I mean, what about finding her little girl?"

"Ma'am, I'm a Greyhound driver. This ain't a tour bus. She can go fix up her ticket right over there across the street. People let their kids go wander off, it never seems to occur to them we got a timetable to follow. . . ."

"But—" my protector wavers.

"I can wait five minutes," he reiterates. "You wanna look around?"

My mouth is dry. "Go on, get my luggage out." I want them gone right now, need their beady eyes off me.

He shrugs. "Up to you. What color are your bags?"

The woman in shorts, alarmed, begs me to take another look. Her husband keeps saying the kid's bound to show. I can see the inconvenienced passengers staring at me from their seats, till it occurs to me to face the other way. No point in letting them memorize my features.

The bags are found, put off. The driver revs his engine. The bus blasts off toward the Golden State.

Here I stand like Ellis Island, worldly goods piled around me. One of two bad things, I'm suddenly convinced. Either something truly horrible has happened, or she's gone to call her father.

I start hauling our things into the coffee shop.

* * *

The minute I get outside I start walking along fast. I'm counting in my head, like, onetwothreefourfivesixseven to keep from thinking. Then I try to concentrate on other things.

I like this town. It could be nice living here.

I just need to be by myself, that's all. I'm not particularly mad or anything.

I'd like to run, but people might look.

Last night. That dog. Send me back, she said.

No. Don't think. Nothing. Nobody.

At home, when I want to be alone I can go into my room and shut the door. Also, when the weather's nice I have this place outside in the yard, behind some bushes. Brenda knows not to bother me back there.

Everyone deserves some privacy.

I can't see the bus anymore. Just like it doesn't exist. I like it a lot here: the trees, the sky, and the spicy way it smells. And the

170

quietness, except when a car comes by, which isn't that often. The sun feels good. I want to be way up there on top of that mountain lying on some grass and looking up at clouds and birds and space, not stuck on earth with all the stupid humans.

Like I was the only person in the world.

I'm getting to where the houses are more spread out. A couple times I notice people in their yards, but I don't look at them in case they'd say hello. I don't feel like getting in any conversations, and they might wonder where I'm going so early by myself. I don't see any kids, except for in this one great big yard that's all, like, junk—there's wrecked cars and old washing machines and stuff, and the house is just a trailer, with this kind of porch built on, and different colored washing hanging out—there's this little blond boy, so blond his hair is white, playing with a magnifying glass. He's squatting down, very serious. There's chickens too, pecking all around, enormous red chickens. I notice he's made a pile of dry grass, he's trying to start a fire. There's no adults in sight.

Just then he looks up at me, like he knew all along I was there. But he doesn't say a word, just puts his finger to his lips, telling me to be quiet. I get this funny feeling he can't talk. He's just a little shrimp, six or seven at the most. Suddenly he grins like I'm his best friend or something, and motions with his hand for me to come over.

I smile back, but I don't want to get mixed up in whatever he's doing, so after a minute I wave and walk on. I wonder what'll happen if he gets that fire started, but it won't be my problem, anyway.

The houses have stopped now. The mountain's on my left. Beside the road there's a barbed wire fence, rusty and dangerous-looking. But I've had my tetanus shot. When I get to a place where it's kind of fallen down, I decide to climb over.

It's hard to climb up here in just my sandals. I wish I was wearing sneakers. Every time I step on a rock, my foot sort of twists, and there's a lot of rocks.

The bus will leave, I guess. That's not my problem either.

It's getting hotter now, I'm all sweaty. At least there's some trees up ahead, so when I get that far I can rest in the shade of them. I'd like a drink, only I don't see any streams, and even if I found one the water could be bad. That's one useful thing I learned from being in camp.

Send me back, she said. All right, so big deal.

It seems like someone's constantly mad at me, except for Leah, and she's just a baby. I should of run away with her, that's who, before they make it so she's against me too. It would serve them all right. They could hunt for us forever.

Okay, I'm sitting down to rest right here, on this nice flat rock. There's shade, and you can't even see the highway. I like to be up high and see far. I wonder who this property belongs to. I'd like to build a hut and live here by myself. I wouldn't be lonely, I'd have animals. Like maybe pet deer and birds, a cat and a bunch of hamsters, and a burro to help me bring stuff up from the valley, when I went down to town to buy food. I'd have to be a vegetarian, I guess, since of course I wouldn't want to eat my friends. Also, maybe I could find berries or something. When I went to town to shop, everybody would point at me and say, "There goes Ericka Krevsky, the Weird Girl of the Mountain," but actually they would realize I'm very brave to live up here alone by myself.

I read a book once about this girl that got left all by herself on this desert island. But that was in olden times. Now they'd probably have condominiums there or something.

I wish I'd brought my bathing suit up here. Then I could lie in the sun and get more tan. It's quieter than I've almost ever heard it, except for this loud zinging noise I guess must be some kind of insects.

Josie will be angry I disappeared and made us miss our bus. But she's mad anyway. It's not my fault. And Daddy will be upset when he gets that letter.

The sun is hotter. Now I'm really thirsty.

Why can't they just make up their stupid minds.

Suppose she got back on the bus and left without me. Like I say to Leah when we go out for walks and she doesn't want to come: okay, I'll leave you there. Only I won't, of course. I just pretend I would.

I don't even know anybody here. I guess they'd put me in an orphanage.

No they wouldn't. I'd go live with Grandma.

I don't know if Josie would leave, but I feel scared anyway. She was so mad at me in Amarillo. I'm wearing my birthday watch, and it says almost nine, and I know the bus must've left a while ago. I knew I shouldn't go away like that, but it wasn't me, it was like something burst.

None of this would of happened if Mommy was alive.

*　*　*

I sit in a back booth and review my options. An hour at most, then I'll have to call the cops.

"Excuse me, er, ma'am, are you all right?"

I jump at the voice, but on sight he seems fairly harmless. He's the classic "nice man" from my childhood: Levis, stiff grey flattop, paunch like a hard small football. He's tall, embarrassed, eager to be of help. He's left his coffee cooling on the counter.

I wipe my eyes and start improvising, telling him how I think my daughter must have wandered off to call her grandmother. The whole thing sounds fishy enough to me, but he doesn't seem to notice. He'll drive me around, he says. We'll have a look. The waitresses will watch my bags for me — not that anyone'd touch them. He gallantly holds the door, indicates his pickup truck. He hopes I won't mind the smell too much. He hauled a load of horse manure yesterday, and hasn't had a chance yet to hose out the back.

A tour of the pay phones of Biddle turns up no Ericka. Back on the main drag, Dwayne — his name, as it appears — pulls the pickup over beside a neat large vegetable and flower garden. "Good morning, Mrs. Sears," he yells across me through the open window, and a small old woman, her head wreathed in yellow-white braids, slowly straightens up to face us. Gripping uprooted weeds in work-gloved hands, she squints from beneath an oversized emerald-green eyeshade.

Dwayne explains as he's already done all over town how this young lady here who got off the Greyhound this morning has lost, or he ought to say misplaced, a daughter. Mrs. Sears feels called upon to commiserate at quite unnecessary length, but then unexpectedly recalls that she did, come to think back, notice a little girl with short dark hair pass by a while ago. She was wearing cutoff jeans? A yellow blouse or top? Had real short hair — like a boy's it looked, from a distance. She'd wondered who that could be, not recognizing the child. In fact, she'd started worrying that her memory was playing tricks again, until it dawned on her that it just might be one of Mattie's Nancy's children — Mattie, she elaborates for my benefit, being her next-door neighbor, whose daughter Nancy in Tucson is sending the kids out here for the summer, since she and the children's father are going through a divorce.

I'm paralyzed with hope and irritation, but Dwayne interrupts, implores her to consider if she can remember anything more about seeing the little girl. Mrs. Sears gestures westward: she went off in that direction, and it must have been about an hour ago. "Really, I could just about kick myself. I almost stopped that child to find out —"

Dwayne smiles, squirms, fondles the ignition, and at last succeeds in extricating us. As we drive off Mrs. Sears is yelling at him he's to stop by again later in the day, she has some lettuce she's been saving for him, she's got a terrible lot of it this year, he'll have to take some home even though she knows he's never been that partial to rabbit food: why, even as a boy —

"Amazing energy Elsie Sears has," he comments ruefully, hanging a U turn. "We'll drive on out the highway, see if anything turns up."

* * *

Once I start in crying it's hard to stop. That's one reason I didn't want to think about stuff before. I want to be with Josie and now I can't. I made us miss the bus and she'll blame it all on me. I know she'll just say she can't trust me anymore and send me back to my father.

Nobody wants me now my mother died. Josie said she did, but she doesn't act like it. All she does is yell and get cross. My father says he loves me, but he's busy all the time. They fight about me, and Grandma's in Florida, and no matter which I choose I'd probably get in trouble with the other one. When I grow up I'm definitely not having kids, because even though I'd take good care of them I could always die and then they could get mistreated.

I can't go back to town, no matter what. Maybe I'll just stay here and maybe they'll search for me. Maybe I won't survive without food and water. Maybe they'll have to come looking with a helicopter or something, that's what they usually do when people are lost on the side of mountains. Sometimes they die of something called exposure, or sometimes they get found and flown to hospitals.

I don't want to think about my mother though. I miss her so much then, even though right after the accident and everything, when we had the memorial service, people kept saying I'd feel better pretty soon. Everybody lied. They always lie to kids.

I wish it was true, what TeriAnn's church thinks. She said I would see my mother when I die. She wasn't lying, she really believes in that.

I guess Josie's worried now. It's so hot. I wish I had a bottle of ice-cold Seven-Up.

* * *

Dwayne drops me back in town, agrees I'd better call the sheriff. He explains he's got some business to attend to, but will be back in an hour to see how I'm making out.

The sheriff's office is in the next town. The woman who answers my call promises to have a deputy out to talk with me in about half an hour. I say I'll meet him in the coffee shop and settle down to wait, but almost immediately realize I've got to phone

Daniel. So long as there's a chance she might have called him I'd better find out about it.

Even amidst my terror for Ericka, the prospect panics me. The sheriff is one thing, official but ignorant; to him we'll be simply Laura and Cindy Cole, a rather bedraggled mother-daughter pair on our way, believably, to Disneyland. Daniel is quite another. I'm afraid of his anger, even through the phone.

We'll have to go back? No time to consider that. All I care about on earth is finding her.

One of the waitresses furnishes me with change. I am fortunate: the phone booth has a door.

I can dial direct. The quarters sing in the slot.

In Brooklyn the phone is ringing. Maybe he won't be home.

*　*　*

The sun makes me sleepy. I'm thinking about a story that Grandma used to tell me sometimes. See, when Mommy was little she ran away from home once. She did something she wasn't supposed to do and Grandma told her to go stay in her and Etty's room for a punishment, but instead she went and broke her piggy bank and snuck down the fire escape and took the subway to Grand Central and bought a ticket on the Harlem-Hudson line. Grandma always said it was a good thing she was stubborn and lasted as far as Croton before she got too scared and decided to come back, because Grandma was so worried and upset that when she got a call from the police saying they found her daughter she was all ready to warm Mommy's tuchus, is how she puts it. She said if Mommy only had to come from Boro Hall or someplace near, she'd probably have done it to her, too. But the trip back took so long, by the time she got home Grandma had mostly gotten over being mad and was in the middle of making lemon meringue pie, which happened to be Mommy's favorite dessert.

Since there's nothing else to do, I start digging a hole. The ground is almost bare right where I'm sitting, and I scrape the dirt out with a flat sharp rock. After a while I take my watch off. It's the only thing I've got that I could use, except of course my star that Mommy gave me, which I'm not taking off. I don't even have any change in my pockets.

It's white on my arm, like a bracelet, under where my watch was. That's how I could tell my tan is getting good. By the time we get to California, it'll really be attractive. If we ever get there, I mean.

I lay my watch in the hole. It just fits. Then I take it out and wind it all the way and put it back again. I cover it with the dirt and press it down. You could hardly tell the spot was dug up.

It's kind of weird to think about it going on ticking, telling the time underneath the dirt. Of course it'll run down in a day or two. I'd get in trouble with Daddy for losing it, but Josie probably won't say anything. Anyway, it's mine, I could do what I want with it. It will mark this for my spot. I could come back someday.

I could come back when I'm grown and build that little hut. Then I could dig up my watch, just like buried treasure.

* * *

Unsteadily, with an odd bumping noise, the receiver is picked up. There's a pause, punctuated by stuffy breathing.

"Hello — Leah?"

"Yeah, this Leah." A toddler's sultry giggle.

"Leah, let me speak to your daddy, please."

Ambiguous sounds are heard of coaxing and command, then Leah's wail as her toy is expropriated.

"Hello. Excuse me a minute. No, Leah, go show that to Mommy. Okay, sorry. Daniel Fein here."

"Hello, Daniel. It's Josie. Look, did Ericka call?"

"No — no, she didn't. Why, was she supposed to?"

"You've been there all morning? You haven't left the house?"

"No, I've been home. What's wrong? Isn't she with you?"

"And you haven't been on the phone for a long time, or had it off the hook?"

"No, I haven't. Christ, Josie, what is all this about? Is something the matter?"

"Yes, it is. Ericka's disappeared."

"Where are you? Disappeared when? Look, start from the beginning."

I remind myself to breathe. It's not easy. "Well, the thing is, we're not camping. I can't go into all that now. What happened was, we had breakfast in a restaurant this morning, Ericka said she was going to wait for me out front, and when I got out there she wasn't anywhere in sight, she seems to have disappeared, I've been looking all over for her. Someone thinks they saw her walking, but we —"

"Did you get rained out? Where exactly are you?"

"Never mind. The thing is, in case she calls —"

"You *are* still in Vermont? What's the name of the nearest town?"

"No, Daniel. We weren't going there."

"Josie, what the holy fuck are you telling me? Ericka's lost, you're not in Vermont? You're not making any sense. Would you *kindly* begin at the beginning and run through this thing so I can—"

For some reason his outrage calms me slightly. "Look, Daniel, I can't explain now. I'll get back to you later. She's wandered away, and I think she might try to reach you. I'm doing everything I can to locate her, and I'll let you know the minute I do, but in the meantime, if she *does* call, try to find out where she is, what the place looks like and so on. Don't leave the phone, and for heaven's sake keep Leah away from it."

"Wait, don't hang up. At least give me your—"

"Gotta go, Daniel. I'll call back in a little while."

I slip the phone back on the hook and return to my booth to wait, prepare my spiel for the cops. Suppose they want my address and phone number? I'll have to give them what I've got on my ID, just gamble they won't check.

The deputy appears, lean and blond and brusque: Authority made flesh, years younger than I. A boy, really. I feel a little better. The waitresses seem to know him, though he barely nods to them; one rushes over to place unsolicited cups of coffee at our elbows. He starts putting questions to me, clinically efficient, not liking to let his blue eyes near my face. He's evidently so new at this, so self-conscious with pride of office, that it's hard to take him very seriously.

I'm in the middle of explaining about our trip, even hamming it up a bit about Disneyland, when I glance up to see Dwayne wandering toward us. His weathered face wears an odd, pleased, sheepish look. "See here—" he blurts, and then I take it in: Ericka beside him, bedraggled, dirty-faced. Miserable and safe, whole and in trouble.

I've never been so glad. And I have to think fast.

Face frozen, she hangs back a step or two. Plainly she declines to answer for anything.

"Cindy!" I manage somehow. It's a hollow squeak, absurd. "Cindy, where have you been?" I insist, willing her to back me up in front of this audience.

And then it's okay. She crumples sobbing into my lap, more like a felled tree than a sad child, arms limp, not appealing for help, but utterly forlorn.

I cradle my prodigal while I calculate: everyone must be taken in by this touching scene. "That's okay, that's all right," I urge, gentling. "It's okay, kiddo, you're back, you're with me, you're all right now. Don't worry, don't try to talk, we'll talk about it later." And then I surprise myself; I'm sobbing with her, overwhelmed, aghast at my good luck.

My collapse seems to hasten her recovery. Soon she's dry-eyed, offering me Kleenex. Dwayne and the deputy have removed to another booth, but the waitresses, made of sterner female stuff, stand by to ply us with soft drinks and other restoratives. After I've calmed down and blown my nose, Dwayne comes back and starts explaining, in a voice loud enough to gratify the curiosity of every customer in the place, how something told him he ought to run over and have another look at that stretch of highway, even though it meant taking the long way back from Pattison's, where he'd been seeing about some hay. And sure enough, he caught up with a little girl who fit Cindy's description, hoofing it back to town.

"But I couldn't get a thing out of her," he admits, shaking his head admiringly. "I didn't even think she was gonna come along with me at first, she really gave me the third degree when I tried to convince her I'd been driving around hunting for her with her mother. And all she'd say when I asked her where she'd been was, 'Up on that mountain over there'—and she pointed to that medium-sized molehill over there by Clement Price's place, you know, that antheap he used to run his horses on before he sold it off to that resort outfit and give rise to such a fuss, not that they've ever done a thing with it after all that commotion was caused by those conservation people."

The deputy, looking disdainful but really far more tolerant than I'd expect any city cop to look under the circumstances, obtains my signature for his report, admonishes Ericka to stay put after this, and takes his leave. Dwayne, however, is relishing the limelight. It's quite a relief when finally he guesses he's got another load of manure to go haul.

I thank him profusely and watch him drive away. Then I hustle Ericka off for a turn around the block. She's bawling again before we've reached the corner.

"Okay, take your time. When you calm down you can tell me."

But it can't wait, not even if she chokes. "I couldn't help it, it wasn't my fault, don't be mad, something burst."

"Something what?"

"Something burst, like, you know, like a balloon bursting or something."

"Where?"

"I don't know. Inside, like in my head."

"I don't get it. You mean, at breakfast?"

She nods. "I had to, I *had* to be somewhere by myself. And I was afraid—afraid—"

"Hey, kiddo, calm down. What were you afraid of?"

"I thought maybe you got back on the bus and left me all alone."

"But how could you possibly think that? Didn't you know how terribly worried I'd be? I couldn't imagine what had happened to you."

"I didn't know. You said you'd send me back."

Despair engulfs me, an ocean I can taste. How will we ever get through all of this?

"What is it," she begs, "Josie, I mean Mom?"

"Oh Ericka, that isn't what I meant."

* * *

Josie and I have a grownup type discussion. She explains to me how scared she was when I disappeared, and how her and that man named Dwayne drove all over town asking people if they'd seen me, and how she would do anything to find me, like even calling the police, even though that's very risky since we've just been breaking the law. She explains how it's not that she wants me to go back and live with my father at all, but sometimes she wonders if I might not be better off, because it's hard to be traveling the way we are, and she's always afraid I'm missing being home, especially when we have fights and stuff like that. And besides, he is my father.

"I'm not sure I exactly get what you mean," I say. "I mean, he's my father, so what. I mean, you're my flommy." Flommy's a word we made up, Mommy and me, when I was little, to say what Josie was. I haven't used it in a long time.

She thanks me and gives me a hug and says even so, she's afraid I might be scared to tell her if I really wanted to go back, but it would be much better to say so if I decide that's what I want, because otherwise we'll both be miserable.

I say I miss them some, but I'm used to that from camp.

"Well, you should at least give it some thought. You might get more homesick, later."

"I won't even have *a home, when they move away."*

"The new place would get to be home."

"Uh-uh."

"Well, we'll see. In any event, even if you just feel bad or something, you've got to tell me after this. You can't go running off like that without saying where you're going. Okay?"

"I promise, honest. I want to be with you. I didn't do it on purpose, anyway."

"All right, enough said." All of a sudden she gets this funny look and plunks down on this big old rock that's by the street on somebody's property, and starts crying, covering her face up with her hands.

I sit down next to her. I don't know what to do. I don't want her to feel bad, and I'm also afraid someone will see us and think we're weird or something. I mean, it was one thing, like, for her to be crying in the restaurant. Sometimes you see a kid crying outdoors, but you don't usually see a grownup. I keep patting her shoulder softly, and her back, the way she does sometimes when I'm upset. She finally blows her nose and says she'll be all right, she guesses she's just tired, and we better see about the bus.

When we're walking back she explains she called my father, and now she has to let him know she found me.

"Why'd you do that for? Now he knows we ran away."

"I had to, kiddo. I thought you might have called him."

"But I promised I wouldn't do that." It hurts my feelings she thought I'd break my promise, but I don't want to start another fight.

We go into this store and I look around at the stuff they have for sale while Josie uses the phone. When she comes out I think she looks depressed.

"Did you get him?"

"Sssh, yes, we'll discuss it outside."

She talks to the salesclerk, who sells bus tickets also. There's a bus for Albuquerque due in about an hour, but the one for Los Angeles isn't till 6:30. We go outside and walk around some more.

I ask her is my father very mad. She says she guesses so. Mad at her, not me. But he knows I'm fine now, and he'll get our letter soon.

I look down at my wrist where it's white from my birthday watch, thinking what he'd say if he knew about it, but Josie hasn't noticed. I heard what that man said in the restaurant. A resort bought that land. So now I guess I won't get to come back and dig up my buried treasure.

I figure I'd better say something. "It's long till 6:30."

"Yes I know, that's been bothering me too. Come on, let's go back to the coffee shop and see about our luggage. We can look at the map and think about our plans. I'll buy you a treat or something."

"I'm still so thirsty, can I have another soda?"

"Listen, kiddo, I'll buy you anything."

* * *

Portland seemed like a great idea at the time.

Suddenly, following the second of my phone conversations with Daniel, the one in which, after I explained what I was doing, he crisply assured me he was quite prepared to throw the book at me if I failed to return his daughter on the next plane, I'd become convinced LA would be a trap. True, this was merely a superstitious hunch – unless they found some way of tracing those calls, in which case my destination would be fairly obvious. But then I had good reasons for not wanting to wait around Biddle all day. The town, it seemed to me, already knew too much about us.

When I scanned the Greyhound map for alternatives, there leaped out at me what I ought to have seen before: the thick black squiggle extending north from Albuquerque, bisecting Colorado, nipping Wyoming, and grazing Utah, then slicing a triangle off Idaho and entering Oregon, where it arced through Baker, Pendleton, and The Dalles: to Portland, city of hills, bridges, and rain; cool, somber-eyed market-town of a blessedly backward province, steeped in a marinade of oblivion. Thick-furred with evergreens, looped with gemlike fruit, blackberry vines running wild in all the vacant lots of summer. Where, yes, are set the cunning snares of freeways, and Trojan holds the north in stern nuclear thrall – but you dream the trees might have a fighting chance. Where *quality of life* is savored like vintage wine. Where *nothing ever happens,* oh miracle. And where dwells Rosemary, my spacey friend from Scrubb College, lately saddled with marriage, a mortgage, motherhood – but perhaps still reckless enough to take us in.

This change of plans would mean extra travel time, nearly two days in fact. But under the spotless sky of Biddle, in the amphetamine relief of having gotten back my lost child, a few extra hours on a Greyhound bus seemed a trivial assignment. Maybe it even had its virtues, guaranteeing as it did two additional nights' lodging and postponement of the hour when we'd run head-on into an ocean and have to face Real Life.

Of course I romanticized that black squiggle – an easy mistake to make, coming as I do of a generation weaned on the surreal transitions of jet travel, used as I am to eastern distances. Once out west, how far can the coast be?

But North America is serious: not so easily chewed, spit out. I failed to anticipate the grinding miles, that grim night stretch that followed Albuquerque the second time around. I didn't foresee the trauma of restroom mirrors, my face looming purplish and diseased-looking in the fluorescent wee-hours glare of Trinidad,

Colorado; nor how Ericka, huddled against me through the night, would stir in half-sleep and piteously murmur, "Josie, I mean Mom, how long did you say till we get to go to bed?"

Back there in Trinidad, I decided we needed rest. Sleepwalkers, I grasped, make clumsy fugitives, and despite my instinctive preference for motion, we'd better stop in Denver. Now, as we wait forlornly on the porch of a ramshackle house in an old neighborhood, I'm having my doubts about the Portland plan—and everything else.

It was pretty early when we hit town. I made some phone calls from the station, found out the Denver Y doesn't allow kids, and that all the centrally-located hotels seemed to be either skid row class or exhorbitantly expensive. Then, having with some difficulty obtained directions to a women's bookstore, I schlepped Ericka and our possessions over there. We sat on the doorstep wearily munching corn chips, waiting for opening time.

Opening time was not as advertised. The woman who finally showed up said she personally couldn't help us, but suggested I check the bulletin board in back of the store. And there, in a haystack of thumb-tacked notices, I ran across a sign lettered in crayon:

SYSTERSEA SHARESPACE. New in Denver? Passing through? In crisis? Looking for Positive, Syster-Centered Space? Come share with us. Pay what you can, stay as long as you want. Also looking to expand our collective. Especially need input from Older Systers, Working-Class Systers, and Systers of Color. ALL SYSTERS WELCOME.

Well, we were certainly passing through. And probably in crisis. I asked the staffer if I could use the phone. She looked put out, and I couldn't really blame her—our stuff was sprawled across the scant floorspace, we clearly had no thought of buying books. Finally she said she guessed if it was a very brief local call. . . .

After eight or ten rings somebody picked up.

"Hello," I opened, "is this the . . . Sharespace?" I couldn't seem to manage "Systersea."

"Yeah," said a child's voice. "Who's this?"

"My name's Laura Cole. I was wondering—I mean, could I speak to—your mother, or anyone?"

"I'm anyone," she hardily replied.

"I've been looking for a place to stay tonight."

"It's okay, yeah."

"Are you sure? Maybe I should talk to someone else. About when I should come over and everything."

A pause, while something loud got chewed and swallowed. "Come when you get ready. I'll be here."

Scarcely encouraged, I thought to ask her name, as one does of unhelpful Con Edison personnel, in case things go wrong later.

"Astarte."

"Oh."

The staffer was eyeing me.

"By the way," I added, "I'll be bringing along a child. I assume that's okay?"

"Girl or boy? We don't allow pricks."

I reassured her on that point, then made what I hoped was a subtle last-ditch bid for contact with her elders. "Is anybody home who could give me bus directions?"

"I don't think so, you'd have to call back in about an hour or two. B.D. and Chamomile went to shop at the food co-op. Mountain's in the hut and can't be disturbed. I don't know where Cascara and Pat are at."

Defeated, I thanked Astarte and hung up.

"We hafta stay there?" Ericka cried.

"Didn't you tell me you wanted to go to bed?"

Brazen with exhaustion, I imposed upon the staffer to furnish a complicated set of bus directions, and we finally set out. The trip, involving two transfers, took about an hour. Ericka yawned and fidgeted and grilled me: What's a "sharespace"? Who ever heard of the name Astarte? Why'd they spell "syster" like that? *She* wouldn't like strange people staying in her house all the time, would I? *Would* I?

"I'm tired, kiddo. Let's just be quiet now."

The third bus we took deposited us in a racially mixed neighborhood of spacious but shabby houses set on ample lots, one that's obviously seen more prosperous days. Clearly on the verge of gentrification, it's probably populated at the moment by the usual lively, edgy mix of working-class families with kids, students, old folks who've lived here thirty years or more, feminists, and longhaired white men marooned by the ebb of the counterculture.

Finding the bell broken, I've been hammering away at the door of a place distinguished from its immediate neighbors by a decrepitude less cosmetic, more structural. The yard is anarchic with dandelion puffballs. I'm sure it's the Sharespace, although the number's missing, for by peering through a thickness of oval glass in the top half of the door I can make out bundled stacks of *off our backs* and *Big Mama Rags* strewn among the boxes of Mason jars, propped bicycles, withered houseplants. Plastic bags stuffed with clothing appear to have gotten lost on their way to a rummage sale. Behind looms a broad, rather grandiose stair.

"No one's home." Ericka seems hopeful.

No such luck, however. Several thumps are heard within, and the door is opened a crack by a husky, barefoot hoyden with unkempt hair, her raspberry-colored robe slit to the thigh.

"Hello, I'm Laura Cole. And this is Cindy."

"You're the one that called?" She doesn't budge.

"Yes. You're Astarte, right?" I say brightly. "You said we could stay—"

"Well, sure. You're women, aren't you? Bring your stuff." We stumble in, hampered by sudden gloom. "Follow me." We climb toward the light.

"How old are you, Cindy?" is flung back at us.

Ericka admits to being ten.

The other baldly states she doesn't look it.

"How old are you, Astarte?" I retort, partly in loyalty to Ericka, partly just curious.

"Twelve in August. I got my bloods already."

We climb to the third floor, a sort of finished attic. "You're gonna sleep here," our concierge announces, indicating a low, narrow, dusty room furnished with single mattresses on the floor. It will do quite nicely, I see: the door shuts. The view from the dormer window is of a backyard half patchy vegetables, half weedy tangle.

"See that?" Astarte gestures toward thick foliage, through which can be glimpsed some sort of wooden structure. "That's our menstrual hut. B.D. built it last year. We can't use it in the winter, though, it's not heated yet. Mountain's out there now, and Pat and Cascara went to chant with her. You can leave your stuff up here and come down. Unless you want to sleep in my room, Cindy. It's farout, it's grownup-free space."

Ericka looks alarmed, so I tactfully suggest that we can make decisions about sleeping arrangements later. All I want in this world at the moment is to unroll my sleeping bag and lie down like a hypothermic surrendering to snow, but I figure I'd better meet the Systers first. I try to suggest a nap to Ericka, but she clearly doesn't want to be left alone.

So we descend the stairs again, Astarte leading the way to the kitchen in the back, where a big barefoot woman in very short blonde hair, her workshirt open over plump tanned breasts, acknowledges us with a nod and continues chopping onions.

"What's for dinner?" Astarte demands suspiciously. "Yuk, all those onions."

"Millet stew. For you, anyway. I'm fasting."

"Ew yuk, millet stew's the absolute pits. Where's Pat?"

"Still out back with Mountain."

"Can I go out? I wanna chant too."

"I don't know, Astarte, I think you'd better not. Your energy's pretty intense for Mountain's first day. How about helping me, chopping a few of those carrots?"

Astarte screws up her face disobligingly, but does grab several of the largest carrots I've ever seen from a gunny sack beside the refrigerator, then dampens them slightly with water from the tap.

"Not like that, Astarte. Really *wash* them."

She goes back and rinses them again, then commences a desultory chopping operation. Ericka and I stand stupidly in a corner.

I decide I'd better take the initiative. "I'm Laura Cole," I announce hopefully, "and this is my daughter Cindy. We're traveling across country, and we found your place through a sign in the bookstore. I really appreciate the chance to stay here."

The cook extends an onion-scented paw, grips my hand firmly. "Howdy, name's Earthdyke. Where you all headed?"

"The coast. We're on our way from New York City."

"Hitching?"

"No, Greyhound."

"Oh, right." But I see we've sunk a bit in her estimation. After a minute she adds, "That gets pretty expensive, doesn't it?"

"Well, we've got month-long passes. You get where you're going."

"There's a dyke staying here, been here about a week, calls herself Railroad Sue. Seems to know quite a bit about hopping freights. She'll be at dinner. Two of you ought to talk. Might be able to save yourself some bread."

"Indeed," I mutter, thoroughly incensed, but forbearing to inquire whether Railroad Sue recommends hopping freights with kids.

Jack Kerouac again, coming back to haunt me. The butch reproach of all those cozy boxcars.

"So you're from New York, huh," she continues pleasantly. "I've been through there myself."

"What did you think of it?" My weary eyes feel as though they could sink right into my skull and be lost without a trace.

She gives a tolerant shrug. "Well, every place has its own energy, know what I mean? I couldn't get into it. But then, I've never been much of a city person. New York messed me over so bad, I had to go on a water fast for about three weeks and meditate like crazy and have healing circles and all *sorts* of shit, you know, acupuncture treatments up the ass, before I could even begin to get some decent energy going, after I left that place! I mean, talk about a left-brain, patriarchal head! And I'd only been there about a week. Think what years of that could do to you!

"Now, I'm not gonna say what's right for everybody. Maybe some dykes can deal, know what I mean? I have enough trouble dealing with Denver. Me and Mountain are fixing to get us some land with a bunch of women, maybe this year if everything works out.

"Once in a while . . . does it ever cross your mind, it might not be so bad if a tidal wave or something, you know, some volcanic eruption or whatever, some natural emanation of the Goddess, so to speak, would just kind of conveniently come along and wipe out all that urban patriarchal bullshit, give us a chance to start over?"

"Well, no," I admit. "But I'm biased, being from Brooklyn."

"Oh, right." My irony escapes her. "Just a thought. Where on the coast are you heading?"

"Seattle," I improvise. "I know some women there."

"Farout. Beautiful place. As cities go. I have some friends there myself. You ever run into a dyke named Ketchikan? Or Twig? Or Blue Whale?"

I haven't.

Fine, fine women, I'm assured.

The conversation lapses; I feel I've done my duty. I ask if it's okay to take a shower.

"Sure, go right ahead. We don't have any hot water, heater's broken this week, but you're welcome to all the cold you can use . . . Say, before you go—"

"Yes?"

"You *are* a dyke, aren't you?"

I avow my affiliation.

"Excuse me for asking. Some people think I shouldn't, but the Space *is* open to bis and even hets, and I like to be sure who it is I'm dealing with. I mean, like, if The Man comes busting in all of a sudden, I'd like to have it clear who my friends are, know what I mean?"

Despite the disclaimer, I feel she doubted me, and suspect our names have a lot to do with it. "Laura" and "Cindy" may do for the outside world, but here they ring absurdly limp and femmy. And as for possessing a *last* name—sheer gaucherie!

I should have been Subway Ellen or Pocatello.

"See you folks later," Earthdyke cheerfully reminds us. "Dinner happens somewhere around six. We ask two bucks a head, more if/less if. Done chopping carrots, Astarte? Don't you want to take Cindy outside?"

"Uh-uh," Astarte grunts—to "Cindy's" clear relief. Half-finished chopping abandoned, she idly gnaws a carrot. Her splay-footed crouch on the dirty linoleum hints she grew up in a world without furniture.

"I don't think I like it here," Ericka whispers on the stairs. "I don't want a cold shower."

"Sleep is what you need. Washing up can wait."

"How come they have those names? And who's Astarte's mom? I don't get it. And what's that shack for, in the backyard?"

Reluctant to get into an exhaustive elucidation of local customs at this point, I say we'll talk about it after we've had some rest.

"But I don't think I like that stuff that what's-her-name's fixing for dinner, and then what am I gonna eat?"

"Look, take a nap. I won't let you starve."

Ten minutes later, back from my bracing ablutions, I find her out for the count on the bare mattress. No amount of effort serves to rouse her when Astarte bellows from the second floor that dinner's almost ready. Finally I cover her with a sweater—the evening is rapidly cooling—and steel myself to meet the multitudes.

The vast, dim, ruined dining room below is full of white, mostly young, mostly crop-haired lesbians who sit jammed on benches around a rough table. Someone is ladling Earthdyke's millet stew into a plethora of mismatched bowls. Someone is slicing a leaden-textured loaf. Hoping to go unnoticed, I claim an empty place; nevertheless, almost immediately—"Hey, wait a minute, women, we've got a new syster with us in the circle, let's everyone go around and say our names," Earthdyke conscientiously insists. And I'm honored by a bewildering litany: "I'm Pat . . . I'm Fern . . . Natalie . . . Elderberry. . . ."

I do manage to attach names to several faces. The one certifiably "older" woman, probably fifty or so, with silvered hair and a riveting blue gaze, turns out to be B.D. Railroad Sue, sitting opposite me, looks more like forty. She's wiry and tanned, white showing deep in the wrinkles around her eyes, a cigarette pack sexily rolled into her T-shirt sleeve above a swell of muscle. Grudgingly, I find myself admitting she *does* look like she'd know about trains.

The two young things to my right, who eat with some awkwardness because they are holding hands beneath the table, turn out to be Cascara and Chamomile. Their drastic-dyke haircuts, men's suit pants, and round wholesome faces are so similar that they bear an unnerving resemblance to a pair of twins. Except for one factor; Chamomile, the one right next to me, is, beneath a large labyris pendant and billowy lavender smock, indubitably pregnant.

I address myself to my bread and millet stew, which I supplement recklessly with a dollop of cottage cheese from the container Cascara holds out with the ominous invitation, "Here, have some, if you're not worried about forming a lot of mucus!" The stew is lumpy and lacks seasoning. When Railroad Sue shoves a bottle in my direction—"Pour yourself a glass, if you're not another one of those drug-less, booze-less, life-less, lez-be-ens they grow around here," she chortles cynically—I'm grateful to fill my chipped, handleless cup with sour red wine.

Earthdyke, ascetically sipping herbal tea, resumes her account, interrupted by my entrance, of her sure-fire method of curing allergies by means of judicious fasting. This soon gives way to a general discussion of food: someone speaks out on the digestive evils of mixing fruits; someone else explains why we'd all be much healthier if we avoided wheat products; it is alleged that the diligent consumption of miso will help neutralize the poisons from Rocky Flats.

Suddenly Astarte begins to fuss, "Pat, Pat, I can't eat this garbage."

"Then go get some of your own stuff out of the fridge," Pat curtly instructs, and goes back to a lively debate about menstrual huts. "The thing, is, though, so many of the ancient rituals have been lost under patriarchy. And we can't just re-*invent* them, we have to re-*member* them. Read Mary Daly, you'll see."

Astarte returns from the kitchen with three naked, wrinkled hot dogs, which she devours banana-fashion.

"I thought someone told me you had a kid too," Chamomile ventures conversationally.

"She's upstairs, sound asleep. We're both pretty tired." The wine is beginning to hit, so I make an effort and add, "Do all these women live in the house, or what?"

"Oh, tonight we have a lot of dinner guests," Cascara replies for her. "We're going to a concert later on. You and Railroad Sue are the only overnighters. See, the Space collective is really just B.D., Pat, Mountain, Earthdyke—well, and of course Astarte. Me and Chamomile are sort of temporary."

"Maybe." Camomile dreamily fingers her abdomen. "It kind of depends a lot on this kid, actually."

"You mean . . . when the baby's born, you'll decide if you want to stay?"

"Well, see, depending what it *is*. They have a very firm Space policy, no pricks whatsoever, not even meter readers, so if it's not a girl . . . but I know it's gonna be. Cascara says she can tell it's a dyke by how strong it kicks!"

At mention of the name, a bit of botanical knowledge forgotten until now pops into my head: cascara is a plant, native to the Pacific Coast, renowned for the laxative properties of its bark.

"Was it hard getting pregnant?" I politely ask Chamomile.

"No, I hit the jackpot right away, it was really farout. But see, I was eating really, really healthy, you know, meditating a lot. And then Cascara would always help me and hold the turkey baster and everything. I think that's what really did it." She turns to kiss her lover on the mouth in a gesture of gratitude.

"And what will you do if—well, if it's *not* a girl?"

"I guess me and Cascara will just have to get our own place. I hope we don't have to, we certainly can't afford it. And it'd be hard, not being able to go to meetings and women's spaces together, or, like, come over here, you know, but one of us would just stay home with him. I figure that's the risk you have to take, just like you hope it's healthy but you'd still love it if it had a birth defect."

"No matter what, it'll still be our kid," Cascara confirms fiercely.

"Actually, though," Chamomile hastily adds, "the collective's been real good to us. They even said we could have the birthing here, which *does* mean the possibility of male energy in the house, for a few hours at least. Earthdyke isn't too happy about it, but . . . but that reminds me, I wanted to ask, what was *your* birthing like?"

Fuzzy with wine, for a second I draw a blank. "My birthing?" Maybe someone who believes meditation gets you pregnant really expects me to remember being born.

"You know, when you had your daughter."

"Oh, that!" I manage not to laugh. "Goodness, let's see, it was quite a while ago, and. . . ." I stall, await appropriate inspiration.

"I mean, I can't remember much about it, the way they knocked me out."

"You had her in a regular hospital?" Chamomile regards me with shocked, respectful pity, as though I've revealed I lived through the siege of Stalingrad, or was a bar dyke before Stonewall. "With painkillers and all that shit?"

"Painkillers!" I'm warming to my fiction. "Not only that – stirrups, forceps, the works. You see, I was overdue, and my obstetrician wanted to go away on vacation, so they induced labor. Then the contractions were coming way too fast, I was lying there screaming, so they came along and . . . first a spinal block. Then they totally put me under. Naturally I don't remember much."

"Oh that's awful!" Chamomile grips my hand.

"Women have suffered worse under patriarchy," I can't resist intoning.

"That's true. But is she – okay now, your kid?"

"Well, yes. I mean, she's ten years old."

"You're really lucky then, because sometimes these horrible violent patriarchal births can do all sorts of damage that comes out later on. You've met Astarte – Pat's kid, over there."

"Oh yes. Definitely."

"Well, Pat had a C-section. And sometimes I suspect that explains a lot of Astarte's problems."

"Hmm, you really think so?"

"I mean, she's just so hostile and negative a lot of the time. I don't know, I guess I sort of believe Nature takes care of things, if you do like she intends. When things go wrong that way – well, maybe that particular baby just wasn't meant to make it."

"But if it was yours, and there were complications – " I begin indignantly. Chamomile's face is peaceful, innocent, her complexion fresh and smooth as Ericka's. It's unclear to me whether she understands that she's just suggested Astarte would be better off dead.

"I try to stay centered," she replies modestly.

Cascara now reminds her they've got to get ready for the concert, and the two of them depart, still holding hands. I wish them all the luck.

Nothing prevents me from following them upstairs. I've eaten all the millet I can stomach, there's less than an inch of wine left in my cup. And still I don't move.

It's the alcohol, of course, on top of the exhaustion. The relief of having a bed, for the night at least. My child is safely sound asleep upstairs and . . . how can I explain?

190

In this ludicrous situation, I'm remembering who I am.

Say it's like this: you live in New York City. You've been out for years. And you're used to the idea; it's stopped being anything like the adventurous old days, when you hoarded your courage for weeks just to walk into some bar; when you looked at women, even on subway trains, and thought: underneath those Levis, those Gloria Vanderbilts. . . . Because, you see, you've stopped being the outsider, latent longer, furtive experimenter. You've joined, you've taken out your party card. Before you know it you're a pillar of the queer community, and *lesbian* is anything but sex: a political position, social nexus, system of supports and obligations.

Everyone you care to know is gay. Your life is a room of women. Of course you forget to hunger and thirst for them.

But, scooped out of this cozy artificial pond, cast into the high seas of a hostile planet, your attitude quickly alters. Out here in the world, they're wearing mascara, dresses. They're getting married. They're talking about their men.

And nowhere may you touch. Nor think about it.

And so, when you spot some dyke on the street in a small town, or stroll into the one gay bar in three states—what a gift, what a thrill, what balm! It's the rare affirming mirror the Village used to be: others have thought of this, I didn't just make it up.

I'm watching Railroad Sue across the table.

What I like: the small but clearly defined breasts, nipples darker circles under the clean white T-shirt. Her capable shoulders, abandon when she laughs, tosses her head back, lips spread over prominent teeth.

How she narrows her eyes, as though troubled by the sun.

How she moves.

Butch.

It could have been almost anything, of course: bare brown tits in the kitchen this afternoon. But it happens to be this.

My eyes graze hers. I wonder what she sees. Nothing, probably. She stands up, stacking dishes.

"Here, I'll help." I trail her to the kitchen.

We dump the dishes on the counter and go back for more. The pileup grows alarming. I know I should start washing, but when she guesses she'll go out back and have a smoke, I ask to bum a cigarette.

Not having smoked in years, naturally.

We sit down on rotten steps, before a vista of lettuce going to seed, the "re-membered" menstrual hut turning its back on us behind ragged shrubbery. She shakes two Marlboros out of a half-full pack. They're my favorite of filters.

I inhale, cautious as a teenage novice. The smoke tastes harsh but good.

"Whew, that's better," she breathes. "I wouldn't dare light up inside, they'd have my ass. They're a fine bunch of women, but they're all so goddamn *good*. Worse than Methodists.

"Even that B.D. And I used to know that woman. Ran into her in bars—oh, eighteen, twenty years back, when I was just a kid. She sure drank plenty then!"

"Maybe it's just as well she gave it up—but I know what you mean," I add. What differentiates all this from my adolescence is nothing much more than a trick or two I've learned: a faith in my talent for dissimulation, the control that separates me into halves—the half that goes on talking fairly normally, and the one that's feverishly conscious of proximity to a strong naked arm; how easily, accidentally, we might touch.

"And everything's goddess this and ritual that. Honest to christ, it reminds me of my folks. They were real big Christians, I guess that's why it bugs me. Every other thing you thought about doing was on their list of sins."

"At least they allow sex. Here in the Space, I mean."

My sally seems mistaken, I feel suddenly embarrassed, and can't think of anything natural to say. Finally I recall her reputation for hopping freights.

"Oh, that." She dismisses the achievement. "Yeah, I tried it a few times when I was younger and dumber, but it's not much of a way to travel. It's colder 'n shit in winter, and it's hard to figure out exactly where you're headed, and if they catch you they think it's a good joke to throw you off in the middle of nowhere. And you can run into some pretty rough customers in those cars, believe me. Man, I love trains—but let me ride with a ticket. If I have to travel cheap, I'd rather hitch. I know I'll get where I'm going quicker, be warmer and dryer at it, and probably a lot safer, too."

Since I don't dare watch her face, I'm watching her long thin hands, wondering why it should be I'm so infatuated with the contrast between a narrow blue-veined wrist and that stretchy metal watchband, the kind my father wears. "Well, that's interesting. I was curious what you'd say. I mean, I *knew* Earthdyke had to be a little over-optimistic, as far as the possibilities of doing something like that with a kid—"

"You've got a kid?"

"Yeah, she's asleep upstairs."

192

"Hey, that's farout. I used to want a kid. But it's probably just as well I never had one."

"How come?"

"I'd probably have made a lousy mother. Besides, I can see *me* pregnant."

"Well, why not? Look at Chamomile." Our cigarettes are out. I can't hope to hold her long.

"She's really into it, isn't she, poor kid. See, I've never been able to really settle down and stay in one place long enough to make much of a home life. Like even now, I can't make up my mind whether to hang around Denver and get some kind of job, or go back out to the coast again, or what. I'd like to see Alaska."

"I bet it's gorgeous there."

"Hey, listen, are you coming to this concert? It's some local dyke, supposed to be all right."

"Oh no. I've really got to get some sleep."

"I'd better vamoose, I guess. See you tomorrow, maybe."

We rise. I walk behind her, free to look. And then that's it, I'm on my way upstairs, breathless with lust, ridiculously wet, to lie down on the floor two feet from my slumbering child, in whose presence I can't even decently jerk off.

* * *

It's our second night in Denver. Josie's going out. Just for a bit, she says, to a women's bar. Railroad Sue and a couple of others are going.

"How come you have to leave me all alone?"

"I'm not leaving you all alone. There's grownups downstairs."

Yeah, plus Astarte, is the main problem. Astarte-Smartie, she ought to be called, or else Astarte-Smartass, since she thinks she knows so much.

"Be sure and come back." I laugh, to show I'm joking.

"Don't worry, kiddo. I won't be late. But you be sure and be in bed by nine. Nine-thirty at the absolute very latest. We have to get early to catch the bus."

I shut our door and concentrate on reading. I've already decided if Astarte bothers me I'll just say I'm at a good part and don't want to be disturbed.

Pretty soon I hear footsteps, then a loud knock. "Who is it?" I say, just like I didn't know.

"Astarte."

"What do you want?"

"Can I come in?"

"What for?"

"Just a visit."

"I'm busy reading. I'm at a suspenseful part."

"Just for a minute. I won't hassle you."

I'd rather not be rude. "Well, just for a minute."

Astarte comes bursting in and plops down on my mattress. She's wearing the top to a two piece bathing suit, so you could see her breasts are starting, and these real short shorts her legs are ballooning out of. Her big fat stomach sticks out about a mile.

She looks and sees I'm reading National Velvet. "I liked horse stories too, when I was your age," she goes. "Hey, where's Laura at, anyway?"

"If you mean my mom," I inform her, "she went out."

"Where to?"

"A bar."

"Who with?"

"Railroad Sue."

Astarte rolls her eyes and starts humming, "Here Comes the Bride." I pretend I didn't notice.

Then she goes, "What kind of a lesbian is she, anyway?"

"What do you mean, what kind of a lesbian?"

"Well, like my mom's a dyke sepertist."

I didn't know there were kinds. "I guess mine is too."

"Does she talk to men?"

"Well, sure. Like my father, and people like that."

"Then she's not a sepertist," Astarte goes in this I-told-you-so sort of voice.

This is getting really stupid. I remind her her minute's up.

Suddenly she gets super-friendly and announces the real reason she came up was to invite me to see her room. It won't take long, she says, and I can read my book later. I say okay. At least she'll be out of here. She might even turn out to have a TV.

We go downstairs. She's got a sign on her door, "Attention, No Grownups Allowed Beyond This Point," and inside it's painted all different colors, including orange, green, and purple, and it's a mess. There's even old sandwiches lying on the floor. I don't see a TV.

"Don't they ever make you clean your room?"

"Are you kidding? I told you it's grownup-free space, didn't I? I only clean it up when I feel like it, like maybe about once a year or so."

I don't say anything, but it smells in here.

"So what do you like to do? Wanna see my books?"

"Don't you ever watch TV?"

"Sometimes I go next door."

"Okay, let's see your books." That's polite—then I can leave.

"I have Rubyfruit Jungle, *you ever read that? It's got some pretty good parts." She starts trying to find it, picking up books and throwing them back down. They're all mixed up with clothes and games and stuff.*

"So what are you guys doing here, anyway?"

"Nothing much. Just taking a vacation."

"Where're you going?"

"We're—" All of a sudden I forget what Josie said to say, we've changed so many times. "We're . . . going to Seattle."

"What for?"

"Oh, just to. . . ."

She's staring. "Just to what?"

"Um, see my grandparents."

I guessed wrong, she jumps on me instantly. "So how come in the kitchen yesterday I heard Laura say you're going to visit friends?*"*

I'm trapped. "We're visiting them at the same time." I'd like to ask why she brings up all these questions she knows the answers to already, but I figure I better keep quiet.

She gives me a funny look, but just says, "Damn, I can't find that book. Where does your father live?"

"Back in New York."

"You see him?"

"Sometimes. Well, anyway I used to. How about yours?"

"I don't have a father," she says, loud, like it was quite a privilege.

"Well, you've got to have one somewhere."

"Not me. And Chamomile's having a baby, and it's not gonna have a father either. Unless you can call a turkey baster Daddy!" Astarte laughs. How she does it gives me goose bumps. "What's the matter, dope, you never heard of artificial insemination?"

"Yeah," I say for some reason, even though I never.

"Dykes take some sperm and stick it in themself. That way they don't have to get near a you-know-what."

"But where do they get the sperm from?"

"Anyplace. Chamomile got hers from this faggot."

"So then he's *the father," I point out.*

"No, he's not, because jerking off in a bottle's no different than peeing or shitting, that's what Earthdyke says, and you wouldn't call somebody a father just because they peed or shit in some toilet. Anyway, he's not going to help take care of the kid or anything. It's gonna be just Chamomile and Cascara's."

"Is that what your mom did, got it from a gay man too?"

"No, back then they didn't have artificial insemination."

"So how'd she have you?" I'm scared of her, she's smart. Maybe if we can just talk about her personal business for a while instead of mine, it'll stop her from asking more of her snoopy questions.

"The regular way." Astarte sounds cross. "But she says since she never saw him after that, he doesn't count as a father."

"But don't you ever wonder what he's like?"

"Uh-uh, not me. I wouldn't want some old prick bossing me around, anyway."

"My father isn't bossy," I inform her.

"Oh yeah?"

"Oh yeah."

"But did you ever live with him, though?"

"Yeah, for about a year. It was neat. My father's a history professor. We had this brownstone on a good block, with a yard and everything. I went to Lincoln Prep, that's a private school in Brooklyn."

I stop. None of that really sounds like what I meant. I wish I could tell the truth and not always be pretending, so I could talk about what it's like when your mother dies and you have to choose between two other grownups.

"So why'd you stop living there then, if it was so great?"

I shrug. "It's complicated."

"Complicated how?"

"I really don't feel like talking about it, it's not that cheerful a subject. I thought you were going to show me your books," I remind her.

She starts hunting again, but she can't find Rubyfruit Jungle. *So she says she'll show me her special secret collection, and goes over in the corner and starts moving all these piles and piles of stuff, toys she probably had since she was just a baby, blocks and puzzles and things. At the bottom of all that there's piles of books. They're paperbacks, brand new, and they mostly have the same kind of covers, a man and a lady in old-fashioned clothes.*

"Where'd you get the money to buy all these?"

"I don't buy *them, dummy. I* liberate *them. They have 'em in all the drugstores and supermarkets. I get candy too that way, whenever I want.*

"Here's a pretty good one, Bold Barefoot Bliss. *Wait, I'll find you a good part."*

I read where she points:

His arms around me, almost crushing me with the tender yet ruthless force of his implacable arousal, his lips groping mine with imperious insistence, he caught me to his heaving breast and, near swooning, I detected the perilous pressure of his inflamed manhood.

"Lord Whitelaw," I cried with all my fainting strength, "thou dost forget thyself."

But it was too late. Insensate with passion, groaning his savage need, like Excalibur into the sheath he thrust home his massive weapon.

"Gross, huh?" Astarte grabs the book back.

"Yeah." I could tell that much, even though I'd need a dictionary to understand half those words. "But how come you keep all that stuff covered up, anyway, if this is supposed to be grownup-free in here?"

"Oh well, just in case. Pat and B.D. and everybody, they don't like stuff, you know, with pricks in it, so I figure why upset them? Besides, I don't want them to know I rip off. But hey, look, what else I've got here. I borrowed this from Earthdyke."

She hands me what looks sort of like a comic book, only the name of it is, How Dykes Do it. *Inside it has a whole bunch of drawings, mostly of women without any clothes, lying on beds or floors or kitchen tables or taking showers or dancing in the woods. Even though it's all just women, it's kind of embarrassing to look at it with someone peeking over your shoulder.*

"That woman that does it draws good," Astarte says.

"Uh-huh."

"I'll show you my favorite one."

She turns to a picture of a person lying on her back, with this other one, no clothes on, crouching down, putting her face between the first one's legs. It looks sort of strange, like she has this curly beard.

"Your mom does that," Astarte goes.

"I guess that's her business," I point out.

Astarte looks disappointed. I don't know what she expects. I tell her I'm going upstairs to finish my book.

I'm halfway to the door when all of a sudden she says, "If you're supposed to be Cindy, who's Ericka?"

Count on that fart-face to make some kind of trouble.

"I'm afraid I don't know what you're talking about."

"Betcha you do."

"Betcha I do not."

"Then how come I heard your mom*"— she pronounces it like it was the dumbest, most ridiculous word in the world, in other words like she doesn't believe it for a minute—"call you that?"*

"You couldn't of. My mom calls me Cindy."

"Betcha I did."

"When?"

"A little while ago. When you were in your room. I heard her through the door."

"You mean you were sneaking around, spying on us!"

"I was not." She acts so innocent. "I just came upstairs to ask you something, but it sounded like you two were having a private talk. I didn't want to interrupt.

"I'm a pretty good sleuth, I practice all the time. And I know when people aren't who they say they are. I heard your 'mom' call you Ericka, I heard you call her Josie, and you both said you were going different places. That's already three clues."

"Liar," is all I can say. I feel scared.

She's such a showoff, she can't stop talking. "We had a woman staying here once that was Underground, you know what that is? I didn't know about it till after she left. She had a fake name too and everything. She'd bombed somewhere, I think, or something like that. What did you guys do? Are the cops looking for—her?"

All of a sudden I'm so furious. "Okay, yeah," I go, "the cops are looking for us, because we're dangerous bank robbers, but they're going to put you in prison instead, when they find out you liberated all those nasty books."

She makes this face, like I'm being unfair. "Come on, please. Honest, I won't tell."

"No!" I almost scream. "And that's final, period!"

I'm so close to her ear, she looks kind of startled.

"And you'd better not say one single word about us to anyone else, either, or I'll tell Pat and B.D. and Earthdyke about all that stuff you rip off."

"Don't get so mad. I was only curious."

"Thanks for showing me your room and everything. Now I'm going upstairs and finish National Velvet."

* * *

"Of course," says Rosemary, when I finally get her. "I'll pick you up at the station."

Simple as that. Saved.

But this is over the phone in the cramped Cheyenne terminal in late morning, thirty-some hours and four states out of Portland. Babies are screaming here and on her end, there's a cacophony of pinball and bus motors, and my light flirtation in Denver is a fast-fading memory. Now we begin the lonely Wyoming arc: Laramie, Rawlins, Rock Springs, the trajectory over into northern Utah.

Ericka dozes fitfully in my lap, then props herself to gaze, rapt as a TV viewer, out the window in facile childish acceptance of the terrifying volumes of space we're now consuming, those sheer gaping pits, townless, which wait to be filled up with whatever free enterprise may invent for the purpose: strip mines, campgrounds, junkyards, bowling alleys, missile sites, mobile home parks. I feel in my bones the peril and grinding effort, us bearing now inexorably down, tearing deep into the flesh of the continent, this west that bore me, that I deeply know, having memorized its double message in earliest sleep, long afterwards unaware it had taught me anything.

"Enough mountains for you now, kiddo?"

She nods. "They're so *craggy*." All around us the tourists are slinging adjectives: gorgeous, exquisite, awesome.

It was all about the land from the beginning. It always is, once you get as far as the Rockies. Here the imprint of trees and sky was on you first; here, beneath the mere outlandish, prodigal *beauty* which parents and teachers incessantly pointed to and visiting relatives invariably gushed over, the earth was reality, was unarguable power. It still could tip the balance with its mass, the sheer ungovernable extension of it, set over against the thin bustle of cities, of scattered farms and scant coast-huddled towns. It wore lightly the brittle trusses of the highways, the preening historical markers which boasted deeds and dates. Here, there was little History for ballast, and the light encrustations of human habitation and commerce might yet be half-expected to disappear with the shrug of an earthquake, the flick of a tidal wave. No matter that you grew up in the suburbs: you were casually exposed to stars and mountains, left to play in sample patches of wilderness.

All of this meant you developed, very early, a nameless, anachronistic sense of connection to things you had no business being in love with, things that would cause you grief, since their days were clearly numbered. For the logical culmination of the process that had given you the land was killing it, not by inches but by miles, not by generations but by years. The mechanisms of extinction were frank and public. When the hillside where you'd played, rolled in the tall grass, eaten the fallen plums from the half-wild tree, was levelled one day for a concrete cloverleaf, no appeal was possible. You watched with a child's stoic comprehension, and knew yourself the spawn of thieves and spoilers – yet knew yourself, too, the heir of conquering heroes, and drank in the pioneer legends, and pitied the Indian kids you glimpsed on the reservations through clouds of dust as the station wagon roared through.

Night quells the tourist babble, but not my thoughts. Our progress is tedious, labored, along the diagonal the map reveals strung from Ogden north to Boise. When I close my eyes and try to rest, I see too much: us locked in the hold of a flimsy metal boat, adrift on the wide, slow swells of the continent, nameless and aimless, about to be engulfed. Was I destined to be swallowed from the beginning, cling as I would to that tiny fleck of rock, Long Island barely moored to America, washed by an always European sea?

Beneath, such depths. And everything falls away. And even wide awake, I shrink from the pale stare of that face hanging suspended outside the glass. I seem to have forgotten exactly who that is, who's Josie, who is she, where's Rhea, where's my life—that life I so deliberately accreted on New York's granite shelf of old world sorrow. In rooms thick with books and streets thick with traffic and menace; peering through rationed windows at the sky; hurtling through the subway's interstellar reaches; always talking, always drinking coffee. . . . Seen from the distance of this Idaho night, its fundamental hush barely disturbed by the drone of the bus motor, that whole cramped, frantic, verbal Eastern seaboard, that gabbing, blabbing, bickering multitude, seems to me to be hiding from the massive grief that reveals itself in silence.

Somewhere after Boise I lose my grip, tumble into the cauldron of dreams. Here the decor is maximum security, the face behind metal Rhea's, delivering instructions in a disciplined monotone, her eyes controlled, impassive; only, once, that smile flashed like ID against the grate, telling me *love*, begging me to hurry. I'm the lucky one, free, my task to break her out. Then long windowless corridors and fumbling terror, culminating in a stylized panorama of the prison yard crosshatched with beams from a searchlight beneath which women inmates perform calisthenics that look like a Chinese revolutionary ballet. Rhea stands at the very center, arms outstretched toward the flying machine that hauls me inexorably up and away from her, its controls mysterious, beyond my reach.

She always said she'd travel west with me.

I wake tasting failure. I can't quite shake the notion that she's out there somewhere; tonight everything in my old life seems equidistant from this mobile island of half-reality, Ericka beside me, my reflection in the window, the heavily breathing bodies all around us, each steeped in its broth of troubles.

Finally, first light. My sense of reality hardens as the hills repossess themselves of their familiar outlines. We're in Oregon now, not the green one of popular legend, but the dry Eastern terrain, sparse settlements strewn about the cracked brown landscape like weeds sprung up in pavement.

Soon after we leave Pendleton the plain begins to drop away beneath us. Cliffs lift rapidly on either side: the Columbia River Gorge. The day is clear with only a few high clouds. After some minutes of watching for the first glimpse of Mt. Hood, I decide maybe I'm remembering wrong, maybe the mountain isn't visible from this angle after all. We parallel the river's downstream course past The Dalles and Hood River, and then we're into the Oregon of postcards, the heights above us thickly treed except for the sheerest faces, narrow waterfalls streaking exposed rock. Then I realize I haven't been able to pick out Mt. Adams over on the Washington side, either, and it strikes me there's been a suspicious thickening of the air. Not coastal cloud cover, for the sky overhead is still blue—yet by the time we reach Cascade Locks, the atmosphere duplicates the haziness of the lower Hudson Valley on a warm, still afternoon.

Well, I haven't been back in quite a few years. Some things were bound to have changed. At least the highway is still only four lanes wide, not too heavily traveled. My companion is uncritical of the air quality, and quite impressed by wonders both natural and manmade: she cranes her neck for Multnomah Falls, exclaims over Bonneville Dam.

And soon we're roaring over the multi-bridged Willamette, toward the West Hills baking in the odd, wrong haze—"This is Portland? It's so *little*," cries Ericka—and through unlittered downtown streets, into the Greyhound station.

We claim our luggage, then enter the waiting room, crowded now at four o'clock but just as musty and small-town as I remember from Scrubb days. I begin checking faces. I hope to avoid being spotted looking stupidly expectant, but Rosemary hails us, "Josie! Ericka!"; advances toward us, baby on one arm, the other extended in welcome.

At her request, we're to use our real names here. Though she didn't hesitate for a minute to say she'd put us up, she did volunteer over the phone that it would make things simpler for her if Peter didn't have to hear the whole complicated story. She'd just tell him, she said, that her old college roommate was traveling with a young friend, and would be paying them a visit.

Naturally I agreed, though I was slightly scandalized at her matter-of-factness about deceiving a husband.

Now I cringe at her public greeting while reminding myself it's quite paranoid to suppose that anyone in the room can care what our names are. Rosemary's style was always demonstrative, and even back at Scrubb I can remember wondering where she'd come by a manner I vaguely recognized as out of keeping with Mercer Island, the affluent Seattle suburb where her architect parents lived. She hugs me as best she can while juggling the baby, then hugs Ericka, who looks shy but not displeased. "God, am I glad to see the two of you! I can't believe I made it here on time, I was terrified I wouldn't find parking. You don't know how they've been tearing up these streets!"

She really does seem glad, and I'm enormously relieved. Though she sounded fine on the phone, I wondered afterwards whether she'd turn out to be entirely in sympathy with my mission, once she'd had time to consider. Timid she never was, but I thought she might have changed, given this new life of hers of which I've formed a partial impression through sporadic correspondence and reports from mutual friends. I haven't actually seen her in seven or eight years, not since she "came in from the cold" as she once wryly put it in a letter about her decision to move in with Peter.

Though her manner seems not to have altered, her look is entirely different. At Scrubb, where her nickname was Queen of the Underground, she aimed for specific effects. She favored diaphanous garments – gowns, wide pants, flimsy gathered tops – augmented by bangles, rings, beads, hats, scarves, and even veils, most of this stuff acquired secondhand in Portland's marvelous thrift stores, the Volunteers of America being her favorite. With her long full legs and unfashionably big breasts, she used to make me think of some nineteenth century courtesan got up like Janis Joplin. It was one of her carefully cultivated eccentricities to avoid displaying flesh. Even after we started living together, I rarely saw much more of her unclothed than one sees of a conservative nun on the street, and the piquant contrast of this outlandish reticence with the well-known fact that she worked as a topless dancer did a good deal to enhance her legend and even won her imitators among the female student population.

She categorically forbade her friends to visit the bars where she was working, but once a bunch of us went anyway for a joke, and I had the thrill of sipping a screwdriver while watching her, clad in a sequined purple G-string, pink pasties, and black spike heels, agitate her naked hips to the inspirational strains of "This Is the Dawning of the Age of Aquarius" before plucking a few crumpled bills from among the footlights that lined the tacky little stage and flouncing off to the dressing room. She was furious at our prank, and I felt rather bad about it, but masturbated for weeks to the memory of her up there.

Her motions seem heavier now, some old elasticity lost. Bra straps show under her tank top, her shorts reveal cellulite. Her famous red-gold hair, which once hung to her waist, is lopped off pragmatically at shoulder length. Like me, she looks young and tired on the way to being middle-aged. She looks like a Portland housewife.

We follow her out to where her battered compact is parked. Ericka and I manage to stuff some of our luggage into the already cluttered trunk, then squeeze into the back seat with the rest. Rosemary buckles the baby into his carseat and apologizes for the rotten shock absorbers. If we decide to go swimming tomorrow, she promises, we'll take the station wagon, let Peter drive this buggy for a change.

Ericka perks up. "Is there a pool?"

"Pool! There's a whole river—several, actually."

It's my mother's polite phrase I find myself uttering: "Look, Rosemary, please don't feel you have to entertain us."

"Come on, Josie, how long since we saw each other? Anyway, you're not interrupting much. Riding herd on one toddler and in-cubating one foetus is about all I can manage at the moment, and I can do both at the beach."

"You're pregnant again?" It comes out a bit ungracious.

"Didn't I tell you? Just about four months. I guess I forgot to mention it when you called, I was so surprised to hear your voice. No, actually you couldn't have come at a better time. Even the weather's been gorgeous. The past two summers were so rainy, last year I don't think we had more than a couple days this warm the whole season."

"Isn't it a little smoggy? Coming in we could hardly see the West Hills."

"Well, yeah, I guess." She seems unperturbed. "It probably *has* gotten a bunch worse since you were here last."

"Do you ever see Mt. Hood anymore?"

"Oh sure, sometimes, especially after a rain. Lots of afternoons you just kind of see the tip, you know, levitating above the haze. You should ask Peter more about it, he'll give you a whole rap. They've got all those statistics where he works in the Office of City Planning."

*   *   *

"*Ericka,*" *Rosemary calls, "I bet Petey would like it if you'd take him out in the back yard while Josie and I finish our coffee."*

It's the morning after our first night in Portland. I guess she means they want to talk private, either that or they think I've watched enough cartoons, but it's okay with me. Petey likes me, I think.

Petey has his sandbox and toys in the back yard. It's fenced in, so I just have to make sure he doesn't go into the vegetable garden and step on stuff, or put things in his mouth. They have a patio with lawn furniture like Grandma does in Florida, only bigger. The house is brand new, all on one floor. It has three bedrooms, I'm staying in one. Josie's sleeping in the rec room.

It's going to be hot again, so we're going swimming for sure. Rosemary also said maybe one day soon we could go pick strawberries at this U-pick place. I didn't know what U-pick was, but she explained it to me. She said we could pig out *on strawberries. I laughed, I never heard that expression before.*

I like her. I think her hair is beautiful. I wish mine could be that color. We had this whole long conversation this morning after Peter, that's her husband, left for work, while Josie was in the shower. She said I could help her make strawberry jam. She can hardly wait till she has a kid like me that's old enough to do stuff, instead of just needing things all day like Petey does.

She'd like her next baby to be a girl. I suggested to her maybe she should have that test like Brenda did, so she could find out in advance, but she said she guessed she'd wait and take pot luck. She can be really funny, how she talks. She has this way of speaking with a cigarette in the corner of her mouth like a real tough lady, only it's just an act. I told her I heard it wasn't that good to smoke if you're going to have a baby, and she said she knew but she hadn't been able to quit, only cut down, so it looked like the kid was going to have to get used to smoking a cigarette once in a while.

We still don't know what we're doing next, exactly. I asked Josie this morning. She said give her time.

*   *   *

"So what do you suppose he'll do?" Rosemary leans back indolently exhaling smoke through her nostrils, a typical Queen of the Underground attitude. Every so often a gesture or phrase of hers takes me back so vividly to our midnight roommate rap sessions—but it's in her alarmingly contemporary kitchen that we're nursing our morning coffee, and beyond the sliding glass, beyond the barbecue, Ericka is to be seen keeping an eye on us while ostensibly tending Petey. She'll be in here any minute on some pretext or other; meanwhile, I'm revelling in the luxury of having another adult to tell my troubles to.

"Her father? I can't imagine. Aside from the fact that I'm probably not exactly the world's most penetrating analyst of the male psyche, I haven't been able to do much coherent thinking. I've just been running since Brooklyn. It's like it's taken everything I've got simply to get us across the goddamned continent more or less in one piece."

"But you don't think he'd actually prosecute."

"Well, I didn't at first. I'm not sure anymore. Like I said, his theme song when I called from Arizona was how he'd throw the book at me if I didn't bring her back – 'safe and sound and in good health' was how he put it, as though if he didn't spell it out I might send her to play in traffic.

"If he could get to us right now, he might do a lot of things. But the point is, he'd have to track us down, and that's not such a simple matter." I summarize Luce's lawyer friend's argument about why the FBI wouldn't want to get involved. "Since local cops around the nation obviously have plenty to do besides tracking down some smalltime lesbian kidnapper from New York, short of Daniel's hiring his own detective – "

"You're sure he wouldn't try that? The dude sounds pissed, frankly."

"He might, I guess. I really just don't know."

"But Luce thought – I mean, aside from that – you'd be safe with the ID and all? I'd hate to see you busted in any case, of course, but especially with a kid along like that – "

"Luce was fairly confident that as long as this is just for a short time and I'm using the aliases and the ID and stuff, I don't have too much to worry about. Of course to her this is very small potatoes."

"How *is* she, by the way? Still quoting Chairman Mao?" Rosemary's sarcasm sounds affectionate. She and Luce never had much use for one another during the brief period when they intersected in Portland, primarily during my last semester at Scrubb when I was friends with both of them. It happened to be the spring of the Cambodian invasion, and Luce flourished on the strike committee at Portland State while Rosemary spent most of her time holed up writing papers, gripped by a methedrineamplified resolve to wipe out several years of Incompletes and graduate on time.

"God, no. She hasn't quoted him in years. But she's still going strong, she's joined a sectarian group. That'll be her life, I guess. It's really too bad."

"Sectarian group?" Rosemary seems surprised. "You mean, like, fundamentalist? I never would have—"

"No, no." Her simplicity is touching. "A political group. You know. Very dogmatic. A waste of her talents, as far as I'm concerned."

"Oh." Rosemary shrugs. "Well, at least she's doing *something*."

Her almost wistful tone makes me look sharply at her, then wait a decent interval to inquire, "What about you? How are things with you?"

Last night we had no time for catching up. The evenings are sacred to Peter, that's clear already—and so far this morning my old friend seems a lot more precise and energetic in talking about the past than accounting for the present.

"I'm just fine." She laughs hoarsely. "Worn out half the time—I had a lot of trouble with morning sickness these past couple months, but I'm pretty much over that. No, everything's okay. I'm really doing great. Peter's really sweet, I guess you—well, I'm sorry you couldn't get a very clear sense of him. He can be withdrawn like that, when he doesn't know people."

"He certainly seems to be a devoted father." After the perfunctory introductions, he virtually ignored Ericka's and my presence at his dinner table last night. As soon as he'd finished eating, he whisked Petey off to play, urging Rosemary to stack the dishes in the sink and join them on the patio, it was such a nice evening. At first I thought perhaps he suspected something, but relaxed a little when it occurred to me that more likely he was simply uptight in the presence of his wife's famous man-eating New York lesbian friend.

"Oh, he's a very involved father. He's crazy about Petey. Actually, he's a lot better parent than I am—more patient and everything. Too bad he has so little time home. God, when I think of the creeps I used to hang out with at Scrubb, how they'd have been as fathers—" We set off on another round of reminiscence, and it's some time before I get around to the question that's been on the tip of my tongue: how long we can stay.

"Oh Joze"—she uses the old form, forgotten since Portland days—"I'm *so* glad to have you. Don't worry about that yet."

"No, let's be realistic. I've got to make plans. And I don't want to cause trouble between you and Peter. I mean, how thrilled can he be to have us crashing here? Does he really buy that story about us flying out to Portland on the spur of the moment?"

Rosemary flings her bright hair back in the old imperious gesture. She's got a silver ring she's been toying with, turning it over and over, tossing it up and catching it in one hand. Seeing I've noticed, she hides it between her knees.

"Actually, I don't care. He owes me one."

"Oh." I'm taken aback by the defiant sound of this.

She perceives the need for further explanation. "Basically, we live his way much more, I mean if you compare what both of our lives were like before we met. He's always been settled and predictable. It's all for the best—well, you know all about that, my life was a mess and I wouldn't go back—but I don't think it hurts him to be shaken up just a little every so often.

"I really do go along with most of what he wants. This second kid—it's fine with me and all, but he's the one that really pushed for it. You should see him, he's just so *into* the whole thing, it's funny in a way, I mean he's so worried about everything I eat now I've got a bun in the oven, bugs me to death if he catches me with a beer. Usually I let him have his way. It doesn't make much difference to me, one way or the other."

This seems to open the door to larger issues—"bun in the oven," I note, sounds positively bitter—but I only ask her for an estimate of how long we'll be able to stay.

"A week, say? I wish it could be a month."

"Fine, that's fine. I'll plan on about a week. It makes a good breather for Ericka and me."

She wants to make sure I understand about Peter. "Actually, he's too good for me. I mean, he's just so fundamentally decent and upright and non-cynical. Not like I always was, bitchy and alienated. Like, he's not just putting it on, he really *believes* you follow the rules and go through the proper channels, and if something's fucked, you fight like hell to change it, but you do it by the book, everything legal, aboveboard. I mean, he believes in the *constitution,* crap like that. . . . I really admire him for it, in a way."

She's fidgeting with her ring again, spinning it like a top, rolling it hoop-fashion across the formica table, then arresting it with a finger. "Joze, I've been meaning to tell you—I guess it's been months since I wrote, hasn't it? I'm sorry, I should have been better. I felt so awful when I heard about Rhea."

I see she means it, so we talk a little. I tell her how it feels like having died myself, like having been run over by a freight train and left without a scratch. I almost start to cry, but Ericka comes in.

"God it's late," Rosemary covers for me, "I ought to get dressed." I blow my nose and offer to make lunch.

But in fact she doesn't get up right away, just sits there in her robe and frowns at the coffee cups, bare knees drawn up beneath her thrust-out chin, splayed bare feet dirty, the red-gold stubble on her pale calves precisely evocative of that damning phrase *poor grooming* which meant something to our mothers. As I lay out slices of bread on the butcher block and hunt roast beef and lettuce, I feel we might almost be two adolescents cheating on our diets, raiding the refrigerator during a babysitting stint in some suitably gilded suburb.

When in fact the burden of proof is now on us. Rosemary's toy, I notice, is back on its proper finger. And this wasn't supposed to happen to us, ever, but it's her wedding ring.

* * *

We went to the beach, which is at the Sandy River. It was lots different than Brighton Beach or Coney Island or Riis Park or any of those. There weren't very many people and most of them were white and there wasn't any lifeguard and the water felt like it had icecubes in it. Rosemary said that's because it comes off of a glacier on the side of Mt. Hood.

People climb Mt. Hood. I'd like to do that. It's neat around here, the mountains and trees and things. I like how you could pick stuff, like strawberries. I found out it used to be an orchard before, where Rosemary's house is at. That's why there's filbert trees in the back yard. The filbert nuts aren't ready yet, though. Rosemary said they'd get more if they'd spray the trees, but her and Peter don't want to spray because Petey plays out there. She said it's too bad what happened to the orchard, they cut down a lot of trees to build the houses. I asked how come they bought a new house. She said Peter wanted them to get an old place which they could have renovated and everything, but she doesn't have the energy right now.

Rosemary reminds me of Brenda in some ways. They both complain about no energy. But she says fuck sometimes, which Brenda never does. Also, Brenda has a job of course, even though she's also pregnant. I don't know if I'd like to be like Rosemary and stay home all the time. I think I might get bored. I asked if she thought she'd ever get a job, and she said she guessed she'd have to eventually, "Either that or it's gonna be curtains."

"What's that mean?" I said. I was thinking of real curtains.

"Death on a Mastercharge. Financial ruin."

I guess she just meant they needed more money. Once when I asked her if it was okay that Petey kept on playing with some dust—there's quite a lot of dustballs around her house—she made some comment about guessing she just wasn't cut out for the life of a housekeeper. "So, you could be a lesbian," I said. I mean, I was just joking, but I was thinking, like with Mommy and Josie and other friends of theirs, they never seemed concerned about housewife type things. They'd just clean when they got around to it. But then I felt bad I said it, in case it was rude to Peter.

*   *   *

"California money. . . !"

Earlier in the day Rosemary employed this contemptuous phrase in explaining to me how the transformation of Burnside came about. That street, its name anciently synonymous with Skid Row in Portland, has undergone the predictable renaissance, and most of the winos and hoboes and hookers are gone, along with the bars and missions and pawnshops. Now, as I trudge past lot after rail-fenced, landscaped lot on the fringes of her raw development, that superior tone seems to me to have been misplaced. Foundations still gleam naked, not yet obscured by foliage. Despite the nationalist pride displayed on bumper stickers ("Don't Californicate Oregon!"), it appears the natives are playing it both ways.

I'm headed for Wyeast Mall and the nearest pay phones. Wyeast, of course, is Mt. Hood's "Indian name." And sure enough, the mountain hangs before me, a presence brooding in the dubious air above a vast, square, shit-colored, hangar-like structure marooned in a sea of asphalt. Snows rose-tinted by the setting sun, it's a fuzzy replica of the old Hood, that sharp, austere duenna of the Willamette they still show off on the postcards.

I cross the parking lot, glide through automatic doors, and come upon a very large sign, a sort of bas-relief in colored plastic: Disney-type cartoon Indians purport to retell "The Legend of Wyeast." *Here, within sight of the venerable Wyeast himself on ground where Northwest Indians once gathered 'round the blazing campfire" to relate his awesome saga, we proudly dedicate Wyeast Mall to the greater shopping convenience of the citizens of Multnomah County.*

Muttering imprecations against western civilization, I hurry through the great, Muzak-suffused concourse, past stores selling every necessity of life from peat moss to bathroom tile. I locate a bank of phone booths, enter one, and empty my pockets of all the dimes and quarters stored up against this moment. Then I unfasten my watch and set it on the shelf where I won't forget to keep an eye on it. Luce thinks calls can be traced in about ten minutes, possibly less these days.

Brenda picks up on the second ring.

"Hello. Daniel, please."

"Who's — sure — just a min —" The panic and, for some reason, embarrassment mingled in her voice indicate she thinks she's recognized me. A hand is clamped over the telephone.

Thirty seconds pass.

"Daniel Fein speaking." Armored, gruff. Boyscout: everything to be prepared.

"Hello, Daniel. Josie. I called to talk."

"Where's Ericka? Let me speak to her."

"She's not with me at the moment, she can't come to the phone. But I want you to know everything's okay. There's really no need at all for you to be concerned, I want you to know that. I just called so we could discuss . . . how to settle all this."

"I demand to speak with my daughter."

"Daniel." I close my eyes. Ninety seconds. "Look, Daniel, I don't have long to talk. Now you must have gotten my letter, you know all about my position, so I won't bother to repeat myself. The important thing is for us to reach some kind of agreement, something where she spends time with you and she spends time with me, so we can be finished with this nonsense."

"Whose nonsense?"

"What?"

"Whose nonsense? I mean, whose fault is all this mess supposed to be, anyway?"

"What difference does that make? We've got to find some compromise everyone can live with."

"You call it a compromise when you get exactly what you wanted in the first place by holding a gun to Brenda's and my head?"

"Daniel, I know this has been no fun for you and Brenda, but remember it's been rough on me too, not to mention Ericka."

"It's been hell for Brenda and me. But we're not going to be bullied. If I agree to talk things over in a general way, it'll be *after* I've had a chance to speak to my daughter."

"I don't think that's advisable at this point."

"Josie, let's get this straight. You and I are not at a negotiating table. You are not Ericka's parent. No court in the land would uphold these claims of yours—"

A recorded, official voice desires more money. I deposit quarters, repeat old arguments.

"Let me speak to her."

"No, Daniel."

"Then how am I supposed to believe she's choosing to stay with you?"

"Do you really think I'd hold her against her will?"

"There's all kinds of coercion."

"What's that supposed to mean?"

"Josie, you are a powerful figure in Ericka's life. You have a lot of influence, and you've abused it."

"What choice did I have? What choices did you allow me?"

"Someone who really loves a child doesn't kidnap her."

"Oh bullshit, Daniel. You read that in a book." Five minutes, my watch says. And I'm losing control fast. "Look, I didn't call you up to listen to a lecture. I think maybe I'd better go for now. I'll call back in a few days."

"No, don't hang up. Listen to me a minute. Bring her back and I won't prosecute."

"Don't do me any favors."

"Now wait, Josie, listen. We could settle this, it'd be better for everyone. You'll correspond with her, talk on the phone, visit us in Cleveland if you want. . . . Though I must say, after this past week. . . . But even now, I'm prepared to be perfectly—"

"I've heard all this before."

"No, wait."

"What?" I shouldn't be listening at all, it's probably just the old glass-of-water-at-bedtime trick: keep her on the line as long as possible, I can hear the helpful man from Ma Bell advise.

Daniel's voice is softer, almost wheedling. "I wish you could see what we're going through with this. Not just Brenda and me. Leah's heartbroken. She can't understand where her big sister went."

I repeat that a tough time's been had by all.

"That's just my point. Consider Ericka. Just imagine the problems this is going to create for her later on."

"I'll take my chances. She's handling it, Daniel."

"But isn't it obvious to you this isn't going to work? You haven't a legal leg to stand on. You can't run forever. Even if I actually were the monster of a father you've chosen to paint me as in your delusional scheme, it's hard to imagine how you justify subjecting a ten-year-old. . . .

"Anyway, aside from that, in a court situation—I mean, *we* move in liberal circles, but in that context . . . it won't be simply any child-snatching. It'll be an adult lesbian who's abducted a preadolescent girl. Explain that to a jury."

I hate him, the coolness with which he covers himself. "No, you mean *you'll* explain it. You're threatening me with—"

"Josie, just calm down, I am not *threatening* you with anything, I'm simply pointing out the fact that the average American harbors certain prejudices. And if you think I'll hesitate to prosecute because—"

I use the only power at my disposal. "Goodbye, Daniel. I'll speak to you again." And flee through the mall's chill wastes like a panicked shoplifter.

* * *

Rosemary and Peter have this neat kind of shower in the bathroom that's connected to their bedroom. Peter isn't here, he's at a meeting, so Rosemary said I could use it if I want. It has a glass door on it that keeps the water in, and this dial you turn to make it hot or cold. There's this peppermint soap of Rosemary's, I'm using it all over.

I get the feeling something's happening, I don't know what exactly. Josie went out for a walk after dinner, and now she's talking to Rosemary.

Wouldn't it be strange if my father and Josie couldn't decide anything and her and me just kept moving around to different places? I think I'd get tired of that. It reminds me of this story I read once in a library book, about The Man Without A Country. See, this man said he didn't like America, so he got punished by having to sail around in a boat and not belong anyplace in particular.

I'm clean now, I'm turning off the shower. The bathroom is steamy all over, like in a thick fog. I'm putting on my nightshirt and hanging up the bathmat and remembering to take my towel with me, so I don't leave a mess. I don't want Rosemary to think we're rude guests! I'd like to stay here as long as we could.

I don't hear those guys. They were in the kitchen before. I'm going and getting a drink of apple juice.

They're on the patio. The door is closed, but I get the feeling they're talking serious—like, you know, the way you could usually tell even if you can't tell the words when grownups' voices get a certain way.

"Bastard," Rosemary goes. I could hear that perfectly.

I want to know who's a bastard, so I close the refrigerator and tiptoe over by the sink, where the window's part way open.

"I'm not sure what to think," Josie's saying, quieter. "On the other hand, he blustered a bit less. That could mean he's softening, or—"

"But you can't count on that."

Josie answers something I can't hear. I lean over the sink and put my ear as close as I could to the screen. They're sitting on lawn chairs facing the other way.

"Who knows what evil lurks, or doesn't lurk." That's Josie again. "Time will tell."

"He's definitely trying to intimidate you."

"Not to mention the guilt trip aspect, which is actually most effective. I mean, of course I worry about Ericka's—"

"You've come this far. Don't listen to the fucker."

It's obviously my father they're discussing. Who Rosemary never even met, so what gave her the right to call him cursewords?

"On the other hand, the . . . psychological warfare doesn't prove anything, either. I mean, how am I supposed to guess what it means when he says . . . it's impossible, absolutely impossible, trying to make these decisions in the dark."

Rosemary snaps her fingers. "Men are such a groove."

"Careful, now, don't go generalizing."

They both laugh. I don't see what's funny.

"But seriously, Joze, I am concerned. I mean, just supposing they managed to trace that call—"

I'm holding my breath to hear. I'm furious. I just figured out Josie went and called my father without telling me, and now she's sitting there talking the whole thing over with somebody who's not even involved.

". . . worries me too. Suppose you could be charged with—"

"Oh, that doesn't bother me." Rosemary again. "I'd say I didn't know. I really don't think they'd mess with that anyway, this is hardly the Hearst case after all. But just in terms of your and Ericka's safety—"

"So, where's safe? Alaska?"

"Good place to disappear."

"Speaking of . . . maybe I'd better go check. Seems like a long time since I sent her to take her shower."

I hop down from the sink quick, but she still sees me.

"Goodness, kiddo, what are you doing in here in the dark?"

"Getting some apple juice." I feel embarrassed. I don't know why, it serves her right I listened.

"Well, get it then, and go watch a little TV if you want to before bed. But make sure you don't spill anything on the livingroom carpet." She says it cross, like she doesn't quite believe me, but she couldn't prove I was doing anything.

* * *

"Goddamn, I'm sick of this beer. I think I'd rather be drinking piss."

We're still sitting out back on the patio, dusk thickening around us. It's a warm night, sticky for these regions. I started monitoring the hedge for fireflies before I remembered there are none on the West Coast.

"I could use a shot of whiskey."

I decline to encourage Rosemary by answering. She's really just showing off, looking for a chance to complain about Peter's strictures, which I consider to be quite reasonable in this instance. Peter himself is still at his Community Board meeting. The children are in bed.

"Do you really think I'm doing the right thing?"

Rosemary squints at me through her Blitz-Weinhardt bottle. "About Eugene, you mean? Yeah, I think it's a good plan." She and I have concluded that maybe the best idea is for me to find a place where Ericka and I can settle down for a month or two. Eugene is near enough to Portland that we could come up for the day, yet far enough away that even if tonight's call were traced, our whereabouts wouldn't be totally obvious.

"No, I didn't mean about Eugene. I meant in general." Now that my plans are settled, I feel freer to probe motivations. Despite my affection for her and considerable gratitude, I've been a bit uneasy all along about her unquestioning support. I want something more than loyalty, and I'm not sure how much she understands.

"You mean, should you have –?"

"Do you see anything in what he said? Should I have left her with him?"

She hesitates just a moment. "No, I'm sure you did right."

"But why? What makes you sure?"

"Just watching the two of you, how you interact. It's obvious there's real caring there, coming from both sides."

"Yeah, great. I guess that would be enough – if I were her mother."

"What do you mean?"

"I mean, in the eyes of the world affection from a parent, a *real* parent, would be sufficient reason. But what would you think," I hypothesize rather harshly, "if you opened up the *Oregonian* and saw a picture of some woman, an utter stranger, in custody, trussed up in handcuffs and the whole bit, looking the way they always look in those shots, like she hasn't slept in a week – and the headlines read, 'Lesbian Kidnap Case'."

"That's a fairly slanted way of putting it."

"Sure. But it's true. What would you think?"

Rosemary seems pained. She slaps at a mosquito. "Joze, look, I know you. You're my friend."

"That's exactly what bothers me."

"How come?"

"Oh, shit." Do I really have to explain? "I can't be everybody's friend. I can't go out on the streets of Portland or Park Slope and introduce myself and campaign on the nonbiological parents' rights ticket. I mean, what you're implying is that's what it would take for people not to go bazooey."

"That wasn't just a rhetorical question, when I asked what you thought. Daniel really upset me. It's heavy, what I'm putting Ericka through."

I stop. It all seems inadequate. Rosemary knows three worlds: Mercer Island, hippiedom, this. She lacks all the requisite political references.

"I admire you enormously," she announces.

"Whatever for?"

"For having the guts to – just pick up and *do* it. Hold your breath and take the plunge. Sometimes I think, man, what's stopping me, *really*?"

I feel uneasy. "Stopping you from what?"

"Anything." She laughs sarcastically. "Heading for the hills."

"I don't understand. Are things – I mean, is Peter –"

"Oh, Peter's fine. It's not Peter's fault. *He's* not the problem. It's me." She picks her beer bottle label like a scab. I await revelations.

"You did know about me and Ilona Matthews."

Ilona Matthews? "What was there to know?" Visions of a tall, pale, speedily gaunt person who was up and down the stairs to Rosemary's crepuscular boudoir rather frequently that last semester at Scrubb, during most of which time, it's true, I was too preoccupied with my own troubles to perceive very accurately what was going on around me.

Ilona was a philosophy major. She was doing her senior project on Logical Positivism – certainly an eccentric project topic, but Ilona was expected to be eccentric. Her fingers were nicotine-stained from the cigarettes she rolled herself. She was said to deal acid, which was thought odd in a woman, and nobody seemed to know whom or even whether she fucked. Still, she somehow escaped the usual Gertrude-and-Alice jokes. And Rosemary's boyfriend then was Stan Scudder, campus dope dealer, village gossip, anomalous son of a Mormon grain merchant from La Grande, Oregon. Stan and Rosemary were considered the perfect couple, sort of the Scrubb equivalent of the football hero paired up with the homecoming queen.

"I always assumed you knew," Rosemary's saying. "It just never occurred to me you didn't guess. I mean, of course I was paranoid as hell, I thought *everybody* knew I was sleeping with her. When I walked across campus I used to feel like I had some kind of brand on my forehead or something. While trying, naturally, to look totally cool. You remember how it was, how we always tried to be cool."

"Oh, I remember," I say, wondering whether to tell her how much I'd wanted her for a couple of months the previous fall. "You didn't tell anyone?"

"Nope, not a soul."

"In the middle of the sexual revolution."

But we get no further with these confidences. There's a click and grinding shudder as Peter, predictable as the clock-ingesting crocodile, signals his approach by activating the remote-control opener on the garage door.

Rosemary snatches up the beer bottle and slips it beneath her chair along with her cigarette pack and ashtray, but when her husband comes along a minute later his first comment after switching on the light and inquiring why we're sitting out here in the dark is a reproving, "Drinking again, hon?" He stands behind her chair, rests his hands on her bare shoulders.

"Girls' night in," she retorts playfully.

"Well, I'm home now. How about hitting the hay?"

* * *

I don't want to live in Alaska.

That's what I wake up thinking, but it takes me a minute to even figure out where the idea came from. Then I remember, like a bad dream, hearing Josie and Rosemary talking on the patio last night.

I'm also thinking about my father. Stuff I like to do with him. Like when we went up to Boston for that seder at Grandma and Grandpa Fein's, and he took me to the museum while Brenda stayed home with Leah. He's so smart, the way he explains things.

"What's the matter, kiddo? Get up on the wrong side of the bed?" Josie asks in this super-cheerful voice, part way through breakfast. I hate when grownups bug you like that. I don't hassle Josie when she's in a bad mood.

I don't say anything, and after a minute she says, well, maybe we can talk it over later, she thought we should do some shopping up at Wyeast Mall, and she might buy me lunch, how would I like that?

After breakfast I start to go outside, but Rosemary asks if I'll take Petey with me. I say okay, but right away I'm sorry. He follows me around like a lost puppydog. I decide to try an experiment, so I pick him up and bounce him on my lap and whisper in his ear any old thing, like, "Your mom's gonna run away and leave you, you're gonna be an orphan." He's such a dummy, he thinks it's something good, just because I use a nice voice. He claps his hands and shrieks, "Ecka, Ecka," which is his idea of how you say my name, till I could slap him if he was my kid. Then I feel bad and give him a horsey ride.

The Mall isn't far. I think it's very convenient, with these stores all bunched together, so you don't have to get wet if it starts to rain. We should have that in Brooklyn, it's also air conditioned.

I ask Josie what we're shopping for.

"Oh, I have a couple things I need from the drugstore, and I thought maybe we could find you some books to read, maybe some games and puzzles, so you'll have plenty to do."

"I've been finding stuff to do. I can help Rosemary."

"We can't stay at Rosemary's indefinitely."

"Why not? Could I get ice cream after lunch?"

We walk all over the place, but we don't see any bookstores, except one that says "Christian Supplies" on the front of it. I ask Josie, are people here Jewish.

Of course, she says, there's Jews everywhere.

"I bet there's hardly any in Alaska."

"Very few, probably."

"I'm glad I don't live there."

She doesn't say anything except ask me whether I'd like to have lunch now before we do more shopping. She buys me a hotdog, which is what I wanted. There's some benches to sit on in the middle of the mall. I start squeezing ketchup out of these little aluminum foil packages they give you, it's tricky to get any out.

"I spoke to your father last night."

"Uh-huh." I knew she brought me here to have a talk.

"It didn't go too well."

"What's he say?"

"Well, he's not really willing to discuss things yet. Mostly he just kept repeating that I should bring you back."

"He's mad at me?"

"No, not at you, kiddo. He's very concerned about you, naturally. He says he's afraid traveling around like we've been doing is having a bad effect on you."

I still don't believe he's really not mad, but I just say, "So why doesn't he work things out with you, then, if he doesn't want me traveling?"

"We'll just have to cross our fingers and hope he will soon."

This lady sitting on another bench has these two twins with her in a twin stroller. They're really cute, dressed identical in pink, so I guess they must be girls.

"I think we need to leave Portland," Josie adds.

I have a hopeless feeling in my stomach. "Where're we going, Alaska?"

She looks at me funny. "Hardly!"

"Where, then?"

"How about Eugene?" She explains how her and Rosemary talked it over, how it's not so far from Portland and all that. She says we'll come back here when she needs to call my father, in case they already traced that other call.

I keep on watching the lady with the twins. She's eating sugar doughnuts out of a paper bag, every so often breaking off little pieces to put in the kids' mouths like a mother bird feeding her greedy babies. She's smoking a cigarette between bites. Every time she bends over the stroller, I'm scared she'll drop ashes.

The subject of tracing phone calls makes me think. "He didn't say he'd ask them to arrest you?"

"Well," she says, "he wasn't specific about it."

"You mean he still might?"

"I'm not sure it's even that simple. I don't know, if he asks the police to look for you he might not have any say-so over whether—over what decisions they make after that."

"It really is just like those TV programs."

"What?"

"Remember, before in Brooklyn, when I asked you if we'd be wearing wigs and stuff, you told me I was watching too much TV. But that's what this is like, those cop shows. I wish you would of told me."

218

Josie looks sad. She just sits there thinking. The lady with the twins has finished all her doughnuts, and they don't understand why they're not getting more. Even though they're barely old enough to talk they're screaming, "Doda! doda!" and you can see her going nuts, trying to figure out how she's going to shut them up. Finally I see her take her purse and go over to the bakery.

I bet she has problems with them when they're older.

"Josie?" *I ask.*

"What?"

"What happens if Daddy doesn't change his mind?"

Her mouth gets like it does when she's upset. "Well, I think we'll have to come to some sort of decision by the time school starts, anyway."

Even though I feel like I'm not supposed to I ask, "What do you mean, a decision?"

"About what to do. Whether you should go back. It's possible we could try to keep on hiding. . . ."

"How come by the time school starts?"

"Because, for one thing, I don't think you can be registered as Cindy Cole. They'd want your old records."

I get this awful feeling, either way. Stuck in Cleveland with the two of them mad at me, plus having no friends and starting a new school and never seeing Josie, or else staying with her and hiding all the time, always lying, always feeling scared.

"Do you think he will?"

"Do I think he will what."

"Change it. By September."

She looks like she's seeing something far away. "I don't know, kiddo. I really can't guess."

The twins are quiet, they've got another doughnut.

"Do you hate my father?" *I ask.*

She shuts her eyes. I said the wrong thing.

"That's a good question," *she says, in this funny voice.*

I just noticed the music they play in here. It's "Raindrops Keep Fallin' on My Head." We sang that in school chorus.

"It's okay, really. You could tell me." *I want her to talk to me like to a grownup.*

"You shouldn't have to worry about all this. I know you care about him."

"He's my father," *I remind her.*

"Yes, I know."

"But he'd never be outlaws like us."

That makes her smile a little. She squeezes my hand. "You do know he might not change his mind. I hope he will, but there's no guarantee."

I nod my head. We went through this already. My mouth feels dried up. It's hard to chew my hotdog.

"Sure you still want to go on? We don't have to."

I feel the tears stinging inside my eyes.

"I know it's tough, kiddo. Awfully tough. No disgrace in turning back, you know."

I'm not going to cry. I clear my throat. "That's okay," I say. "Do we have enough money?"

*   *   *

"Well now, I don't know," says Mrs. Nellie Swenson, dubiously eyeing Ericka, who sits stiffly beside me on a print-covered couch behind a large, claw-footed, glass-topped coffee table. "I never had a mother 'n child stay up there before. In that little place? Seems like there's barely room for one person to turn around in. Won't you be wanting something a bit bigger?"

"Eventually, maybe, but —" I rest my hand protectively on the offending child's shoulder. She radiates resentment, I can feel it. "For now, the space wouldn't be a problem. I can pay in advance, of course, plus any deposits you require."

"I see." Mrs. Swenson folds her large blue-veined hands in her broad lap. Patiently she waits for further enlightenment.

It is not a difficult task to make my voice hesitant, deferential. I haven't even set eyes on her "furnished upstairs studio, separate entrance" yet, and I want it desperately. "The thing is, we're just getting to know Eugene. Cindy has to get used to a new neighborhood, and I'll be finding work. I think a quiet little place might be just the thing for now."

"I see, I see. You said you'd come down from Portland?"

This is small-town tact. Of course she wants my credentials, but she's quite content to get them through a process of indirection. Which suits me perfectly, for a gradual revelation of my touching circumstances is one of the strategies Rosemary came up with as we sat around the picnic table last night in the campground where we're staying. She drilled Ericka and me on our interview technique, much to Ericka's amusement; what was left of juvenile good humor waned early on, however, in the round of calls from pay phone booths and fruitless forays into living rooms which has taken up the better part of today. Some of the advertised places had already been rented, some were in bad locations if you didn't have a car, and a number of landlords said flatly that they didn't want kids. This is the last place on a long list, and I'm devoutly hoping that my much-practiced pathos will help compensate for our bedraggled condition. The showers we took in the pay stall at the campground early this morning wore off long ago, and I'm more and more conscious that the slacks Rosemary loaned me, which are really too short, call attention to my sneakers. Also, as I can't resist confirming by a quick glance in the mirror above Mrs. Swenson's tidy grey head, the fact that my hair has grown out in recent weeks, while it has the advantage of making me look less dykey, instead has produced a layered, tufted, most unmatronly effect.

Nervously I twist the cheap ring, next-to-pinkie on my left hand. (Rosemary really got into the dramatics.) "Yes, Portland—we've been up there in Portland for several months, staying with my sister. You see, I'm from the West Coast, California originally. But we lived in New York, my husband was from there. He recently . . . passed away." From the moment Mrs. Swenson answered her door I've been telling myself that if I can just think of her as one of my mother's mother's friends, the women whose talk I listened to day after day during summer weeks in Boise in the Fifties and early Sixties, I'll know how to behave. And they all said *passed away*.

"Oh. Oh my, I'm sorry." Mrs. Swenson's tongue flickers like a lizard's, wetting her pale lips. "So young, too. Course I been widowed three times myself . . . Say, wouldn't you like a cuppa coffee or some iced tea while we talk?"

"Thanks, iced tea would be nice." And quicker than coffee, I hope. Evidently my reference to tragedy has awakened Mrs. Swenson's interest, but I'm not sure of her yet.

"How about you, little girl. I don't suppose you like sugar cookies?"

Ericka looks to me for permission I'd be a fool to withhold. Mrs. Swenson, stooped but vigorous, bustles out to her kitchen.

"Little girl!" my accomplice indignantly mouths. I frown and shake my head.

Outside the day is bright; within, dim, everything shaded and covered. The room itself is paneled in dark wood. Its numerous windows, all of them rather small, are rigged with an elaborate flurry of shirred and sashed curtains over plain blinds. There are a few leafy houseplants, flourishing but ugly, and a row of tubular cacti like spiny green cocks set on one high window sill. The odor of the place is – what? Pine Sol mixed with baking? Furniture polish, too, and floor wax: I'm sure Mrs. Swenson waxes and polishes weekly. And I'd lay ten to one she crochets, for there's an otherwise inexplicable extravagance of afghans, while the end tables are thronged with multicolored doilies. On the backs of gloomy overstuffed armchairs are elaborately worked coverings designed to protect from greasy masculine heads which presumably might loll there, perhaps after a heavy Sunday meal. The lamps have shades like prissy starched tutus. A few issues of *Reader's Digest* and *National Geographic*, and an upright piano with yellowing keys, suggest the place of culture in this scheme. The old house, an ample though plain wooden structure on a quiet tree-lined street a few blocks from Eugene's main shopping area, is itself clearly a well-tuned instrument.

I take note of an open bible on a stand. And then it dawns on me what's missing, what gives the room its truly archaic cast: there's no television set.

Mrs. Swenson comes shuffling back, in her hands a tray with pitcher, glasses, and a plate of cookies. "Yes," she reminisces dispassionately, "I was married three times, and buried all three. A soldier, a fisherman, and a logger. One Polack, two Scandihoovians. See them pictures, over on the buffet? That there on the end is my son."

There they sit in a row, the men who were her fate. Four pale mugs, one an ill-favored boy's. Of the three husbands, the first is solemn in an army uniform; the second stands grinning on a boat's prow; the third, in a color snapshot, poses on the stump of an enormous redwood tree.

"Ed there, the Pole, hubby number one – well, I called him a soldier, but actually he was a salesman, before the War come along. That's our son, the boy. Ed did pretty well, selling, considering it was the Depression and everything. We had some hard times, moved around a lot. But then, just about when things seemed to be looking up, along come Pearl Harbor. Old as Ed was, he up and joined the army. Of course they didn't want him for combat duty. So what do they do but send him up there to these Aleutians – you know, them islands almost over there by Russia. Godforsaken land, without a tree or hardly so much as a bush on some of 'em, to hear Ed tell it. I guess they might of had some Indians over there, but they moved 'em to someplace else. Well, I took our boy, Tommy – he was in high school by then – and we moved right up to Anchorage to be closer to Ed.

"Things went along okay for a few months. But the winters up there, you know—there's months out of the year where the sun'll hardly rise, 'cept to turn around and sink right down again. Even in Anchorage it could get pretty tiresome, after a spell of that. But up there where Ed was—see, there wasn't much for the boys to do up there, really, other than wait for the Japs or whoever to show up, and it kind of got to some of them. Well, one of these fellows, anyway, who was stationed up there with Ed—one dark night, or dark day, as the case may be, they happened to have a little disagreement about some silly thing, and this soldier takes and clobbers Ed with a crowbar.

"Course they court-martialled the guy for it, but it was too late to do Ed much good. The fellow got off in the end, anyway—temporary insanity—all that darkness drove him plum berserk, they said. He was from back East and couldn't stand it. Well, I don't know about that, I just know a man lost his life. And the thing where I felt so sorry for poor Ed—you know, ever since he found out he was posted up there, he'd been talking about wanting to see that midnight sun. And he never got a look at it. He died in February. I've always thought what a shame that was.

"Well, you can imagine I was pretty shook up, but I stuck up there around Anchorage a year or two, waitressing and that, and then I met my second husband. That's him there, in the middle. Finnish, and a fisherman out of Kodiak. Fins to the Finn I used to say—hah, hah, that was our little joke. It always tickled him. He had a pretty good living out of that, see—owned his own boat. Well, we got married, and that didn't set too well with Tom, so soon's the war ended he quit school and joined the merchant marine, shipped out overseas. Then my second husband was lost in a storm one day, after we'd been married three, four years. Wave come right up on deck, they said, and swept him clean off . . . how're those cookies, honey? Would you like a glass of milk?"

"No, thanks. They're good," replies Ericka primly. But I note signs of continuing strain beneath the veneer of model child deportment, and am beginning to be more nervous about handling her than I am on account of our hostess, who after all probably wouldn't be rambling on at such generous length if she weren't inclining to take us in. I'm determined to rent the apartment, and in no mood at all to deal with dissent from a junior partner who is, I'm afraid, rapidly forming the impression that Mrs. Swenson is terribly peculiar, a natural conclusion if one judges by New York standards of efficiency in business and in social intercourse.

"Anyway," Mrs. Swenson continues, thoroughly at ease, "after being widowed a second time, I decided the state of Alaska was jinxed for me. Here I'd lost two husbands and one son – Tommy didn't write me, after he left home. So I took the insurance money I had coming, and come down here and bought this place. And I've never been sorry – it's built good and solid – though we did have quite a time with these, what they call carpenter ants, a couple years back. You ever seen what happens when they settle in a place? Lord, don't make me think what I had to do to get rid of them.

"Then I married John Swenson, number three over there. Like I say, he was a logger, but retired already by the time we met. He's just posing for a gag on that big old stump – took that picture myself, one year, someplace down there on the coast near Eureka. We was happily married until he passed away, seven years come September. Died in his sleep, quiet as a mouse. Cor'nary, they told me, afterwards. I woke up one morning, and. . . . " Suddenly she seems to recall something. "But that can't be very cheerful for you to hear about, here you've lost somebody."

"That's all right."

Ericka nudges my foot with hers. I studiously ignore her.

"John was steady – didn't drink, even, but an occasional beer. Didn't smoke, though he did chew that snoose. You wouldn't of thought he'd a been a logger most of his life, probably, just to look at him. Kind of a smallish fellow, quiet-spoken. Went to church fairly regular. I guess he was wilder, some, in his younger days, before I ever knew him. But then I have to admit I'm a faithfuller Christian now myself, than I ever used to be. Religion has a way of growing on a person. I never used to understand what my mother meant when she used to tell me that, until I saw for myself. All's well that ends well, anyway. But I can't help thinking, if we'd been more a church-going family, things might of went differently with Tom.

"Course, he turned out all right, too. Came back to the States eventually and settled out in Missouri. Worked at this and that. Most recently he's become a preacher himself, strange as it is to think of it if you knew him as a child. Hardshell Baptist, but I'm not complaining. I'd rather that, than hardshell atheist, which is what you'd pretty much have to say his dad was. I get a letter from him now, every year at Christmas. I think of going out there to visit, but I hate to leave the house.

"It *is* a funny thing, though. Reminds me of the parable of the disobedient son, you know, the one that said no when he was s'posed to go work in the vineyard, but later on he did after all?"

Mrs. Swenson pauses. It seems time to change the subject. Ideally, of course, I'd like some way to bring the conversation back to my interest in the apartment, but I don't want to invite any more personal questions. "Did you grow up around here?" I temporize.

"Oh, no. I was born in South Dakota." To my surprise, she doesn't elaborate, and her manner as she leans forward and places her empty glass decisively on the tray almost suggests she has some reason for reticence. "That's enough of that!" she announces briskly. "Now we've had a chance to get acquainted, would you like to come up and take a look at the place? No, don't bother with those things, just leave them on the tray. I'll go get the keys from the other room."

"Are we going soon?" my child perversely hisses.

"Behave yourself," I hiss back furiously.

"I gotta pee."

"Well why didn't you say so?"

Mrs. Swenson returns, points the way to the bathroom. Ericka departs down the hall, a small grubby figure who will undoubtedly leave muddy pawprints on the towels—if she remembers to wash her hands in the first place.

"Poor little girl. It must be hard on her. A youngster that age needs a father," the landlady observes, succumbing to the natural temptation to discuss a child's fate the moment it's out of earshot.

"Yes," I sigh cunningly. "I worry about her. She's been so quiet since my husband . . . passed away."

A few minutes later, as we ascend the outside staircase leading up to the apartment, Mrs. Swenson mentions innocently that, this being a university town, there are plenty of young people in the area. She's had several very nice young men stay up here, though you have to be careful these days, renting to students—after one or two bad experiences she's begun requiring a cleaning deposit, something she never would have dreamed of once upon a time. "I think you did right, coming back," she adds as we reach the door. "This here's God's country. New York never sounded like much of a place to me." And I congratulate myself on my good sense in having established that I'm a West Coast native. I can see the whole thing taking shape in her mind, how she reads my future from her own past. I will rent the apartment, settle down in

Eugene, and meet a nice young man – perhaps a graduate student – and my welfare, and my child's, will be secured, largely thanks to her good offices.

I am amused at this self-centered brand of kindness, but I need kindness, and I am also touched. I only worry it may be hard to keep the necessary distance.

The apartment is more or less what I expected: a large room with drab, serviceable furniture, including a hide-a-bed. The kitchenette has a two-burner stove. There's a nice view out to the backyard vegetable garden with its neatly staked beans and dominating squash plants, their yellow trumpets and spayed green foliage.

Ericka wears a look of veiled disapprobation. I make a mental note to teach her the song about the logger lover, the one who stirs coffee with his thumb and would eat a bale of hay if you'd just pour whiskey on it. The tune started running through my head while Mrs. Swenson was describing her third husband; perhaps its silliness will charm her out of her grumpy mood.

For now I rest my hand admonishingly on her shoulder. "So you'll be wanting a month's rent plus – what for a cleaning deposit?"

"You'll take it then?"

"If you want to rent to us."

"Well, I guess," our benefactress allows, as though a bit reluctant before the ultimate commitment. "Cindy, I'm sure you won't be running and hollering on those stairs, will you now? They go right past my kitchen window, so I'll know if you make a racket."

Outwardly all meekness, Ericka promises she won't.

Fifteen minutes later, on our way back to meet Rosemary, who has been waiting with Petey in the car parked two blocks away, she skips and hops in expression of long-pent energy. To my relief, she seems resigned to our new quarters, and reserves her criticism for their owner. "She sure is strange. How come she talks so much? And how come she keeps mentioning religion and stuff? And what's God's country mean, anyway?"

"It's just an expression. It means . . . a beautiful place. Somewhere fit to live, in her estimation."

"She said her son only writes her once a year. I could see why! Anyway, I guess he probably doesn't really want to see her that much. Didn't you think that?

"Josie, I mean Mom, what's a Jap?"

I was hoping this had slipped by. No such luck. " 'Jap' is a racist term for Japanese. It was used a lot especially during World War II."

"Oh."

"Thousands of Japanese-American families were taken away from their homes and put in concentration camps then, just because their ancestors had come here from Japan. A lot of that happened right around here."

"Yuk, that's no fair. What's a Hardshell Baptist?"

"I don't know exactly. Some very strict kind, I guess, one who believes in a literal interpretation of the bible."

"Then what's a Hardshell Atheist?"

"Just something she made up. She meant her first husband was not her notion of a good Christian."

Ericka pirouettes, pronounces cynically, "Guess I'm a Hardshell Atheist too then. Josie, do we *have* to stay with her?"

"We're not staying *with* her. We're renting an apartment." Mrs. Swenson has her drawbacks, but I feel protective of her. She reminds me of those old ladies in Idaho, pious and house-proud, whose fussy affection and fussier decor once put me off, too.

"How come we couldn't rent some other apartment?"

"Don't kvetch, Ericka. I think you know."

"No, really, why?"

"Have you ever heard the saying, 'Beggars can't be choosers'?"

PART III: BEGGARS

I like Mrs. Swenson better than I did. Sometimes now I watch TV in her place. Josie was surprised when she found out Mrs. Swenson even had a TV set. The thing is, she keeps it in her kitchen instead of the living room, so she could watch it while she's working. During the day she usually watches stuff like As the World Turns and Days of Our Lives. Those shows don't interest me that much, I'd rather go down in the evening when Josie's at work to watch Hawaii Five-O.

Sometimes, though, I help in the vegetable garden. Mrs. Swenson has this gigantic vegetable garden—well, pretty gigantic, lots bigger than Rosemary's. She has a little of everything, she says, all in neat rows. The different things look nice, all bunched together. Corn, my favorite, but it's still pretty short, just like fat tall grass. Zucchinis, but they're just starting, smaller than grownup cucumbers, these pale green things and there's a little mark on the end like a scab or a belly button where the flower dries and drops off. You can watch the flowers turning into squashes. And peas. And little tomatoes, hard and green. She said you could make a pie from green tomatoes. And beets, which I hate, but I like how the leaves look, with red veins just like they had blood in them. She even grows some potatoes, even though she says they take up too much space, cause she loves new potatoes. New potatoes are the little round baby ones, smaller than store potatoes. She's got some ready already. I like how they grow all globby under the dirt, I never saw that before.

Sometimes she has me pick a bowl of leaf lettuce and carrots and radishes to take up to Josie. And she pays me with cookies, after I help out. She makes me take off my sneakers by the door. "Now Cindy," she says, like I will've forgotten from last time, "don't track up my clean linoleum, I just got everything all spic 'n span." She uses some strange expressions. That one gives me a kind of a creepy feeling, in case it means something bad about Puerto Ricans, since she said that other thing about Japanese, but I decided it probably doesn't. Anyway, I don't think there's very many Puerto Ricans in Eugene. When we go to stores I only hear people talk English.

Mrs. Swenson usually lets me pick from a couple kinds of cookies. She bakes a lot. She collects cookie jars. She also collects these glass things, sort of like glass balls but flat on the bottom, with tiny adorable little scenes of people and houses and churches and trees and stuff, like, frozen inside. Some of them, if you turn them upside down, you can see "snow" fall.

She says she'll show me canning later on. She calls it putting up—"I put up a lot of tomatoes, and fruit, and that." But I wonder if we'll even be here that long. She says she might take me blackberry picking, in August.

She reminds me of Grandma Krevsky a little bit. Like, they both like to grow things, and they're good at sewing and stuff. But Mrs. Swenson's much more superstitious. I think she's also a Republican.

Sometimes she treats me younger than I am. Like one time she told me there used to be this little girl living next door who would come over and help her out like I do now, who used to call her Aunt Nellie, and would I like to call her that.

I didn't know what to say. Finally I just acted like I didn't hear her, the way I do whenever she mentions God.

*   *   *

I am working swing shift at Dexter's Do-Nut Depot. The job is perfect. It pays minimum wage. I work five days a week, with variable days off. I punch a clock for the first time in a decade, and wear a daffodil-yellow pants uniform, the cost of which is to be subtracted from my weekly paychecks in five-dollar installments. The uniform top has appliquéd on it a large smile-button shape with a doughnut hole in the middle. Inside it, I am a smiling "counter girl," and feel myself more effectively disguised, cloaked in sweet anonymity, than even my fake wedding ring or my counterfeit daughter can make me.

My job helps us keep up the pretence of normal life – for which, since the bus trip, we've developed quite a craving. I applied, however, not only with that benefit in mind but because our money is running low and, though I don't expect to have to hold out past August, I want to be prepared for anything. Also because I would clearly have lost my marbles, along with my last shred of patience, if Ericka and I had continued to spend twenty-four hours a day in each other's company. And finally because getting hired was so easy. I simply presented myself in response to a newspaper ad and was accepted on the spot by Mrs. Dexter – "I guess you'll do," she said resentfully, with the air of making the best of a bad bargain – without even the bother of lying about my past on an application form.

The shop is only a few blocks from Mrs. Swenson's. At first I was nervous about leaving Ericka, especially since we don't have a phone, but, thanks largely to her surprising new friendship with that good woman, she's proved quite cheery and self-confident. I don't have to be at work until four, so we're able to spend most of the day together. I cook in the morning and leave her food to heat up, though in practice I often come home to find she's eaten downstairs. I have instructed Mrs. Swenson to pack her off to bed at a reasonable hour, and of course to send her home anytime she's in the way.

Fortunately our landlady seems terribly literal-minded; I judge her unlikely to nurse subtle suspicions. As for Ericka, reminded to be careful of her tongue, she replied quite blasé-ly that if awkward questions were asked, she knew the way to get the subject changed.

"What's that?" I inquired.

"Act sad about my father. My poor dead dad, who I don't like to mention."

In two or three evenings of moderate application, I have mastered the basics of doughnuts. Plain or frosted cake; crullers, applesauce, or old fashioned; but above all, raised (glazed, bars, or filled), they repose in a long glass case at the front of the shop. The decor of the place vaguely echoes the "depot" theme, with a few clumsy stencils of steam engines on the walls. All service is at the counter, but there are six formica tables for those who wish to ingest their sugar "in."

My main job is doling out doughnuts and cardboard containers of coffee, but I'm also responsible for light maintenance – for instance, clearing the tables once an hour or so if the shop is not too busy. (However, in light of the fact that I'm alone at my post till the night baker comes in at ten o'clock, I've also been cautioned not to venture out front if the shop is too empty, or if suspicious characters lurk – with the result that the tables are almost never cleaned.) At one point during the evening I'm also obliged to clean the display case, inside and out, with Windex and paper towels, first removing the merchandise. (I have been told that one of the lapses which led to my predecessor's ignominious dismissal was her neglect of this basic precaution. Customers did not appreciate the taste of Windex.) I am also to fold a supply of cardboard boxes, pre-measure coffee grounds into paper filters, start up the fryer at a given hour, wipe down the proof-box, and fill the jelly pump which the night baker, in a curiously sexual operation, will use to inject raised doughnuts with glops of scarlet jelly.

Mrs. Dexter – who, as her husband's deputy, oversees the three shops he owns here in Eugene – comes in every evening around five to pore over the receipts. Already she has summoned me to her desk in the back room and, peering up from beneath her fringe of bleached bangs, tartly complimented me on my efficiency. Hers was, I thought, the crude ruddy face of a smalltime madam appraising a new whore. She hinted that if I fulfill my initial promise I may soon be eligible to receive baker's training, which would bring a raise of forty cents an hour.

I smiled, of course, and tried to look ambitious. But I lied—I'm not at all. When last spoken to, Daniel was a shade more conciliatory—that is, he conceded we may have a thing or two to discuss once I bring Ericka home—but the basic situation remains unchanged. The horizon of my ambitions at this point is to become the perfect Dexter's counter girl.

*   *   *

Sometimes it seems like we've lived here our whole life, even though it's just a couple weeks. Everything's so quiet. The days take so long. I like it, though, it's better than the bus.

Before I go to sleep (I get the folding bed—Josie has a mattress on the floor), I try to think of everything I could remember about New York. What our block looks like, and the kids in my last year's class. I pretend I'm cleaning my room and go through all the drawers and shelves.

Sometimes it's hard to remember what everybody looks like. I had that problem after Mommy died, sometimes I couldn't remember how her face went. Then I got a picture and looked at it a lot, so when I wanted to think about her I'd have it in my mind. But I don't have any picture of Daddy with me, or Brenda or Leah, or Grandma and Grandpa Krevsky. I don't even have my watch. But I wear my Jewish star and woman's symbol.

Josie and I do things on her day off, like once we rented bicycles for the day. Even on the days she has to work we could go to the library in the morning, or take a picnic lunch to this little park near here. Sometimes I go there and play in the afternoon, after she's left for the shop. I see some kids there, but I don't talk to them. I'm scared if I got to know them they'd ask a lot of questions.

I wonder if Daddy would hire a private eye. That's what I'd do if I wanted to find my daughter. I keep looking out the window to see if the house is being watched. Sometimes I play different pretend games, like what I'd do if Josie went to jail. I'd run away so I could visit her.

I wonder did they sell the house yet.

*   *   *

Chandelle, the night baker, is the Dexters' daughter-in-law. Her job makes her the central figure in the shop, for the "day bake" is a limited affair; everything depends on the night's output. She is two years younger than I, a sharp-nosed, full-hipped blonde; has a couple of kids at home, and a husband who works days. When she gets her sleep is a mystery to me. Perhaps she's on uppers, she seems so enthusiastic, evenings when she comes in to start her shift. Or maybe she's just relieved to get out of the house. Her marriage, I'm informed, is a "disaster area."

This gossip comes from Dana, the counter girl on days, who stays to change out of her uniform in the bathroom, and then to sit on a stool in the storage area, next to the giant mixer, sketching great blue targets around her small dark eyes with the aid of a pocket mirror, smoking Virginia Slims, and chattering nonstop. Dana graduated from high school in June. By her own account, she's unsure "what to do with herself." It is from her comments I've gathered that to be a Dexter (or to marry one) is to have one's life as fatally involved with doughnuts as a Wallenda's would have to be with the high wire. Or at least this seems to be the case for the females. For in addition to Chandelle there are three Dexter daughters, all living here in town, working at the other shops – handy that way, as Dana points out, since it means there's always someone to fill in, should an employee quit or be fired. Only Chandelle's husband, the sole Dexter son, has taken a tough stand and become a bricklayer.

Dana warns me not to trust Chandelle. Nice as she seems, she's a spy for her mother-in-law. "I have to hand it to her as far as baking, she's a real pro. You ever watch her cut her raise? But just don't let her find out anything you don't want the old lady to hear about. That's how the girl on swing shift before you got fired, you know. Naw, they wouldn't've let her go just for a little Windex, it's too much trouble to train a new girl. She had her boyfriend coming here evenings, after Mrs. Dexter had been in to look at the receipts and left for the night. She was letting him in the back, which is a *real* no-no – don't ever let anyone in there. Well, Chandelle came in early once and caught them. Nobody in the shop, it was a Sunday, slow – and he's dry-humping her on a pile of flour sacks!"

After pausing to let the drama of this sink in, Dana adds that in her view it was rather hypocritical of Chandelle to get all worked up. "You should see her, married and everything, making time with the cab drivers. Long about four, five in the morning when she's got her bake out . . . I've been here two or three mornings real early, you know, days I had off, when I'd been out dancing late. I found out what goes on. You should see her twitching her fanny, those tight uniforms she wears. I'd love to hear what the old lady'd have to say if she knew about that one. Her son's dear little wifey! Bad as they need her nights, old Chandelle'd be yanked off graveyard quicker'n you can say day-old maple bars!"

Speaking of which, we really do sell maple bars, a confection I was fond of in my youth, and hankered for in vain in the capitals of the East. I love a fresh maple bar every so often, and my quiet, companionable mornings with Ericka, and the Eugene paper, soothing, almost devoid of news. I love my job, though it bores me to distraction and makes my feet ache. And the proper grey-green hill color of the hills, Douglas fir like the first forests I knew.

I love my peace, my anonymity, out here in America: Mrs. Swenson overheard explaining, over the back fence to her next-door neighbor, that yes, she has a young widow and her daughter living up there in the apartment now. And the sight of Dana's charming little ass in her tight designer jeans, twitching out the door as she finally takes her leave just in time to miss Mrs. Dexter's supervisory visit.

*   *   *

Mrs. Swenson knows how to make a lot of stuff. She said she might teach me how to knit. I'd rather learn that than crocheting. We don't need all those round things she has on her tables and chairs.

I wonder what she'd think if she knew who we really are. I guess she wouldn't like us anymore. Or maybe she would. I can't make up my mind.

She's kind of dumb sometimes. Well, not dumb exactly. But I mean, like one day I was wearing this top with a kind of low neck, and she was looking at my Jewish star. "That's a cute little charm you've got there," she said. "Don't you have a charm bracelet, though? You should ask your mother to start you up one."

I finally asked Josie: do you know what we're doing yet?

*   *   *

Ericka is right to be concerned. I'm playing it by ear. Faking it. And it sometimes does occur to me to wonder—for there's suddenly plenty of time for such reflection—whether I haven't simply made an enormous fool of myself, committed a blunder so obvious it seems incredible.

If that is the case, I wish I did not have this witness who regards me with the gravity of a polite passenger reluctant to ask questions of the driver as the car speeds over the dark and tangled roads and the destination recedes – but who nevertheless is clearly wondering: shouldn't one inquire at a service station?

Well, there are no service stations on this route, and certainly it's better to dismiss such thoughts, which can serve no constructive purpose – and relatively easy to dismiss them, where the streets are so pleasant and clean, where the weather's so bright and obliging. It hasn't rained once since our arrival. The citizens of Eugene are marvelling at the drought.

Every four or five days I phone Rosemary. She insists I call collect, swears Peter won't see the bill. I always dial rather nervously, half-expecting to hear that some sinister crewcut type has just been knocking on the door, and am then relieved (and oddly disappointed) when she turns out to have only the most inconsequential domestic traumas to report. But even five minutes of this provides a welcome break from the rigors of my current incognito, which is, I'm discovering, like even the most lenient of girdles, a relief to take off.

I have written a letter for Wendy to forward to Daniel. It doesn't say anything I haven't already said over the phone, just spells my position out as clearly as possible. I wrote it partly according to the theory Rhea and I employed when dealing with landlords and other petty tyrants: repeat what you want over and over again, never minding how ridiculous it sounds or your own embarrassment at their stubbornness and denseness; perhaps you'll wear them down eventually. Also, Ericka seems to feel that my being in touch with her father is a positive sign rather on the order of cultural exchanges with the Russians, and keeps pestering me about when I'm going to phone him. The letter seemed a way to demonstrate my exertions on her behalf without the risks of another fruitless phone call.

As it turned out, it involved its own risks. She decided to include her own letter, a letter she said she wanted to keep private. I let her seal it in the envelope with mine, and contented myself, perhaps foolishly, with questioning her in an effort to make certain she hasn't let slip anything that could give away our whereabouts.

I'm increasingly fatalistic about these things. Either they'll get us, I figure – or they won't.

*   *   *

I started a diary. It's my first one ever. I got the idea from this Nancy Drew book. I've been checking out all these Nancy Drew mysteries on my temporary library card. There's zillions of them, so when you finish one you don't have to worry about what to read next! Anyway, I took my allowance money—I got Josie to give me an allowance, only not as much as I used to get from Daddy—and I went to the little store where you get popsicles and bought a notebook and a Bic pen. I keep them under my shirts in my drawer now. No special reason. It's just like having a friend you could tell anything to. Stuff I might of wanted to tell Mommy. Or just private stuff.

I started out like this: Dear Diary, My name is Ericka Krevsky. (That's my mother's name, my father's name is Fein, but they kept their separate names when they got married and I got to have Krevsky since I turned out a girl.) Anyway, I'm ten since last March. I'm in kind of an unusual situation for a kid to be in. You see, I'm here in Eugene, Oregon, with Josie (Mommy's lover), who used to live with us all the time after my mother and father got divorced, she's my flommy, that's a word we made up. But then my mother got killed (instantly in a car crash) and now I'm supposed to live with my father but he's going to move to Cleveland with Brenda that's my stepmother and Leah and Jeremy that's going to be the new baby when he gets born in fact maybe he did already, this is August. Then I noticed this was a runon sentence like they always tell you not to write in class. Then I didn't know if I should write it over, but I suddenly got scared because what if someone saw it, they'd find out who we were. But then I realized it's probably okay because who would be looking in my dresser drawer unless they already knew who we were?

I've been writing a lot lately. I wrote a letter to my father. I said I love him and want to see him soon. I asked him please to settle things with Josie, so I could start school on time. I also mentioned about losing my birthday watch when I was lost on top of a mountain in Arizona, and asked him please not to be mad. I promised to be a help around the house, if he works things out with Josie.

* * *

Ericka has been cultivating her tan. Ritually each morning she dons her bathing suit and descends into the sun of the back yard, where she spends an hour or two tastefully arrayed on a towel, reading her mystery through heart-shaped plastic sunglasses, turning every so often to grill more evenly. Mrs. Swenson maneuvers the garden hose around her. From upstairs I can hear them talking back and forth aimlessly like comfortable old friends.

In light of Ericka's sensible inclination to ignore our landlady's pronouncements on most political and religious topics, her faith in the woman's judgment in smaller matters surprises me. For instance, when I included watermelon in one of our recent picnic lunches, she set about painstakingly divesting her portion of every single seed before taking the first bite. When I finally asked her about it, she revealed that Mrs. Swenson holds swallowing melon seeds brings on appendicitis. I argued against this, but unsuccessfully: she continued to pile up the dangerous black seeds until her melon was reduced to a watery pink mush.

* * *

Mrs. Swenson tells me about Alaska. She told me about this big sled dog race they have up there every year, and lots of bear stories. One time, for instance, she was about three feet away from this grizzly. She was picking berries and the bear was too! She said scram, which was all she could think of, which the bear did, luckily. I like her stories, but I still don't think I'd want to live up there. It seems further away than Oregon does, even.

Josie's going to call my father soon. Then I guess I'll find out whether Jeremy's born yet. I don't know what we'll do if Daddy's still mad. I think we might need more of a plan or something.

What we're doing now feels strange if you think about it, like playing hide and seek, only you're not sure if anyone's coming to seek or not, that's the weirdest part. I asked Josie what I should do if a policeman or someone ever comes to the door if she's not at home. Do I have to let him in, or only if he has a search warrant, the way they do on TV?

Josie said I shouldn't let anybody in if she's not there. If anybody comes, which there's no reason why they should, I'm to tell them to go downstairs and speak to Mrs. Swenson.

On TV programs they break down the door. But they only do that, like, for armed robbers and stuff.

There's this graveyard near here I pass sometimes, if I go out for a little walk when Josie's at work. It's new, I mean newer than ones you see back East. Everything's newer here, the buildings too. I don't go in, but I could see through the fence, and all the stones are standing up nice and straight. They look polished and clean, not broken like Vermont. And you don't see so many tiny stones either, like where kids died, or even little babies, like they used to all the time in the old fashioned days.

Sometimes I try to imagine what it's like being dead. To not think or feel or remember. To be just one big nothing. I know that's dumb, since nothing's just nothing, and even if you try to concentrate on nothing, you're still thinking of something, instead.

I used to have these scary dreams about the dead place. But I know that isn't real, everybody said so.

Sometimes I don't get it, I don't get it at all. Sometimes I wonder, like, if I'd been in that car with Mommy.

* * *

I've finally figured out why Dana stays after her shift is over. It's not simply out of boredom, and it's certainly not out of any particular fondness for me, though it would be pleasant to think so, since I'm getting rather attached to her overpainted face and her engaging chatter. No. It is on account of a balding blond deliveryman who comes in every day between 4:15 and 4:30. He's about my age, I guess, and his name is Bert, according to the scrawl of machine embroidery on his dark blue coveralls. He has blue eyes, too, and wears a wedding ring. He has short, strong, hairy forearms and longish sculpted sideburns, is beginning to thicken around the waist and hips. He always wants the same thing: two jelly doughnuts and a carton of milk. I get them out now when I see him coming.

She and Bert are just good friends, Dana has volunteered. She has added, as though feeling a need for further justification, that he has a CB radio in his van. She prances out frankly now to sit with him at one of the littered tables while he wolfs his snack down. Then she comes back for her things, mentions she's got a lift.

"That Bert guy been around?" Chandelle demands, when she shows up at ten in a new pink uniform. (Apparently it is one of the privileges accorded to her as night baker—or perhaps as a member of the ruling clan—not to wear the yellow smock with the leering doughnut.)

"Every day. He's a real regular."

"I bet. Was Dana still here when he showed up?"

"Well, yeah. She hadn't finished changing. You know Bert?"

"He used to work nights. That little two-bit. . . ." She turns out dough on the floured board, lets the epithet dangle.

240

I'm dying to hear more, naturally, but out of some ancient habit of discretion I refrain from encouraging her. After a while she adds anyway, "I figured the minute I saw that little tramp she'd have them sniffing around like dogs after a bitch. Lifting their legs all over the parking lot. Damn, I don't feel like cutting my raise tonight."

Finding her harshness a bit unsettling, I decide to go out and clear the trash off the tables, which turn out to be heaped with sordid drifts of waxed paper, cardboard, napkins, and half-gnawed doughnuts. When I come back Chandelle is bent over the cutting board punching out her "raise" with her usual precision.

* * *

Mrs. Swenson taught me how to iron. She was surprised when I said I didn't know how. She started me out with napkins and placemats, which are easy, and then an apron to learn how to do gathers. Then after she said she thought I was getting the hang of it, she went to a closet in the extra bedroom and got out an old shirt—she couldn't remember which husband it belonged to, either the Alaskan or the logger—so I could practice shirts. She said every girl needs to learn how to iron them, even though they're the hardest. I didn't mind, it was sort of interesting, and anyway Daddy wears ironed shirts sometimes. I could help Brenda out, like I promised in my letter.

Mrs. Swenson showed me all the different steps. There's a special way to do it. First, of course, you have to sprinkle the shirt. Then there's this part in back you iron first. Oh, and the collar—you spray starch on that. Then the cuffs. Then the sleeves, or else the main part. It's hard to do it without making a wrinkle in the wrong places. But she said I did a good job for my first time.

After I got done and turned the iron off, we went in the kitchen to have my cookies. Usually then she turns on the TV, but this time she didn't. All of a sudden she asked if I was baptized.

I didn't know what to say. I'm not even exactly sure what it is, except I know it's a thing Christians do to babies. Maybe it's sort of like a Christian bris, except for girls too.

She asked me again, and I had to say something. I said I didn't think so.

You must know, she said.

I couldn't think how to explain it to her. I wanted to say I'm Jewish, but I didn't know if I should. Finally I said we don't believe in God.

*"Oh Cindy," she said, "you don't really mean that. Who do you sup-
pose could have made this whole big wide wonderful world if it wasn't
for God? Could anyone you know have done all that?"*

*Then she said some other stuff about Jesus, like couldn't I feel his
love, that wraps around the planet like a big electric blanket.*

*As quick as I could finish up my brownie I explained it was time
for me to go upstairs.*

* * *

I am chopping onions, browning stew meat. (I've reverted to all-
American menus here: no tofu, but meatloaf, fried chicken.) I
want only to be left alone to do this. It is the evening of my day
off, a rare hour for me to be at home, and I want to allow my mind
to wander at random, to sift through a mesh of silence the impressions of the day, the week past. But an importunate child hovers
near my elbow.

"Did she tell you yet what days you get off next week?"

"Monday and Thursday."

"We're going up to Portland?"

"I told you we were."

"When, though?"

"One of those two days."

"When are you gonna know which?"

"Later this week. After I talk to Rosemary. It depends on her
schedule, when it's best for her to see us."

"Which bus will we take? A real early one?"

"I haven't got that far yet. I have to call the station."

"Will we stay all day?"

"I don't *know* yet, Ericka, all right? I have to talk to Rosemary
and find out schedules and stuff. Can't you find something to do
for a while now, while I'm cooking? I see Mrs. Swenson down
there watering. Aren't you going to help her?"

A short, dark, curly hair shows up among the onions. No doubt
whose. I'm horribly annoyed.

How many times have I told you not to comb your hair near the food
. . . I want to say. But bite the words back.

My eyes sting from onions. I crave silence.

"But what if my father isn't there when you call? Hey, you're
sure crying from that onion."

And so on and so forth. That ancient leaden sense (but from
where is it familiar?) of wading through a swamp, murky matters

neither one of us will acknowledge lurking beneath our surface affection or surface snappishness.

And I am the grownup. Supposed to fix things.

Feeling her eyes on me.

To live with a child is to be watched. To watch yourself.

* * *

I try to think what Mommy would say to do. Of course I know she'd want me to be with Josie. But I mean, I guess she probably never imagined this kind of a situation.

Or Grandma, what about her. She said I could always have a place with them. She told me that right away after Mommy died. I guess she didn't realize how the law says my father gets to keep me.

I like it in Florida pretty much, I think. Grandma and Grandpa have some good friends there that they used to know in New York. I like them, they teach me Yiddish words sometimes. Anyway, when those friends of theirs come over, they sit around and talk about how things used to be in the bad old days. That's what Grandma calls them. I couldn't understand a lot of it. She says it's a mercy I never heard of HUAC.

I didn't say the days seem bad enough now, otherwise why were we always going to demonstrations and stuff. But maybe Grandma thought of that too, because then she said it looked like I was going to have to grow up quick and fight this rotten system all over again.

"What if I don't feel like fighting?" I asked. See, I was joking.

"Well," she said, also joking, "your odds of avoiding it don't seem very good, do they? You're female, a Jew, and you come from a long line of troublemakers.

I guess she meant lesbians too, though she didn't say them.

* * *

Our trip to Portland goes like this:

All the way up on the bus Ericka pesters me with pessimistic forecasts—which she clearly desires me to contradict—that her father won't have changed his mind at all. Meantime, I'm assailed by fantasies that we'll be nabbed the minute we set foot in the station. Rosemary, however, meets us as planned and obligingly whisks Ericka off to do some errand while I go find a phone.

But of course it turns out nobody's home at Daniel's, and we attempt a picnic in Laurelhurst Park. Finally Rosemary gives up, says Petey's too impossible, she'd better go back, put him down for his nap, and can some apricots she U-picked the other day, which are in danger of spoiling. I have her drop us downtown, near the bus station.

I call again and get Daniel immediately. He seems to be furious. Even his hello is laced with venom. He starts in berating me for "putting Ericka up to" something—what, he seems to think I ought to know.

"That sweet little note you dictated to her!" he gets around to explaining.

"What are you talking about? I never saw that letter."

"Well, maybe not, but you obviously had some input. Manipulative piece of crap—don't try to tell me she cooked it up on her own!"

It emerges that what infuriates him so is a plea of Ericka's that he compromise with me. Evidently he regards this as the rough equivalent of the letter a hostage may compose at gunpoint which requests a horrified family or government to comply with the captors' demands.

All the time I'm prying this out of him and inserting endless quarters, I'm thinking of the danger: how absurd it would be to get busted for this. I avoid looking out through the smudged glass, for whenever I do I can see Ericka hovering at the small distance to which I banished her before entering the booth. She strains to read her fate in my moving lips.

I don't get anywhere at all with Daniel, though I do discover incidentally that Brenda has not given birth and that, thanks to me and my disruptions, they haven't yet started showing the house, either. The minute I hang up, my captive rushes over. Immediately I dread the coming evening, the close bus, her vigilance, her questions.

"N-O spells no, right? What did I tell you?"—with a kind of grim triumph.

*   *   *

"What happens to us now?"
I ask Josie that on the way.
"I don't know, kiddo. It's too soon to tell."
"But school's gonna start in a few weeks."
"Let's not borrow trouble, okay? It's too soon to be sure what your father's going to do. And I need some time to think about our choices."
"But so far he just says the same thing."
"I know it's hard, but try to be patient. He may still change his mind."

244

"But what if he sent a detective to look for us?"

Josie doesn't answer for so long I start to think she's not going to answer at all. Which gets me mad: it's my life too.

Finally she says in this sad weird voice, "Kiddo, I don't know. I'm doing the best I can."

* * *

Things take a turn for the worse following our Portland excursion. The good weather, for one thing, is abruptly at an end. The clouds hunker down around the dark hills, and they soon set about raining on Eugene in serious Oregon fashion. Around the shop there are many tired jokes about the "liquid sunshine," at home the usual rainy day complaints.

And then there's trouble involving our landlady.

Ericka comes to me wearing a peculiar expression and inquires, trying to make it sound casual, what the word *sheeny* means.

"Where did you hear that?" I hear myself demand in the sharp-anxious voice, the guilty voice, in which a mother asks where her toddler acquired some dangerous plaything.

"Mrs. Swenson said it."

"About whom?"

"Well, see, she was telling about when she was little. First they lived on a farm but then they moved to town and her father had to work for this . . . what I just said."

"It's a very ugly expression for Jew."

"Like Jap or something, right? I never heard that before."

"I'm glad you didn't."

"Last week she asked if I was ever baptized."

"She had no business asking a thing like that. What did you tell her?"

"I wasn't sure what to say. I didn't know if I should say I'm Jewish. Finally I told her we don't believe in God."

So she's sensed a need for caution all along. The revelation stands as a reproach. I never fully realized in New York what complications might lurk out here in the country.

"I'm afraid I'll have to have a talk with Mrs. Swenson. You know, Ericka, you don't have to keep going down there."

"I know. And I'm not, either. What are you gonna say?" In her listless face, a lively interest kindles. There's going to be some action. Mrs. Swenson will get in trouble.

* * *

I had a logger lover
There's none like him today
If you'd pour whiskey on it
He would eat a bale of hay

Josie taught me that a while ago, and I sing it now on my way downstairs. I don't know if Mrs. Swenson could hear, and I don't care either.

I avoid Mrs. Swenson. Like, I try not to go down if she's working in the garden, and if I see her by accident and she says hello I just say hello back and then go where I'm going as quick as I can. One or two times she asked if I'd like to come in for cookies, but I said I wasn't hungry. I'm very disappointed in her.

Josie told her both of us were Jewish. Which was simpler, of course, since people are usually the same thing as their kids so it would be weird to explain how come your kid was Jewish if you weren't. She explained how come she was mad at Mrs. Swenson, but she thinks Mrs. Swenson didn't really understand. But anyway, she told her not to talk about religion. Which she won't get the chance to, since I'm not going down there.

I got this book out of the library, it's called The Jewish People in Song and Story, *and I read it a lot, since there's not that much to do. It's boring not to watch TV at night, and I was just in the middle of this Reader's Digest book of Mrs. Swenson's, which now I can't finish. I wouldn't mind so much, only sometimes I get scared when Josie's gone at work. Just because I can't stop thinking about policemen coming to arrest us and things like that. Every time I hear a strange sound I wonder if it's them, and what to do.*

I didn't know people still didn't like Jews. I guess I thought that was just in long ago days, like with Hitler and the Nazis and Anne Frank.

*   *   *

Mrs. Swenson's betrayal comes at a bad time. We're frightened of the future. We're tired of the rain. Mornings, Ericka now mopes more pointedly than ever around our single room, and complains more monotonously of lack of things to do. Knowing her misery is genuine hardly fortifies my patience.

After some hours of this, I go off to work and worry. I find I worry about her especially while I'm cleaning the doughnut case, around nine o'clock when I used to be able to reassure myself with the thought that she'd be downstairs watching trash with

Mrs. Swenson. It wouldn't be so bad if I could just call, and I've been on the point of having a phone put in despite the steep deposit, but the prospect of being grilled about previous phones and residences has kept me from following through.

At first I thought Mrs. Swenson might be pardoned, but after a week it begins to look doubtful. I'm proud of Ericka's pride, lonely as it makes her, but despite myself I sometimes feel a little sorry for the Christian miscreant, who evinces (as I notice from my window) a certain hovering tendency, a habit of emerging from her back door just as Ericka is heading off for groceries or to the library. She makes me think of some feckless wicked witch lurking wistfully in her kitchen, hoping to lure a youngster with a disarming sweet. But this particular youngster has made up her mind, and is not to be tempted.

I've bought her a pacifier, a transistor radio. At midnight, my shift finished, I rush home through peaceful residential streets that no longer seem without menace, to find her always asleep, the light on in the bathroom, the radio playing low beside her pillow, tuned to the same Golden Oldies rock station that's kept perpetually playing in the shop. More than once she's had her thumb in her mouth.

Mornings, we make an effort to get out. The other day we happened on a rainy August 6th memorial vigil in front of the post office: a dozen or so grave matrons dressed in white, several of them holding aloft a dripping bedsheet which bore the smeared appeal: No More Hiroshimas. Ericka wanted to join them, more I suppose out of nostalgia for the rituals of protest than any comprehension of the particular issue. But I didn't want to stand there in the rain, or contemplate the fate of those terrifying cities, so I said that demos belong to our other life, and we went off to do our shopping. That night I was punished with a dream about the proper way to educate children for activism in the modern world: when a small boy with stomach flu suffers severe nausea, his mother, rather than comforting him, explains, "Fallout from bombs will make you feel like this."

An epidemic of Christianity seems to be ravaging Eugene. Or perhaps it's coincidental that this very week Chandelle should be reported (by Dana, naturally) to have located Jesus. So far the alleged convert hasn't directly confirmed the rumor, but it's true that her hectic vigor has been replaced by what seems an almost unearthly cheerfulness. I haven't heard her swear in ten days at least, and she hums wordless but obviously uplifting tunes as she goes about her "bake."

I am intrigued, but Dana is sarcastic. She tells me a story about a boyfriend she had in high school who'd had a strict fundamentalist upbringing. He'd rebelled and gotten heavy into drugs, and once when they were driving in his car, he started to freak on LSD. He kept on repeating his soul was damned to hell, and she couldn't talk him out of it. He wouldn't stop driving around, either.

Finally he pulled into a driveway where a man happened to be out washing his Buick. They screeched to a halt and he staggered out, sank to his knees on the concrete, and began howling, "Baptize me, you dirty motherfucker," while Dana cowered in the car. The man with the Buick, however, was only momentarily nonplussed; then he hurried over and baptized the bellowing stranger with a bucket of soapy water. He explained very seriously to Dana that what they had just witnessed was a clearcut case of demonic possession, and gave her the phone number of the something-or-other Pentecostal Church, in case of further emergencies. The boyfriend afterwards allowed himself to be driven home quietly.

Dana thinks Bert might get her a job in Reno through a friend he has there. It's legit—no sex or dope, doesn't even involve gambling. And she'd love to get out of this dump. She's sick of rain and doughnuts. But suppose she goes all the way out there and it doesn't pan out? What do I think she should do?

I inquire just what the job *does* involve.

Oh, it's being a hostess in a club of some sort. They have topless dancers there, but she'd be able to keep her clothes on. The pay's shit, but you make it on tips. . . .

I start thinking how I might confide in her, how disguise myself while revealing my situation. I could use the old ploy, "I have a friend," and solicit her advice.

In the end, of course, I do nothing of the sort.

For the first time since Brooklyn, I've caught myself in daydreams straying down that treacherous avenue of speculation that begins, *after Ericka* —

* * *

Me and Josie have been having some arguments.

At first when we were here we got along. Now she's more cross. We had this one argument about me playing my radio in the morning. She said I had to turn it off after one more song. I didn't think that was reasonable. You have plenty of time to listen when I'm out, she said. I said, why don't you go out right now, then. You're always never home, anyway. She said it's not her fault she has to be at work.

It went on for a while. Then we were just quiet. I started to read my book.

I couldn't concentrate. Then I said, "Are you going to send me back?" I've been wondering that.

She didn't even look at me, just said in this voice that sounded mad still, "Do you want to go back?"

"I don't know," I said. I felt bad.

"You know what I told you," she said, "right from the beginning. Anytime you decide you really want to leave you're free to go. Only you'd better be sure first, because you won't get another chance."

It made me mad how it seemed like she didn't care. "You're just trying to get rid of me," I said.

"Oh don't be tiresome!" she snapped at me.

"I'm not being tiresome!" I yelled back. "How would you like it if the people you had to stay with didn't really want you?"

"What is this shit about not wanting you? What do you suppose I schlepped all the way across the fucking country for if I didn't really want you? What does this look like, some kind of fucking picnic?"

I was yelling at her and she was yelling back. Then all of a sudden we remembered we had to be quiet, in case Mrs. Swenson or somebody would hear.

* * *

I used to be Rhea's lover. I used to be a musician. I used to be from Brooklyn. I used to have politics.

I used to go hear Betty Carter at BAM and Alberta Hunter downtown, Jean Pierre Rampal at Carnegie hall. Crazy Brazilian musicians, and Verdi at the Met. Count Basie and John Lee Hooker, Suni Paz and Cris Williamson. Nina Simone once, but she cancelled the performance.

I used to attend meetings. I used to have ambitions.

I used to read books. I used to love women.

* * *

It's late afternoon. Josie's gone to work.

I watch Mrs. Swenson out the window. She pulls up in the driveway and climbs out of her car. She's carrying a brown grocery bag.

I stand back a little, so she won't notice me. Once she looked up and waved when I was watching.

Yesterday when I went down to the store she came out of her kitchen before I could get past. She said hello, and I had to say it back. "Cindy," she said, smiling, "how come you don't come down to visit me anymore? Have you been too busy? Hmmm?"

Like she didn't know perfectly well why not.

I can see her working in the garden sometimes, now it's stopped raining. She gave Josie some green beans, but I wouldn't eat any. Let her keep her old anti-Semitic green beans to herself.

*   *   *

My sense of distance from the dykes I spot on the street borders on hostility. I glare at them, athletic and collegiate on their ten-speeds, or just in off "the land" in their battered, butch pickups, mutts crouched in the back. What do you know, I think. They do not recognize me. And though it has certainly crossed my mind that I might drop by a bar on one of my nights off, I haven't followed through. I don't like to leave Ericka more than necessary.

It's getting hard to remember the reasons for all this. What was it that made me think Daniel was going to change his mind? Maybe, in fact, it was I who counted on magic, as I've accused Ericka of doing. Maybe I thought we'd get along so well, she'd love and need me so much, that life on the run would prove possible after all. We'd never go back.

In retrospect our first weeks here in Eugene seem like a short remission in the course of a fatal illness. And I have other metaphors. On bad days, in especially trying moments, our misery together makes me think of the unhappiness of impoverished romantics who have eloped together in the naive expectation that passion will suffice. Or I compare us to a city under siege: defeat assured, some sense of honor rests in managing to hold out a little longer.

I'm getting overanxious. I don't like to admit it, but one reason I avoid going out is my fear of being spotted.

In the night there are too many questions, I sleep badly. Suppose I'd chosen to stay and keep working on Daniel? Might I have gotten Belle and Sam to help?

Where further could we go? Alaska, maybe?

A Jewish girlhood in Alaska. Underground.

I should not have brought her here.

I wish I knew if I have to go back. Sometimes I think I sort of want to, now. I know I would miss Josie, but when I'm older I could see her. Till then I'd have everybody else. It would be nice to go more places and play with kids when I want and not have to use my pretend name. I guess Daddy and Brenda would get over being mad. I didn't want to move away from Brooklyn, but Cleveland probably wouldn't be any differenter than here. At least those people wouldn't have to know about my mother. I'd just say my parents are divorced. I learned how to lie good on this trip. I never make a mistake anymore.

If I did that, though, Josie'd be alone. First Mommy dying, then me going back. It seems like no fair.

I finally met this one girl in the park. She said hello, and I wanted to be polite. Besides, she seemed nice. She started showing me how to make daisy chains with these little daisies that grow in the grass there. You make a slit in the stem with your fingernail and pull the next daisy through.

She looked Chinese. I asked was she from here.

She said she was, and asked where I was from. I told her New York. She said her father teaches at the U. Her parents came here from Vietnam.

"I heard of there. Wasn't a war there or something?"

"Yeah, that's partly why we had to come. But I was born here, in Oregon."

I said I was Jewish, and showed her my star. She said her name's Amy. I forget her last name.

We made enough daisy chains for two necklaces and four bracelets. Then we decided to go to the store to get a Fudgsicle. On the way there I asked her what she'd do if she had this problem: having two different people you were supposed to be living with, and those two people didn't get along, and you had to decide whether to stay with one person or go back to the other one, and you didn't want to not live with either of them.

"I guess you'd have to decide who you like the best," Amy said, taking a bite off her Fudgsicle. I don't eat it that way, I like to lick mine.

"But suppose you liked both?"

"Both exactly the same?"

"I don't know." It was too hard to explain, especially when I couldn't say everything. "Like, suppose the law said you had to live with one of them, and you wanted to, because he was your father. But you didn't want to not live with the other one. And also, you didn't want to leave that one alone, because you thought they might be lonesome. But they might get in trouble if they kept you."

"You mean, if your father's got custody?"

"Yeah."

"Who's the other one? Your real mother?"

"Uh-uh. It's—another relative."

"I don't know." Amy bit her Fudgsicle. She was saving it, taking little tiny bites. "I guess you'd probably belong with your father, though, if it wasn't your real mom."

"Even if you'd never get to visit the other person?"

"Beats me. I guess you'd have a problem. Wow, these stupid daisies are wilting already. Anyway, people can't always get to live where they want to live. Look where my parents had to move to."

*   *   *

Rhea strolls into my night, a heartless stranger, the young housewife who rented me a room. But before morning she holds me, declares I'm safe.

I come awake sobbing, surprised, then concerned: supposing I managed to wake Ericka. But she lies still sleeping her promiscuous child-sleep, mouth agape, sheet knotted around her far-flung limbs. It's a week now since she's roused me complaining of one of those nightmares she's somehow never able to reconstruct.

The dream renews my physical memory, sex inseparable from the comfort of Rhea's nearness. In this I feel disloyal to our child. Sadness might take me from her, seal me off. How many losses can one mourn adequately?

Our life does seem calmer. Perhaps we've simply adjusted. The rain has let up, though it remains overcast and chilly. Ericka has relented a little bit in the matter of Mrs. Swenson. She now volunteers a greeting when they meet down in the garden, and several days ago when the woman presented me with a two-pound coffee can full of wild blackberries (I've had an inordinate number of food gifts since issuing my rebuke), she consumed the pie I made without a murmur.

The third week of August is half spent. On the hills around town, scattered vine maples are turning. Dana continues to weigh the job in Reno. Chandelle has begun to speak eagerly of Jesus. The stores downtown are pushing back-to-school; Oregonian mothers throng them, with herds of tanned offspring.

I plan one more call to Brooklyn, then a talk with Ericka. I really don't see us hanging on past Labor Day, not unless something changes.

* * *

I make myself go in that cemetery. I know there's really nothing to be scared of.

It has this big high fence around it, but you could walk right in the gate. Only I'm sort of nervous somebody's going to come along and tell me I shouldn't be in there.

I go on a little ways, but I don't see a single person, which is spookier in a way. It looks so normal, it's weird to think about all the skeletons underneath the ground that you could see if your eyes took x-rays. There are lots of little daisies on the grass, like the ones me and Amy used for chains. It's so pretty there, I'd like to sit down and make a daisy chain again, only I feel nervous, so I just pick one flower and walk on. Then I start peeling off petals to find out something I want to know about Josie calling my father again tomorrow. I go, "Okay, not okay, okay, not okay, okay. . . ."

The last petal turns out on not okay. *But the petals are so little, I could've made a mistake. Anyway, I said before I started that this time wouldn't really count.*

I try again. It comes out on okay.

I keep thinking there must be a solution to every problem.

Only suppose there isn't.

If a person could be a person and then nothing.

They burned her up. They threw away the ashes.

* * *

Daniel has come up with a new approach. He says he's not interested in talking anymore, and desires me not to call again unless it's to inform him I'm bringing Ericka back. He makes no further mention of leniency. He's pursuing "other channels," in his phrase.

Rosemary, glimpsed only briefly in Portland this time, then consulted on the phone, implores me to be careful. It would be terrible, she points out, to be caught at the last moment; therefore I should be both speedy and cautious in negotiating the surrender, which she agrees is necessary at this stage.

I expressed last-minute doubts. "Maybe I'm chickenshit. . . . Who really *needs* fathers and schools and all? Why *not* Alaska?"

"But could you decide that for her?" she asked, unanswerably; then gratuitously added, "Look, Joze, have you ever thought about having your own kid?"

I keep showing up at Dexter's, purely out of habit, a sort of reverse example of the phenomenon that sometimes keeps janitors working for months after they've won the lottery.

We haven't talked yet, but I think Ericka knows. In a way I imagine we'll both be relieved.

* * *

I have a dream. Mommy and Josie are in it.

It's in our old apartment. Everything seems regular, except Mommy doesn't live with us. She's just visiting.

We have moussaka for dinner, like she always used to make. After dinner she says, while we're all here together, why don't you give your Grandma and Grandpa a call? We haven't talked to them in a long time. Ericka, how about dialing? You remember the number, don't you?

Of course I remember the number.

* * *

In the abrupt way she has of voicing a thought she's been spinning out privately for some time, while we're sitting at breakfast Ericka comes out with, "Do you think someday *flommy* will be in the dictionary?"

"In a hundred years I guess it's possible," I answer drily, hiding my sudden pleasure.

"It's no fair. You ought to have a title."

* * *

Josie and I finally sit down and have a talk. According to her, she doesn't think my father will change his mind now.

"So that means I have to go back I guess." I'm not surprised.

"How do you feel about it?"

"I dunno."

"Well, I feel rotten about it, but I can't think what else to do. School's going to start. It's just too hard, hiding."

I knew all that. "I guess I better, then."

"I'll miss you a lot, kiddo. But who knows what'll happen. Maybe your father will get over being mad and let us spend time together when you're a little older."

I doubt it, that's the same thing she said already. But I don't say anything. I know she's trying to cheer me up.

"Anyway, I want to make sure you know this isn't what I want. You do know that, don't you?"

"Yeah."

"One time a while ago you said you thought I'd like to send you back."

"It's okay. I was upset then. I know you didn't, really."

"We could stay till Labor Day. I'd like that. I guess I might as well give them a week's notice at the shop. Then we could maybe . . . is there something you'd like to do? Go to the ocean or something? We don't have camping equipment, but we could stay in a motel for a couple nights."

"Wouldn't it be expensive?"

"I don't think we have to worry about that now."

"That's okay." *I wanted to see the ocean. But it doesn't seem important anymore.*

"Well, you think about it. We'll go if you want to go."

After that we both start doing other stuff. I'm thinking about Cleveland, what it'll be like, if I really have to go. Meeting new kids, and what I'd say if the teacher makes me write a composition about my summer vacation. Maybe I could just tell about this trip, and not say who I took it with. Mostly I'm just waiting for Josie to go to work so I could be by myself and listen to my radio and try and make up my mind about my plan. Which probably won't work, but it's all I could think up.

Josie doesn't talk much the rest of the morning. She makes us a special lunch. I guess she probably thinks I'm mad at her. But that's not it really. I just don't feel like talking.

After lunch I remember there's something important I didn't ask. "What will you do? Will you go back to Brooklyn?"

"Good question, kiddo. I don't know."

"But you won't have a job or anything."

"That's the least of my worries. I can always get one. Maybe I'll . . . who knows. Save up my money and travel around for a while. Go see how people live in Peru, or Nigeria."

Those places sound far. "How will I know where you'll be? Will you write me? I want to come visit you the minute I'm eighteen."

"Of course I'll write you. Don't worry about that. I'll always keep you posted on where I am, what I'm doing."

"If Daddy lets me get letters."

Then another thought occurs to me. "Did you ever consider maybe having a baby?"

Josie starts to cry. I don't know what I did.

"I only meant, then you'd have a kid to be with."

She blows her nose. I'm also almost crying. "I know, kiddo. It was a good thought. It's just . . . well, everyone seems to ask me that."

* * *

These last days are peculiar, so little happens in them. I keep feeling I should be priming my child with good advice, wisdom packed like provident sandwiches to sustain her on her journey. But I don't feel very wise, and we don't talk very much. We read, swim, take daily walks together.

I have gone through the formality of giving notice. Despite her early enthusiasm for my talents, Mrs. Dexter heard the news calmly. In fact, everyone seemed indifferent. Counter girls are expected to come and go. Only Dana said enviously how lucky I was to be leaving. The Reno thing appears to have fallen through.

I've informed Mrs. Swenson when we'll be out. She looked hurt, I thought, but maybe I simply misinterpreted her dismay at having to advertise for a new tenant. "Going back up to Portland?" she inquired.

"No, actually we'll be heading back East."

She pursed her lips. I could see she disapproved. But she's scared of me now, and kept it to herself.

I have made plane reservations. Later I'll call Daniel, make him promise not to bust me at the airport, and let him charge the tickets on his card.

* * *

It's Josie's last day of work. She left an hour ago. Raining again — just when I have to go out.

It's later there. They should be home by now. They never go anywhere, hardly, after dinner.

I take a dime out of my allowance money, then fifty cents in case I want a treat, even though it's not real popsicle weather. The pay phone is over by the store.

There's no umbrella. Josie took it with her. It's raining hard. I run all the way.

The booth's empty. I go in and shut the door. I feel nervous and weird, like I'm in a performance or something.

I read the writing on the telephone and follow it exactly. I put my dime in. I listen for the tone. I dial zero, then the other numbers. It makes me feel old to be doing this.

The operator answers. I have to clear my throat.

"Hello, I want to reverse the charges, please. This is Ericka Krevsky calling Belle Krevsky."

PART IV: AFTERWARDS

Ericka sighs. "Aren't we *ever* leaving?"

The question, oft-repeated, is so obviously rhetorical I no longer bother to answer. But this time, as though in reply, the cabin lights flicker. The Muzak halts mid-phrase with an inelegant squawk, and a professionally upbeat voice starts in, "Ladies and gentlemen, on behalf of Captain Kellogg and our crew, I'd like to welcome you aboard Delta Airlines Flight 451."

My seatmate's pointed chin has been pressed to the window glass. Now she turns to me, excitedly gripping my hand. "Listen, that means we're going!"

"Relax," I advise. "It may be a while yet."

"Our flight today will take us to Atlanta, with a brief stopover at Chicago's O'Hare Airport. If there is anyone aboard *not* planning to travel to Chicago or Atlanta, will you please deplane at this time?"

A pause. Nobody moves. A faint ripple of derisive laughter washes through the half-filled, stuffy cabin. We've already been delayed without explanation nearly half an hour beyond our scheduled departure, and the restive passengers, many in business suits, know perfectly well where it is they want to go.

"At this time, we'd like to ask that you make sure your seatbelts are securely fastened, all carry-on luggage is stowed beneath the seat in front of you or in the overhead luggage compartments, and all seatbacks and traytables are in their full upright —"

"Hey, what mountain is that?" Ericka points. We have begun to back slowly away from the gate, and a sharp, eccentrically-chiselled peak — from some angles, the summit appears slightly hooked — has come into view to the east, above the rosy, low-lying smog of a Portland summer morning.

"Hood," I say. Today is the first of September, the snow cover at its sparest. Even quite near the top, black rocky ribs show through.

"Are we flying by there? I want to see it up close."

"I don't know. It depends what route we take."

The man sitting to my left in the aisle seat smiles knowingly at me. He's been listening to Ericka for some time, and now ventures to ask, "Her first flight?"

"No. But still, an event."

"You're not from the Northwest?"

"We're from New York City."

That encourages more questions, to which I supply brief answers. He's just about my age, it shocks me to realize, despite the business suit and attaché case. Not the suit, nor the *Forbes* he's got open in his lap, nor his fresh-faced, healthy look, nor the fact that he clearly supposes me a mother, endears him to me.

He doesn't seem to notice my curtness, or at any rate is unhindered in his determination to make available to benighted Easterners the natural glories of his native land. "Keep looking out that window," he instructs, "and you'll get a good view as we're taking off. Usually on this run they bank around to the north and make a full circle, counter-clockwise, before heading east. On a morning like this, we should see all the mountains. Right up north of the river, that lumpy-looking rockpile will be Adams. Then St. Helens—that's the regular cone. They say it's the nearest to a perfect volcanic cone this side of Mt. Fuji. We might even get a look at Rainier."

I find it irksome to be lectured, particularly since I know all this already, but Ericka, who probably realizes she's about exhausted my patience with her inquisitiveness, plies him with eager questions until interrupted by the flight attendants, who launch into their bizarrely choreographed demonstration of emergency exits and oxygen mask procedures. To this she attends with terrific seriousness, and when they reach the part about how parents should position their own masks before putting on their children's, she nudges me and whispers I needn't bother, she understands how to do hers.

At last they announce we're cleared. We start our run for it.

She grips her armrests, awaiting the miracle. We're screaming, too fast for earth, too slow for air.

"Josie, look, we're flying!"

The treacherous runway slips from under us. We labor upward, over water now. The Columbia. It has small boats on it.

Intent at the window, Ericka is quiet. I'm counting to myself: one thousand one, one thousand two, one thousand three. . . . when I hit sixty, I'll figure we won't die yet.

Really, though, it's only an old habit. I feel superstitiously invulnerable today, and am not afraid of crashing.

Sure enough, beyond my companion's small dark head the mountains pass in review, all present, accounted for. On their slopes, made invisible by haste and distance, are the glorious meadows I've described to her.

We wheel sharply over Portland. On our right, to the northwest, the confluence of Willamette and Columbia; then below us many bridges, the West Hills like a stage set.

Now we rise more rapidly above mist clinging in grey-green forest crevices. Eastward we nose toward the brown terrain: wheatfields, sagelands, desert.

Without turning from the window, Ericka asks, "What time did you say we get to Florida?"

"I don't remember exactly. Somewhere around your bedtime. Your bedtime here, that is. You know there's three hours' difference."

"How long will we be in Atlanta?"

"About an hour and a half."

"Do we have to get our stuff?"

"No, it's checked through."

"That's good. I bet we're late, the way this thing is flying." She subsides once more into her window reverie. The eager Oregonian beside me has whipped out a pocket calculator and begun to jot figures down on a yellow legal pad. Gratefully I close my scratchy eyes. I didn't sleep much at Rosemary's last night.

Tonight, at least, I'll be able to collapse. Belle and Sam are to meet our plane in West Palm Beach. At first I tried to persuade Belle we could spend the night in a motel, but she wouldn't hear of it, though the airport is quite a drive from their place and Sam's health is shaky. I know what a production the trip will be, how they'll fuss at one another in their fond-irritable way, making sure all the appliances are off and the right lights left on, how Sam will inflame Belle with suggestions about her driving.

It was three days ago that Ericka came bursting into Dexter's just about the start of the evening rush. Brandishing a dripping popsicle, she announced she had something to tell me.

"What is it?" I demanded. Since she wasn't supposed to visit me at the shop, her very presence suggested some cause for alarm.

"You'll probably be mad," she defensively asserted. Looking closer, I gathered she'd been crying.

"We'll see about that. What's up?"

"I called up Grandma. She wants to speak to you."

I was confused. Customers were waiting. "What did you call her for?"

"I told her . . . I wanted to see if maybe I could stay there for a while."

"You what?"

"I can't explain. You better talk to her. Call collect, right away she said."

I was, as she'd predicted, momentarily irritated that Ericka had taken it upon herself to flout my most basic rule, even though it no longer seemed to matter much. But I had to figure out what the whole thing meant. Fortunately Dana was still hanging around, and I got her to wait on people while I went into the back room to perform the daring feat of making a personal call on the shop phone.

It wasn't a pleasant prospect. I expected Belle to be upset and angry, even thought it possible she might be cooperating more or less directly with Daniel – whom I hadn't yet informed of his victory. On the other hand, maybe she could help out with negotiating the terms of our disengagement. . . .

In fact, she barely took time to accept the charges before she began scolding in the unmistakable tone of relieved mothers everywhere. Why hadn't I called? Why hadn't I written? Didn't I know how concerned she and Sam had been? Thank goodness *someone* had finally had the good sense to get in touch. If there were problems developing between me and Ericka's father, why hadn't I let her know?

Startled that she seemed to suggest herself as an ally, I ignored the complexities of our history and merely said I wasn't sure she could have done anything. "And then, these past few weeks – well, you know we've been hiding."

"Hiding!" she scoffed. "Run away from the problem! Now there's a constructive solution, Josephine!"

I'd forgotten that Belle uses my full name, something very few people in my life have done. It's nothing personal. She simply has a habit of calling people what she thinks they should be called. "What did Ericka say?" I inquired.

"The poor little thing, she sounded so grownup at first I hardly recognized her. Then she broke down and started crying till I thought she'd never stop. She sounded like a little lost . . . I don't know what, without a friend in the world. Then she poured out a bunch of nonsense about police and arrests and jail. I think she's really afraid she may never see you again! And at the same time, she's convinced her father's furious with her.

"You can see the child's being torn in two. It's a dreadful situation. She practically begged to come down here and live with Sam and me."

"What did you say to that?"

"Well, of course she's always welcome, as I made clear to her. But I don't believe that's the main issue. She seems to see that as her only means of avoiding this absurd, childish *contest* between you and Danny."

264

"She might be right," I said, galled at the parallel. As though Daniel and I had equal power.

"I'd certainly hate to think so. I can't believe things like this can't eventually be worked out between a couple of rational adults."

Lovely, I thought. "How would you suggest?"

"Well, granted Danny is not your favorite person. For that matter, Sam and I sometimes had our differences with him, as I know you're aware, when Rhea and he were married. And I know she resented his actions later on. But he *is* a human being, and he *is* Ericka's father. He might have been reasoned with."

"Don't you suppose I tried?"

"I'm sure you did. But why all by yourself? Why didn't you discuss things with Sam and me, have one of us speak to him at least, before you went flying off into the wild blue yonder, scaring us half to death?"

Too disheartened for tact, I blurted, "I didn't know you would."

"Why on earth not?"

"Because—oh, plenty of reasons. An awful lot of people seem prepared to support a father in anything he does, just because he's the father."

"Do I look like one of those people?"

"And then, there's who *I* am."

Belle was indignant at this, and hurt, evidently. "After you helped raise my granddaughter all those years? After what you were to Rhea? Do you really mean to tell me you thought of me as a reactionary old fogey who's side with Danny on account of *that*? Don't you suppose I realize my own child was also . . . gay?"

"I didn't know what you'd do." I perceived I'd blundered, but at the moment I really didn't care much.

"It wasn't even worthwhile finding out?"

"Look Belle, I'm sorry," I said. "You're right, but it's too late now."

She wasn't listening. "Rhea surely would have wanted—"

"None of that matters. It's what Daniel wants."

"Well, the man can't have everything he wants! There are Ericka and her wants and needs to consider."

"Not legally. I assume you've been in touch?"

"He *is* pretty upset," she admitted. "Of course, he's been under a strain. Things have been so up in the air. But the baby was born three days ago, and she and Brenda are doing just fine. . . ."

"*She*? But I thought it was going to be a boy."

"Yes, isn't that something? Apparently they made a mistake with the lab report on the amniocentesis."

This cheered me a bit, for some reason. "What did he have to say last time you talked to him? Is he really serious, do you think, about pressing kidnapping charges?"

"Oh, stuff and nonsense! Is that what he told you?"

"It's been his classic line, pretty much from the beginning."

"I can't believe he'd ever go that far."

"You don't understand. He can go as far as he wants." For a former Communist, I thought, this woman sometimes seems to have a remarkably naive analysis of power relationships. "Frankly, right now my biggest concern is how to get Ericka back there without his—with some kind of guarantee he won't do anything drastic."

"There's an optimistic attitude!"

"Realistic, however."

"Don't give up too easily," Belle urged. "I still say Danny could be worked on. Though our position would be much stronger if you hadn't run off with Ericka, of course. I can't dispute his being furious at that."

"Worked on—how?" Despite my cynicism, I found encouragement in that inclusive "our." At the same time, I wanted to let her know that she reminded me of the folks who used to be all in favor of fair working conditions as long as getting them didn't involve nasty strikes. But I figured we could argue theory later.

"I think he might respond to—the pressure of public opinion."

"Public opinion! Yours and Sam's, you mean?"

"What's wrong with that? And Danny's mother, too, I could try giving her a call. Rose and I always got along all right. I won't say she's what you'd exactly call progressive—as I recall, she thought she was doing something really adventurous when she voted for John Lindsay—but she does have a basic sense of decency. I doubt very much she'd go along with this legal nonsense, and I might even be able to make her see how important it is for Ericka to maintain her relationship with you, Josephine.

"Then who knows, possibly even Brenda. . . . After all, I *am* Ericka's grandmother. If I can't pull rank every once in a while, what's the point of having the lousy title, anyway?"

I was both touched and amused by her typical zest, so obviously that of the old warrior who hears in the distance the familiar battle call. An organizer: that's what this struggle needed. And another thought struck me: I ought to suggest to her that if she wanted to exert any kind of influence over her former son-in-law, she'd better stop calling him "Danny." Rhea had told me how he hated that.

At this juncture there intervened a fearsome apparition; Mrs. Dexter came bearing down on me, her florid coloring heightened even more by righteous indignation. "What's going on here, Laura?" she cried. "Is this a *personal call* you're making? Don't you know the shop policy? What's Dana doing out there in her street clothes, waiting on customers?" I had to tell Belle I'd call her back in the morning, when we could talk strategy.

It was quite a task to placate my employer—not that I'd have bothered, but I didn't want Dana to get in trouble for aiding and abetting. "You girls are all alike," her highness fumed. "Start out so eager to please, and after six weeks you're actin' like you own a friggin' franchise. Wish they'd invent a machine to replace the bunch of you." After she finally calmed down and left, I still had to report to an amazed Ericka that she had a new sister, set her up with a chocolate frosted doughnut, and convince her I wasn't "mad" about the call.

Next morning Belle proposed that she should call Daniel and inform him I'd contacted her and would be bringing Ericka to West Palm Beach. She would then tell him she felt this provided an ideal opportunity for us to have a much-needed talk about Ericka's future, that he should fly down for the purpose.

"Suppose he won't come?" I objected. "Or refuses to discuss anything with me?"

"Well, he doesn't have much of a choice about *coming*, now, does he, if he wants to see Ericka. As far as *talking* goes, he's not talking just with *you*. This is a family conference I'm calling, to deal with a subject which vitally concerns Sam and me—the welfare of our granddaughter. As a member of the family, you're obviously included. And I'm not inquiring whether he cares to show up—I'll handle it, you know, like you do with a little kid. You don't ask them do they prefer to have broccoli for dinner or not, you just put the broccoli on the plate. It works—well, a good deal of the time, anyway.

"Of course I'll try to be tactful. No need for Danny to know—"

"Better call him Daniel," I remembered to suggest.

"Very good. Thank you. Daniel. There's no need for *Daniel* to know that I've gone into the whole business with you like this. Better let him think I'm simply acting out of—well, concern for Ericka. Which I am, of course. In fact, once he arrives I think both you and he had better stay in motels. That makes things clearer. I'll get someone to take her to the beach during the day, so we can all have a chance to talk."

Though I liked Belle's energy, and was willing to try her plan, I was far from being converted to her relatively generous view of patriarchy. Earlier she'd admitted that Daniel had mentioned something about having hired a private investigator, though she'd insisted her impression of this was that it had to do merely with finding us, not with any plan to arrest me. Now I tried to warn her. "You realize he simply may not listen. He can tell you to go to hell with your family conference. He's got custody, that's all it takes. You don't have any more rights than I do."

"Well," she shot back tartly, "if he wants to be a *prick–*" She hesitated before the epithet in such a way as to emphasize that while it was far from being her everyday usage, in this case she employed it deliberately.

Ericka pokes me, interrupting my reflections. "Mom, I mean Josie, what are you smiling at?"

"Nothing. I was thinking about your grandma."

"What about my grandma?"

"It's difficult to explain. Just her . . . the way she has of fooling you by acting like such a solid citizen most of the time, when really in lots of ways she's still a rebel." Come what may of her efforts on our behalf, I'm glad I'll be spending time with Belle again. And I need someone to talk to about Rhea.

"Oh." Ericka is bored by this sort of analysis. She gazes again toward the distant country, its wrinkled contours still plainly visible through a floor of gauzy cloud-cover. "Imagine if people had to walk this far."

"They used to," I remind her. And we remember them in airplanes–the ones who belonged, and the ones who supplanted them, what they saw on their toilsome journeys. The harsh and beautiful miles we stride over, like shallow gods in our seven-league boots.

"Josie, what do you think's gonna happen?"

Obeying a playful impulse, I take her hand, turn her palm up toward me. "Let me see, this line here indicates–my, this hand is grubby, how long since you washed it?–indicates, I say, the following fortune: you will be met late this evening at the airport in Florida by a short, plump woman with beautiful blue eyes and grey hair pulled back in a straggly bun. She will have a peace symbol and perhaps some other buttons prominently displayed on her handbag, and will be accompanied by a man of advanced

268

years, of medium height and with a receding hairline. He will have a kindly if abstracted look on his tanned wrinkled face, and a little alligator on his short-sleeved shirt. They will conduct you to a haven near the water, where you will sleep between spotless percale sheets. In the morning, you'll have fresh-squeezed Florida orange juice, and—let's see—I forecast cream cheese on a bagel. Maybe even lox. How's that?"

Ericka squirms with pleasure; but she was, after all, serious. "No, I meant . . . when all you guys talk."

"I know what you meant, kiddo. I just don't know the answer."

"It's good I called Grandma, though, don't you think?"

"Yes I do. It was a terrific idea."

"I tried to think what Mommy would have said for us to do. And then I had this dream—"

"What kind of dream?"

But she's reconsidered, doesn't want to tell. Instead, she asks quickly, "Do you think Grandma thought it was okay . . . that Mommy was a lesbian, and you?"

I have to stop and weigh my answer. Finally I say, "I'm not really sure what her feelings were at first. I know it bothered your grandpa, and it may have bothered her. Now I believe she understands better."

"Oh. How high up in the air do you think we are now?"

"I have no idea."

The businessman beside me glances up from his columns of figures to consult his digital watch. His voice comes out in an odd, stiff croak. "We've reached our cruising altitude by now. Somewhere between twenty-seven and thirty thousand feet." His ears are red, I see, but it takes me a minute to put it all together, realize what he's heard that makes him blush.

The flight attendant comes staggering up the aisle, on her face an harassed smile, in her hands our plastic trays of microwaved breakfast. Twenty-seven to thirty thousand feet below, in North America, it's morning. The continent's energy pulses up to us. The engines groan and heave us ever forward, at our backs that inexorable wind that brings the East's weather.

"Mom, I mean Flommy—" She's silly with happiness. Tonight, Florida. Her grandparents. In the morning, fresh-squeezed orange juice.

We're off, we're going somewhere. She has always loved this feeling.

My life rushes toward me. I can't imagine it.

"Josie—" She really is wound up today. She could rattle on about nothing and everything, but, flommy-like, I soon intervene. "Eat your eggs, kiddo. They'll get cold."

She wrinkles her nose in travestied distaste. "I think I'd rather starve. Airplane food is gruesome."

"Gruesome or not, eat it. Dr. Muller's orders. No starving allowed. You and I have work to do."

ABOUT THE AUTHOR

Born and raised in the Pacific Northwest, Jan Clausen moved to New York in 1973. Over the past decade her poetry, fiction, and criticism have appeared in a wide range of periodicals and anthologies; she has been active in feminist publishing and in several radical political organizations and community groups. She was a co-founder and for five years a co-editor of *Conditions* magazine. In 1981 she received a National Endowment for the Arts fiction fellowship. She is the author of five previous books, among them *Mother, Sister, Daughter, Lover* (stories, The Crossing Press, 1980); *A Movement of Poets: Thoughts on Poetry and Feminism* (essay, Long Haul Press, 1982); and *Duration* (poetry and prose, Hanging Loose Press, 1983). *Sinking, Stealing* is her first novel. She lives in the Park Slope section of Brooklyn with her lover and their teenage daughter.

Sinking, Stealing is part of The Crossing Press
Feminist Series. Other titles in this Series include:

Abeng, A Novel by Michelle Cliff

Clenched Fists, Burning Crosses, A Novel by Cris South

Folly, A Novel by Maureen Brady

Learning Our Way: Essays in Feminist Education, edited by
  Charlotte Bunch and Sandra Pollack

Lesbian Images, Literary Commentary by Jane Rule

Magic Mommas, Trembling Sisters, Puritans & Perverts, Essays
  by Joanna Russ

Mother, Sister, Daughter, Lover, Stories by Jan Clausen

Mother Wit: A Feminist Guide to Psychic Development by
  Diane Mariechild

Movement, A Novel by Valerie Miner

Movement In Black, Poetry by Pat Parker

Natural Birth, Poetry by Toi Derricotte

Nice Jewish Girls: A Lesbian Anthology, edited by Evelyn
  Torton Beck

The Notebooks of Leni Clare and Other Short Stories by Sandy
  Boucher

The Politics of Reality: Essays in Feminist Theory by Marilyn
  Frye

The Queen of Wands, Poetry by Judy Grahn

Sinking, Stealing, A Novel by Jan Clausen

Sister Outsider, Essays and Speeches by Audre Lorde

Triangles, A Novel by Ruth Geller

True to Life Adventure Stories, Volumes I and II, edited by
  Judy Grahn

The Work of a Common Woman, Poetry by Judy Grahn

Zami: A New Spelling of My Name, Biomythography by Audre
  Lorde